Danger in the Shadows

"Dee Henderson had me shivering as her stalker _____ _____ to his victim. The message that we have nothing to fear as long as God is in control was skillfully handled, but I got scared anyway! I highly recommend this book to anyone who likes suspense."

TERRI BLACKSTOCK, BEST-SELLING AUTHOR OF *EMERALD WINDOWS*

"A masterstroke!… Dee Henderson gives the reader not one but two irresistible heroes."

COMPUSERVE REVIEWS

The Negotiator

"Solid storytelling, compelling characters, and the promise of more O'Malleys make Henderson a name to watch. Highly recommended, with a cross-genre appeal."

LIBRARY JOURNAL

"Dee Henderson has deftly combined action, suspense, and romance in this first-class inspirational romantic suspense."

AFFAIRE DE COEUR

The Guardian

"An entertaining thriller-cum-romance-cum-conversion story is what readers get in this fast-paced novel…. Christian readers will relish this intriguing tale."

PUBLISHERS WEEKLY

"More than an investigative thriller, this is a great romance dealing with complex matters of faith."

ROMANTIC TIMES

"Another exciting new thriller from an up-and-coming talent in Christian fiction."

LIBRARY JOURNAL

The Truth Seeker

"Another fantastic, page-turning mystery by Dee Henderson! Heartwarming romance and exciting drama are her trademark, and they'll be sure to thrill you a third time!"

SUITE101.COM

"Read one book by Dee Henderson, and I guarantee you are gonna be hooked for life!"

THE BELLES AND BEAUX OF ROMANCE

"For a complex story and profound statement on Christianity, read *The Truth Seeker.*"

THE ROMANCE READERS CONNECTION, INSPIRATIONAL CORNER

The Protector

"There are very few books that touch the soul and the heart while trying to deliver an inspiring message but Ms. Henderson always manages to accomplish this feat."

BOOKBROWSER

"*The Protector* is vintage Dee Henderson."

WRITERS CLUB ROMANCE GROUP ON AOL

True Devotion

"Dee Henderson has done a splendid job mixing romance with the fast-paced action of a Navy SEAL platoon."

STEVE WATKINS, FORMER NAVY SEAL

"Action, adventure, and romance! *True Devotion* has everything a reader could want!"

ANGELA ELWELL HUNT, BEST-SELLING AUTHOR OF *THE JUSTICE*

"A truly stunning tale of love and devotion to God, country, and to those left behind when the missions are done."

COMPUSERVE REVIEWS

"A wonderful story with real and entertaining characters. Ms. Henderson's gift with words makes this book impossible to put down."

WRITER'S CLUB ROMANCE GROUP ON AOL

True Valor

"With its behind-the-scenes look at military deployments and a setting taken straight from the headlines, *True Valor* will have special appeal for military families and anyone searching for heroes in these uncertain times."

BOOKPAGE

"Dee Henderson writes with the skill of an F/A-18 Hornet pilot! *True Valor* is certainly an eye-opener into the unique and courageous world of those who so bravely serve their country, while the romance is brewed at just the right pace."

ROMANTIC TIMES

"The high-tension action scenes make a jarring counterpoint to the 'easy' pace of the romance. Ms. Henderson pulls off the seeming dichotomy with dispatch.... I honestly believe Ms. Henderson could make a grocery list interesting to read."

SCRIBES WORLD REVIEWS

THE
HEALER

Book Five — the O'Malley Series

Dee Henderson

Tyndale House Publishers, Inc.
Carol Stream, Illinois

Visit Tyndale's exciting Web site at www.tyndale.com

TYNDALE and Tyndale's quill logo are registered trademarks of Tyndale House Publishers, Inc.

The Healer

Designed by Ron Kaufmann and Dean H. Renninger

Previously published in 2002 by Multnomah Publishers, Inc. under ISBN 1-57673-925-2.

ISBN-13: 978-1-4143-1060-2

ISBN-10: 1-4143-1060-9

Printed in the United States of America

13

19 18 17 16 15 14

To my mom,
who is the best friend an author could have.

———∞———

I am the LORD, your healer.
EXODUS 15:26B

TITLES BY DEE HENDERSON

THE O'MALLEY SERIES

Danger in the Shadows (prequel)
The Negotiator
The Guardian
The Truth Seeker
The Protector
The Healer
The Rescuer

UNCOMMON HEROES SERIES

True Devotion
True Valor
True Honor

Kidnapped
The Witness
Before I Wake

Prologue

Carol Iles pulled on tennis shoes to replace the heels she'd worn at work and tossed her shoes down the hall toward her bedroom.

"So where are we going for dinner?" Her friend Amy asked, digging through her cosmetic bag for a lipstick tube. She had come over directly from work, bringing a change of clothes to replace her suit with jeans and a sweater. Amy stepped into the bathroom to use the mirror.

Carol looked at the clock on her kitchen wall. "I was thinking Charlie's Grill at the mall; then we can walk off dinner and spend some of your vacation money before you leave." She opened the refrigerator to see what she had available to offer her guest. "I've got Sprite, Pepsi, and several sports drinks."

She had bought the sports drinks for her son when she went grocery shopping last night, and it looked like he'd managed to gulp down two before his father picked him up tonight. She should have suggested he take them with him. It would be two weeks before her son would be here again. His absence was a painful reminder of what hadn't worked out in her life. Divorce left everyone struggling to make new routines work.

Carol touched one of the bottles. It was one of the few traces of her son's presence left in the house. He insisted on bringing his things in a duffel bag and leaving with everything, as if to put roots down here in her house through his clutter would be to admit that he too had been split apart by the divorce. He lived with his father; he was always quick to point that out.

"A Sprite is fine."

Carol forced aside the melancholy. She set the can on the counter for Amy and got a Pepsi for herself. Amy was making a special point to stay in town on Friday night just to cheer her up when Amy could've made an early start on her vacation. Carol was determined to make the effort to enjoy tonight.

She took the soda with her to the dining room and flipped through the day's mail. Amy rejoined her and put her lipstick and hairbrush away in her cosmetic bag. Carol offered Amy three catalogs that had come the day before. "I found that blouse in one of these."

"Thanks." Amy carried them over to the kitchen counter and opened her soda. "I'm hoping they have it in a soft peach." She dug through her purse for a pen. "Oh, I found the card I had told you about." She held up a blue business card.

"Brian would blow his top if I asked him to let us get professional help for our son."

"You have to think about what is best for Mark. It's normal for divorce to be hard on kids, but Mark is taking this rougher than most," Amy replied.

"Brian keeps insisting it's a family problem."

"Carol, I know your son hates my guts for convincing you to leave Brian. And if he knew I was the one suggesting this, he'd dig in his heels, but I really do think it would be good for him to see someone. It's been over a year. He's not getting better on his own. Would you at least talk to Rachel O'Malley? She's very good at what she does."

Carol felt exhausted at the idea of bringing yet another person into this trauma, of having to once again explain. Amy was so hopeful this could get better. Carol smiled. "Leave the card. I'll think about it."

"You won't regret it."

The doorbell rang. Carol wasn't expecting anyone. "Just a minute." She went to get it.

Carol opened the door only to stop, surprised. "Was the basketball game canceled?" She stepped back to let her visitor in. She hoped Amy would be smart enough to stay in the kitchen when she heard his voice so they could avoid a confrontation.

"Not exactly." The gunshot hit her in the chest. She went crashing back into the living room table.

One

We need to go, Mrs. Sands." Rachel O'Malley stopped the elderly lady from turning toward her living room and instead steered her toward the front door and the waiting Red Cross volunteer. Shutters rattled and a misty rain blew in the open door, dampening the hallway. The Des Plaines River was surging through the levee; and getting people to safety was the priority. It was Tuesday, March 13, and rains across Chicago had triggered rapid flooding along six miles of the river.

"I need my pictures."

"Yes, ma'am. But I'm afraid there isn't time." Rachel shifted the birdcage and medicine bag she carried to help Mrs. Sands with her raincoat. "This wind is strong, so let Nora and the officer help you."

With twenty minutes warning to leave their homes, residents were able to grab a few clothes and personal items but that was it. Nora took Mrs. Sands's arm and helped her walk to the waiting rescue vehicle. Rachel handed her personal items to the officer.

In the twilight, torchlights bobbed like fireflies along the block as three police officers and two other Red Cross workers took part in the evacuation search. Rachel worked disasters for a living, but she would never get used to floods. Little could be done once the flooding took ground. Rachel placed a red fluorescent square on the garage door of 58 Governor Street to mark it as confirmed empty. Cold, muddy water swirled over her boots and reached to her jeans as she waded into the water to cut across the yard.

The next house was set back from the road, with sloping, land-scaped grounds. Located closer to the river, the house was suffering the most damage of any so far as water poured in through the backyard and rushed around the house to flow down Governor Street. Rachel fought against the water to walk up the driveway. It took her feet out from under her. She instinctively threw her arms up to protect her head as she was swept downhill toward the street. It was her second dunk-ing of the day.

She slammed up against fire boots.

"Got you." The reassuring words came moments before hands slid around her jacket and hauled her to her feet. Captain Cole Parker stood in the rushing water with his feet braced apart and let the current break around him. He'd been buttoning his fire coat.

"Thanks, Cole." Everything on her was wet. She leaned forward and dried her face on his shirt. It was rough blue denim and she could see the white T-shirt beneath it. He had planned for the reality of this weather better than she had, with layers to fight the chill. The breadth of muscles on the man stretched the fabric taut.

"My pleasure, Rae." His hands pushed back her dripping hair as he laughed. "You are really wet. The water bang you up any?"

"I'm okay." She was embarrassed and annoyed that he'd seen her fall, but she couldn't do much about any of it. Her short haircut was new, and when it was wet it lost any definition and simply became straggles of hair. She blinked water out of her eyes and sniffed, then reached for his hand and dried her eyes on the back of his cuff.

"I wish I'd brought at least a hand towel."

She tilted her head to dislodge the water in her ear. "You're enjoy-ing this."

"I'd love to have a camera right now," Cole confirmed, his smile widening. He put his hands on her shoulders and helped her turn against the rushing waters. "Go with Jack. I'll check the last house."

Her brother was crossing the street toward her. He was a lieutenant in the same fire company where Cole was a captain. Cole said his pre-mature gray hair was at least partially Jack's fault. Jack was a careful, safety-conscious firefighter but invariably led his men in a firefight from the front lines, especially when there was someone at risk. Jack was here, and Cole, so Company 81 must have been dispatched to the scene. "I didn't know firemen fought floods."

Cole tugged straight the now sopping Red Cross jacket from being bunched around her back. "It looks like we're going to learn how. The Corps of Engineers guys are stretched thin. The bridge is ours to defend."

She raised startled eyes to meet his. "Whose blacklist are you on?"

Cole laughed. "I hope it only looks impossible. Jack said it sounds like fun. You have a change of clothes at the shelter?"

"If I don't it's going to be a miserable couple hours drying out." The water was inching up around them. She glanced at the house that had been her original destination. "You'd better go check the house while you can still get to it. But please, be careful."

"Always," Cole promised. "Can you get me a head count at the emergency shelter and ask around about pets? I'll be pulling my guys back from this street in about twenty minutes."

"Will do." Rachel grabbed Jack's hand to keep her balance in the fast-moving waters and headed up the street toward the truck, which was on higher ground. Cole was defending the bridge. She smiled. Well at least she knew where to find him in the foreseeable future. The idea of working at the nearby shelter suddenly had more appeal.

By Friday the rushing waters were a roar in the night that grew louder the closer Cole got to the Des Plaines River. One of the residents of Governor Street forced out by the floodwaters had raised an American flag to fly over the sandbag levee that workers had named "the Alamo line." The flag waved in the night breeze, backlit by the emergency lights that enabled workers to keep an eye on the bridge, which was now cut off and surrounded by water. It was a defiant symbol. It fit the attitude of those dealing with the disaster over the last three days.

Today had been rough. When he hadn't been hauling sandbags or fixing pump equipment, he'd been working with the guys who were doing the dangerous job of breaking up and hauling out debris that had gotten stuck and piled up beneath the bridge. As he made his evening rounds, Cole felt a bit like a general inspecting the state of his troops. Fighting water was far from his specialty—he led the arson group—but his men had met the challenge. They'd fought the river to a draw today, and it felt great.

Cole kept a lookout for Rachel as he walked. She'd been supplying them with hot coffee and sports scores. Her caramel-colored hair had dried with a flyaway curl to it, and when he happened to catch her during the rare moments she had her reading glasses on, Rae reminded him of a studious college student, years younger than her real age.

She was thirty-five if her brother Jack was to be believed, and given the intensity of Rachel's job working disaster scenes nationwide, Cole wasn't surprised her hair had begun to show signs of gray. She was aging elegantly. If he couldn't have the pleasure of her company on a date tonight, he'd settle for a few minutes to talk with her and enjoy that smile that lingered in his memory.

Cole didn't see her and hoped that meant she was finally tucked away somewhere getting a few hour's sleep. She had been staying at the emergency shelter rather than returning to her home a few miles south, her sleeping bag and duffel bag well used. She carried odd things in that duffel bag she considered her emergency kit. He'd seen fingernail polish and stickers and all kinds of colorful hair ribbons alongside aspirin and envelopes and postage stamps. He had slipped in a funny Hallmark card he'd picked up at one of the few businesses in the area determined to stay open. He wanted her thinking about him with a smile and a laugh tonight.

Spotting the yellow smiley face on the back of Jack O'Malley's fire coat, Cole changed directions and headed toward the blue pump engine. The engine had been retired and replaced by more modern equipment years ago, but in a fight like this one, anything that could pump water had been called out.

Jack was working on the top of the levee, pushing thirty-pound bags around. Beside him a six-inch-main fire hose was taut, stretched up and over the wall of sandbags, dumping water into the river as fast as the pumps could throw it back. Cole stopped by the front bumper of the pump engine, curious as to what was going on, cracking open another peanut while he waited for Jack to finish what he was doing. His pocketful of peanuts was turning out to be dinner tonight.

His friend hauled the hose into the new cradle he had made. The shoot of water became a water fountain with spotlights illuminating the flood area. Jack reached down and lifted a flat cardboard box onto the sandbags. Moments later a yellow rubber duck with black sunglasses dropped into the shooting water and reappeared in the middle of the river.

Jack was playing.

The swift-moving water carried the yellow duck downriver and under the bridge, where it disappeared.

"Nice shot."

Jack turned on his perch. "We've got ten thousand of them. I figure they won't miss a couple dozen." He dropped another one and the water shot it into the river where it bobbed upside down, righted itself, and got slaughtered by a tree branch it slammed into.

The local chamber of commerce had been planning a duck race as its opening event in a charity fund-raising drive. They had ten thousand ducks stored in the fire department's maintenance garage. It looked like they would be stuck with them for a good long time—the event had been canceled.

"Hold on to a box for Adam tomorrow. He'll love them," Cole said.

"That's what I was thinking."

The boy's home was visible through the trees during the day, the water now up to the middle of the living room windows, the mailbox at the roadside underwater. Adam was down here every day, helping them. He had to watch the river destroy his home. They were all trying to make the situation a little easier on him.

"Does the river look like it's picking up speed?"

Jack reached for his inside pocket and pulled out a stopwatch. He timed the next duck as it raced between two poles they'd marked with red flags. "Eight-point-two seconds. It's really moving now."

"The crest should hit in another forty-eight hours."

"I saw what looked like a small propane tank go by that was rolling like a cork. Someone's backyard grill probably got ripped apart."

"The cemetery off Rosecrans Road flooded this evening. That ground was as much loose sand as dirt. I bet this river current is eating it up like mulch," Cole said.

"You know about the most ugly things."

"I work at it." Cole didn't mention that Jack's sister Lisa had stopped by to drop off two body bags. Lisa's boss, the medical examiner, remembered the last time he'd received a body pulled from the river. It was wrapped in a curtain for want of a better covering. He'd sent out his central staff today to make sure rescue crews were prepared. It was inevitable that someone would attempt to drive across a flooded street, try to reach a flooded home, or otherwise act before they thought. The river would have no mercy.

Cole gestured toward the pump engine. "How's it holding up?"

"Beautifully. This baby could pump the whole river if we asked her to."

Jack was wet and tired. The hyperbole was getting a bit thick, but he had cause. He'd been keeping the old pump engine in top shape through scraped knuckles and frustrating part replacements. This was her moment to shine. And so far she was holding her own against the heavy seepage.

The sandbags were slowing down the river and forcing it to soak rather than slam through the levee. The pumps still had to keep up with the fact that unless the water working its way through was repelled, the river would flood the city sewers.

"I'm laying a new line of bags around the bank just in case. It's going to rise at least another six inches before the crest. Anything you need?" Cole asked.

"Coffee. Dry socks. Cassie."

"Interesting order you put those in. I won't tell Cassie you made her third." Cassie Ellis and Jack had been dating since last fall, and Cole was looking forward to seeing them married someday. A former fire-fighter, Cassie had been badly burned in a nursing-home fire. Cole admired the way she'd dealt with that tragedy and rebuilt her life.

"Coffee and socks are not a problem. I've got Cassie supervising the hauling out of the library historical documents. If it can't be replaced, there's no use taking chances." Cole glanced at the ducks. "But I'll send her down later if you want to put her name on one of those." He dug out a black waterproof marker from his coat pocket and tossed it to Jack. "She'll get a kick out of it."

"Thanks, boss."

"Don't fall in."

Jack laughed and picked up a duck to start his artwork.

Cole moved on to check the rest of the guys working the front line.

Rachel's legs were numb and her left arm ached. She would not have moved for the world. Nathan Noles was finally asleep, hiccup-sob-sighs still occasionally shaking his small frame. Tear-drenched lashes covered his big, brown, break-her-heart eyes. Life was rough when you were three and your favorite blanket was missing, swallowed up in the fast moving waters that had swirled into his home on Governor Street.

Rachel rubbed her thumb in small circles on his back. They were buddies. The teddy bear she had offered him to take the place of his blanket was now muddy in spots and still clutched under one arm. Nathan had latched on to it and refused to let go.

She didn't have a family of her own, but she had her dreams. A lump rose in her throat as she looked at the sleeping child. She wanted a son like him. She kissed his forehead and smoothed out the wrinkles in the warm pajama top, then tucked the blanket around his shoulders.

Nathan's family had arrived at the emergency shelter while Rachel was setting up tables for the Red Cross help desk. She found her duffel bag, which she had tossed in a corner, and pushed aside her blue sweatshirt to retrieve the bear tucked in the corner. "This is Joseph. He's old and kind of beat up, but would you like him, Nathan? He's a friendly bear."

The boy's eyes glanced from her to the bear. Nathan sniffed and reached out to wrap his hand around the bear's arm. He tucked Joseph close and sighed, then leaned his head back down against his mom's shoulder.

A shared smile with Nathan's mom and Rachel had made her first friend of this tragedy. Ann Noles was a single mom who worked emergency dispatch for the 911 center. She was staying optimistic that something in her house could be salvaged. Rachel found in Ann a kindred spirit.

Nathan's brother Adam was asleep now, his sleeping bag spread on top of one of the gym mats. Rachel reached over and picked up the paperback he'd been reading with the help of a small flashlight, marked the page he was on, and slid it in his backpack. A teddy bear had helped Nathan; she was still working on something for Adam. The flooding had destroyed a four-year collection of comic books he had mowed yards and run errands to be able to buy.

Ann would be moving her family from the shelter to stay with friends tomorrow, for it would be some time before they could get back into their home to start the cleanup. Adam wasn't thrilled with the idea of going back to school on Monday. The guys working on the levees had made him welcome. It was much more exciting than school.

Rachel leaned her head against Nathan's, closed her eyes, and sought a few moments of rest. Her days began before dawn. Floods were harder to work than tornadoes because they first exhausted people with a fight against the water and then presented them with nothing but devastation. The tragedy would strike home anew when people could see the loss—chairs punched through ceilings, furniture smashed and piled up by the water, plaster collapsed, appliances destroyed. Exhaustion and dashed hopes would overwhelm people.

Rachel had built her life around helping hurting people, but she just wasn't as young as she used to be, and the pace wore at her. Being a trauma psychologist for the Red Cross was a young person's profession. Not everyone was able to remain as optimistic as Ann, and keeping other people's spirits up inevitably drained her own.

How is Jennifer doing?

Whenever Rachel paused in the midst of her day, her thoughts returned to her sister. Jennifer's cancer had gone through a brief remission, then came back more aggressive than before. It was around her spine and had moved into her liver. This return stay at Johns Hopkins was lasting longer than her first admission a year ago. The news wasn't good. Rachel had to get back to Baltimore to see her.

Having a close family was one of those dreams that had come true with the O'Malleys, and the idea of losing her sister to this cancer… The thought was enough to make tears return. Jennifer was the most precious friend she had.

"He's in love."

Rachel opened her eyes and blinked away the moisture before turning her head and offering a smile. She hadn't heard Cole come into the gym. "So am I."

He sat down on the mat to her left. Mud had stained the shirt he put on this morning. She was tempted to reach over and try to brush some of it off. It would dry stiff and be uncomfortable, but she knew he wasn't done for the evening. He'd be walking the sandbag levee several times through the night.

He opened the duffel bag he'd left near hers and found dry socks. "Did you get some dinner?"

"They brought in chicken tonight."

"I'll buy you a real dinner when this is over."

"It's a deal."

He paused to look over. "Really?"

She chuckled at his reaction. "How many times have I pleaded work as an excuse lately?"

He smiled at her. "Three, but who's counting?"

She'd spent enough time with Cole since Christmas to know that she more than just enjoyed his company. She was looking at a guy she could spend the rest of her life with. And as hopeful and joyous as that idea was, as much as she wanted to explore what their relationship might become, she just didn't have much time or energy to offer at the moment.

She knew the other O'Malleys would catch wind of their relationship soon. She had done her best not to mention Cole too often around them to avoid the speculation. But in trying to save herself and Cole from some of that family attention, she'd probably been more cautious with him than warranted. "Let's not do Mexican."

"How about Chinese?"

"Sounds good."

"I'll look forward to it." His gaze shifted to the boy she held. He reached over and tucked Nathan's teddy bear closer. "He looks comfortable."

"I like kids."

"Me too."

She smiled and rested her head against Nathan, choosing to let the comment pass.

"Ann is just finishing up at dispatch," Cole mentioned. "Are you okay with the boys for another twenty minutes?"

"Yes."

Cole leaned his head back against the wall, folded his arms across his chest, and closed his eyes. "Wake me when she gets back."

Rachel hesitated for a moment, doubt creeping in just for an instant that she was reading Cole's interest in Ann correctly. "Sure."

He didn't open his eyes but he did smile. "She's a friend, Rae. I like her boys. But it's your brother who has his eyes on their mom."

"Stephen?" She had only one brother not involved in a serious relationship at the moment. Her surprise woke Nathan.

"Hmm. Only reason I can think of for why a paramedic hangs around dispatch on a Friday night."

She could think of another, but still… "He offered to help them move to her friend's tomorrow."

"I heard that too."

Ann had mentioned that she'd met Stephen, but she hadn't asked anything beyond a couple of general questions. Rachel thought about it as she rocked Nathan back to sleep. "Stephen?"

Cole chuckled and reached over to pat her shoulder. "You've been busy."

Rachel saw a sliver of light appear as the door to the gym opened and the person entering the room paused to let her eyes adjust to the dim light inside. Ann crossed the room with care and eased down on the air mattress beside her.

"Nathan woke and realized you were gone," Rachel whispered. She waited until Ann was settled, then eased Nathan onto his mom's lap, immediately missing the weight and comfort of holding him. Rachel tugged a tissue from her jean's pocket and wiped away a tear trace from the boy's cheek. "How was work?"

"Hectic." Ann lowered her head against her son's and closed her eyes. "I'm so tired the air mattress will feel like a featherbed tonight."

"I put your ice pack in the freezer. Want to use it for twenty minutes before you crash?" Ann had waded into the flooding to help a neighbor and had unfortunately taken a hard shot from a floating tree limb.

Ann nodded. "I could use it. Thanks."

Rachel went to get the ice pack. She snagged two tapioca pudding cups and spoons on the way back. It was nice having a friend to share the quiet moments with at the shelter. Pausing inside the doorway, she searched among the three-by-five cards on the corkboard with her penlight. She found five messages for Ann and took them with her across the gym. Ann was cuddling with Nathan.

"A few messages were left for you today. And Cole said he needed to talk to you." The man slept so soundly he hadn't stirred at their quiet conversation. After three days of fighting the river, his exhaustion had to be complete. Every time Rachel had seen him he was in the middle of the work.

"Let him sleep. He was passing on a message from my cousin, and I got it just before I left work." Ann leaned around Nathan and settled the ice on her knee. She sucked in a breath at the cold.

Rachel winced in sympathy. "You need to see a doctor."

"It's just bruised. I should have gotten up and walked more today. Sitting just made it stiffen." Ann relaxed and opened the pudding cup.

Rachel offered the Hallmark card Cole had left for her. Ann laughed as she read it, glancing at the sleeping Cole, then back at Rachel. "He's sweet on you." She handed back the card.

"I hope so." Rachel tucked it in her bag to make sure it got home with her. "I'm thinking about being gone for a couple days," she said, testing out the idea.

"Going out East to see your sister?"

"Trying to figure out the logistics of making it happen."

"You should go."

The kids needed her. Her sister Jennifer needed her. Rachel was stuck with the reality that she couldn't be two places at once. "I'll be back before the water recedes."

Ann smiled. "Trust me, the water will still be here." She laid Nathan down and stretched out beside him. "I heard a rumor today."

"What's that?"

Ann reached over and rubbed Adam's back. "Jack was behind my son's desire to toss a ship in a bottle into the river."

Rachel licked the lid of her pudding cup. "My brother is a kid at a heart."

"I noticed that. Adam talks about him all the time. Jack's a good man."

"All my brothers are. Stephen is the responsible one." Rachel bunched her pillow behind her head and stretched out on her own sleeping bag.

"I've noticed. He brought me flowers tonight."

"Did he?"

"Hmm," Ann murmured.

Rachel hesitated, wondering if Ann would say more. "If you'd like to go out, I'll baby-sit for you."

"He didn't ask me."

Rachel pushed herself up on her elbow. "Why not?"

"Good question. Will you ask him for me?"

Rachel reached for her jacket and her phone.

Ann stayed her hand as she smiled. "Tomorrow is soon enough."

"You're ruining my fun."

Ann chuckled. "Thanks, Rae."

"For what?"

"Telling Stephen to bring me flowers."

She'd been found out. "You're welcome. I kind of figured you needed something to brighten your day."

"Don't apologize. A nice guy bringing me flowers and flirting fits the bill beautifully."

"I didn't tell him to flirt."

Ann smiled. "Exactly. It was nice for morale. I'll take you up on the baby-sitting. Tell Stephen I like a good steak and salad."

"Done." Rachel had never met a crisis that flowers couldn't help. It sounded like sending Stephen on that errand had turned out to be a good move. Rachel tucked her arm under her head and closed her eyes. It was after eleven, and in six hours she would be starting another long day.

Rachel woke to the sensation of someone tickling her wrist. She moved her hand, smiling. "Cole, that—" she murmured, opening her eyes. No one was there. Her pager was going off. She had clipped it to a sweatband on her wrist to ensure that she would wake if it went off. She tugged it free and looked at the number. Her heart broke at the special number, suspecting what the page meant. She slipped from the sleeping bag, left the gym, and returned the page in the quiet hall.

"Rachel, he didn't come tonight."

Marissa was crying.

"Oh, honey, I'm so sorry." Rachel walked outside and sat down on the steps, hearing the hurt and wishing Mr. Collins could see past his own grief to understand what he was doing to his daughter. Marissa was a junior in high school, and her music competition had been tonight, the top awards included scholarships to college. Tonight had mattered.

"I got your message. Mom said I should call you back in the morning."

"I asked you to call," Rachel said. "Trust me, friends don't care about the time. How did you do?"

"Second."

"I'm proud of you, Marissa."

"Linda took first. Her solo was wonderful."

"There's always next year."

"I wanted Dad to be there."

"I know, honey. He gave his word. He should have been there." Marissa had lost her leg in a car accident two years ago. Traumatic enough for a young girl, but her dad had been driving and he'd never been able to get past his own grief. He had walked out last year. Broken promises hurt when you're an adult, but when you're a child and it's done by family— Rachel had been there, and even decades later the hurt didn't entirely fade. The only thing she could do at this point was be a friend and listen.

"Mom took me out to eat afterward. I was too nervous before then."

"What did you have?"

"She talked me into trying the scampi. It was pretty good." The girl's tears were fading. "I just thought he might come."

"Love always hopes," Rachel said softly. "He's still hurting over the fact that he was driving."

"Yeah."

Marissa had fought for two years to get her life back. But family wounds hurt so much deeper than physical ones.

"Am I doing something wrong?" Marissa whispered.

Rachel closed her eyes. "No. Your dad always wanted to protect you. Now he feels a need to protect you from himself. It will eventually get better, Marissa. Remember when we talked about how time changes people? Keep giving him opportunities into your life. There will be a day when he'll feel able to come. When he does, just start with 'I love you.'"

Silence lingered. "Thanks."

"Time, M. It will help."

Rachel leaned over to pick up two jacks a child had missed.

"Greg Sanford asked me to the prom."

"Did he?" Rachel was pleased to hear the news, for she knew how much Marissa had hoped to be invited. "I've got to meet this gentleman. I already like him. What did you say?"

"I said yes, as long as he wouldn't ask me to dance. We'd just go."

"Greg has been there for you this last year. Trust me, you'll have a wonderful time."

"I wish he didn't graduate and leave in four months. I'm going to miss him."

"Did he receive his acceptance papers yet?" Rachel asked, feeling out the changes coming for her friend.

"From the Air Force academy. He wants to become a pilot like his dad." Marissa hesitated. "Do you think we could maybe have a soda next time you're in town?"

"I'm nearby," Rachel said. "I can meet you tomorrow, or we can do something next week when I get back from visiting Jennifer."

"After school next week would be nice."

"It's a date." Rachel wrote a note on the palm of her hand until she could update her day planner for the month of March. This kind of fatigue shot holes in her memory. "Anything you need or want me to tell your mom?"

"Everything there is okay."

"Anything you're not telling me that I should know?"

Marissa paused to think about it. "I'm okay there too."

"Then I'll see you next week. If you want to talk before then, promise to call me?"

"Yes. Thanks, Rae."

"Honey, I'm proud of you." Her pager went off again. "I'll call your mom tomorrow to confirm arrangements for next week," Rachel said as she got to her feet. It was a page from Jack, and that meant trouble at the levee.

"Cole." Rachel shook him gently, wishing she didn't have to wake him. He'd fallen asleep sitting against the wall with his chin tucked against his chest, arms folded. She admired his ability to close his eyes and drop off. If he worried about things, she'd never been able to figure out when. They certainly didn't affect his sleep.

Cole opened his eyes, blinked, and focused on her.

"Jack paged. They need you at the levee."

He took a deep breath and sighed. "Okay, I'm awake."

"It's 1 A.M."

"I didn't ask."

She let her hand settle on his forearm as she smiled back at him. "I know, but your watch stopped. It's blinking this strange pattern of red and white numbers. Nathan thought it was your night-light."

"Water and watches do not mix. It's never going to dry out."

She stepped back as Cole rose to his feet.

"What's going on?"

"Jack said something about too much mud in the water—it's clogging the pumps."

Cole reached forward and rested his hand on her shoulder. "You were up?"

"I had another call."

"If you need a place to hide so you can get some sleep, try the front seat of one of the fire department vehicles. No one will find you."

He was taking care of her in the same way he took care of his men. It was nice. "Thanks."

"Take me up on it. And bring Adam down to the levee later this morning. Jack's got something he should see."

"I'll do that."

"You really said yes to finding time for dinner?" His thumb rubbed her shoulder blade. "I would hate to think I had been dreaming."

She chuckled. "Chinese. And hopefully an evening with no interruptions."

He was stalling, not wanting to break this moment. She didn't either. He was so good-looking half asleep—she wanted to give him a hug and get swallowed in one in return. "Go to work, Cole."

"Yes, ma'am." He smiled at her and headed toward the door.

Rachel watched him leave and then settled back on her sleeping bag. She reset her pager and wrapped her arm around her pillow. When she closed her eyes, she was still smiling. A smile from Cole and an invitation to dinner was nearly as nice as getting flowers.

"What's happening, Jack?"

Cole found Rachel's brother in the parking lot where they had the flat-bottom fire rescue boat parked testing brake lights on the trailer. "I didn't want to worry Rae. Lisa needs us. She said to bring a body bag."

"Where is she?"

"Rosecrans Road."

Cole squeezed the bridge of his nose and tried to get past the fact that it was 1 A.M. "Please tell me she knew I was joking with her earlier. Is the body embalmed?"

"Lisa's first words when I returned her page were, 'the water is destroying my crime scene!' Then she got testy. It sounds real to me."

"You've got interesting sisters."

"Tell me about it."

Cole pulled out his keys. "I'll drive. Do we need more than the two of us?"

"It sounds like she needs us for transport. Company 42 is working in the area."

"Okay. Let's go see what she's gotten herself into."

Two

The intersection of Rosecrans Road and Clover Street had become a parking lot for emergency vehicles. A hundred yards further east, Rosecrans disappeared into standing water. Men were wading through the water around a brick house three blocks down, visible in the improvised lighting set along the edge of the roof. The house was on a slight rise, but the front yard and the driveway had disappeared underwater. Cole saw a man leaving the garage lose his balance. "Another few minutes and those men are going to find themselves unable to get back here to safe ground."

Jack swung down from the truck. "Cops are just like civilians when it comes to underestimating rising water. How are we going to float the boat?"

Cole walked into the water until it reached his bootlaces. The roadway flooding appeared to be backwater with the current coming toward him. "I'll back up the truck."

Jack buckled on his life vest. "I was afraid you were going to say carry it." He released the straps across the boat, climbed up on the hitch, removing the locking pin on the winch. "Okay, let's do it."

Cole backed up along the road until Jack was able to shove the boat off the trailer and float it. Cole returned the truck to a safe distance, parked it, and picked up the body bag they'd brought along in the truck bed. He waded back to where Jack was idling the boat. The water quickly deepened.

Jack steered the boat right up the driveway of the house in question and gently beached the flat bottom of the boat on the concrete. Cole stepped off the front of the boat and tied the rope to a brick planter by the garage. Men were working to build a break wall across the front steps with bags of dirt, birdseed, and anything else they could find in the garage.

"Who's in charge?"

"Detective Brad Wilson, inside."

Cole knew the name. "Wait here, Jack." He stepped over the improvised wall to enter the house. Four men were in the hallway, and he could see another two in what looked like the dining room. With the power out, the lighting inside was established by bright flashlights.

"Cole, good timing." Detective Wilson came to meet him, picking his way around evidence markers. "This situation is getting away from us. I didn't want men walking back through the water in the dark."

"Jack can take five at a time."

"You know this river better than I do. Can you handle the water battle and arrange the evacuation? I need what time is left to work the crime scene."

"Sure." Cole stepped into the living room. Halogen flashlights had been set around to provide basic lighting. He dealt with fire deaths, but murder was something else. A woman, probably in her thirties, who appeared to have been shot once in the chest, was lying on her side near the coffee table. It was a sight that made Cole feel nauseous. He couldn't see her face and he had no desire to. This memory would already be hard enough to shake. Lisa O'Malley was bending over the body, slipping paper bags around the lady's hands to protect evidence.

"I've got your body bag."

Lisa looked over and rose to cross the room and get it. "Thanks, Cole. I went through the three I had with me at a car accident." Her shoes squished. "Would someone please stop this water? Sandbag the doorways or something."

"It's coming up through the flooded basement," one of the officers working the problem called.

"Then block the basement doorway. Start a bucket brigade and haul it out. I need more time."

Cole stepped around the man dusting for fingerprints and went to see the problem. Two inches of water stood in the kitchen and had made it across the dining room floor. The water was beginning to soak the living room rug. He tagged the two nearest men. "Check under the kitchen sink and in the utility room. Garbage bags, freezer bags—grab whatever there is. Fill the bags with water and stack them—create a barrier at the basement doorway, another at the kitchen doorway, and a third at the dining room doorway. If you can't stop it, try to control it. Lisa, prioritize. You've got ten minutes max."

"Make it fifteen."

"Ten, and your time is running."

"You're killing me here." She had the body bag open. "Wilson, let's get her out of here."

Cole sent five men to the boat and then turned his attention to helping create the final barrier into the living room. The cushions from the dining room chairs worked as a fast sponge to stop the water from crossing the boundary. One of the officers tossed him some of the empty plastic bags they'd found.

"Does anyone have a name for her yet?" Lisa asked the room at large.

"I just found her purse," an officer said. "Carol Iles. 32. Her driver's license expires in July."

"What else does she have in her billfold?"

"Seventy-nine dollars in cash, credit cards, library card, and what looks like an electronic key card—to the federal court building no less."

"Great. Marcus is going to love to hear that." Lisa's brother was a U.S. Marshal, a job that involved protecting the federal courts and those who worked in them. Lisa pointed to an officer. "An address book, bills, files from her desk—shove them in a box and get it out of this water. Find me as much as you can about Carol's life."

"I'm on it."

"Do we have pictures of the blood splatters on the wall?" Lisa asked the crime lab photographer.

"Got 'em."

"I need as many pictures of this room as you can take, then get the hallway and doorways. And if you can get out there, I need photos of the garage and her car." She pivoted on her heel to look around. "Someone start bagging these couch cushions and throw pillows. If it's fabric and it moves, I want it sealed and out of here."

"What about the bloody lamp shade?"

"Take it."

Lisa rose and with Detective Wilson's help lifted the body bag. They carried the woman to the hall.

Lisa came back to examine the scene afresh, shining her light around the living room walls and floor. "She was shot, but where's the gun? Where's the shell casing?"

"This room is a hiding place for small objects," Wilson said.

"Then let's start moving furniture. We need that shell casing."

One of the officers working to keep the water away from the front door stepped inside. "The boat is coming back."

Cole sent two cops and two of the coroner technicians transporting the victim out to the boat, along with all the bagged evidence they could carry.

"Lisa." Cole waited until she turned. "We can take the living room rug if you want it. But we've got to do it now."

"Yes, I want it. See if she has clean sheets in the hall closet. I want something as a control barrier before we roll it. Who checked her bedroom?"

"I did," a technician called out.

"Have sheets been gathered to take, toothbrush and hairbrush, medicine bottles?"

"Bagged and ready to go."

Cole helped Wilson move the couch into the dining room to free the floor rug. "Four minutes, Lisa." The house was groaning. He could hear the water gurgling up into the floorboards under their feet. It would be pouring out of the heating ducts any moment.

Lisa spread out the sheets. Cole had done some unusual things in his job, but rolling up a bloody rug by flashlight was a first. Wilson helped him lift it. "Let's set it on chairs until the boat gets back." Water began cascading into the room from the floorboard ducts. Lisa jumped back as it swept across her feet.

He heard Jack's call. "There's the boat. Everyone is leaving this trip."

Cole let the technician and Detective Wilson take the carpet out. He helped Lisa gather up the last of the evidence bags.

"So much stuff I didn't get..."

"There's no choice, Lisa. We've got to go."

Cole waded to the boat, unloaded the items he carried, and came back for Lisa as she stepped outside. He grabbed her as the floodwaters hit her feet and tried to knock her over. "We stayed too long." He carried her down the flooded drive to the boat. Jack helped her over the side. Cole heaved himself into the boat and took a seat on the bench beside Lisa.

"Someone is getting away with murder because of a flood."

Cole leaned around Lisa and got them both towels. "Who found her?"

"A cop checking on the mandatory evacuation. From the rigor mortis, it happened probably three to four hours ago."

"As bad as the scene was, it could have been worse. She might not have been found until after the floodwaters subsided."

"I know." Lisa tried to wring water out of her denim pant legs. "Man, I hate wet socks. Wilson, do you have any ideas?"

"The mail on the dining room table was in two stacks, one opened and one unopened, with one envelope dropped on top half-opened. There was an open soda can on the counter, still cool enough that the can was sweating. I didn't see signs of forced entry. Her purse still had cash in it."

"She opened the front door and someone shot her," Lisa offered.

"Could be that simple."

"I saw nothing in her home that suggested two people lived there—milk was bought in a half gallon; the shoes I saw were the same size; the sink had one cereal bowl and one glass. There were no pictures of her with someone, not even one that looked like a family picture. Did you see anything in the house that suggested otherwise?"

"No." Wilson braced the rolled carpet as Jack swerved the boat to miss a floating tree limb. "She lived alone; she was shot for a reason other than robbery. It's probably domestic trouble."

"Maybe." Lisa shook her head. "Her car was in the middle of her two-car garage. The soda was on the counter, not at the table where she was opening the mail. A second person could have been there and tried to get outside. There may be another victim we didn't find. Until the water recedes we're guessing." Lisa leaned over and tapped her forehead against Cole's shoulder.

He smiled and squeezed the back of her neck, understanding well how an O'Malley reacted to being stymied. "Time will tell."

She sat back with a sigh. "I want the murder weapon found."

"Cole." Jack pointed to the north.

A dog was swimming in the water, trying to make it to dry ground, his eyes the first thing visible as the torchlight reflected on the dark water.

Cole leaned over the side of the boat and called the dog. The mutt changed course toward them but the current impeded his progress. Jack steered to meet the animal. Cole hauled the animal aboard. He got a lap full of wet, exhausted dog. The animal was shivering, his fur wet and plastered to his body, appearing to be nothing but skin and bones. There was no sign of a collar.

"What are we going to do with him?" Lisa asked.

Cole stroked the mutt's tattered ears. He had room for a dog at his place, and he wouldn't mind keeping him if no owner could be found. The animal could also use some immediate help. "For tonight, take him to Rae."

Three

Rachel snapped her fingers to get the dog's attention. She offered him a breakfast biscuit one of the children had dropped by the picnic table. It was taken carefully from her fingers. He looked like part sheepdog for the curly coat, part basset hound for the ears, and part German shepherd for the nose.

Cole had been like a little boy in his delight, lugging the wet animal up the stairs of the community shelter last night. It had been a labor of love to try to clean the dog up. She'd sacrificed some of her no-tears shampoo and a blanket taken from her car trunk. She banished the animal from staying inside but had made a bed for it in a box that she set in a sheltered spot of the breezeway.

The animal slapped his tail against her jeans. "I know; you love whoever feeds you."

The dog took off to rejoin Adam. It'd been sticking like a shaggy shadow to Adam's side this morning, for the boys were lavishing the mutt with attention.

Rachel watched Stephen shift boxes in the back of his truck, helping Ann pack the few belongings she had been able to get out of the house and bring to the shelter. He was giving them a lift to their temporary home. Nathan was standing in the bed of the truck, peering over the side at his brother Adam, who was lobbying to ride in the truck with Stephen.

Ann paused beside Stephen, crowding his space, her comment making him laugh. Rachel had already seen at least one wink from Stephen to Ann's boys. Cole was right. Something was going on between Stephen and Ann. If her brother hadn't already corrected that lapse of a missing dinner invitation, she knew he likely would before he dropped them off.

Rachel rested her chin on her fist, a rush of emotion leaving an ache of sadness in its wake. She was glad for Stephen, but if he found someone special, she'd be the last of the O'Malleys officially unattached. She didn't want that distinction.

"That frown is going to stick."

She glanced over. Gage Collier took a seat across from her at the picnic table. He was hanging around because he was a reporter and smelled a story in the flooding, but also because he knew she was here. The last two years had refined their friendship into gold. He would have been celebrating his son's first birthday this year if his pregnant wife hadn't died in a fire. It had been a hard couple years, for his wife had been one of her best friends.

Gage didn't mean to miss her sadness now and incorrectly assume it was the thousand details of this flood getting her down. He would probably even understand if she explained. "Did you bring a newspaper?" Rachel asked.

"Hello, Gage. It's nice to see you, Gage. You're here early…"

She heard the gentleness under his teasing. The care she remembered him taking with Tabitha was now being directed toward her. He knew how hard the last few months of Jennifer's illness had been on her. She smiled back. "Hello, Gage. It's nice to see you, Gage. I haven't seen a newspaper. What did you write about this week?"

"The proposed tollway fare increase. You're not into politics so you would just read it and ask me, 'what?' I did bring you an early mock-up of tomorrow's comics."

"Bless you."

He handed over the folder. "You're so easy to please."

She opened it, drew out the pages, and started reading the comics.

Gage tugged out the notebook that went everywhere with him and flipped to a back page. "I checked your apartment and put the mail on the kitchen counter. Nothing urgent there, but your neighbor asked me to tell you, 'Kathy said six on the third and bring Crock-Pot potatoes,' whatever that means."

She glanced up. "A birthday party for a five-year-old, want to come?"

He made a face at her and drew a laugh in response. "Your fern was dying. I probably drowned it."

"It's the thought that counts."

"I'm a thoughtful kind of guy."

She tugged over his plate and speared his pineapple slice. They had shared breakfast many times over the years. He thought yellow fruit should be banned. He only got pineapple because he knew she liked it.

"Eat your eggs," he suggested.

"They're cold. I was on my way to reheat them."

He pushed his plate over and offered his fork. "Eat. I'll go get another tray."

He left his notepad and crossed over to the serving table. The Red Cross had made arrangements with a local restaurant to set up and serve food on picnic tables outside under the breezeway. It gave parents a chance to relax and not worry if a child dropped something, and it let crews working on the levees come and go. The menu this morning was cereal or fruit, scrambled eggs, toast, and hot blueberry muffins. She'd made the rounds of picnic tables earlier, pouring coffee and asking questions, listening. Breakfast was a good time to stop and talk with people, pass on news of progress, and note new problems that needed to be solved.

With little warning of the evacuation, most people had been able to get out with only their children, pets, cars, and what they could carry. Rachel had been able to solve the hot shower and toothbrush problems. Prescription refills. Shoes. She was working now on the more complex items: where to go for temporary housing—friends, family, or a hotel—photo IDs so some people could pick up their mail at the post office, temporary checks, replacement credit cards, insurance agent contacts. Small steps but they mattered.

The loss of little things amplified the sense of having lost control of their lives and was often the point when the stress overwhelmed. A mom would break down in tears because she didn't have her fingernail file. A dad would lose it when he wanted his change and didn't have pennies. A child would cry because shoelaces on borrowed tennis shoes were not tied right. Rachel couldn't restore to people the valuable things they had lost—pictures and keepsakes and memories—but the other items she could help replace. And by solving the small things, a reservoir of trust was built that the bigger obstacles coming could also be solved.

Gage returned, jelly-smothered toast stacked beside his eggs.

"Did you know they think this flooding could have been prevented?"

"Don't ruin my breakfast." She looked up from the comics. Gage was predictable: he was either seeking news or passing on news. "You're serious."

"Yes."

She glanced around. "Keep your voice down. What did you hear?"

"When they built the bridge, they narrowed the river to save some money. But because that speeds up the water flow, they were supposed to extend the concrete along the riverbank to the original river width. They took it only half that distance. It was the dirt around the ends of the concrete that gave way and brought down the levee. Who lives in the house nearest the river? There may have been some warning."

"Don't make it worse, Gage. They just lost everything."

"It's a story. It's breaking. If not by me, it will be someone else. I'm just going to ask a few questions. What did you see that night? That kind of thing."

She could steer him or let him go out on his own, but she couldn't get him off the story. "Mrs. Sands will talk with you. She lives in the brick house with the ivy on the chimney, two houses down from the bridge crossing. Nice lady, in her seventies, still sharp. She has lived in that house for thirty years. The house one closer to the bridge—the owner is out of town. He's coming home to a mess."

"Where can I find Mrs. Sands?"

"She's staying with her sister Eva Grant in Mount Prospect. I've got her address in my reference book."

"You're sending me an hour away and you're enjoying this."

She just smiled and finished the fruit.

Gage closed his notebook. "What did you hear about the murder Lisa was working last night?"

"Just that Jack and Cole took the boat down to help her out with transportation." She tried not to dwell on what her sisters did for a living. Lisa was a forensic pathologist, Kate a hostage negotiator. The aftereffects of tragedies were hard enough to deal with.

"It was one of three shootings overnight. Someone shot an off-duty cop as he was leaving a restaurant, and a taxi driver was robbed and killed."

"You're full of good news today."

"Which is why I left mentioning them until after you ate breakfast." Gage got to his feet. "Cassie Ellis sent you a package. It's in the backseat of the car. Do you want me to get it before I chase down this lead?"

"Please. Cassie was looking for a rare comic book to be the linchpin of a new collection for Adam. Did she say which one it was?"

"Just that he should like it."

Rachel shoved keys and cash into her pocket on the off chance she'd have time to stop and buy Cole a Hallmark card in return. She picked up the package for Adam and headed toward the levee where she'd last seen the boy. She found Adam with Cole saying good-bye to the firefighters. Cole's new dog climbed over a mound of sandbags, chasing the smells.

"How fast is it going?"

Adam scrambled down from his perch on the levee carrying a clipboard. He came to join her and show her. "Cole showed me how to graph the river's speed based on how many seconds it took for the duck to travel between the poles. It's slowing down today. See? This was early this morning; this is now."

She looked at the careful graphs made on a grid. "Excellent job." Adam beamed at the praise and she ruffled his hair. He was a bit shy, careful, and eager to get things right. She was going to miss him. "I got you something to take with you." She held out a hand towel she'd thought to grab from the general resource box. "You'll want to dry your hands first."

After he did so thoroughly, Rachel handed him the sack.

Adam opened it with care. "Wow."

She'd seen Cassie get that same fascinated look on her face when she held a hundred-year-old book. He held the old comic book reverently, careful not to bend the pages as he turned them. "Mom said it was okay?"

The hope in his voice made her smile. "She was the one who gave me the issue and date."

He hugged Rachel, catching her around the waist while holding the comic to the side. "Thanks."

She circled his shoulder and hugged him back. "My brother Jack, the fireman who has that smiley face on the back of his fire coat? His girlfriend Cassie owns a bookstore with rare books. She said she'd help you find some more comics so you can rebuild your collection."

"I've got to go show my mom."

"One more thing." She held out a blue business card. "For you. Since you're going to stay with friends, I might not see you for a couple days. If you have a question or just want to tell me about your day, your mom said you could call me anytime. All you have to do is punch in the special numbers on the back, and I'll know it's you."

"I've heard about your cards."

"You have?" She squeezed his shoulder. "I only give them to special people. If you need anything or if Nathan or your mom need anything, I'll help. That's a promise."

He carefully put the card in his back pocket.

"Adam." He turned at his mom's call. "Ready to go? We're packed."

Rachel nodded. "Better join them."

Adam walked backward two steps, holding the comic book. "I'll treasure this forever."

"You're very welcome. I'll see you soon."

The boy raced to where his mom was waiting. "Mom, she got me a comic. A rare one."

Cole stopped beside her. "Nice of you, Rae."

"It might help when he actually sees what he lost. Thanks for letting him come down here and help out."

"He's a good kid. I've met some of his friends at the middle school. It will be good for him to get back into his routine."

"Anything I need to know about in Adam's network of friends?" She knew Cole was often in the schools teaching fire safety classes. Arsonists tended to get started early.

"A couple pranksters, but nothing to worry about."

"He'll take some ribbing about his stuff being underwater and about sleeping on a gym floor for a few days."

"Sure. He'll also be a hero among his real friends because he's got cool stuff to talk about, not to mention making friends with a rescued dog. This hit him hard, but he's bouncing back fine."

"Did you guys make him an honorary member of Company 81?"

"Who, us?" Cole smiled at her. He nudged a LifeSaver from the roll he held, offering her the orange one at the end.

"How are you doing after last night?" She studied his face, looking for the signs of strain around his eyes that she had begun to recognize when he'd had a lot on his mind. Helping Lisa couldn't have been easy.

"It was a bloody tragedy. I frankly don't know how Lisa handles walking into scenes like that." He shook his head. "Your sister is intense at a crime scene. Trying to collect evidence before the water surged inside made it chaotic."

"Did the water ruin any chance of solving the case?"

"It didn't help. As much as we got out before the water forced us to abandon the scene—it probably wasn't enough. But knowing Lisa, she'll figure it out."

"Lisa will take it personally if she can't. She'll do her best." Lisa was known for her ability to think outside the box and find connections in the evidence that could make a difference. "Thanks for not sending the dog to the pound."

"You're not the only one with a soft heart. He needs to stumble into a few soup bones and see a vet." Cole tossed a dry pair of gloves to a man joining the levee crew. "You were the one who suggested I needed a dog."

"You picked an interesting one. That big three-bedroom house all to yourself, a backyard with shade trees—you could probably use more than one. Have you named him yet?"

He rebuttoned his fire coat, getting ready to rejoin the men resetting the pump lines. "I have to come up with something better than Dog?"

She laughed. "Yes."

One of the pump lines being moved hit the pavement with a sharp crack, and the dog disappeared under the blue pump engine. Cole kneeled to coax him out. "He spooks at sudden noises and darts under the nearest vehicle as if his world was coming apart."

"I've seen it before. A tornado goes through a farming community and the next storm that comes, the animals will crash through fences to find shelter. The poor thing must have been swept into the water."

Cole rose as the dog crept out. "Why don't you name him?"

"Me? I don't know good dog names. I've never had one."

"Think about it for a few days."

"He'll end up with a name like Spot."

The dog barked. Cole laughed and ruffled the mutt's ears. "Sounds like he approves."

"No. You can't name him Spot."

"Naming isn't easy. Can you imagine Adam from the Bible being asked to name every animal on earth? No wonder we ended up with *aardvark*. God probably asked Adam how to spell it and Adam replied two *a*'s."

She smiled because it was funny. And she knew she'd find that fact in the Bible when she looked, for Cole was comfortable with the book she was just beginning to learn. "I can come up with a name somewhere between Spot and aardvark. Give me some time to think about it." Rachel took a step back and slipped her hands in her back pockets. "I'm going to be gone for a few days. Can I take you up on that dinner when I get back?"

"Going East to see Jennifer?"

She nodded.

He searched her face, and she tried to keep the worry under control. "Wish her well," he said gently. "We'll have dinner when you get back. You have my number?"

"Memorized."

"Call collect if you want to talk, okay? It won't be an easy trip."

"Thanks."

"Do me a favor and take me up on it."

The offer helped. "Would you pray for her?" Rachel was a new Christian, and she knew she had so much yet to learn about prayer. She didn't want anything she might not understand to hinder an answer.

"You know I will," Cole said. "Remember, God cares about the small things as well as the large, okay? I know the prayers that Jennifer be healed haven't been answered so far, but if the big prayers don't seem to be getting answered, try the small ones. God really is in the midst of this."

She rested her hand on his arm. Cole was helping her bear this burden in so many ways. The steady, dependable calm he had about life headed the list. There weren't words to say thanks. "I'll call you when I arrive."

Rachel had no idea what the temperature was like in Baltimore. Mid-March, turning into spring…she added two summer-weight shirts and a sweater to her bag. Her bedroom was in chaos as she tried to pack. She pulled more tissues from the box, slipped most in the suitcase, and used the last one to blow her nose as she fought tears. She had been with Jennifer through chemotherapy and radiation treatments and had stepped in to help with arrangements for Jennifer's wedding. One remission had come and gone. Her options were shrinking. The idea of seeing Jennifer and having to find something rosy and positive to say… She simply had nothing left to draw from inside, and the last thing Jennifer needed was more sadness. Her brother was on the speaker-phone. "Marcus, I'm bringing the family scrapbooks. What else?"

She was so grateful her brother was already out East with Jennifer. "Just you, honey. I'll meet you at the airport."

She picked up her tickets to check the flight number and time. "It's a 9 P.M. flight, but it'll probably be delayed."

"I'll have a book with me. It's not a problem."

Rachel sank down on the bed, holding the package that had been waiting for her, brought in by Gage with the mail. The return address was from Jennifer. "You can tell Jen I'm obeying her note, but it's killing me to wait to open it."

"It's for the flight out here."

Rachel placed it with her purse. In her job when a crisis erupted and she could do something, her coping skills were pretty good. But when unable to help, her defense mechanism was to freeze. She was doing it now, finding it hard to put one step in front of the next. Marcus was reading her correctly and doing what he could to help her out. It was the second time he'd called this afternoon.

Lord, Jennifer has to get better. Please. There has to be some way for that to come true.

Marcus hadn't called in the entire O'Malley family, and he would have done so if things had changed seriously in the last ten days. Rachel had some hope in that. They were a unique family. All seven of them were orphans. They had met decades earlier at Trevor House and later legally changed their last names. They were a family related not by blood but by choice. The O'Malleys thrived as a group by depending on and being there for one other.

Rachel transferred what work she had to take with her to her brief-case. She added the composition book she'd been using as her log for the flood so she could update her notes during the plane trip. Six months from now a glance at the book and she'd be able to see a person's network of friends and neighbors, see in her notes the small things that would matter the most—birthdays and anniversaries—days when this tragedy would really sting.

"How's Jack doing?" Marcus asked.

She smiled. "Working around the clock and playing in the water. Stephen snapped a few pictures at the levee of what is going on. I'll bring them with me."

"Shari arranged a room for you at the private bed-and-breakfast near the hospital. If you want the company, we brought Jennifer's puppy in for a visit."

Another dog in her life… "I'd like that. Thanks."

"Thank me after he hides your shoes. I'll see you in a few hours. I'll be by a phone if you have any problems."

"I'll see you soon, Marcus." Rachel disconnected the call.

She added the Bible she'd started to read in the last few months to her briefcase. *Jesus, I want so badly not to face this.* She had been tugged toward belief by Jennifer, who had such a joy in her life these days even as she fought the cancer. *I can't figure out how to have that joy in suffering that Jennifer describes. I just wish doctors would call and say the cancer is back in remission and heading toward nonexistence. Having her healed would be such a celebration.* The Bible had numerous accounts of people who were very ill being healed by Jesus. She read those passages and had so much hope that maybe Jesus would heal Jennifer too. Her sister believed He would.

Believing in but not seeing that improvement come—Rachel was accustomed to accepting hard things, but this open question of what Jennifer's future held haunted her. When Jennifer smiled and said it was okay, it was going to be so hard to smile back.

Rachel was afraid she was going to Baltimore to help her sister die.

Four

Rachel waited until the flight east was at its cruising altitude and the flight attendant had brought refreshments before she reached for the package Jennifer had sent with a note that said: 'Open on the way here.' With hesitant hands she tore open the wrapping paper. The box was old and inside it, nestled in tissue paper, was a fabric-bound book whose plaid colors had faded. The words stamped in gold were still readable: *Diary* and a date. It was Jennifer's diary from the year she had come to Trevor House. Rachel picked it up with care. She remembered the day she'd given the gift to Jennifer.

Trevor House

Two Decades Earlier

The group assembled in the third-floor library. The room was musty, the few books on the shelves worn, curled, and warped from heat and humidity. It was a forgotten place, the encyclopedia set even several decades old. Rachel was late to the gathering. She found a seat beside Kate as she offered an apology. Jack and Stephen sat in front of the window taking advantage of the only breeze available. Lisa perched on the edge of an old table. The room was a quiet place to gather, and they had made it their own assembling point when they preferred not to have others listen to their discussions.

"There's a new arrival today," Marcus said, explaining the reason for the meeting. "What do we know about her?"

"A drunk driver hit her parents' car, killing them both," Kate replied. The others winced, for a family with two parents was itself rather rare, and losing both at once was a tragic loss.

"No one wants her?" Stephen asked, his quiet question reflecting what they all felt at the idea.

Kate shook her head. "No family. Not even a distant cousin. She's been staying with neighbors. The court heard the case last week, and no one offering to be her guardian came forward."

Marcus looked around the room. "Do we want a seventh person in our group?"

Rachel tried not to catch his eye, not wanting to be the first one asked to offer an opinion. They must have had a meeting like this to decide on her. It felt selfish to suggest that they had to limit the group size at some point if they wanted to keep it special. Marcus and Kate had led the group for years, and Stephen, Jack, and Lisa were settled in. Rachel was still trying to feel her way. They liked her—why she wasn't quite sure—but they liked her. She wanted to help the group as her thank-you, and if they kept adding numbers, it would be tough to fulfill her role.

Lisa leaned over and tapped Kate's shoulder, whispering something. Kate nodded. "Is she a whiner?" Lisa asked. "We don't need to add a whiner to the group."

Rachel smiled at her roommate. She had never had a more loyal friend in her life, and they had known each other only a few months.

"If she is, I'm sure she'll grow out of it around you," Marcus replied to laughter around the room. "Do we want a seventh person?" he asked again, then looked at her. "Rachel?"

She wasn't sure why he had known she was ambivalent about it, but he was making her decide. "Yes."

"Are you sure?"

She nodded.

"Is that a group consensus?"

There were more nods around the room.

"Then the question becomes, do we want *her* as the seventh?"

"It would make it four to three, gals to guys. I suppose they deserve the advantage in the basketball games," Jack offered.

Kate turned in her chair to smile at him. "You just need another excuse for when we beat you."

"Let's add her," Lisa said. "She'll be the youngest of the group. If she has to endure several years here at Trevor House, we ought to at least make it less hard on her than it was on us coming in."

"She can be our group project."

More laughter met Jack's pronouncement. "Don't get too carried away, Jack," Marcus said. "We're still working on getting you to grow up. Who does she bunk with?"

"Put her with Kate," Lisa suggested. "Kate needs practice at being a mommy."

Kate threw a wadded-up page of notes at Lisa.

"Good idea." Marcus nodded to Kate. "I'll handle talking the office into putting her with you. We need to assemble a welcoming kit. Don't be stingy on items from your stashes."

"Rachel," Kate said, "we need a gift."

She nodded. "Something pretty but useful. I'll find it. And I've still got wrapping paper left."

Marcus stood up. "Let's meet downstairs at one-thirty to greet her."

Rachel had given Jennifer the new diary as her welcoming gift. She opened the small card Jennifer had put in the box.

Rachel,

On a day that was one of the hardest and loneliest in my life, you met me midway up the outside steps before I even reached the front door of Trevor House and asked one question: 'What's your favorite flower?' And by the time I reached the third floor bedroom I had been assigned to, the vases were full of carnations. Kate was sitting on her bed reading a magazine. She glanced up and said hi, then pretended to ignore me so I could wipe tears without being noticed. Lisa stopped by to show off a new gerbil she was searching for a place to hide. Pretty jewelry in a box was on the dresser and a stash of cookies were in the nightstand drawer. Stephen brought artwork for the walls, and Marcus—he came with a VCR so I could watch the videotapes I had of my parents. I got swallowed up and made welcome. And the fact that you sat with me on the stairs that first night and just listened to my story—I have never forgotten what it was like to be loved like that. Remember that as you read this diary and share some memories.

Jennifer

Rachel found her reading glasses, slipped them on, adjusted the reading light, and opened the diary and began to read.

The flight attendant came down the aisle one last time before touchdown, checking trays and seat backs and that people had seat belts buckled. Rachel stowed her items into her briefcase. No matter how much she flew, she would never get accustomed to the disorientation it caused. She had brought one bag and a briefcase, having long ago learned that it was easier to buy what she needed if she ended up staying longer than planned. The plane landed and taxied to a gate. She followed passengers from the plane, Jennifer's gift protected against her chest.

Marcus met her by the gate and took her bag. She leaned into her brother's hug. "She sent me her diary from her first year at Trevor House."

"I know."

"I think I cried and laughed the entire flight here."

"The headache has your eyes practically crossed."

"Add to that I'm hungry."

Marcus stood still, holding her, letting people flow around them. He led the family and there was a reason all of them turned to him: Marcus was a U.S. Marshal. He could handle any trouble that came his way. She hugged him, grateful that he was in her life.

"Kate called. She swung by to see Lisa and the guys. All is quiet on the home front."

"Good. I brought pictures of Jack's ducks."

"I'd ask, but you said Jack's name. They weren't alive, were they?"

She giggled. "Rubber ducks. But I'm sure if someone had suggested the real thing, he would have located them somewhere." She stepped back. "Let's get to this bed-and-breakfast. What time is Jennifer expecting me tomorrow?"

"She asked if I'd bring you over to the hospital about ten. She's got something planned, but she's keeping it a secret."

"How's she doing?"

"Jennifer? Trust me. She hasn't changed. She talked me into wearing a tux and tails and taking a special dinner to her friends in the pediatrics cancer ward."

"I bet you looked...spiffy."

"Shari laughed. Putting my fiancée and Jen together is trouble," Marcus replied, his voice softening at the mention of his fiancée's name. Rachel was glad he had found Shari as his partner for life. Someday she was going to have that too. She thought about Cole and wondered what Marcus would say about him. His opinion mattered to her, more than he knew.

The airport was busy but the parking lots had cleared out. Once seated in the car Rachel opened her briefcase and removed her composition folder for the flood. She clicked on her penlight to make sure she had her to-do list for tomorrow in order. She had a list of calls to make in the morning. She understood the bureaucracies involved in emergency assistance, and just getting people status updates could eliminate a lot of stress.

"What's coming up on your calendar?"

Rachel reached for her day planner. The latch had given way, so she had used sturdy rubber bands to hold it together. "Pretty light. I've got a commission meeting in Washington on May 10. Clayton, Georgia, is dedicating a memorial on May 6 to the five who died in the tornado last year. I'm planning to go. On the come-if-possible list are—" she counted—"twelve graduation and three birthday parties. Denver, Chicago, and Miami. I'll make most of them."

"When's the commission report being released?"

"July. We're already passing around drafts." The Presidential Commission on School Violence had held two public hearings this year and had another two scheduled. She'd been serving on it since December. Kids killed kids. She knew it. She'd counseled kids forced to live through it. But she wished she hadn't said yes when the president of the Red Cross asked her to serve. It was a tough assignment.

"The bottom line?"

"The chain of events leading to a shooting can be broken at a thousand places. But parents, adults, or friends have to intercede. The signs of trouble are there—kids are poor at hiding that kind of pain and anger—but adults and friends often don't step in for just as many reasons. Shootings will keep happening. A report isn't going to change that."

"Not an easy fact to live with."

"No, it's not."

He took her hand and squeezed gently. "Let it go. You've only got time to fight one battle at a time."

"That from a man whose pager goes off more often than mine." Rachel returned the notebooks to her briefcase. "I'm wearing out."

"And I worry about you. Anything I can do?"

She rested her head on the headrest. She wished there were. "A vacation would help. A few days of solid sleep. I'll be able to get both next month."

"You said that last month too."

"I mean it this time."

Marcus slipped a card from his pocket. "I got you something."

She took the plastic card he offered her.

"It's a guarantee of a room at any hotel in their chain, anytime you need one. The bills come to me, so order room service."

She turned it over and laughed at the sticker on the back. There was a badger sticking its nose out of a hole. "I like your gift."

"You better use it."

Marcus had a way of offering just what she needed when she needed it. "I will. Thanks."

Rachel knew hospitals in a way few others outside of staff could. As a trauma psychologist she spent about a third of her life in them—visiting with patients, sitting with relatives, talking with doctors and rescue personnel. When on the job it wasn't uncommon for her to be the one getting direct updates from the hospital personnel to convey to the families involved. She'd learned what to expect and the questions to ask, but it didn't make her any more comfortable spending time in one. She carried the family scrapbooks and wondered what Jennifer had planned for their Sunday.

"Marcus, go ahead and make your call." His partner Quinn Diamond had paged him as they were coming inside.

"You sure?"

"Room 3212. I can find it."

"I'll be up in five minutes."

Rachel was relieved to be able to go up on her own. It was one thing to keep a steady expression for Jennifer, another to fool Marcus who saw her just before she entered the room. She knew how critical it was to keep her composure during the first few minutes.

She found 3212 and leaned around the doorway.

"Rae!" Jennifer beamed at her and waved her into the room. She was sitting up in bed, a newspaper spread across the blanket.

It wasn't the loss of hair covered by a colorful scarf, the jaundice, or the thinness that threatened to freeze Rachel in the doorway. Jennifer looked so incredibly young. Rachel crossed the room to the bedside and hugged her sister, in no hurry to let go. "Hi." She leaned back, relieved to find Jen's blue eyes clear of pain. There was joy there. "Marriage looks like it suits you."

Jennifer grinned at her. "Tom just went to check on something for me. Sit, Rae, sit. Marcus didn't tell me a fraction of it." Rachel eased down on the side of the bed. Jen laid her hands lightly on either side of Rachel's face and studied her. "The stress is showing. The missing sleep shadows are growing and we need to get some hair color. You've got gray hair appearing."

"I've been working around Jack recently."

Jennifer laughed. "That would do it."

Rachel tugged a strand. "I've been hoping it would come in as a nice white."

"Just gray, I'm afraid." A quiet moment lingered as Jen still held her face. "Don't worry about something you can't change. Do that for me?"

Rachel didn't have a good answer to that request. "I like to worry." She was struggling with a new faith that said it wasn't necessary. It felt so foreign not to worry.

"I know." Jen smiled at her. "I love you for it, even though I want you to stop." She rubbed Rachel's arms, then nodded toward what Rachel held. "What did you bring me?"

"Photo albums."

"Oh, excellent! The old ones too?"

Rachel nodded. "I thought Shari might like to see the ones of Marcus as a teenager."

"She'll love it."

The door opened. "I found a blanket, but they only had pink, I'm afraid, so we're going to stand out for a mile." Tom came into the room pushing a wheelchair. "I had greater success on the pillows and beach towels though. Hey, Rae."

"Tom." Rachel smiled as she turned. She was enveloped in a hug by him.

"You ready to bolt from this place for the day?"

Rachel looked over at Jen. "What do you have planned?"

"An adventure. Bring the albums."

"Marcus is on the way up," Rachel commented.

"Good. He's going to get my puppy for me. Shari is bringing lunch."

Tom pushed the wheelchair next to the bed. Jennifer rested her head against her husband's shoulder, wrapped her arms around his neck, and he carefully lifted her from the bed to the wheelchair.

Rachel blinked away tears. Jen was no longer walking. It might not be official, but Tom made the move with an ease that said he had done it many times.

Blanket, pillow, beach towels...Rachel was glad they were getting out of the hospital for a while. She already found herself at her limits and the day had only just begun.

Rachel had forgotten how relaxing it was to be with her sister. For the afternoon Rachel's attention barely went beyond the fact that it was a comfortable temperature, sunny, and she was in love with the puppy scampering around her feet. For the first time in months there was peace inside. "He's wonderful."

"You need a dog of your own," Jennifer said.

Rachel was already coming to that conclusion. If she couldn't have kids in the forseeable future, at least she could have a dog.

Jennifer reclined on a blanket to enjoy the day outside. The Johns Hopkins complex was behind them, this grassy park area held for future expansion. They were just a few of those who had come out to enjoy the day. It was a place of normalcy for those otherwise having to fight against serious illness.

"My Washington apartment doesn't allow pets, and the Chicago one—I'm not home enough."

"Then it's time to move."

"You make that sound so simple. Maybe next year." Rachel struggled to stop a yawn. Lunch followed by the warmth of the day was making her sleepy. Marcus's fiancée Shari was already dozing lightly, a book resting open on the blanket beside her.

Jennifer's attention turned to Tom hustling over the grass tossing a Frisbee back and forth with Marcus. "Is my husband good-looking or what?"

Rachel laughed. "You don't want me to answer that. You get jealous."

"I love being married."

"I've figured that out. Tom spoils you rotten."

"He tries to." Jennifer tossed the sunscreen she used out of habit to the side. "How's Cole?"

"Jen."

"I'm not the only one who would like you to be married."

Cole was one of the most intriguing guys she knew, but Rachel didn't want to mislead her sister. "He's Jack's boss. He's a friend. Let's leave it at that." She had so many knots in her past, and her present would never fit a definition of orderly. As much as she hoped something might work out with Cole, she knew better than to assume anything. Her past wasn't as tough as Kate's or as tragic as Jennifer's, but it had still left scars.

Jennifer dropped the towel over her face. "Where'd I go?"

A bark, and the puppy set to joyfully digging with his front paws at the towel. He lifted the edge and shoved his nose underneath to pull it off Jennifer. The little guy gave her face a bath as she giggled. "I taught him this game."

"So I see."

The puppy tried to climb over Jennifer and got stuck. She helped him with a push. "He is so much fun."

Rachel held out her hand and the puppy came to climb all over her. "He still looks a bit like a butterball." He settled across her lap, panting.

"Butterball is his unofficial name since my lapse in speech with Jack." Suffering from a bad fall and confused by medicinal side effects, when Jennifer had first seen the golden fur and a very round puppy, she told their brother that Tom had bought her a butterball for Christmas. Amid the laughter, it had stuck.

Jennifer returned to studying the album and the loose pictures

Rachel had slipped in the front. "Who's this?" Jen held up a picture.

"Adam Noles. Jack was teaching him the finer points of skipping rocks in the river."

"One of yours?"

"He got a card," Rachel confirmed.

"I thought so. Think anything from their home will be salvageable?"

"Not much. If it was just rising water in the house, it would be one thing, but there's a strong current through the floodwaters doing a lot of damage. His mom Ann is hopeful, but it's going to be a mess."

"How long before you know?"

"Once the water recedes they have to get the structural engineers in to look at the homes. It will be at least a week before cleanup can start. Have you found the pictures of Jack and his rubber ducks yet?"

"I just did. These are priceless."

Rachel looked at the picture Jen held up. "That duck was his tribute to Cassie." She settled her hands behind her head and closed her eyes against the sun. "Summer is going to be here before we know it. And this sun is going to give me freckles."

"You look good with freckles. You know what we need this summer? An O'Malley ladies only weekend. A hotel, pool, girl talk."

"What a wonderful idea," Rachel agreed.

"Maybe we can talk Kate into setting a wedding date."

"She wants to elope."

"It takes two. Dave's sister Sara would kill him."

"Very true." Rachel wasn't sure which O'Malley wedding would come next. Lisa and Quinn's probably, but Lisa wanted to wait on Marcus, and he and Shari didn't want to set a date while Jennifer was in the hospital. Everyone was trying not to make plans so as not to complicate things for Jennifer.

"Ouch."

Rachel turned sharply, for it wasn't a soft sound. "What's wrong?" She had watched Jennifer closely enough through the day to know that the pain was constant and her energy didn't last long. Her health was precarious at best, all the upbeat talk notwithstanding.

"Just a twinge. I moved wrong." Jen was leaning back on her elbows, cautiously moving her toes.

"Tom!"

"Did you have to—?"

"I had to."

"Here, Jen, lean back against this." Shari offered her pillow.

Tom came hustling over. "Good plan. Lay back, hon."

"The meds are wearing off. That's all."

"Any numbness?" Tom asked.

"Just that all-too-familiar pinch followed by a case of the tingles."

"Since we've been out here for three hours and I've been run ragged by your brother, it's just as well." Tom leaned down and kissed Jen's forehead. "Let's go, darling." He scooped her up and settled her carefully in the wheelchair.

Rachel hurriedly gathered up the blanket and pictures.

"It's no big deal, Rae," Jen tried to reassure. "The meds wear off and it's like an adrenaline letdown. It caught me by surprise is all. I just need a nap."

Rachel smiled at Jen because her sister didn't want this to be a problem. "We both could do with an afternoon nap."

"Who's got the puppy?"

"I do, Jen," Marcus said. "Go with them, Rae. Shari and I will bring the stuff."

Rachel paced in the lounge down the hall from Jennifer's room, feeling like the walls were closing in on her. By the time Jen was settled back in bed, she was no longer trying to insist that it was no big deal. She was in severe pain and the numbness had spread.

Rachel drew in a deep breath, fighting the fear. *Jesus, I can't do this.* How many people had she sat beside who were having to accept losing a loved one? She knew what it would be like toward the end and what the aftermath would do to the O'Malleys. *I see so many lives cut short—by illness, natural disasters, tragedies caused by men. I don't have it in me to lose family. Please, Lord, be merciful.*

Tom stopped beside her and rested his hand on the window glass.

"Is she going to die here?" Rachel whispered.

"They'll tell her to go home first."

"How long does she have?"

"She won't die in a hospital, Rae. I've promised her that."

She leaned against Tom and hugged him. Jennifer had married such a good man. The fact he hadn't even offered a guess for how much time was left… "How can I help you?"

He drew in a deep breath. "Pray. She's still got the heart to win. She doesn't want to talk yet about that not happening."

"She's a realist under that optimism."

"She's not talking about that reality because she knows I can't handle it."

Rachel tightened her grip. She was hurting, but for Tom…this must be agony to daily watch Jen's decline.

"Rae, she's getting better in some ways. Her blood work is finally improving. Another remission is possible."

"But is it likely?"

"No."

The silence lingered. With a child she knew the words to help, with a woman she understood how to communicate with the silence, but for a doctor watching his wife die… "Jen mentioned she was craving peanut butter cookies."

Tom kissed her forehead. "I know why she loves you so much." He tucked a tissue in her hand. "She'll sleep for the rest of the afternoon. Marcus will take you back to the bed-and-breakfast if you'd also like to get a nap. Why don't you join us for dinner around six? Bring the photo albums. It was good to hear her laugh today."

"My pleasure." She hugged him. "Six o'clock."

Rachel was glad Marcus was driving. She wiped her eyes, grateful she didn't have to hide tears from him but doing her best to stop them.

There was a place deep in her heart where an ocean of tears was waiting to fall if she let them start.

"You want to talk?" Marcus asked.

They were almost to the bed-and-breakfast. Rachel shook her head and quieted the puppy she held.

"You need to."

"Is it going to get worse than this in the next week? Do we need to get everyone here?"

Marcus rubbed the back of his neck. "No. Jen is stable. Not doing great, but stable."

"Then I think today I just want to sleep."

Marcus reached over and squeezed her hand. "Kate's coming in on Wednesday for a quick day visit. Jen doesn't have the energy for a bunch of us. We'll have one of us with her at all times, with Tom."

"He needs that support."

"It's there." Marcus glanced over. "You heard about Lisa's tough task during the flood, but did you hear about Kate's evening last night?"

"No."

"She got called out on a domestic squabble, a guy threatening to shoot his elderly mom. It goes on a couple hours; she isn't getting anywhere negotiating with the guy, so she has the SWAT team guys dig up the cable line going into the house and cut it. She got the man so mad at her for making him miss the ending of the ballgame that he came out of the house to go after her. They cuffed him while he yelled at her."

"It sounds just like Kate."

"She called me when she got home and wanted to know if I had heard the game's final score. She'd been following the game while negotiating with the guy and wanted to know how it ended." Marcus shook his head. "I trust her instincts—she can figure out a way to end a standoff short of a tactical response in more creative ways than I have ever seen—but every time she gets one of those calls…"

"She'll never change that take-control attitude when a hostage is involved." Rachel agreed. "The best thing you can do is just keep close contact."

"Anything I can do for you when I get back to Chicago? I know you were rushed to get out here." Now that they were both engaged men, Marcus and his partner Quinn had arranged to split their time fifty-fifty between Washington, D.C. and Chicago, where their respective fiancée's Shari and Lisa worked.

"I think I'm covered," Rachel replied. "Jack's going to call if the river gets away from them. And Gage is keeping an eye on my place for me; he'll handle mail and the rest."

"If Jennifer needs anything, just let Kate know and she can bring it out with her on Wednesday."

"Will do."

"We'll get through this, Rae."

She wondered if he was saying it for her benefit or his own. They had no choice.

The puppy disappeared under the bed with Rachel's tennis shoe. "It won't fit under there." She gave up and held out her favorite belt. The end was taken, shaken, and the belt disappeared after the shoes. "And those were new shoes, just for your information."

She couldn't sleep and she was talking to a dog. Rachel tugged the pillow over. Grief was hitting so hard it was difficult to breathe.

Jesus, what do I do? I need to sleep. I really need to sleep.

Was she going to be facing a family funeral this summer? The thought was terrifying. *Why don't You heal her? Why are the prayers answered with silence? Am I doing something wrong?*

She could counsel Marissa through that question, but she didn't know how to answer it for herself. Through the past year Jennifer had shown a joy and confidence that didn't waver. Rachel would have pegged it as denial—the safe place that people went to when the tragedy was this huge—but now she knew it wasn't denial as much as it was hope.

What am I going to do when Jennifer's hope wavers?

She wasn't ready for this.

Rachel thought about Cole and the way he so easily fell asleep. She wished she was more like him. Did years of believing lead to that calm trust, or was she missing something more profound? Rachel thought about calling him, but he'd likely be at the levee and busy. Besides, she couldn't think of anything to ask him; she'd be calling just to hear the comfort of his voice.

The comfort of his voice... She buried her face in her pillow. Cole had slipped through her defenses over the last year. He'd shown himself to be a man able to help her carry the weight of nights like this one.

Her relationship with Cole was so different than most in her life. He didn't need her for anything, not really. It was disquieting to realize she consciously tried to keep the scales balanced in most of her relationships. With Gage it was a balance of helping him with his grief and her getting back in return someone she could absolutely trust. With the O'Malleys it was helping them with anything they needed as a thank-you for the deep family loyalty she had that survived any pressure.

With Cole...he might seek out her company, enjoy it, but his life was pretty complete as it was. He was ready to settle down, and he needed someone to love who would love him back. If she missed fulfilling that, then there weren't many other things he needed to take up the slack.

Jesus, this is scary. An unbalanced scale with Cole—I need him more than he needs me. Does he realize that? Does it matter to him? Or is my desire to have a balanced scale part of my own habit of trying to stay safe in a relationship? To ensure that I am needed and thus not going to be abandoned? It's old territory, Lord, and I wish I were past this. It complicates my life and my relationship with Cole. I trust You. I know Cole is Your man. Help me figure out how to trust You for my security without attaching that emotional weight to Cole.

Rachel looked at the clock and didn't know if Cole was working the day shift or still working nights. She'd feel awful if she woke him up when he most needed his rest, but she needed to talk about Jennifer and this grief.

She leaned over and picked up her Bible, seeking a deeper source of comfort available tonight. There was a slip of paper in the front where she'd been collecting verses on suffering and comfort and prayer. Jennifer understood the subjects as did Cole, but Rachel couldn't share this with Jennifer unless she understood not only the words but also what they meant.

> *"After you have suffered a little while, the God of all grace, who has called you to his eternal glory in Christ, will himself restore, establish, and strengthen you"* (1 Peter 5:10).

> *"These things I have spoken to you, that my joy may be in you, and that your joy may be full"* (John 15:11).

> *"Is any one among you suffering? Let him pray. Is any cheerful? Let him sing praise"* (James 5:13).

She loved the first verse and was puzzled by the second. The verse in James was clear, but what was she supposed to pray for regarding suffering? Relief from it? The verse in 1 Peter suggested that God would step in when the time was right.

Jennifer had often said that prayer was simply the honest expression of what was on your heart. Cole said to pray for the small things when the big things didn't seem to be answered.

Jesus, I'm thankful that I have so many incredible people around me—Jennifer, Marcus, Kate, Cole, even Gage, who has taught me that anything can be endured if necessary. I'm suffering because I love Jennifer and the cancer is taking her from me. I know heaven is real and a day is coming when all of this will go away, and there will be no more illness or evil or suffering in our lives. Heaven sounds so gloriously peaceful. But I don't want heaven to come yet. I want more time with my sister. Please, don't let her die.

The puppy started pushing his bed around the room. Rachel held down her hand and snapped her fingers. He scampered over to join her. "Are you going to wear out soon?"

He rolled over to have his tummy rubbed.

"That's what I thought."

She obliged. It was comforting to have him around.

"Lisa? It's Cole." It had taken him more than two hours to track her down on a Sunday night. "Sorry to interrupt." His secretary had gone to Post-it notes with messages across the back of his chair because his desk was overflowing with incoming mail. Arson investigations didn't stop just because he was wading through water for a few days. Cole pulled them off, read them, and either deep-sixed them for later in the week or added them to his list of calls to make tonight.

"Don't worry about it," Lisa replied. "I'm between trips to the lab. It's been a busy night for people dying. What's happening?"

"Your murder at the house that was flooding out—"

"Hold on." She shifted the phone. "No, I need that blood panel tonight. Her kid is in the hospital with the same symptoms!" she hollered back in answer to another question. "Sorry, Cole. Carol Iles. Okay. I'm with you now."

"I knew her." It hadn't clicked until he read the obituary in the newspaper this afternoon, and forty minutes of hunting through archived files had confirmed it.

"How?"

"Five years ago, a house fire. Her son was playing with matches. Her name was Carol Rice then, which is why it didn't click."

"That fits. Detective Wilson's been looking at her background. She'd been divorced less than a year with joint custody of one son. Wilson jotted a note that the boy lives with his father."

"Her son—that would be Mark."

"Was it an accidental fire, or the first signs of future trouble?"

"My notes show that he was playing with matches in her closet. He had all her expensive shoes piled together in a mound with one of her silk blouses balled up under them."

"He'd have been what, eight, nine? This kid is trouble."

"Home had been a battleground and the fire was just the latest round. I'm not surprised to hear the marriage came apart in divorce. His dad dismissed the fire as 'boys will be boys.'"

"Has Mark started any other fires lately?" Lisa asked.

"He got through middle school with a lot of stuff I suspect but can't prove—a trash can fire, bottle rockets, pulling the fire alarm. I'm more worried now that he's a freshman in high school. He's hanging out with a bad crowd. The boy strikes me as an insecure kid, a bully, looking for attention even if it's for being a troublemaker."

"Would he be violent enough to kill his mom?"

"I'm no expert on what a kid might do. But no, I think this info is just background noise," Cole said.

"I'll pass it along to Wilson."

"Making any progress with other leads?"

"Not much. No luck matching the bullet to a gun."

"The river will crest soon. Let me know if you need a lift back to the crime scene."

"I'll do that. Thanks, Cole."

"Talk to you soon, Lisa." He cradled the phone with one hand and closed the Mark Rice file with the other. He'd have to get by the high school Monday and talk to the counselor. It was hard to tell how Mark would react to Carol's death. Cole didn't want to deal with another arson fire set by an angry boy.

Cole dialed home and checked for messages. If Rachel had called, she hadn't left a message. He hoped she was handling today okay. She had called from Baltimore to let him know she'd arrived, but he hadn't heard from her since. He wished she would call. He could do so little from here. The next trip Rachel took East to see Jennifer, he would figure out a way to go with her.

Five

D id you ever plan to become a doctor? Or did we just decide you'd make a good one?" Rachel asked Jennifer, idly paging through one of the photo albums. The lights were dim and Tom was sound asleep in the hospital chair by the window. Rachel was keeping one eye on the clock. She had moved her flight to nine o'clock Tuesday night, and she didn't want to leave one moment before she had to. It was getting close to that time.

"The way I remember it was I wanted to be a surgeon and you and Lisa kept taking me by the hospital nursery to see the babies."

"I remember now. That was around when Lisa got fascinated with what they did with dead people."

"I did not enjoy that visit to the morgue."

Rachel didn't think she would ever forget her glance into the autopsy room. "Don't tell Lisa, but I nearly threw up." She held up the list they had written over twenty years ago when they were meeting to decide on a last name for their new family. "I forgot we had the name Lewis on the list."

"Who suggested that?"

Rachel held the list close to see the handwriting. "Lisa."

"She wanted matching initials."

Rachel read to the bottom of the list and laughed. "Jack suggested Magnificent."

"Jack Magnificent." Jen let that draw out. "What a fantastic name. Who suggested O'Malley?"

"I don't know. It's not on the list. There is a list of nationalities. I wanted an Australian connection. Ireland is not on the list though."

"You need one of the later lists. That sounds like our first meeting on the topic."

Rachel studied the list. "I think you're right. If you find the last list, set it aside. It would be a good memento."

"I'll keep an eye out." Jen slid over the pad of paper she held. "That's everything I can think of that I could use sent out here. The pistachio nuts are the most important item. They are Tom's favorites and he needs something to munch on."

Rachel scanned Jennifer's list. Most items could easily be bought here, but that wasn't the point. Jen knew it helped if there was anything tangible she could let family do for her. "I'll send the stuff out with Kate." Rachel closed the photo album and looked over at Tom. "Do you think I should wake him up before I go? He's got to be uncomfortable in that chair."

"Let him sleep."

Rachel reluctantly got up from her chair and gave Jennifer a long hug. Rachel leaned back, searching her sister's face, very aware of the fact that it might be the last time she saw her alive. She didn't want to forget so much as a curl of an eyelash, and she was afraid that over time this memory might dim. "I'll call you when I get back to Chicago."

"Please do. No matter what the time."

"God bless, Jen."

Her sister hugged her back tightly. "He already has. He gave me you for a sister." Jen leaned back. "And I want to hear about this dinner with Cole."

She should have never mentioned it. "It's not that big a deal."

"Right. You'll tell me everything?"

Rachel smiled. "Maybe not *every*thing."

It would have been cheaper just to buy a new picnic table. The sander jammed and kicked back at him. Cole shut it off, wiped the sweat from his hands, and reached for the ringing phone. "Cole." The bugs around the garage light swarmed in a hum. His second chance to get a few hours at home, and he'd felt like taking out some of his weariness on wood. Ann's patio furniture had likely been washed away, and this table would at least be a start in replacing it.

"Hello, Cole."

The voice was faint but just hearing it filled him with pleasure. He settled on the bench he had been sanding and pressed the phone close. "Jennifer O'Malley. This is a surprise."

"A good one I hope?"

"You're now the bright spot of my day."

"That bad?"

He laughed. "It's been a long one."

"I've only got a minute, I'm afraid. Could you do me a favor?"

"Done."

"You're a trusting man."

"I just know you."

"Rachel is on her way to Chicago. She's trying to sneak back into town."

His smile disappeared. "Jen—"

"I can't call family. I gave her my word."

The bonds between the O'Malleys went deep. If Jennifer had given her word, she wouldn't break it. But she couldn't leave a problem alone either.

"Rachel just left the hospital. I'm worried about her. I was trying not to cry on her shoulder too much, but she's so good about being empathetic that I probably did more than I realized. They stuck me in a wheelchair for good."

Cole wanted to help, but for all the time that he and Rae had spent together, she had yet to call him when she was in trouble. And he knew he wasn't the one she would necessarily turn to when the pain hit this hard. "Call Gage."

"I did," Jennifer said softly. "He's not home."

So much for hoping Jennifer would say he was wrong about the way the wind blew. Gage had several years of history with Rachel, and in the past Cole had himself called Gage on Rae's behalf. For Rae trust was the hardest emotion to extend, and she trusted Gage with her tears. Cole wanted that role in her life, but he was very aware that he would have to earn it.

In the last few months Rachel had let him into a lot of her life, but the relationship was still progressing slower than he'd like. He understood part of it. Rachel didn't take major risks in relationships; she inched her way to find out if the ground was safe before stepping forward. He wanted forever with someone; he had chosen her; and he was trying to proceed at her pace. She had heavy burdens to carry right now with Jennifer's illness and her own work. He'd tried not to step into the time and energy Rae had left and take it for himself when she really needed some breathing space. "What time's her flight getting in?"

"After midnight. Northwest flight 712."

"It's not a problem. I'll meet her."

"I appreciate that."

"I'm sorry about the wheelchair," Cole offered, at a loss for better words to express how sorry he was for what it represented.

"So am I. Tom wants to get me one of those horns they put on kids' bicycle handlebars so I can warn people I'm coming through. I've got to work on left turns. You'll help Rae, Cole? With whatever she needs?"

There was more going on than what she was saying. "You know I will, Jen. I'm glad you called."

"So am I. Thanks, Cole."

"Anytime, Jennifer." Cole said and hung up the phone. Rae had so much on her plate right now. She wouldn't want company tonight. Not when she had just left her sister, not if the news there was bad. He had observed Rachel long enough to know she was a hider by nature, wanting to curl up with her own thoughts until she gathered perspective on what to do. But Jennifer wouldn't have asked if she wasn't concerned.

Lord, what should I do?

Rachel might not want the company, but she needed it. Giving her twenty-four hours would leave the situation twenty-four hours older, but it wouldn't heal the hurt on its own. Cole went to call the airline for the exact flight arrival time.

Rachel glanced up from her book as the seat belt light chimed and flashed off for the fourth time during this return flight to Chicago. Given the repeated turbulence, adults ignored the freedom because they knew the seat belt light would be back on soon for landing.

There was a scramble behind her. "We're going to crash."

She turned to look at the young girl pulling on the back of her seat, peering over the headrest. "If we do, I'll get you out." Rachel was sitting in the emergency exit aisle. She'd worked too many plane crash aftermath's to voluntarily sit anywhere else.

"And Mommy?"

"And Mommy."

"What are you doing?"

She half closed the book to show the cover. "Reading a teenage girl's diary that was published."

"She's pretty."

"Yes, she is." She was also dead. The Columbine High School shooting had been memorialized in several ways, *The Journals of Rachel Scott* one of the more poignant. Rachel's namesake had been murdered, and all the dreams written in the diary would remain just dreams.

Setting aside the book, she reached for the sack in the empty seat beside her and offered a gummy bear to her new friend.

"What do you say, Kelly?" the girl's mom said.

"Th'k you."

Rachel shared a smile with Kelly's mom. Traveling with an infant and a bored, bright young girl who was not interested in sleeping was a challenge. "Is someone meeting you at the airport?"

"My father," Kelly's mom said.

"I'll give you a hand getting down the causeway if you'd like. I'm traveling light; I checked my bag."

"I'd appreciate that. I worry about Kelly getting away from me in the crowd."

"I stay close, Mom."

"You try to, honey."

The infant went from sleep to scowl to tears. Rachel winced, knowing painful pressure in the ears was an unpleasant way to wake up. "We're descending."

The offered pacifier eased the infant's pain. "Buckle your seat belt, Kelly."

The girl scrambled to fasten her seat belt again and then looked out the window. "That's Chicago?"

It was hard to see the city lights through the haze and light rain, but there were glimmering twinkles down there.

"That's home," Rachel agreed, stowing her book in her briefcase. If she could slip into town unnoticed, she just might get twenty-four hours to herself before she returned to the site of the flooding. She had plans to curl up on her couch in a nest of pillows with a homemade milkshake and watch reruns of *Quincy* she had on tape until her mind was numb and she fell asleep.

"Grandpa."

Rachel released Kelly's hand to let her join the gray-haired man getting up from the first seat in the waiting area.

"It looks like we're not the only one being met." Kelly's mom nodded toward the concourse.

Rachel turned to look. Cole stood a few feet away blocking traffic, people flowing around him like he was a rock in the middle of a river. She held his gaze for a long, searching moment, then looked away. "So it appears. That's Cole." Her rock. Immovable. And not supposed to be here.

Kelly tugged on Rachel's jeans. "He's a fireman?"

Surprised at Kelly's question, Rachel glanced back. He wore his old jacket, wet at the shoulders, faded jeans, and then she saw the boots. Only Cole would think nothing about wearing steel-tipped black boots with yellow stripes on the sides outside of an arson scene. "Either that or a sewer repairman."

Cole heard her and chuckled.

Rachel touched the child's shoulder. "Have fun with your grandparents, Kelly."

"We're going to go see the big fish aquarium this week."

"That's a good plan."

Rachel said farewell to Kelly's mom and moved to join Cole. "I didn't realize you knew I was coming back to Chicago tonight."

"Jennifer called me. Gage apparently wasn't home."

And her sister didn't have time to be subtle—she was matchmaking from a hospital bed. *Oh, Jennifer, did you have to call Cole?* Rachel knew that Jennifer's focus on seeing the O'Malleys settled could come across as pushy if presented wrong. "I could have caught a taxi." She never knew how long she might be gone on a trip, so she had a habit of taxiing back and forth to the airport.

"Nonsense. You want to spend the next hour in a smoky taxi with a stranger? Tollway traffic is always a mess when it rains," he said easily.

Cole had a point, but she struggled to offer him a smile and thanks. She wanted this man to see her at her best, and right now she was far from it. If exhaustion was not written across her face, the sadness probably was. She was ready for the anonymity of strangers.

"Not that pleased to see me?"

"It's not that, Cole. I'm just overwhelmed right now," she apologized. "I'm afraid I'm not adjusting well to even good surprises today."

"That I can understand." Cole held out his hand for her briefcase. "Why don't we see if we can't make life a little less overwhelming."

She stepped forward, gave him the briefcase, and wrapped her arms around him in a hug. "I missed you."

She heard her briefcase hit the floor beside him as his arms came around her. He was such a solid, steady man, and it felt good to close her eyes for a moment and just enjoy the comfort he offered. He cared so much about making this better, and she leaned into that strength and emotion, using it to let go of the trip and the weight it had pressed into her soul.

"Forget my phone number?" he asked softly.

"I thought about calling just to hear your voice."

"Why didn't you?"

She was wondering the same thing and sighed. "I didn't want to interrupt your work."

Cole rested his head on hers. "Work I get 365 days a year. It doesn't hold a candle to you."

She smiled as those words reassured that they were okay. "I'm sorry I didn't call," she whispered.

"You're forgiven." He stepped back and tipped up her chin. "How's Jennifer really doing? She dodged my question." She held his gaze as his searched hers, seeing in his eyes the same sympathy she heard in his voice.

"Jaundiced. On morphine. Spending what time she's out of bed in a wheelchair. We cruised the pediatric cancer wing at Johns Hopkins last night reading bedtime stories and hearing 'bless my mommy and my daddy and my kitten' prayers. The kids giggled at the fact that their visiting doctor had no hair."

His hands soothed hers. "I'm sorry you couldn't stay longer."

"Three days was enough. You could tell Jennifer was trying to be up for me."

Cole reached down and picked up her briefcase. He turned her toward the concourse. "Feel like eating?"

"Another time perhaps."

He rubbed the spot on the back of her shoulders where her headaches were born. "Let it go."

"It's not that easy."

"You can sleep in, watch cartoons in the morning."

The man had passed forty and stopped apologizing for liking Road Runner and Wile E. Coyote. "I appreciate the suggestion. I'll stick to my newspaper, coffee, and a morning walk."

They had to wait for the luggage to appear on the carousel. Since Cole had bought her the luggage for Christmas, she let him retrieve the bag. He was a practical man. Gage bought her a Christmas wreath; Cole bought her luggage. She thought he spent too much, but a quiet word from her brother Jack had stopped her from mentioning that. She hadn't known the autographed baseball she gave Cole for Christmas to replace one destroyed by a vandal had been worth a small fortune. She'd had it in a drawer. She hadn't looked at the value of the gift and neither had Cole.

"You're doing it again, Rae."

"What?"

"Worrying a problem in circles."

She slipped her hand under his arm, squeezed his forearm, and offered a smile. "A bad habit of mine." She really was trying to take those worries to God and then let them go. "Take me home."

"Home it is."

Cole led the way through the tunnel to the parking garage. He unlocked the passenger door for her and the faint smell of charred wood filtered out. His fire coat had been tossed on the backseat. "You came here from a fire scene?"

"Left over from this afternoon."

"Was it serious?"

"No injuries, moderate damage. Repairs to an attic fan sparked and caused an insulation fire." He pulled out into traffic.

"I came up with a name for your dog," Rachel offered.

"You did? I've been waiting with great expectation."

"Hank."

Cole laughed.

"Have you ever met someone named Hank?"

"Besides a famous pitcher and singer? No."

Rachel swatted his arm. "I like it."

"Hank. Okay, I suppose the mutt can grow into it. It's an old dog name."

The rain was intensifying. Rachel watched the wet darkness. She had missed Cole, and his calm presence. Just seeing him was enough to help her relax. It meant a lot that he had set aside his plans for the night to come and meet her. "I changed my mind. Think you can find carryout at this time of night? I need to talk."

"This storm is drifting east over the lake. If you don't mind eating in the car, I'll find us Chinese carryout and a place to park and watch the storm."

"Please."

Lightning hit the water. The blinding flash destroyed Cole's night vision.

"Wow."

Rae had disappeared into the darkness, but the awe in her voice told Cole she'd seen it too. She emerged from the shadows as his eyes adjusted again to the night. She had folded her jacket into a temporary pillow behind her against the window and turned in the seat to angle toward him. She'd finished her sweet and sour chicken. It wasn't the elegant Chinese dinner he'd hoped for, but it was hot and she'd been hungry. He was pleased to see her relaxing.

Cole set his shrimp-fried rice carton on the dash. "It's a good show tonight." Lake Michigan was spread out in a vast expanse from this parking lot at the south end of Illinois Beach State Park. Rae said she'd nearly called just to hear his voice—he let that one linger, pleased to realize she'd been thinking about him. And his new dog had been on her mind. *Hank.* He was not letting her name their first child.

"The storm is scary."

"Powerful."

He let the silence return. He had no desire to push, not about her family. But it was late, and after what Jennifer had said when she called, Cole felt he didn't have the option to take a pass on this one. He rested his left arm across the steering wheel, picked up the special issue North Carolina quarter he'd received in change, and walked it through his fingers. "What's going on, Rae? You told Jennifer not to call family. You don't hide like a turtle from them unless the pressure is fierce."

She sighed. "It's easier to have these conversations over the phone than in person."

"Then I'll take you home and you can call me."

It earned him a brief smile. She pushed the remnants of her meal into the sack. "Jennifer still thinks God is going to heal her."

He paused the quarter between his third and fourth finger. They had talked about this problem too many times before for him to have a new answer for her tonight. "Don't do this, Rae. Don't search to understand what can't be understood." She'd only been a Christian a few months. He'd been one for over thirty years, and he didn't have an answer for why Jennifer was still dying from cancer despite their prayers. There was just a God to trust.

"I doubt that God means what He says," she whispered.

Cole tossed the coin back with the other change. He wasn't surprised at her words, but he wished he could take away this moment that most new Christians experienced. Doubt was like smoke—it found cracks and worried its way inside until it clouded the joy that was there before. A little could fill a big volume of space. "Christianity isn't what you thought it would be like. Okay. So change your expectations."

"You said there would be peace; Jennifer says there's joy."

"There is both," he promised, trying to reach through her turmoil. "What Jesus actually said was, 'These things I have spoken to you, that my joy may be in you, and that your joy may be full.'"

"I've read that verse several times, but I don't understand it, Cole."

What were the right words to explain it? Cole had never felt more challenged in his own faith than when he tried to help her see some of what had taken him years to grasp. "A few verses earlier He said, 'Peace I leave with you; my peace I give to you.' Jesus said *My* joy, *My* peace, Rae. He said that even though He hardly had an easy life. Crowds pressed in on Him; the authorities hated Him; Jesus had no place to call His home. He died on the cross, but He had a joy and a peace in life that was absolute. At its heart, the concept is simple—Jesus trusted His

Father. He didn't doubt God's goodness, His control of the situation, or the fact that His plan would lead to everlasting glory. That's what Jesus is asking you to do too. Trust God, even in this."

He wished he had the wisdom of Solomon to give her an answer. "You can see only one answer to Jennifer's cancer—a cure. God may see another. A verse in Psalms says, 'The LORD will fulfill his purpose for me.' If God has to choose between His purpose for our lives and a long life, I believe He'll go with the purpose every time. Jesus died when He was thirty-three."

"Jennifer's a pediatrician. She has a life ahead of her helping children. What purpose could God have in not curing her?"

"When you choose to trust despite the circumstances—it's called faith, Rae. And sometimes it's so hard that you wonder why God demands it. Think about this: Is a promise made that's not yet delivered on any less of a promise? God is trustworthy. It isn't easy to take that on faith when circumstances are tough, but that's what He asks of you." Cole went to the heart of it. "You love Jennifer, and her suffering is pressing hard. Leave the questions for later. You can't fix this. It will break you to try. And Jennifer is worried about you."

She rubbed her eyes. "You had to add that last point."

He covered her hand with his. The bond between the sisters was so great that he knew to Rachel this felt like it was happening to her. "Were you going to call Jen when you got in?"

She nodded.

"Then let me take you home so you can call her." He started the car. "Tell her we talked. She'll worry less."

"You mean she'll just ask me about you."

Cole smiled, hoping that would be the case. "You can tell her I still owe you dinner. Eating in the car doesn't count."

"This dinner is becoming like the event of the year. Don't set your expectations too high. It's likely going to be our typical meal grabbed in spite of a busy day."

"Rae, it's time with you that makes it special, not the circumstances. I'll make sure it's Chinese—not in a carton this time."

Six

Rachel leaned against the wall of sandbags. The stagnant water stank, the current gone. The sun was out on Saturday morning, reflecting off the muddy water. The floodwaters had crested and receded in the last two weeks and were down to a mere foot. The workers were repairing the initial breach in the retaining wall, hauling rock and sand out to the now visible break. Cole was out there in one of the boats, helping Jack move heavy bags that rocked the boat as they dropped them into the water.

Her brother Stephen stopped beside her. "Another day and the break will be repaired. It will then just be a case of pumping out the last of the water."

It was better progress than she had hoped. Governor Street had been drying out for the last week. Structural engineers were in the houses now, finishing their inspections. People were lingering at the community center, waiting for word that they could return to their homes for the first time.

"It's going to be a mess," she observed. The emergency shelter had transformed itself into the headquarters for the cleanup, the Red Cross giving way to the local Emergency Services Agency. Plywood sheets were already piled and waiting. Six large dumpsters were lined up, ready to be taken in and placed near driveways to allow for expedited removal of destroyed belongings.

"The damage isn't as bad as it could have been. Rather than be a trash pit for the floodwaters, the moving water kept the worst of the debris from building up here. About three miles south is apparently a real mess. Twenty minutes, Rae, and the chief inspector said they'll be letting residents in. I've heard Ann's house is bad but recoverable."

"Thanks, Stephen."

Having worked numerous flood cleanups, Rachel had dressed in old jeans and a bleach-stained shirt, thick socks, and heavy boots. She wore an unbuttoned long sleeve shirt over it to protect her arms. She was already hot. She retrieved the water bottle she'd let chill in the freezer for an hour and tossed it into her bag.

She'd checked at the command center to make sure there were plenty of volunteers for the block. It was well organized. Since other needs were covered, Rachel put herself down to help Ann. With Cole, Jack, and Stephen already on the list to help Ann, someone needed to keep them in line.

"Hi, Rachel." Adam was the first to reach her, racing ahead with a friend he had brought with him, Cole's dog running alongside.

"Hi, Adam." Rachel knelt to pet the dog. The boy with Adam looked to be about the same age as Adam, but shorter, stocky, with red hair and freckles. A healing scrape on the boy's chin suggested a recent collision with pavement. "Who's your friend?"

"This is Tim Sanford."

"Hi, Tim." She offered her hand.

"Hi."

Rachel offered the boys pieces of gum from a new pack she had tucked in her pocket that morning.

"Tim goes to my school," Adam said, dancing around the dog as Hank tried to knock him over. "He's staying with me today, and next weekend I get to go stay over at his house."

"Fun."

"Are they still pumping water?"

"I think so. Why don't you join the guys at the blue engine."

"Come on, Tim. Let's go see."

With a smile Rachel watched them go. She tucked the gum back into her pocket and unwrapped a cough drop for herself.

Ann joined her. "The idea of staying at the sitter's with Nathan was the worst idea Adam had ever heard of, so I let him come. I told him he couldn't enter the house until we called him so if it's real bad I can warn him."

"Good plan. As was letting him bring a friend along." Rachel looked at Ann. "Are you ready to do this?"

"I don't think reality could be any worse than what I've been imagining."

Rachel offered her one of the licorice hard candy drops. "The taste is sharp enough it will at least help counteract the odors."

"Thanks for the warning. I brought buckets, mops, bleach, and lots of garbage bags."

"Let's haul the supplies down to the checkpoint, and the guys can carry them the rest of the way."

Cole, Jack, and Stephen joined them as they brought the last items from the car. The inspectors opened Governor Street to residents, and in small groups people began to see what was left of their homes.

The walk up Ann's driveway was an adventure. It was covered in a muddy river flowing down to the street. Rachel walked beside Cole, ready to grab his arm if necessary to keep from falling. A demarcation line of dirt, wrapped around the house's siding, displayed the crest of the water. The sun had been working at it for days as the water receded, and the residue looked baked on. Grass remained in the yard but it poked up through a muddy swamp. The ground had acquired rocks, stray branches, and odd-looking leaves now wilting in the sun.

The front door had been propped open by the inspectors and windows around the house opened. Rachel followed Ann inside. The living room carpet was under two inches of standing muddy water. Furniture had floated. The sofa and television and heaviest items had not moved, but it was as if a powerful hand had shoved everything else to the east side of the room. Books had swollen and now lay curling as the pages dried. The smell was of mold and humid mustiness.

"Is the house still structurally sound?" Ann asked softly.

Stephen came up behind them and settled his hand on Ann's shoulder. "Yes. Once we dry things out, the inspectors want to look again at wiring before they restore the power. We'll be able to run off generators for now, start fans blowing to assist with the drying out."

Cole walked through to look into the kitchen, then turned to look at the guys. "It's best if we divide and conquer. I'll take care of hauling out the spoiled food. Stephen, if you can start with the clothes, take them out to the truck, we'll take them to the cleaners. Jack, why don't you tackle the generator and get fans blowing, and then hose down the drive. We'll carry out furniture and wash it off there. The sun will help things dry, help us figure out what we can recover first."

"I'll also see about cleaning off the back patio," Jack offered. "We can bring in the picnic table you sanded and fixed up so there is a clean place to sit and take a break."

"Good idea."

"Ann." Rachel could see that her friend was fighting tears, for this devastation was huge. "I brought lots of boxes. We can start in the kitchen and take the dishes and pans out today. The restaurant next to the bank offered to let us run items through their industrial-sized washer. We can at least have them washed and ready to unpack once the kitchen cleanup is done."

Ann nodded.

Stephen hugged her. "We'll get your house back together."

"Can we start with Adam's clothes? He needs options for school," Ann said.

"Sure."

Rachel picked up a bucket and a bottle of bleach. "Jack, when you can get to it, will you thread a hose into the house? It will make it easier to clean walls than if we have to haul water in."

"Glad to."

"Someone find a good radio station with music, something peppy," Ann requested. She headed toward the kitchen, and Rachel followed after her friend. This would discourage even the most optimistic lady.

Rachel worked from the top of the cabinets down, washing the wood with the bleach water twice, letting it dry, and then coming back a third time with soap and water. She turned her head and wiped her eyes on her sleeve as the smell overwhelmed her. The open windows and fans were not keeping up with the fumes. Smelling bleach was going to ruin her sense of taste for days.

Cole had the stove tugged out and was working on removing the side panels. It was comforting to work with him, for he was a man who assessed the job and then dug in to do the work.

"Rachel, look what we found." Adam came in the back door with Tim. She leaned over to see. In his hands were three silver dollars, still crusted with dirt. "They were in the mud out in the flower bed." The boys were having a great time discovering all the strange things left by the water.

"Excellent finds, guys."

"Would you keep them for us?"

"Sure. Put them in my burlap satchel. I'll get them cleaned up and put in coin sleeves for you."

"Thanks."

Ann came into the kitchen and Adam hurried to show his mom their treasures. "We'll be with Jack, okay? He's going to start washing the siding."

"As long as you don't get in his way."

"We're helping, Mom."

Ann smiled at her son. "Have fun."

The boys rushed out as fast as they had come in.

Rachel hauled another bucket of soapy water to the corner cabinet. "It's a treasure hunt out there."

"Boys and mud. They are having fun," Ann agreed. "It's looking good in here."

Rachel wet a new rag and started on the next cabinet. "How is Adam's room?"

"Most of his clothes can be recovered, probably his chest of drawers. Stephen is hauling out the mattress and is looking at pulling up the carpet and padding. If you're okay in here, I thought I'd start cleaning some of the furniture they've carried out."

"I'm fine."

"Cole, can I get you anything?"

"I'm good. Thanks, Ann."

Rachel watched her friend as she left the kitchen. "She's handling this better than I would."

"You handle what you have to," Cole replied. He got the second panel off the stove.

Someone turned the radio up. Rachel hummed along with a song as she tried to distract herself from the aches. She finished the final cabinet.

There was so much to do. She sat down on a stool to begin sorting out items under the sink.

Rachel jolted as a hand touched her shoulder. Cole leaned down. "Call it a day. I'll help the guys finish hauling items to the dumpster and move furniture to the garage, and we'll start again tomorrow."

"I'm okay. I want to do one more round on the cupboards in the kitchen."

"It's five o'clock. If you don't leave, Ann won't think of leaving. She needs to take Adam home."

Rachel had had too much on her mind to realize the time. "Good point." She got to her feet and stretched to take the ache out of her back. "I need to take a walk around the block anyway, see how others are doing."

"In that case—" he offered the full roll of LifeSavers from his pocket—"got tissue with you?"

She tapped her pocket.

He smiled. "Go walk the block. I'll make my own walk-around of the levees and bridge and catch up with you."

———∞∞∞———

Cole would never fail to be surprised by what the floodwaters left behind.

"How did a golf cart get under there?" Gage asked.

"Great question." Cole leaned against the bridge railing next to Gage. They were both spectators. Four guys from City Services were down there wrestling to get it out of the weeds. Cole kept a close eye on the men's safety lines but otherwise left them alone to figure out the problem. "It doesn't look like much of a golf cart anymore."

Gage leaned too far over the edge for Cole's comfort. He tugged the man back. "Let's not have a casualty." The river was rushing by within its banks, but it was still violent.

"Is the bridge going to reopen soon?" Rachel called out.

Cole turned around to see Rae coming across the improvised walkway made from sheets of metal. The flooding had washed away and collapsed sections of the roadway. Cole went to meet her. "Another two weeks at the earliest for repairs to get finished."

"Hey, Rachel LeeAnn. Come give us your opinion. What does that look like on the bank to you?" Gage asked.

Cole reached over, grasped her by the waist, and swung her over the last few feet to more firm ground. He wiped a spot off her chin with a grin. "Chocolate?"

"I was sharing cupcakes with the kids."

"So I see. Hold still." He tipped up her chin with a finger and wiped away the evidence, thinking seriously about kissing her. Their first kiss was going to be a forever memory for both of them, and he liked the idea of it being on a day they worked together. He'd been looking for that perfect moment—one that had both their undivided attentions but not so obvious for the kiss to be expected.

A soft blush tinged her cheeks as she caught the direction of his thoughts. Her eyelashes dropped and then swept up again. "Not here," she whispered.

He settled for tightening his hands on her waist and leaning down to rest his forehead briefly against hers. "Later," he promised. "How was the walk-around?"

"Most are relieved just to be able to get in and do something."

He stepped back and when he did, she slipped her hand in his and stayed in his space leaning against his arm. "Tell us what you think," he asked. "The riverbank, just beyond where the breach has been repaired."

She reluctantly turned to look where he pointed.

"Does that look like car tracks to you?" Gage asked.

"Gage, you can't look at anything without seeing a mystery. It's two deep valleys cut into the muddy bank. Are you sure it's not just the results of one of those boulders that got shoved around by the water? Or for that matter, the first landing of the golf cart?"

"That's what I told him," Cole replied.

"What's on your plan for the evening?" Gage asked. "If I buy the steaks, Cole offered to fire up the grill. Want to join us?"

Rachel looked between the two men, her surprise that they were getting together showing. "Sure."

Cole understood her reaction. He and Gage respected each other, but their jobs had often put them working on opposite sides with his job in investigating arson fires and Gage's to find news. It was slowly becoming a friendship. They both recognized that for Rachel's sake it was important that the tension end. Gage had a story running this weekend about the flooding, and Cole was in the mood to be generous when asked to comment. "How do you like your steak?"

"Medium. Not too charred on the edges. With a baked potato that is falling-apart done."

"Can do. Eight fit your schedule?"

"I'll make it fit."

Cole cut the French bread in thick slices. He could get used to this. Rachel sat at his kitchen table occasionally spearing a strawberry with a toothpick, keeping him company as he fixed Texas Toast to go with the steak and potatoes. The steaks on the grill were coming along to perfection under the watchful eyes of Gage and Hank. It was the kind of night that made memories.

"You have a quart of 1 percent milk in the refrigerator, oatmeal in the cupboard, and enough vegetables to start a market, but we're eating steaks and potatoes. I sense a contradiction. Now I wonder which one is really you?"

He could get used to her teasing. She'd relaxed with him. "It's called balance."

"I'd say you were trying to impress me with your discipline but you forgot to take down your shopping list, and it's more of the same."

"One of the realities of a desk job is to adapt or pay the price. I don't mind working the weights, but I'd rather not have to add another session to my workout schedule."

"I handle it by never being home to buy groceries." She rested her head on her arms.

"You're falling asleep."

"You should feel flattered. I no longer feel like a guest. The days when I could handle the pace of keeping up with kids and doing a flood cleanup are long gone."

"Age teaches you to think more and act smarter. It's good for you." He set a glass of iced tea beside her.

"Why didn't you get married a decade or two ago?"

She didn't censor her questions when she got tired. He tucked away the observation, knowing it would be useful. "I was too young to realize what I was missing, too busy to make time, too stupid to take my mom's advice. You would have liked her Rachel LeeAnn."

"I was hoping you didn't hear Gage call me that."

"It's not a bad middle name."

"What's yours?"

Cole chuckled. "Something worse." He slid the toast under the broiler.

"I'll be nice and not ask."

He got out the fixings for the salad. She was idly moving her glass of iced tea on the table, watching the moisture form a circle.

"What?"

She shook her head.

"You're biting your lower lip. What's the question?"

She glanced over and gave an apologetic smile. "Your middle name isn't Clarence is it?"

He burst out laughing. "Clarence? No, it's not anything that bad. It's Joseph." He stepped back to the table, leaned down, and kissed her. He was smiling as he did so, intending it to be a casual kiss. He knew she'd been waiting for him to keep his promise from that afternoon, and he didn't want the first kiss to become such a huge deal she got tense expecting it. Casual didn't last, though. He wanted to linger in that kiss and deepen it. He let himself do so briefly. She was sitting at his kitchen table where he would love to have a chance to greet her with a kiss every morning. He reluctantly opened his eyes to find hers still closed.

She curled her hand in his shirt rather than let him move back. "What was that for?"

"You need a reason?" He had several, not the least of which was the fact that she was adorable and he fully intended to win her heart in the coming months.

She blinked at him, and he loved the fact her eyes still weren't quite focused. She shook her head slightly. "Come here." She slid her hand around his neck, pulled him back down, and returned his kiss. The memory of their first kiss got swamped by the emotional wave from the second. "One to dream about," she whispered. She smiled at him and slid her hand around to touch his jaw, her hand soft against the end-of-day roughness of his face. "Breathe, Cole. You want me to help fix the salad?"

He took a deep breath. "Okay, sure, whatever you like." Her smile was incredible when there was laughter behind it. He chuckled and pulled her from the chair. "You're precious, Rae." He wrapped an arm around her and hugged her, then stepped back and let her go. He held out the paring knife. "Not too many radishes."

Seven

isa."

Hearing her name and having nowhere to set down the blood-stained shirt, she carried it with her to the door of the conference room. "Back here, Marcus."

So much evidence had been collected from the Carol Iles murder scene that Lisa had taken over the room to manage the processing of it all. She returned the bloody blouse Carol had been wearing to its plastic evidence bag.

Her brother came to the doorway where he paused, looking around. "Detective Wilson called and said you needed to see me. How's it coming?"

She rubbed her forehead with the back of her arm trying to eliminate an itch, avoiding using her hand still in the rubber glove. "Since I haven't seen much daylight because of this case, I suppose it's relative. Wet stuff molds and my allergies have been going crazy. I hate mysteries."

"You've got one."

She nodded and walked over to the wall of enlarged photos she'd been using to try and recreate the crime scene from the evidence. "Tests are finally coming back on some of this stuff. It's like a Chinese puzzle. You checked the federal court building and the office where she worked?"

"I ran down the information for Wilson. Carol didn't have access to anything classified, didn't work on any profiled cases. Just routine paperwork in the criminal division. I sent over the box of personal stuff we found in her office. There wasn't much."

"Wilson brought it over," Lisa confirmed. "Thanks for sending over the fingerprints from her file."

"No problem. I figured it would save you some time. Any ideas at this point?"

"Carol's murder was either domestic, work related, or random. I'm ready to rule out random. It's too neat of a scene and there are no signs of burglary or other violence. Wilson is getting nowhere on domestic. She'd been divorced about a year, shares joint custody of her son who primarily lives with his father. Her ex-husband and son were at a high school basketball game that night. I don't have a good time line yet, but so far their alibis hold. And there is no indication Carol was dating anyone. That leaves work related, and you've pretty much ruled that out."

"Anything coming from the evidence?"

"That's why I wanted you to stop by. The bullet that killed Carol is in pretty good shape. No shell casings, so I'm limited in info, but it's typing as a Smith & Wesson .38 caliber." Lisa tapped two of the photos. "And my puzzle: I think someone else was there. This mail being opened at the dining room table had Carol's prints on it. But this soda can on the kitchen counter? The prints are unknown."

"Her husband or son?"

"They both offered prints and neither matched. One other thing." She crossed to the table and lifted a plastic evidence bag. "This cosmetic bag? One of the officers cleared everything on the dining room table into a box, and this was in that set of items. You can see it on the table in that photo." She lifted out the brush. "Long, blond hair. Carol was a brunette with a pageboy haircut."

"You're looking for a woman shooter?" Marcus asked, obviously intrigued at the idea.

"Someone brought over a cosmetic bag, had a drink, and then shot Carol? No. I think Carol and another woman were going out that evening, shopping, dinner, something. Her guest brought in the bag to retouch her makeup and hair, and while she was there someone knocked on the door and shot Carol."

"Then there's a second victim."

"We never explored the basement. It was flooded." Lisa leaned against the table and tugged off her gloves. "Want to go play detective with me?"

"I'm federal not state, remember?"

"Wilson won't be free for another three hours. He said I could draft you. And technically I don't need company to go back to a crime scene, but even I have a bit of a problem walking down into a flooded basement with just a flashlight."

"I'll go along, but I'm calling Quinn. If you're going to get spooked by a ghost, I want him there to see it."

Lisa smiled at the idea of her fiancé going along. "Call him. But you two are going down into the basement first."

"This is creepy," Quinn protested. The stairs creaked as he walked down them, his halogen flashlight peering into the darkness.

Lisa tugged the back of her fiancé's collar. "There's creepy and really creepy. It doesn't smell like a decomposing body's down there," Lisa mentioned, keeping her hand on his shoulder for extra balance as she came down behind him. "Let's just get down there and get it over with."

Marcus went down ahead of them and hung the lantern he'd brought along on the staircase banister. It dimly illuminated the room. "We've still got some standing water down here. The pump lines dropped in those basement windows to pump out the water weren't weighted to reach the floor. Walk carefully."

Quinn paused near the bottom of the stairs. "What is that?"

Lisa leaned her head against his shoulder to see around the rafters and follow his flashlight. "A dead rat."

Quinn stepped off the last step and shone his light around. "Why don't you stay right there, Lisa?"

"And miss all this fun? How do you want to do this, Marcus?" It was her crime scene, but by asking the question, she knew Marcus would select the toughest part of the task for himself.

"You two work clockwise from the steps; I'll work counterclockwise," he decided, taking the deepest segment of water. "Let's get this done."

Lisa circled with Quinn, looking for anything that suggested evidence. They found a workbench, boxes of stored Christmas decorations, and a couple pieces of furniture Carol had moved downstairs that she didn't need. Items that had floated ended up on the floor in strange places. Lisa knew from the lack of the distinct smell of decomposition that this idea hadn't panned out. They finally met up at the other side of the room.

"Ready to call this search done?" Marcus asked.

She reluctantly nodded. Their search had been thorough. She led the way upstairs.

The kitchen and living room still showed the rapid recovery of items they had made the night of the flooding. She looked out the kitchen window. "The body could have ended up in the river, but it's going to take a lot of convincing before Wilson agrees to dredge."

"The river doesn't hold things forever," Quinn reassured. "You want to look around some more while we're here?"

"Let's assume Carol's company is in the kitchen when the gunshot goes off in the living room." Lisa looked around. "She only has two options of escape: the garage or the back patio door. I want to walk the grounds."

She pushed back the vertical blinds on the patio door. It was unlocked, but she had to wrestle it open. Draining water had left a place mat, candle ring, saltshaker, and several pages of a wall calendar plastered against the glass. She pushed the items away with her foot. "See if you can find me a garbage bag, Quinn. If it looks interesting, let's take it." She stepped outside. "I bet the shooter threw the gun into the river as well. It's close and it washes everything away."

"We'll start walking the riverbanks," Quinn offered.

"We may have to." Lisa rubbed the back of her neck. She wanted this case solved, but she had a bad feeling about it. So much evidence had been lost in the floodwaters.

Marcus stopped beside her. "Let's walk."

Lisa nodded and led the way into the yard.

Eight

A dam, listen to Rachel and help with Nathan. You're a guest in her home so be helpful. Don't just watch TV."

"Mom…"

Rachel smiled at Ann and shifted Nathan against her hip. She was going to have a great time baby-sitting. "We'll start with Battleship and then play Scrabble."

"We're just going to pick out carpet and paint. We won't be long."

It was Friday night. It had taken days, but the cleanup had finally turned the corner, and it was time to start restoring rooms. The electricians had been in; the furnace and ductwork had been cleaned out. Drywall had been replaced and new subflooring put in where needed. Stephen thought they could start painting Saturday and lay carpet down midweek. Ann's home would feel new although rather sparse, as most of the furniture would have to be replaced. "Stay out as long as you like," Rachel said. "I'll page Stephen if I need you."

Stephen set down the backpack with things for the boys, Nathan's now worn teddy bear poking out of the top. "Expect us about eight, Rae."

She nodded to her brother.

"I appreciate this," Ann said.

Nathan reached for Rachel's necklace, and she caught his hand, kissing it. "I'm glad you took me up on the offer. Say bye, Nathan."

The boy waved to his mom. "Go. Wanna play."

With a laugh Ann kissed her boys and said a final good-bye.

Rachel closed the door behind Ann and Stephen and from years of baby-sitting experience immediately offered a distraction. "Adam, I've got a question for you."

The boy was looking around her apartment in a curious kind of way. Nathan could get into all kinds of things, and she could imagine Adam wondering if he would constantly have to stop his younger brother. Her apartment wasn't very kid-proof. Knowing that, she held Nathan rather than setting him down. Adam turned to look at her.

"Cassie brought over a box of stuff she found at an auction. She needs it sorted and items put into those plastic sleeves. She said if you wanted to do it for her, she'd pay you for your time—you can choose an item for yourself. There are a few comic books in the box."

"I'd love to."

"Help me clear off the table and we'll lay everything out. Does pizza sound good for an early dinner?"

Nathan leaned back. "Pizza, yes!"

"Can we come stay more often?" Adam asked.

Rachel laughed. "I'd like that. Come on, let's get this evening started."

The sounds outside the hospital room carried through the closed door. Evening rounds were being finished, medicines given. The hospital corridor was bustling. Jennifer reached to take hold of her husband's hand. He interlaced his fingers with hers. She found such comfort in his strength. "I love you. Have I told you that lately?"

"Yes, but you can keep saying it. I'm storing them up." He smiled at her, the gorgeous smile that still turned her heart to mush. The first time she met him had been in an emergency room over a screaming two-year-old. Tom glanced up and gave her that smile, then returned his attention to her patient. She'd remembered him for that smile.

Tom used the cuff of his sleeve to wipe her chin. "Cookie crumbs and icing."

"It's pretty awful when homemade cookies don't have much taste."

"Do you want me to call your family for you?"

Jennifer felt like her heart was breaking. "It's going to kill them. You saw how hard it was on Rachel and Kate to see me like this. If I call now and tell them this…"

"Marcus is coming in on Tuesday. He'll take one look at you and tell the others to come. If you want to make the decision, you'll have to make it soon. We're out of time, honey."

"The doctors were wrong before. Why do they have to be right this time?" She so desperately wanted them to be wrong.

"All they said was that your body needs a rest from the treatments." He kissed the back of her hand where the morphine line had been removed. They had put her on a constant pump she now wore on her belt.

"I don't want them to be done." She loved this man, loved her family, and she wanted something that could help her fight this cancer. Having her primary oncologist say that they recommended a break in treatment was terrifying. She didn't want Tom to have to watch her die.

"We're not done yet, hon."

"Spontaneous remission is another name for a miracle," she whispered.

"So we'll pray for a miracle."

"I'm losing faith that there will be one." She'd been trying so hard to trust God through this. She knew God had a plan. The O'Malleys had turned to Him because of this cancer; only Stephen was left to make that decision. Time had been her ally, but now it was going against her.

Tom turned her wedding ring around. "Does God love you more or less than I do?"

"He gave me you."

"Good answer. God will give you all the faith you need. You don't need to wish harder or do more."

"I trust Him. I just don't want to die. And I'm dying."

He leaned over and kissed her. "Don't cry, Jen. He hasn't forgotten you." Tom rubbed his thumb across the back of her hand. "Good-bye is still a long way away. I have today with you, and I plan to enjoy it. You want to sneak out tonight down to pediatrics and see a movie with your buddies?"

She struggled to smile. "I'd love that."

"And the next days? We can do whatever you want, Jen."

"I could use some better scenery."

"Then let's leave. This hospital is a lousy place for getting rest, and you're just surrounded by germs. There are better places to spend our time."

"Maybe Chicago?"

"Let's do that. I like your family, and they need time with you. Who do you want to talk to first tonight?"

"Rachel. She can handle me crying while I try to talk."

He kissed her again. "You're my wife. You don't even get out of that by dying, remember? We struck the *till death do us part* phrase from the wedding vows. Trust me, Jen. We are far from finished with this fight."

She could rest against the determination she heard in his voice. He wouldn't let this fight end. And just hearing that made it easier for her to breathe and think about tomorrow. There was one bright spot in this change—not having to spend hours focusing on the medical treatments and side effects of medications, she would have more time to focus on her family. It mattered now more than ever. "Try Rachel at home. I'd rather not have to page her."

Nathan was asleep. Rachel moved pillows on the couch so he would settle back farther in the cushions. The game of Twister they had squeezed into the living room had probably been a little much, although the laughter had been worth it. The two boys had made up rules that all too often put her at the bottom of a pile of giggling boys.

She picked up the plate beside Adam. "Very nice." He was carefully writing tags for the items he had put into plastic sleeves.

"These comics are really old. Are you sure Cassie meant me to have one?"

"Yes, she did. You can choose the one you'd like."

"If I take it with me before shelves get rebuilt in my bedroom, it might get damaged. Could I leave it with you?"

"Sure, sweetie."

"I made Cassie a thank-you card."

"She'll love it." Rachel hugged him. "I'm so glad you came over." She heard the outside door close and footsteps on the stairs. "I think that's your mom now."

"We were good tonight?"

Rachel laughed. "Yes. And you've got a standing invitation to come over anytime. Let's get your stuff together. Now where did Nathan hide his bear?"

"Behind the couch."

"Of course."

Rachel leaned against the car window. Nathan had already gone back to sleep in his car seat. "I'll be over to help paint tomorrow, Ann. You want to start about ten?"

"Yes. I'll bring lunch for us."

"I'll bring the ice chest with drinks and dessert," Rachel offered. "I'll see you then. Good night guys." Rachel headed back to her apartment.

The phone was ringing as she unlocked the door. She hurried to answer it, hoping it was Cole. "Hello?"

"Hi, Rae."

"Jennifer." Rachel carried the phone into the living room, reached for the notepad of messages she had for her sister, and then she slowly paused. Her sister's voice was soft, heavy, like she had been crying. Rachel settled on the couch and tugged a big pillow over into her lap, leaning back against the cushions. "How are you doing tonight?"

"The doctor recommended I go home."

No. Not this. Rachel closed her eyes and felt blackness deeper than any disaster tragedy swallow her. "Come home to Chicago, Jen," she whispered. "If it wouldn't be too hard on Tom, come here."

"Yes. I need to." Jen stopped.

Rachel waited while Jen fought for composure, wishing she had stayed out East rather than come back here. Her sister needed her. "What did the doctors say?"

"That my body needs a rest from the treatment."

"How bad is the pain?"

"It's under control."

"You can rest here. I'll share my mountains of pillows, and we can pull out that box of videos from under my bed and have a Cary Grant movie night." She was reaching for anything that Jennifer could still look forward to.

"I'd like that." Jennifer went quiet for several moments. "It isn't fair, Rae. Why is God allowing this?"

Jesus, please. I'm failing her. How do I help her?

"Come home," Rachel whispered again. She struggled to keep her voice level.

"We were thinking about maybe flying back on Wednesday night. I'll call you tomorrow with travel plans."

"I'll meet you at the airport," Rachel said.

"I've got to call the others."

"We love you."

"I love you too," Jennifer whispered and drew in a deep breath. "Tomorrow, Rae. I'll call you early."

"It's going to be okay."

"I know. Good night."

"Night, Jen."

Rachel hung up the phone. Her hand shook. She lowered her head and her body shook. She would have to be breathing to make a sound. The only thing more devastating than this call would be the one saying Jennifer had died. She lifted the pillow and pressed it against her face. *Jesus, it hurts.* The sobs came hard and lasted a long time.

She didn't want to talk, but she didn't want to be alone either. Gage would walk with her. Cole. She needed someone other than family while she waited for Jen to make the other calls. She'd known this day was coming and yet it was shattering. Rachel picked up the phone and her hands shook again as she dialed.

Cole pulled into the drive and drove around his house to the detached garage. He reached in the back for his briefcase. He had to testify in an arson case next week and had preparations to do. He locked the car and walked up the path to the house.

Rachel was sitting on the back steps. Cole slowed. He would have to leave one of his lawn chairs out so she'd be comfortable when she waited, since she wouldn't accept a key. Something was wrong. One of her kids had paged, work... He walked up the path but didn't ask. It was enough that she had come.

"Jennifer called."

There was such sadness in her eyes. He brushed a finger along her cheek. "Will it help to talk?"

She lifted a shoulder in a shrug. Cole saw in her gesture what he had feared was coming. How much could Rae carry before it overwhelmed her? Jennifer's illness was the one weight that would break her. He clicked off the back door light to stop the gathering bugs and settled beside her on the steps to share the silence and the night. He would invite her in, fix her a cup of coffee, but he was afraid she'd shift to guest mode and feel a need to ask about his day.

"Jennifer's coming back to Chicago."

He blinked back tears that came when he heard the news. "When?"

"Probably Wednesday. Details will come tomorrow."

"I'm so sorry, honey."

"I need a hug," she whispered.

And she chose to come see him. Cole wrapped his arms around her. Under the pain he felt at the news she had to share, he knew they'd just crossed a point in their relationship that would change it forever. Suffering the deepest level of hurt, she'd chosen to trust him.

She felt fragile in his arms. He shifted positions to tuck her closer. Her head rested against his shoulder, and she began to shake as she silently began to cry. In another setting having her in his arms would be a memory to treasure. Now he simply wished there was some way to help her through the hurt. Jennifer's dying…this tore at the heart of the O'Malley family.

He sat holding her for a long time—his leg went to sleep, his back ached. He was lousy at dealing with tears. There was nothing he could fix. He wanted to say something profound, but the reality was tougher than that. There were no words he could offer that would take away this hurt.

He settled for silence, grateful she had come. There was strength in this woman that went deep enough to handle this. Faith would get her through when she had to face tomorrow, but her grief needed the tears to fall. There was healing in those tears.

She took two final shuddering breaths, lifted her head from his shoulder, and eased back. "So, what's happening in your life?"

If she could still smile like that…she'd found the strength to get to tomorrow. Sometimes that was all that could be done. "I'm dating this really nice woman."

"Cole."

He tucked her hair behind her ear. "I'm thinking about asking her to go for a walk if she's interested." He gently wiped her eyes.

Her hand lifted to his and sought comfort in the contact. She offered a watery smile. "Let's walk. That's what I came over to ask anyway."

"Really?"

"Yeah."

"What, Gage wasn't home?" he teased, trying to lighten the emotions of the moment.

She lightly punched his arm. "I called you first, then decided to just come over."

He wasn't sure what to say.

She smiled at him. "That's sweet."

"What?"

"Your assuming you might be my second choice."

He rose to let his dog out of the house. "I've found that life goes smoother if I don't make assumptions where a woman is concerned." Hank threatened to knock him over in his excitement at company. It was good to hear Rae's laughter. "I don't know about sweet."

"Unexpected. Nice. Charming."

"I can go for charming." He snapped the leash onto Hank's collar and offered it to Rachel. Hank danced around Rachel's feet as she knelt to greet him.

They set out for an ambling walk. When they reached the sidewalk, Cole pointed north. "You and Gage have been close for a long time."

She nodded. "Gage is the man I call at 2 A.M. when I'm mad at the world and want someone to tell me I'm right. He has a dry sense of humor, a black-and-white right-versus-wrong mentality. And he's the only one I let get away with calling me by my middle name. Since Tabitha's death...he's become a cross between a cynic and a realist."

Cole knew some of that history, for the fire that killed Tabitha had been one his department worked. "He's a friend."

"A good one," she said quietly. "But that's all, Cole. And that's all he was ever destined to be."

He squeezed her hand.

The silence lingered past the point either had something else to say, and it became a comfortable silence, broken only occasionally as Rae corrected Hank's enthusiasm, which threatened to tangle his leash into a knot.

"Would you come with me to the airport to pick up Jennifer and Tom?" Rachel asked.

Cole rubbed his thumb along the back of her hand. "You know I will, but your family will be there."

"I know."

He heard something under the question and tipped up her chin. "What is going through that pretty head of yours?"

"I like the word *pretty*."

"Rae—"

"Jennifer doesn't have much time left."

"Maybe not," he said gently.

"Probably not."

He nodded, conceding.

"Jennifer has had two dreams driving her the last few months. First, that all the O'Malleys would come to believe in Jesus like she does and would understand heaven and the hope she feels. Only Stephen is left to make that decision, and there isn't much I can do for that beyond what she's doing."

"And second—"

"She wants all of us to be happy, wants to see our dreams come true. It would help if Jen knew you and I…" She stopped and closed her eyes.

"What, Rachel?" He thought about her words. "That we're seeing each other? That you're special to me? Trust me, your family already knows that." He rubbed her hands, trying to reassure her.

"Jennifer's been my best friend for so long; she knows all my child-hood dreams."

"I'd like to know them too."

She smiled at him but didn't take the tangent. "Would you be com-fortable being part of the family gathering over the next few weeks, let Jennifer get to know you better? I'm happy around you, and I want her to know that. Regardless of what the future holds, I want her to know she doesn't need to worry about me. That's the only gift I have left to give her."

"Rachel, I already like your sister, and I would certainly enjoy get-ting to know her better." He searched for words. "I want to be part of your life, all of it. Trust me with this part too, the weight you carry regarding your family. This isn't going to be an easy time for any of you."

"It's not such a little thing, being part of the O'Malley clan."

"Spending time with you the last few months has begun to make that obvious. You've got an interesting family, Rae."

She hugged him. "I appreciate this, Cole."

He tipped up her chin and kissed her. Her lips tasted salty from the earlier tears. He took his time with the kiss, letting it soften and comfort. It was as much for him as it was for Rachel; there was so much emotion inside. His hands soothed hers. "I know what the next months are going to be like, how hard it will be to have both intense grief over Jennifer's situation and also let yourself build new joy with me, but you need to trust me and try. Life is going on."

"Cole—"

"Are you crying again?" he asked, struggling with that.

She wiped her eyes as she tried to smile. "You don't know what you're walking into."

"I think I do." He wished he knew how to convince her. "I'm a safe gamble, Rae. I promise not to break your heart."

"Oh, now you've done it. Hold on. I need a Kleenex." She searched her pockets and found one. "I don't deserve you."

"Probably not," he agreed, relieved her tears were only threatening this time. "But I don't deserve you either."

She smiled at him and he felt his heart skip a beat. He was definitely falling in love with that smile…with her.

He rested his arm around her shoulder and turned them around to start the walk home. It was time to lighten this conversation. "So you think Jennifer might be interested in telling me stories about you? She must know a few."

Rachel laughed. "Knowing Jennifer, probably."

He couldn't resist. "Any embarrassing ones?"

Rae pushed him off the sidewalk.

Nine

Rachel woke early, her eyes still puffy from the tears of the night before, but her heart was unexpectedly light. She hugged a pillow close. *Jesus, is this going to work out with Cole?*

Their relationship was so different from most she had ever had. There was a steadiness about him that gave her hope they could indeed work out this relationship even while the rest of her life remained chaotic.

Cole was right about the struggle it would be to balance the heavy heart that came from accepting Jennifer's cancer, while at the same time trying to build a long-term relationship. Rachel was glad he was willing to take the lead. To her it was a scary undertaking, while he seemed comfortable with the challenge. She should have sought him out for a hug and poured out her tears a long time ago.

Did Cole understand how huge her dream was to be married and have children? He was great with kids; she only had to watch him with Adam and Nathan to see it in action. He'd more than once made a point of mentioning he looked forward to having a family someday. It was a wealth of little things that said he wanted to be a husband and father.

Marriage was her deepest dream, and yet she had held off on it the longest. She'd lived through her own parents' bitter marriage and been abandoned by so many people that she trusted through the years, she'd put work ahead of settling down. The odds of seven O'Malleys succeeding in strong marriages were long. She couldn't afford to be the one who made a mistake.

Rachel pressed the pillow tightly against her face, then tossed it aside. As much as she wanted to daydream about what the future would be like, it was time to get moving. She rose and got dressed.

Rachel was reading the newspaper when the doorbell rang. She carried her coffee with her and went to get the door, expecting one of the O'Malleys to come to talk about Jennifer. Marcus had already said both he and Quinn had made arrangements to work in Chicago indefinitely while Jennifer was here. Sometime this weekend they were sure to assemble somewhere to make plans for the coming week.

"Gage, hi."

"I got your message." When she got home she'd called him with news about Jennifer. He handed her a copy of his newspaper. He knew she did the unthinkable and subscribed to the rival city paper. She leaned into his hug and peeked into the sack he held. "You brought me a chocolate-covered donut."

"Only because I wanted to make sure my muffin was safe. I'm fixing breakfast. What do you want in your omelette? I brought the eggs and my brand of coffee."

"Whatever you can find. You may have to settle for scrambled eggs."

He headed toward the kitchen and opened her refrigerator. "A vegetarian omelette it is. I can live with that."

"The peppers are going mushy."

"So are the tomatoes."

Saturday morning breakfast was something of a tradition. She normally met him at a restaurant somewhere. He liked to hear her reaction to the piece he wrote. She settled back at the table as he began working and opened the paper he had brought. There wasn't room in her kitchen for two people. "The flood is almost over and now you write about it?"

"You haven't been down to the really bad section. About three miles south, by the bend of the river, homes are still underwater. It's becoming the trash pit of the floodwaters. One house has already collapsed, and they think another one is about ready to fall down. It's dangerous enough that they haven't even let engineers go in by boat to look at what's going on. Some think the ground has collapsed in a huge sinkhole under the homes. It was new construction too, the expensive homes."

"I'm glad I haven't been down there. Governor Street was a big enough disaster."

He brought over breakfast plates. "You want to talk about Jennifer?"

"She's coming home."

"So you said in your message."

"I don't know, Gage. I swing from relief that she'll at least be here with family to fear over what each day will be like. Will her energy hold up? Will she be bedridden soon? The situation has too many unknowns to be able to do much planning."

"How can I help?"

She knew he would offer; it was one of the things she loved most about him. "She mentioned wanting to do a ladies' night out. I may need some help with logistics. Swap cars possibly. Yours has more room."

"Whatever you need."

"I appreciate it."

They ate breakfast sharing the paper.

"Gage, do you ever think about getting married again?"

He set down his fork. "Since we normally have these conversations late at night over the phone when you want to hide what you're thinking, I'll assume this is a hypothetical question?"

She lightly kicked him under the table.

"Oh, one of *those* conversations." He leaned back in his chair, holding his coffee, smiling at her. "Tabitha used to start these with her famous 'what would you do if...' questions that drove me crazy. She once asked me what would be easier: having to spend a year living with the in-laws or a year apart from her. As if there was a safe answer to that question. Sure, I think about getting remarried. Every time I get up and have to face a morning alone. I've even turned on that classical music Tabitha loved to listen to in the morning even though I can't stand it. Life is boring without a need to constantly compromise with someone. Always getting my preference is no fun." He set his coffee back on the table. "Rae, I'm still married in my heart. It doesn't matter that I haven't heard Tabitha's voice in two years. She's still a huge part of me. I don't know when that will change, or if it ever will."

"Your marriage to Tabitha was the first truly happy marriage I ever saw."

"Considering the competition I was up against in O'Malley history, I don't think it was such a huge target to hit. It's not like we didn't have problems."

"Yeah. I heard about some of those too. But you gave me hope again that a great marriage wasn't a myth."

"It didn't last as long as I would have liked."

She was careful with her next comment. "Cole and I—it's getting serious."

He didn't give her a quick answer, just looked at her, and then he smiled. "Rae, there is no one I know who deserves to be happy more than you. Dress up, turn on that megawatt smile, and go spin his head around."

"Somehow I don't see that being Cole's reaction. But it's a nice compliment."

"You don't see the guys who turn to watch you cross the room."

She gave a slight smile. "I see them." She looked at him and her smile faded.

"Going to tell me the rest of it?" he asked gently.

"The grief is heavy, facing this with Jennifer. Cole is…helping balance the other side of the scales."

He thought about that. "How long have we been friends?" Gage asked.

"Please, don't remind me of my age."

"Exactly. I know you, better than even your family in some ways. Tabitha didn't have many secrets either. If you two talked about something, chances are I heard about it. You're doing the right thing."

"I don't know."

"Cole's got a reputation for honesty, hard work, and loyalty. He's got a house. Now he's even got a dog. He's a settled type of guy. Give yourself a chance, Rae. And I say this to my own detriment here."

"It's noted. Thanks, Gage."

"I haven't had the fun of kidding you about a date in what? Three years?"

"Larry was a nice guy."

He laughed. "Sure. Which is why you never let the O'Malleys meet him." He rose from the table and picked up his plate.

The phone rang, saving her from further conversation. She went to take it in the living room. "Hello?"

"Hi, Rae."

"Jennifer."

Gage stepped into the room on hearing the name.

Her sister sounded in good spirits; Rachel gave Gage a relieved okay sign with her fingers. "I'll head out and let you two talk," Gage whispered. "Call me later."

"Thank you," she replied quietly.

Gage let himself out.

Rachel settled on the couch with the phone.

"I'm sorry it was a tearful call last night," Jennifer said.

"It was probably good for both of us. It gave me an excuse to bawl for you."

"I hope you weren't crying alone. Tom was mopping my tears for me."

"Cole did a pretty good job last night, and Gage came over to fix breakfast this morning."

"We have very nice guys in our lives."

"Very nice."

They had been sisters for a long time. The silence was peaceful.

Jennifer broke it. "God is my doctor, Rae. It's not like He doesn't know what He's doing—He created this body. If He wants to heal me, He knows how. I'm going to quit having a pity party now. I've got some living to do. And since getting released from the hospital is actually a pretty nice change, I'm going to enjoy it."

"Good for you." Rachel knew her sister; she had known today would bring that optimism back to the forefront. "It was hard to believe in miracles before today, Jen. But I believe in them now. Because we're at the point we need one; it's the only thing left. God is good. His answer to this will be good."

"I don't want to be the trendsetter, to be the first O'Malley to enter heaven. I'm sure it will be better than here, but I'm just not ready to go."

"How did the others take the news?"

"A lot of quiet. No one sounded surprised. And it helped when I said I was coming back to Chicago."

"We all want your company."

"Kate asked if I wanted to go back through old haunts—Trevor House and the rest."

It wasn't an easy question to think about. "What did you say?"

"Let's leave the past in the past."

Rachel found herself relieved at that. She didn't want to go back either. "Jen, do you really think God will cure you?"

"It's a feeling, Rae. A confidence inside that He's got more people for me to help. I'm a doctor; it's how I answer who I am. And I'm convinced I'm not done yet."

"Then that's what we will pray for. That you get well enough to go back to work."

"So you went to see Cole last night."

Rachel settled deeper in the cushions. "How did I know you would pick up that fact in this conversation? He's a nice guy, Jen. You'll like him."

"Something going on I should know about?"

Rachel hugged the pillow. "Cole kisses great."

Jennifer laughed. "Tell me about last night."

Ten

ole drove Rachel to the airport to meet Jennifer and Tom Wednesday night. He kept one eye on traffic and the other on her, not quite sure how to read her retreat into silence. They had spent the afternoon helping Ann paint and were invited to stay for dinner. Rachel had been keeping her spirits up during the afternoon, but now... Cole knew how tough this evening would be for her. He was still having to guess a bit on how best to help her. "Are you ready for this?"

Rachel had roses for Jennifer balanced on her lap and her head resting against the headrest. She didn't open her eyes. "Did I really eat hot dogs and purple Jell-O for dinner?"

"I wondered how many times you were going to nod when Nathan asked 'more?'" Nathan was attached to Rachel, and the evening had shown in vivid ways that it was mutual.

"I thought he was asking 's'more?' The chocolate graham cracker things Adam was fixing for dessert."

Cole reached over and rubbed her knee, appreciating more than ever the way she opened her heart to kids. He was sure over the years she had said yes to more than one odd dinner because a child asked for her company. "I picked up a soda for you if you'd like it."

"When we get to the airport I'll gladly accept it." She took hold of his hand and looked at it. "How's your thumb?"

The bruise under his nail from the accident while hanging shelves was turning black. "Nathan swings harder than Adam."

"It will ache for days."

"He's not the first boy I've taught the hard way. It will heal." He reluctantly turned the conversation back to the coming evening. "Marcus said Jennifer and Tom had decided to stay at the hotel across from the hospital."

"It's a hard decision because we all want them to stay with one of us rather than in an impersonal hotel, but it makes the best sense. Her doctors would like her to continue with the daily pool therapy so that she keeps as much muscle strength as possible, and they have mutual friends on staff at the hospital. As it turns out, Kate's fiancé Dave's family owns a major part of the hotel. The best suite is theirs for as long as they like."

Rachel sighed. "I'm beginning to accept the fact that a month ago I still thought in terms of having months if not years with Jennifer. Now I'm adjusting to thinking about the next ten days. I know she's going to be limited in what she is able to do, and I don't want to add to her stress by showing the sadness I feel. There will be time for sadness later."

Cole squeezed her hand. "A day at a time."

She squeezed back.

"Have you talked about plans for the next few days?"

"We'll give her a day to sleep. The rest of the weekend—it will depend on Jennifer's energy. We'll probably have an O'Malley gathering. You're invited."

"I'll be there." He reached the airport exit. "At which gate are they arriving?"

"You'll want to circle around to the private terminal. Dave is flying them in."

"You meet him in a suit and tie, a badge and a gun, and you forget the fact that the man is rich enough to live comfortably."

Cole parked and paused Rachel with a hand on her arm. "Stay put. I'll come around and get the door so you don't tip those flowers."

They walked toward the terminal together. "Do you want to make an impression on Jennifer tonight or let her draw a few conclusions over the weekend? Say the word and I'll not let you get a step away from me tonight," he offered, smiling.

"The suit and tie already make a pretty big statement," she teased.

"You noticed?"

"I did. You dress up very nice, Cole."

He rested his hand on the small of her back. "There's the rest of your family."

Then he spotted Jennifer. And any question he had about Rachel's sense of urgency disappeared. Jennifer was a shadow of who she had been just months ago. His heart broke at the sight. "There they are." Tom was pushing Jennifer's wheelchair.

Rachel's grip on his hand tightened, and then she released it and hurried forward.

Cole relaxed in the lawn chair in his backyard later that evening while he waited for Rachel to finish a phone call. She was twenty minutes into a conversation that sounded like it would continue for another twenty. His dog had given up on the walk starting and had stretched out to sleep sprawled across Rae's feet. Cole tossed the baseball into the air and caught it on the way down, the feel of the ball comfortable. He had dug it out of a storage box to give to Adam next time he saw him. Cole's love of baseball went back to his childhood, and he enjoyed sharing it with Adam.

He knew Rachel had a gift for helping people; he had experienced it himself. But tonight he observed something he hadn't anticipated. He'd watched Rachel open her heart and literally pour it out. With her family, she held nothing back. It was there in the quiet words with Marcus, the laughter with Jack, the private moments with Kate, the questions for Lisa and Stephen. She had eased each of them over the pain inherent in Jennifer's homecoming, and they'd trusted her enough to let her take that burden.

It had cost her in energy. After seeing Jennifer and Tom settled at the hotel, Rae had barely said two words on the drive back. If she ever opened her heart like that toward him… He wasn't sure he deserved something that precious.

Rachel was talking to Marissa. Rae had seemed relieved to have the page come in, and as he watched and listened, he understood why. For Rachel work was a distraction. One of Marissa's school friends had gotten into trouble and Marissa needed a sounding board. Rae listened with her full attention, and when she did speak it was most often to ask a question. She had a nice blend of calmness and realistic advice. She cared. Rae would do everything she could to help, but she could compartmentalize the needs. With family she never released the weight, and Jennifer's cancer had continued as a building burden for a year now. The strain was telling on her.

She reached for her day planner and confirmed a date for next week. The call finally ended and she leaned her head back against the lawn chair. "Sorry, Cole."

"First rule of couples—no need to apologize for your job."

She half smiled. "Are we going to be making these up as we go along?"

"Very likely."

"Then you'll let me replace this lawn chair. It's got a hole in the webbing that is tickling the back of my arm."

"I'll even let you put your name on it so Jack won't stretch it out," Cole offered.

"Can we just sit here awhile before we walk? I don't think I've got the energy to get up at the moment."

"As long as you like." She was far from ready to go home. And he was in no hurry to have the day end.

"How did Jennifer look to you?"

There was no good gained by ducking the honest answer. "Like someone alive by strength of will."

Rachel let that reply sink in. "I'm not ready to say good-bye."

"How can I help you, Rae?"

"You already are."

"Seriously. How can I help *you*?"

She turned her head toward him and thought about it.

"I don't want to be alone," she whispered.

"You won't be, through any of this."

"It feels very alone. Death is like a cloud coming near that shadows and blocks the color from life."

"I'll be here, Rae. Whatever you need. And God promised He would never leave you. He meant it. For the rest of eternity you will never be alone."

"How am I supposed to be praying? Death is the one thing everyone fears: dying alone, afraid, before we are ready, leaving things undone. It feels like a betrayal to pray for God both to heal Jennifer and to give her a peaceful death with people she loves around her."

"Do you think God doesn't understand that duality? Loving Jennifer means you pray for a long, healthy life. Loving Jennifer means you pray for a peaceful death when the time does come. Rae—" he waited until she met his gaze—"if there is one person it's safe to share what's inside your heart with, it's God. All of it. His love is steadfast and He describes it as stretching to the heavens. He cares. And He knows what tonight took out of you."

"Stephen has taken it on the chin losing patients in accidents, and tonight hit him like that. He was struggling not to cry when he saw Jennifer. It's not fair, Cole. This family can't handle a funeral."

There was nothing he could say that would help. He knew Rachel couldn't handle it either.

She reached for Hank's leash. "Let's walk. I need to set this aside if I'm going to be able to sleep tonight. And I'm a long way from learning your habit of setting stuff aside."

Cole offered her a hand up. "You'll get there."

"Thanks for being there tonight."

He hugged her, taking the moment to reassure himself as well as her that they would get through this. "My pleasure."

"Would you keep Saturday morning free? It sounds like the O'Malleys are getting together about ten."

"I'll be there."

Eleven

I f Cole had known why Rachel had asked him to keep Saturday morning free, he would have made a point to get more sleep first. He was playing baseball, although the rules appeared to be creative. Someone should put warning signs around that woman. Cole bent down and picked up the baseball that had dropped like a rock and stopped in front of the pitcher's mound as Rachel took her place on first base with a flourish. A shout of delight from the bleachers rose as Lisa and Cassie scored another two runs for the O'Malley women.

The catcher came jogging out to the mound. Marcus shot a look at Rachel on first base, now pausing to adjust the folds on her socks to be even over her brand-new tennis shoes. Marcus took the baseball from Cole and made a point of checking it for smudges. "She hasn't officially started dating you yet. It's okay to get her out."

"The sun got in my eyes."

"Sure it did." Marcus nodded toward Gage playing third. "*He* wouldn't let a little thing like a wink work on him."

"She wasn't winking at him."

Marcus dropped the ball back into Cole's glove, his smile growing. "I noticed that too. One more out and we can take them to lunch. They have a tradition of folding after five innings so neither side has to admit defeat."

"Good point. Besides, you just told me to get your fiancée out."

Marcus glanced toward Shari stepping up to home plate. "No, I just told you to walk her. You can strike Kate out."

"Come on, guys, give me a pitch. I'm ready to add the icing to the cake."

Marcus grinned. "If she doesn't get on base this game, she'll want to spend this weekend practicing in a batter's cage. A walk is purely self-preservation."

It was an elaborate baseball game being played for one person. It was worth it to hear Jennifer's laughter. Tom had transferred her from the wheelchair to the bleachers and swallowed her in a blanket to prevent her from getting chilled. They were all stretching themselves, and the humor of this game was to give Jennifer a day of laughter.

Cole pitched Shari a soft lob way outside of the box, and she still went after it. She swung like a girl and spun all the way around with a clear miss. She pouted, laughed, and stepped back into the hitter's box to try again.

Kate rushed out from the women's bench and showed Shari how to choke up on the bat. She whispered something that made Shari laugh. The next pitch Shari hit and it dribbled six inches in front of home plate.

Shari looked at the ball and then back at her fiancé. "I'm not getting it," Marcus assured her. Shari took off for first base with a delighted hop and a run.

Cole looked at the ball, then at Shari, and decided it was better not to move.

A glance around and Gage decided it was time to dust off third base. When Shari rounded first and the bleacher seats were screaming for her to keep going, Jack playing right field loped in from the outfield to get the ball. A tag-team race ensued between home plate and third as he tried to tag Shari out. He finally caught her in a hug and a fit of laughter. "Out. That's the inning." He picked her up to carry her toward home plate. "I caught a Shari."

"Toss her back," Marcus called.

Shari blew him a kiss over Jack's shoulder. "I nearly stole home."

"Nearly."

"I'm hungry, guys, let's call the game and go eat," Jennifer called.

The guys made a production of showing their disappointment, but they turned their attention to packing up gear.

The pizza shop was busy on a Saturday afternoon, crowded with families and kids. Cole slid in beside Rachel on the bench. She was toying with her straw while watching Tom and Jennifer play an arcade game together. He replaced her empty glass with a full one. "I like your family."

"The guys made you pitcher. You should feel honored."

"They didn't want to strike out their girlfriends."

"I noticed I was on base more often today than ever before." Rachel gave a small nod toward Jennifer. "She's happy."

Cole looked at Jennifer, leaning back in her wheelchair to share a laugh with her husband. "She's getting rest and a lot of laughter. Without the medicinal side effects her body is getting a chance to rally. This is a good week for her."

Rachel tucked her straw into his pocket. "Got any change? I want to play some pinball."

"I've got a pocketful of quarters just for us. Couple play, a flipper each?"

"How are your reflexes?"

"Better than yours."

She grinned at him. "Your age tends to regress around my family."

The carefree morning had lifted a burden from her. Rae was happy. Cole leaned over and kissed her, capturing the moment.

"What was that for?" Rae whispered.

"Because you make me happy." And he wanted to make a memory of this day for both of them.

"Half my family was watching."

"Only half? Remind me later to make up for that lapse."

She laughed softly. "I'll do that."

"I still owe you dinner out; Chinese I think it was. Want to go out this Friday?" he asked. "Just the two of us? Good food, movie, take Hank for a walk to end the evening?"

"I would love to."

He slid off the end of the bench and caught her hand. "Let's beat Jack and Cassie's score."

"It's impossible. I watched them play for four hours one afternoon on one quarter."

Cole rested his arm around her shoulders and steered her around the kids. They joined Jennifer and Tom. With her wheelchair angled to the side of the game she was handling the spinner and timing it perfectly. "The points are racking up."

"A lot of practice with video games in the hospital," Jen mentioned. "You should see me slaughter Pac-man."

"They still make that game?" Rachel asked.

"The version I play is the one they have on the children's ward. It has cancer cells and big, happy red blood cells eating them up."

"I hope you maxed out the counter."

"Twice," Jen replied, amused.

Rachel took the quarter Cole offered. "That one," she pointed out an open game.

Twelve

Rachel met Marissa Tuesday at the ice cream shop down the street from the high school. Arriving a few minutes early, she chose an outside table and worked on a chocolate malt. The Franklin High School complex was new and had over seven hundred students. When the bell sounded and the exodus began, the teens merged into a sea of backpacks, jeans, and small groups of friends holding together in the moving crowd.

Minutes later, bells rang at Quincy Middle School across the street. Parents were lined up along the sidewalk and the edge of the parking lot to meet the younger kids. Adam was somewhere over there with his friends. Rachel had plans to meet him after soccer practice.

Marissa appeared from the crowds of high school students, walking with a rocking gait as her prosthesis threw off her stride. Her friend Janie carried her backpack for her.

"Hi, M."

"I knew you'd be early."

"An excuse to sit and remember my own high school days. Hi, Janie."

"Miss O'Malley."

"Would you like to stay and join us for a soda?"

"I have to get home. I watch my brother in the afternoons." Janie glanced inside toward the counter. "Greg is working today."

Marissa pulled the chair out and carefully sat down. "I saw him." Rachel saw the hint of a blush along with the fact that Marissa did not turn to look for herself. Without having to turn more than a fraction, Rachel took a glance at the boy now moving behind the counter, talking with the manager who had made her malt. A nice-looking young man, a senior from what Marissa had said. They'd make a good couple at the prom.

"I'll meet you in the morning at the corner?" Janie asked Marissa.

"Early? I've got a council committee meeting."

"Early. Bye, Miss O'Malley."

"Bye, Janie."

Marissa's friend headed home. Marissa tucked her backpack under the table.

"I love your earrings," Rachel mentioned.

"I made them."

"Really?"

Marissa slipped one off and offered it to Rachel.

"I'm impressed. You could go into jewelry making if you wanted to."

"It's a hobby Janie is teaching me."

Rachel handed it back. "You should make your mom a pair for her birthday."

"Really?"

"Trust me, she's still young at heart." Rachel picked up her heavy glass. "I'm going to get another malt. I forgot how much I love these. What's your pleasure?"

"A cherry Coke with a scoop of vanilla ice cream."

"Coming up."

The ice cream shop was a popular stopping point after school. Rachel took a place in line. She watched Marissa as she waited. The girl called a couple hellos to friends passing by, picked up and absently twirled the paper from a straw. Twice teens left the sidewalk to cross over and talk. Rachel smiled when she heard Marissa's laughter. If there were problems at school, they were not the major ones of not being accepted.

Rachel reached the counter.

"Yes, ma'am. What can I get you?"

Greg had blue eyes. He was lanky, tall, and had a smile that compelled a smile back. "Another chocolate malt, and for my friend, a cherry Coke with a scoop of vanilla ice cream." He glanced outside to where she nodded.

She caught the smile when he saw Marissa. "Coming up."

He was fast, efficient, and generous with the ice cream for both of them. Greg told her the total with tax before he rang it up, and she wasn't surprised to see it ring up to the penny he quoted. She paid with exact change.

Rachel nodded her thanks, took the drinks, and saw Greg's attention get caught by someone behind her.

"I got a gold star."

"Good for you, squirt. Grab your stool and I'll fix your reward." His smile told her it was family.

The girl was maybe six. "I want a swirly today."

"Do you?" Greg nodded his thanks to the lady who had walked the child to the shop.

The girl rounded the counter and climbed up on the stool by the small counter with the phone and the order pad. "Mom said she'd pick me up at four."

"I get you for almost an hour?" Greg asked in mock horror. "Guess I'll have to put you to work then."

Rachel said a quiet thanks to the teen who held the door for her and carried the glasses outside. She could see why Marissa blushed when Greg was mentioned. The choice of the ice cream shop on Marissa's part had not been an accident.

Rachel set down the glasses and took her seat. "I like him, M. How did you two meet?"

"I baby-sit for his sister sometimes."

"She's cute too."

"Clare is a gem." Marissa ate the cherry atop her ice cream. "It's sad. Their parents split up last year. Clare lives with their mom, and Greg and his younger brother live with their dad two blocks away. Greg's been kind of the go-between, looking out for Clare and Tim."

"It must be hard on Greg, thinking about leaving them in order to go to the academy."

Marissa nodded and dropped her eyes.

Rachel worked on her malt.

"Mom wants me to go to college for a music degree."

"I know."

"But I don't want to."

Rachel hadn't seen that coming. "Go to college or major in music?"

"Both. Mom won't understand."

"She knows your singing could take you places. She knows that's been your dream for most of your life."

"I can't walk across a stage like I used to. People feel pity before they even hear the singing."

Rachel wished she had been at the concert, wished she had asked Marissa's mom more questions when they had spoken. Something had been said, done, that had touched a raw memory for the girl. "It's not an obstacle to your dream of recording music." She knew that was the real dream Marissa had, to make records of her songs.

Marissa nodded. "I know."

"What are you thinking?"

"If I leave town, it's going to be very hard on Mom. And Dad might leave town entirely if I'm not around. I know he keeps this job because it lets him provide health insurance for me."

Rachel nodded.

"I'm known at the high school. No one asks what happened to me because everyone knows. I don't want to go to a four-year college and start over."

"It's not easy to go into new territory, to face people who don't know you, who notice your leg first."

"I'm not afraid of that."

"M, I would be more surprised if you weren't scared."

"I'm just not ready to go away to college yet."

"That's a good place to know you're at."

"I want to help people like you do. Only in my own way. I could get a job at the medical clinic as a receptionist and go to the local college here for two years to get my basic course work."

"Have you talked to your mom about doing that?"

"She'll be disappointed with me."

Rachel smiled. "Trust me; she's working hard to be able to send you to college in another year without crying all over you when she sees you leave. If you want to stay local for two years of college, maybe you could transition to your own apartment after you graduate. You could get in the habit of going home for dinner twice a week and calling her early on Saturday mornings to wake her up and say let's go shopping. I can tell how you're going to make your mom miserable by staying here."

"That sounds fun. That's what I want. A couple years of not having to push so hard. I just want to relax after the last two years before I dive into something huge like a competitive college music degree. I'd have to start the scholarship work this summer, and I'm just not ready."

Rachel would have been concerned had Marissa been changing a long-term dream without that kind of thought behind the decision. But what she was hearing was an honest assessment of what Marissa wanted and why. She'd had two years dealing with the amputation, her dad's grief, and a struggle to catch up on schooling to be able to still graduate with her class. Deciding she wanted a couple years without major life changes was a very grown-up decision. "That sounds reasonable." Rachel turned her glass, thinking about it. "Most of your friends will be going away to college."

"I'm okay with that."

"Marissa—" The door to the ice cream shop pushed open. Clare struggled to hold it. "Can I show you my drawing?"

Marissa turned in her seat. "*May* I. Sure, Clare." She waved at Greg, he nodded, and Clare came out to join them.

"Mom's hair curls at the bottom. I don't think I got it right." The child automatically came around to Marissa's good side and climbed up on her lap with an ease that said she had done it many times in the past. "I'm doing the picture for Greg so he has one of Mom at Dad's house."

"It's a good picture. I can help with her hair." Marissa took the brown crayon.

The child leaned across the table. "Hi, I'm Clare."

Rachel took the offered hand. "Hi, Miss Clare. I'm Rachel."

"You're pretty."

"Thank you."

The child smiled back. "Welcome." Clare leaned back against Marissa. "I wanted to draw your picture for Greg, but he said he already had your picture."

"Did he?"

"He showed me. You were at his football game. With Janie."

"Oh."

Rachel relaxed. Marissa had a pretty full life back. A boyfriend. Her own ideas of what she wanted for the future. The progress was good. And if in another couple years her father got past his own sense of guilt—the hope was there. It was good to see. Marissa was nearing the end of her process of healing.

Rachel finished her malt as she watched Clare and Marissa. From one case nearing its end she'd change to one still in process. Adam was still working through the losses he'd suffered in the flood.

When Clare took the picture to show Greg, Rachel shifted the conversation. "Marissa, would you happen to have some earrings I could borrow that would go with a jade dress for Friday night?" Cole was taking her out to the dinner. She needed something to make a better impression than the jeans and sweatshirt she'd been wearing the last few times she'd seen him.

"Spinners or maybe hoops?"

"I was thinking I'd pull back my hair and have wisps around my face."

"Something long, gold, with a hint of jade. I've got just the thing. You could use a matching hair barrette with a fine ribbon woven into it. Do I get to hear details of your date?"

Rachel smiled. "Maybe. You don't know him."

"Your reporter friend?"

She shook her head. "Cole—he's with the fire department."

Marissa rested her chin on her fist. "A nice guy?"

"Very nice guy."

"You'll have a good time."

"I hope so."

Marissa grinned. "You're nervous."

Rachel laughed. She was, for she'd never set out to turn Cole's head as she hoped to for this date. "Absolutely."

"Kate, if I knew you were going to stress out over this, I would never have mentioned it." Rachel shifted the towel over her wet hair to look back at her sister. Her sister's bathroom was small, and the exhaust fan in the ceiling was out of balance and whining. Rachel shifted her feet carefully. Kate's cat was rubbing her ankles and making her sneeze, had already sunk its claws in her socks twice trying to force attention to his desire to be fed.

"You are going on a date," Kate replied. "We're doing this."

"It's hair color. You put on those plastic gloves and use the stuff."

"Quiet. I'm reading."

"I'm getting tired of staring at sink fixtures that have toothpaste specks on them."

"That's soap specks, thank you, I cleaned in your honor. Okay, we're going to try this. Close your eyes."

Rachel squeezed them tight. "Did you turn off your pager? You get paged in the middle of this and we've got a problem."

"We've already got a problem. The directions look like Greek to me."

"I trust you."

Kate gently pushed Rachel's head farther forward. "Loyalty was never a problem. Common sense, yes. Tell me about this date. Have you chosen the dress?"

"The jade one," Rachel mumbled through the towel, trying not to breathe in the awful smell.

"It's gorgeous. Want to borrow my bracelet and pearls?"

"Just the pearls. Marissa had the perfect earrings." Rachel wiped liquid away from her forehead with the corner of the towel. She turned her attention to the real reason for this visit. "How did Jennifer seem to you?"

Kate's movements didn't slow, but her words were sad. "She'll be bedridden soon."

"Is there anything we can do for her we're not already doing?"

"I can't figure out what it might be."

"It feels awful."

"I know. We do whatever we can to make her happy. She needs time with Tom—that's the most important thing now."

Rachel jerked as Kate's cat tried to bite her toe. "Marvel, I'm going to bring Cole's dog with me next time I come. Kate, you feed the cat too much; he weighs a ton. What's his problem?"

"You're in his bed. He's taken to curling up in a ball inside the sink for some strange reason."

"Your cat is dumber than a rock."

"About as hardheaded as one too."

"Then you'd better get married and let Dave teach him some manners."

"Soon."

"You've been saying that for months."

"Hold your breath. I have to do your bangs."

Rachel held her breath. If she didn't know Kate loved Dave an incredible amount, she would suspect that her sister had cold feet about getting married. Kate wanted to be married; she just didn't want to go through the headache of getting married. She figured if she stalled long enough for Marcus to marry Shari and Lisa to marry Quinn, she could talk Dave into eloping. It would never happen. But Kate was as stubborn as her cat.

Thirteen

I t had been a hot house fire. Even the caulking around the windowpanes had coiled up. The windowsill wood gave under the force of the crowbar. Cole jolted back as a cooked cockroach tumbled out. Arson and bugs. It made for a memorable Friday.

"Cole?"

"Back here."

Cole poked a pair of grill tongs down into the wall between the joists to fish out the evidence he was after. He had to give this homeowner credit for originality. He had spliced a string of fireworks into the outlet to start the fire. The explosions had sent the strand dancing around within the wall and dropped the evidence into a crevice out of the way of the resulting flames.

"So this is your idea of a date."

He turned his head to look back toward the door. Rachel crossed the scarred flooring where the burnt carpet had been ripped back.

Rae was the classic beauty in the O'Malley family with an innate sense of how to dress well to make an impression when she chose. She was making one. She'd chosen ivory and jade, and the vibrant color looked gorgeous on her. He could look for hours and simply enjoy the sight. Even if it did leave him with a permanent crick in his neck.

She smiled. "You should have said you needed to cancel."

"An evening out with you—I'm not canceling. You look gorgeous."

"Thank you, sir."

"I'll be about ten more minutes."

"Take your time."

He reluctantly looked back to the task at hand. "I wasn't comfortable the tarps would hold for tonight."

"Cole…you stood me up for work, not another woman. We're fine."

"Sure?" He didn't know which he appreciated more, Rachel's looks or her common sense.

"It will cost you the larger cannoli."

"Italian? I thought we had settled on Chinese."

"I changed my mind."

"Then it's a good thing I happen to love Italian."

She laughed and started to wander around the room. "What happened here?"

Cole finished gathering the outlet wiring. "My initial guess, the owner got behind on his bills and wanted to collect the insurance."

"So he burned it down."

"Tried to." Cole sealed and initialed the last evidence bag. He'd seen just about everything in his years leading the arson squad. This fire had been an obvious arson attempt, interesting but obvious.

Cole picked up the box with sealed evidence bags. "Want to follow me to the fire department while I drop this off, or head to my place? I'll change and you can leave your car there."

"I'll meet you at the house."

Cole took Rachel to Antonio's. The Italian restaurant was tucked into a hard-to-find circle drive near Sterling Lake and the owner was a friend. He watched Rae in the candlelight toy with her salad. She could push away the weight of what was going on in her life up until the point she paused, then the details rushed back to take her attention. "How did your meeting with Marissa go?"

"Good. I always enjoy seeing her. She's wrestling with college plans."

"And Adam?" He wasn't sure where to take the conversation

tonight. He wanted her to have a relaxing evening. But until he got her out of silence mode, it wasn't easy to know how to accomplish that.

"Adam wants to know when the bridge will be reopened so he can watch the water up close."

"Another week at least. I'm thankful. Kids on the bridge would not be a good idea with all the interesting things still floating in the river just begging to be grabbed."

The waiter brought their dinner and another basket of hot bread. Rachel tore in half a piece of the bread and buttered it. "I'm fading on you already. I'm sorry; Friday night was probably not the best day to suggest."

"On the contrary, this is the perfect time. A good meal, a walk afterward, a chance to sleep in tomorrow—" He raised an eyebrow.

"My schedule is clear," she confirmed.

"Then consider this the start of a chance to relax. That's the definition of a good date." Her smile made the evening worthwhile.

"Your mother taught you wonderful manners, Cole."

"Thank you, ma'am." An idea occurred that might lift her spirits. "Hey, I've got a question for you."

"Sure."

"You helped Jennifer make the arrangements for her wedding. Do you still have your notes?"

"Two notebooks of them. Why? Do you know someone who's getting married?"

"I heard from Marcus that Kate wants to elope."

"He's working the problem now?"

Cole nodded.

"Then it has become more than a rumbling rumor that she might just talk Dave into it."

"I was thinking it would do Jennifer good to be part of planning a surprise wedding."

She blinked, and then her smile bloomed. As tired as she might be at the end of a week, Rachel still blossomed at a suggestion of something she could dive into. "Dave would have to like the idea."

"A given." Cole watched her as the idea developed. He found it fascinating the way her fatigue disappeared.

"Kate's been avoiding setting the date, but the problem is simple—she doesn't want to plan a big wedding, doesn't want to face a day fighting tears trying to keep her smile in place. If it was just her preference, she would have eloped back in November." Rachel thought some more and nodded. "You know, it might work. I've got a pretty good idea what Kate wants at her wedding. We've been sounding her out for months about it. And if she arrived and found Dave had made all the arrangements for them to essentially elope without leaving—" She grinned. "Jennifer will love this, and it will give her something fun to focus on. Thanks, Cole."

"Put those candy mints on your list. I like them."

"Glad to. I wish I had Dave's home number memorized. If he likes the idea, I could call Jennifer."

"Is your phone in your purse?"

She nodded.

Cole slipped out his address book and thumbed through it, looking for the card Dave had given him. "Try this." He gave her Dave's unlisted phone number scrawled on the back.

"You're helpful to have around."

He grinned at her. "Sure am."

"I owe you one." She turned her attention to the phone call. "Dave? Got a minute? Kate's not there is she?"

Lisa had the crime lab to herself as most people in the building had already gone home. She shifted the phone against her shoulder. Rachel and Cole were going out tonight; it was the best news she had heard in days. "Really, Jen? Where was Rachel at when she called?"

"She was just meeting up with Cole. I hear it's going to be Italian tonight."

Lisa brought down the next photograph from the Carol Iles murder scene from the wall and slid it under a magnifying glass and bright light. She was looking for anything that might help give her another clue to work on this case. "Italian sounds wonderful. I think Cole's perfect for her."

"I know she's perfect for him," Jennifer replied. "Rae lights up when she talks about Cole."

"Very much like you do when Tom comes into the room." Lisa spotted something in the photo of the kitchen counter that puzzled her. "Jen, let me call you back."

"Sure. I'll be here."

Lisa called Marcus and asked him to come over with Quinn.

She took the photo with her and went to locate the negative. She took it with her to the image lab. Twenty minutes later she had a twenty-by-twenty blowup of the kitchen counter. She pinned it to the board. Her eyes hadn't been fooling her.

She started looking through the evidence for the box collected from the counter.

"What do you have, Lisa?"

She turned as Marcus and Quinn joined her. "The blown-up photo on the board," she indicated, letting them see for themselves.

She found the right box and pulled off the lid. She pushed aside two pot holders, a napkin holder, salt and pepper shakers. The cop that had cleared the kitchen counter had swept his arm across it to put everything into a box. "This box has already been sorted once already, but the photo said it was here."

"Find it?" Marcus asked, joining her.

She started pulling out each napkin from the holder. "Got it." She gingerly held up a blue business card by the edges. "Carol had one of Rachel's cards."

Fourteen

Rachel finished off her list of Kate's favorite foods. "Timing is going to be a challenge. If we wait too long, Kate will get wind that something is being planned." She ate another bite of her dinner and nodded to the waiter who had come to refill their coffees.

Cole leaned over and added strawberries to her list. "Three to four weeks max," he agreed, "especially since you're going to want all the O'Malleys involved in pulling it off."

"It will be tight. Dave's going to ask his brother-in-law Adam Black to be his best man, and the two of them will come up with a good cover story for us." She stirred cream in her coffee.

Cole smiled at her. "What?"

"I need a date for the wedding." She had a feeling Cole would look really sharp in a tux.

"You've got one. I wouldn't miss this for anything." Cole looked beyond her and set down his coffee. "We've got company." He leaned back, his words and actions catching her by surprise.

She turned and was stunned to see her brother Marcus coming toward them. She nodded to her brother and met the gaze of his partner. "Quinn."

"Ma'am."

She loved the way he said ma'am with his Western drawl.

Marcus pushed his hands into the pockets of his slacks. He looked ill at ease. "Can we talk for a minute, Rae, outside?"

She slowly set down the pen and closed the pad of paper. "Of course." She glanced across the table. "I'll be back in a minute, Cole." She followed her brother, confused by what was going on. Lisa, waiting by their car, raised her hand. Rachel nodded to her and looked back at her brother.

"Lisa's got a murder case. And your name came up."

"How?"

"The victim had one of your cards."

Marcus offered her the card encased in a plastic sleeve.

Rachel took it and turned it over. The ink was faint but readable. "Yes, it's one of my cards. But the number—it's very old. 930710. It's my original numbering sequence. It was the seventh event in 1993, the tenth card I gave out there."

"Remember back that far?" Marcus asked.

She held up her hand and walked away, looking at the card and thinking back to that year in her life. She remembered incidents and children in detail, but putting a number with an event took more thought. She circled back. "9307 was a shooting at a federal park in Colorado. A man walked into a gift shop carrying a handgun, looking for his wife." She had it now, clear in her mind. "It was early May, a sunny day, but cool. A group of school kids were at the park on their way to see the sulfur springs. Police coming in to surround the building were forced to get the kids out one at a time from where they hid behind the counter." She remembered the children's fear of what they had gone through and their fear that their friends wouldn't get out safe.

"Anybody hurt?"

She shook her head. She thought about the event and she could see those kids. "It ended peacefully. But the kids were badly shaken up. Since they got trapped together, the fear one felt transmitted to all of them. They collectively started to be afraid of the outdoors and the strangers who might be out there watching."

"Carol Iles. She's thirty-two," Marcus offered.

"The shooting murder during the early days of the flooding?"

Rachel thought about the name. "No. The name is wrong, and the age. I gave this card to Amy Dartman. She'd be in her early twenties now."

"You're sure."

Her memory tag for names was vivid. "Dean, his friend John, Paul and Brad, Cheryl, Emily, Leah and Lucy. The teacher was Nicole. The tenth card went to Amy Dartman." She felt silly explaining it. "A DJ eating a peanut butter sandwich while talking on his cell phone saying awesome deal: DJ, PB, CELL, AD. Those were the cards."

"Any idea how Carol got this one?" Quinn asked.

"It's not unusual for kids to still have the card years later. But why Amy would have dug it out and passed it on? I have no idea."

"When did you last talk with Amy?"

Rachel shook her head. "A long time ago. It will be in my log book back at my apartment."

"I hate to interrupt a night out, but it would help if you could get the book. Amy must have given Carol the card, and it's not something that would be passed on for no reason. I'd like to locate her if possible," Marcus said.

Rachel looked back at the restaurant. "Let me go tell Cole. I left my car at his place."

"We'll take you by the apartment and then over to get your car."

"No. I came with Cole; I'll leave with him." She patted Marcus's arm. "Give me a few minutes." She nodded farewell to Quinn and smiled at Lisa, and walked back into the restaurant trying to figure out how she was going to explain this to Cole.

He was still at their table, but both plates had disappeared. He rose when she returned. "The plates are being kept warm. Trouble?"

"Remember Lisa's murder case the night of the flooding? One of my blue cards turned up among the victim's things."

"Rae, you live an interesting life," Cole murmured. "How can I help?"

She appreciated the man more every time she was with him. "Take me home? They need my old files."

"Of course."

"I'm sorry about dinner."

Cole smiled at her and spoke briefly to the waiter who had come over. Their dinner became to-go. "Don't worry about it, Rae. We'll try this again next week." He offered her one of the chocolate mints left with the credit card receipt. "How old was the card?"

"From '93. I'm amazed the ink was still readable."

"Your place to get the log book, and then stop for ice cream on the way to get your car?"

"I'd like that a great deal. I am sorry. This wasn't what I thought the night would be like."

"Don't worry about it. Interesting dates are much more enjoyable than boring ones. Besides, the evening isn't over yet."

"I don't like this, Marcus," Quinn remarked, turning over the card. "Amy Dartman. We've heard that name before."

"Criminal division, down the hall from Carol, mentioned as one of Carol's friends. She was on vacation the day we were there," Marcus confirmed.

"My missing blond?" Lisa asked.

"Maybe," Marcus replied. "Let's get Rachel's file and check out Amy. I'd rather not tell Rae more than we have to until we understand this. She doesn't know one of her special kids from years ago is missing and may be dead. She was having a good evening with Cole. Let's try not to totally ruin that."

"Agreed," Lisa replied.

Rachel unlocked the door to her apartment and turned on the lights, hoping she hadn't been in such a rush this morning she had left her housecoat in the living room and her cereal bowl on the desk. She didn't want Cole getting a bad impression.

Her home was cozy, filled with furniture, the walls crowded with pictures of kids she had helped, and pillows dominating the couch and chairs. It was her haven. She loved every inch of it. And with four guests crowding into her living room, it got distinctly small. The material she had been reading in preparation for the upcoming commission hearing was spread out on the floor by the couch.

One wall of the living room was solid bookcases. Rachel crossed over to them. She kept the composition books in chronological order. She searched the bottom left shelf, tugging out books and reading the front labels. "Here it is. 9307."

She opened the book. Over time it had developed into a detailed log. There were factual accounts of the events in the words of those who had lived through it—the children and adults caught up in it, spectators, officers on the scene. Accounts had been underlined to show unique facts brought out by each individual. Spider webs of circled names and interconnections showed relationships among those present. There were neat pages of addresses and phone numbers for family members and friends, records of her follow-up calls with detailed notes. And inside the cover, an index listing of cards given out. "930710 was Amy." She handed the log to Marcus.

"Is this phone number beside her card number Amy's parents?" Marcus asked.

"Yes. Check the center of the book for names and address. Would you like me to call them?"

"Let us check the address, make sure they still live there. Thanks, Rachel."

"I hope it helps."

Marcus smiled at her. "It's a lead. There have been few. I'll let you know what we find."

"How *did* you know where we had gone for dinner?"

Marcus smiled. "You called to talk with Jennifer while you waited for Cole. She happened to mention it to Lisa."

Rachel glanced at her sister. "I hate being on this end of the grapevine."

"Give me interesting news to share—"

Rachel laughed because Lisa was stating the obvious. "Turn the locks on your way out. Cole and I are going to get dessert and then my car. And Marcus, if you've got a minute. The kitchen window is stuck. Could you elbow it down again?"

"What broke when it jammed?"

"I knocked over two flowerpots and broke the string on my sun catcher."

"Ouch. Sorry about that. I'll see if I can fix it permanently this time."

Cole held the door open for her. "How many events are recorded in those books?"

"Forty, sixty, something in that range."

"Amy held on to your blue card for years. When she was scared, she called you." Cole looked over at her.

She nodded. "The incident really shook her up. Amy was scared of the dark and sounds in the night for years."

"Maybe Carol had a reason to be scared about something. Amy gave her your card and told her to call you."

"She never did."

He unlocked the car door for her. "What would you have done if a stranger had called you out of the blue?"

Rachel wasn't sure how to answer that.

"Would you have called your family first? Or just gone?" He started the car.

"If it was a woman, I would have just gone."

"You work with kids. Marcus and Lisa and Kate deal with the crime. Remember that, okay? Call your family before answering a page like that."

The protective words touched her. "Thanks, Cole."

Her pager sounded. Rachel glanced at the numbers. "Okay if I make a call? It's family."

"Sure." He turned down the radio.

She knew the number by heart. "Jennifer. Hi."

"Tell Cole I'm sorry to interrupt tonight of all nights."

"You can tell him yourself in a minute," she offered. Jennifer's voice was soft, but she sounded good. They had spoken a couple hours ago about planning Kate's wedding. Jen should be asleep at this time of night.

"I need a favor."

"Anything."

"I just talked to Stephen. He worked a tollway accident this afternoon. A child wasn't buckled into a safety seat. He sounded pretty down."

She hadn't heard the news yet. "I'll stop by," Rachel said quietly, knowing how hard the day would hit her brother. For a paramedic, a child dying from what may have been preventable was the call they dreaded the most. Stephen talked at times about moving from Chicago to a small town where he would get calls to treat bee stings and broken arms more often than tragic deaths. The years were wearing on him.

"Thanks, Rae. Enjoy tonight with Cole."

"I plan to. You want to say hi?"

"Maybe another time."

"Good night then. Sleep well." Rachel put away her phone and double-checked that her pager was reset. She changed the radio station to the all news station to see if she could get a name for the family involved in the accident.

"Do you need to go directly to get your car?"

She turned to Cole. "This will wait until the morning."

"You're sure?"

She knew Stephen. The first hours after such a death, he wouldn't want to talk about it. Tomorrow would be better. "It will wait."

"Then if you don't mind a suggestion—plan what you will do, and then set it aside until tomorrow," Cole said. "You tend to worry things in circles. Try to worry in a straight line."

"You make that sound so simple."

"Actually it's just the opposite. But it's worth learning how. You'll sleep better."

"I'm trying to pray and let go, but it's hard. Who taught you the wisdom of how to do it?"

"My dad."

"He sounds like a good man."

"Dad was a civil engineer; he built roads. He called it permanent job security because a good road got used the most and always had to eventually be rebuilt. You would have liked him, Rae."

"I'm glad you have that memory."

"What do you remember of your parents?" Cole asked.

"I didn't have a good home, Cole. You don't end up at Trevor House because life has gone smoothly."

"Were there good memories in that mix?"

Rachel had tried over a lifetime to sort out the emotions. "Mom was a good cook. Dad could fix a car no matter what was wrong. They just weren't a couple; you know what I mean? They would rather fight with each other than work together to find a solution. And I was all too often caught in the middle." They'd divorced, and Rachel had gone with her father, but it hadn't worked out. She ended up at Trevor House. "Trevor House wasn't so bad. It was lonely, but I was already that. And the O'Malleys solved that problem."

"Is that past what made you go into the profession you did?"

She took a risk no matter how she answered that. "Kate says my childhood was such a crash course in how to survive a crisis that I now spend my days teaching others who don't have the skills. The reality is much more basic. I work in disasters because I learned how to be good at cleaning up a mess. That's all people really need, a helping hand to get started and a reminder that they did survive."

"You have to admit, not many people can hear news that a tornado came through town and rather than freeze, have a prioritized list in mind for what needs to be found, starting with blood supply, doctors, generators, and water."

"I'm a gofer, Cole. I know enough about what has to be done to be able to plug in where they are shorthanded."

"You fill the need, no matter how big it is or how huge the commitment on your part."

"You exaggerate that a bit."

"Rae, you would do your job even if no one paid you."

She smiled. "It's my own version of job insurance. A disaster will always be around to work."

"Let's hope not for a few months. I've enjoyed having you in town."

She reached over and squeezed his hand. "I'm enjoying it too."

Marcus pulled up to the federal court building, leaned across the seat, and opened the car door for Quinn. His partner was juggling a cardboard box and a laptop. "You were persuasive."

"Judges are a tight group when it comes right down to it. Judge Holland called Judge Reece, and the order was issued. Security unlocked Amy Dartman's office and I collected everything that looks personal," Quinn replied.

"Amy's seventy-two hours late getting back from her vacation; if she actually made it to her vacation. We can't even prove she's missing." Marcus checked traffic and pulled back onto the road.

"We can prove she was at Carol's that day. It's Amy's prints on both the soda can and the blue card. Amy hasn't called anyone lately that we can find, including her parents. She had a vacation plan that comprised a full tank of gas and a map, but sometime in the last few weeks she would have had to use a credit card. I don't buy a coincidence, not when they both worked in the criminal division."

"How does a twenty-three-year-old manage several weeks leave for an unpaid vacation?"

"Call it work for a master's degree," Quinn replied. "I want to see her apartment."

"The warrant came through. Wilson and Lisa are already on their way. I told them we'd meet them there." Marcus looked at his partner. "What do you think?"

Quinn held up a picture of Amy. "Blond. Nice smile. Twenty-three. She's probably dead."

Marcus opened the refrigerator at Amy's apartment, studying the near empty contents. She had tossed anything that might spoil during her vacation. "What are we missing, Quinn?" He wasn't sure what he was looking for that would suggest a lead, but this was the place Amy had called home. Looking around should at least tell them more about her.

His partner turned on lights in the living room. "What's the first thing you do when you return from a trip?"

Marcus thought about it as he opened kitchen drawers. "Park the car, bring in the luggage, toss my jacket, and probably kick off my shoes. Get something to drink. Listen to any messages. Turn on the TV while I look through mail to see what's urgent."

"I don't see evidence that she did any of those things."

"Confirming the suspicion that she never got back from her vacation." Amy was neat to an extreme. There wasn't anything approaching a junk drawer. The phone book was in the drawer near the microwave with a blank pad of paper, one pen, and one pencil in the drawer. There were no coupons for restaurants in the area, no pack of matches, a rubber band, a garbage bag tie—the inevitable items discarded in such drawers. Had she moved in recently? Marcus made a mental note to check that out.

"You know what else would be here if she had gotten home?" Quinn wandered around the living room, turning over cushions on the couch, the chairs. "Pictures, souvenirs. The first trip upstairs to the apartment she would have probably been carrying at least one or two valuables with her that she wanted to take extra care with and not leave downstairs unattended."

"If she never got back from her vacation, we're now at the more critical question: Did she ever leave for vacation? The refrigerator has been cleaned out."

Quinn turned on lights in Amy's bedroom. "Her closet is noticeably missing clothes." A few minutes later he added, "There isn't a toothbrush or hairbrush in her bathroom. That cosmetic bag recovered at

Carol's is going to prove to be Amy's."

The small second bedroom had been turned into an office. Marcus pulled out the desk chair. Starting clockwise, he started checking drawers.

Lisa entered the apartment. "In the morning I'd like to walk around the block."

"See something?"

"Just curious. Her car is missing from the apartment garage. Wilson is checking to see if security tapes are left from that day that might tell us when she was here, if someone was with her."

Marcus uncovered a card from someone named Diana and a bill from a hair salon. Amy had probably gone to get her hair done before she left for vacation. Women talked while they got their hair done. It would be worth tracking down.

"Marcus, come look at this," Lisa called.

Straining to read the date on the receipt, he went to join them.

"This was on her nightstand." Quinn opened a folded plain white envelope. "Do you know anyone who keeps old movie ticket stubs?"

Lisa leaned against him. "I'm planning to hold on to the stubs from the movies we see."

Quinn bent down and kissed her.

"Break it up, you two." Marcus wasn't sure if he was ready to see them married. He took the envelope from his partner and looked through it. There were about fifty movie ticket stubs. "Amy's got a boyfriend."

Quinn reluctantly leaned back. "Any idea who?"

"Someone she trusts. You're talking a couple years' worth of movies."

"So if Amy has truly disappeared, there might be another person out there with motive than whoever shot Carol."

"First, are we in agreement that she was indeed planning to go away on vacation?"

"Everything here says she was," Quinn said. "Even her mail had been stopped."

"Second, we're agreed that she was at Carol's the night of the murder?" Marcus asked.

"Yes. She might be my missing body tossed in the river," Lisa added.

"Maybe. If we can track Amy's movements that Friday, we can firm up the time line for the earliest Carol could have been murdered."

"Let's go find Wilson," Lisa recommended. "Maybe there are also security tapes for the elevators. We can find a boyfriend a lot easier with a picture."

Fifteen

Marcus covered the phone as Lisa joined him at the marshal's office Monday night. "Quinn wants to know if you'd like to do a midnight movie with him."

"Absolutely. You can afford to give him a few hours off?"

"It's the only way *I'm* going to get a few hours off," Marcus replied.

Lisa laughed and took a perch on the corner of his desk.

"She said yes, Quinn."

Lisa took the phone from Marcus. "Not a murder mystery, Quinn. Make it funny." She laughed. "I'll hold you to it. I love you too." She hung up the phone.

"Hey, I wasn't done talking with him."

"You can call him back." Lisa handed him a folder she had brought. "For you. Morgue reports. This is every Jane Doe that was found since the day Carol was murdered that was roughly Amy's age, in this and the surrounding states. Two are slim maybes, but I looked at the dental work. I'm no forensic dentist, but they don't come close. You'll have that officially in a couple days."

He scanned the list.

"Amy's in the river somewhere," Lisa offered again her most likely guess.

"And her luggage? Her car? We should have found something by now."

"There are a couple stretches of lowland still to be searched where the flooding is at best contained by sandbags. And for all we know, the car was buried in a mud bank somewhere with a foot of water now running over it."

"True." Marcus held up the list. "Can I keep this?" Lisa nodded. He added it to his briefcase. "For what it's worth, at least you have a body to work with. I can't even prove I've got a crime. For all we know maybe it was Amy who shot Carol."

"No motive."

"But at least we've got the two of them placed at the scene of the crime. Any luck breaking the ex-husband's alibi?"

"Wilson reinterviewed people, but with his son Mark saying Brian was with him, and with others who were at the basketball game confirming they saw Brian there, it appears solid." Lisa spun the pen on the desk. "What about this being work related? Someone watched the house or followed them and intentionally murdered both Carol and Amy?"

"We're burning the midnight oil to see if we can find something. Any luck on finding the gun?"

"None. We need to talk to Rachel some more about Amy."

"Not yet. She's having her first break in weeks, and I don't want to interrupt that."

"It has been nice seeing her with Cole."

"Exactly."

Lisa slid off the desk. "I've got a car wreck to go look at, and then I'm heading over to the hotel to see Jennifer. Tell Quinn to meet me there later?"

"Will do."

Laughter filled the hotel suite Jennifer had made home Monday night. Lisa had brought a movie with her called *Down Periscope,* and it played in the background as they made secret wedding plans for Kate and Dave. Tom had met them at the door. He kissed his wife, and with amusement told her to behave, and then he had disappeared to join Marcus for a few hours to give them the run of the suite. Jennifer was dutifully lying down on the couch as promised.

"I think we should go with these napkins."

Rachel leaned over to see Jennifer's choice. The floor by the hotel couch was crowded with open books of cards and napkin samples. Between Lisa's ideas, Rachel's notebooks, and Jennifer's lists, they were actually trying to do the impossible and plan the wedding in one evening. "Those would be great."

"Which ones?" Lisa called from the suite's kitchenette.

"Medium size, white, with a red ribbon border, and a heart in the center."

"Yes, great choice. Get matching tablecloths."

"Do they have tablecloths?" Jennifer asked.

"Got it." Rachel found the page and added the stock numbers to their master list.

Jennifer found the wedding cake book. "Did you hear, are we on for the ladies night this weekend?"

Rachel added streamers to her list. "Lisa and I will be over with Kate about 2 P.M. Friday, so make sure the wedding stuff is hidden. Shari and Cassie are going to meet us here about five. We've got dinner reservations at the restaurant downstairs, and Kate is in charge of the movie selection. She promised to get something that was dramatic and romantic, but her taste has been pretty interesting recently, so I may slip one into my bag as a backup. I hear the guys are going to have a night out of their own to occupy Tom."

"I think they are starting with basketball," Lisa added.

"He'll come home with a black eye and look sheepish about it." Jennifer held out the book. "What about this cake?"

"That is beautiful." Rachel looked closer. "It's the cake you had at your wedding."

"I knew it looked gorgeous."

"Kate would go for something with even more roses. She likes frosting."

Jennifer turned pages. "How about this one?"

"Nice. Lisa, what do you think?"

Lisa set down the coffee tray. "Excellent. Did Dave say what he was thinking about for a honeymoon? He's got to make a decision soon."

"He's going to take Kate somewhere her pager won't work. Beyond that he hasn't given much away," Rachel replied, curious about it herself. She had no idea where she would like to go if she were planning her own. "Have you and Quinn decided about yours?"

"We'll go back to Quinn's ranch." Lisa sat on the floor beside the couch and reached for sugar for her coffee. "We need another cake."

"Another sheet cake beside this one?"

"A second wedding cake."

Rachel glanced at Jennifer and both looked at Lisa.

"I want to get married too," Lisa said simply. "We'll have a double wedding. This way if Kate stumbles on some plans, we can just tell her they're for Quinn and me. He and I talked, and we don't want to wait anymore."

Jennifer leaned over, wrapped her arms around her sister, and squeezed until Lisa giggled. "A double. This will be so much fun."

"This way we get a Chicago wedding in and Marcus and Shari won't feel so guilty about having theirs in Virginia where it will be more convenient for Shari's family," Lisa offered.

"And then Jack and Cassie's," Rachel said.

"They get the huge public wedding with all of Company 81 there to help them celebrate," Lisa said.

Jennifer looked over at Rachel. "Let's find two great cakes."

Sixteen

Rachel could barely remember what it felt like not to have aching feet. She shifted shopping bags between her feet trying to get comfortable as Kate pulled around to the restaurant drive-thru window to pick up their order. The Tuesday afternoon shopping trip that had begun as a quick trip by Rachel and Jennifer to the local department store had mushroomed into the four O'Malley sisters going to the mall. Jennifer's brief stretch of renewed energy wasn't likely to last, and they were determined to make the most of it. They had shuffled work schedules to get the afternoon of April 24 off.

The four of them shopping together was an adventure. There was barely room in the car for them on the return trip because of all the packages. Rachel turned in the front seat to check on Jennifer. "Comfortable back there?" Lisa had as many pillows as Jennifer did. The two doctors were having a good time together.

"Just fine." Jennifer looked at Lisa and the two of them cracked up laughing. Lisa had taken charge of Jennifer while they explored the mall, pushing her wheelchair through stores and often stopping to compare ideas on clothes with Rachel. Four times she had found herself being sent to the dressing room to model something they had found for her. Several of the packages she now carried were gifts from her sisters.

"Who ordered the coffee that looks like fudge sauce?" Kate asked.

"Back here," Lisa replied.

"That stuff will kill you."

"As long as someone else has to do the autopsy," Lisa said cheerfully.

Rachel handed the coffee to Lisa and the cold soda to Jennifer.

Rachel's pager went off.

"We're off duty. All of us," Kate reminded her.

Rachel tugged the pager free to see the number. "It's Adam."

Kate turned down the radio as Rachel reached for her phone. She had wondered if Adam would ever use the card. She was surprised—it was at two-thirty on a school day. He should be in class. "Hi, Adam."

"You called me back." He was breathing hard like he had been running, but he didn't sound like he was crying or scared.

"Always." Rachel took the large iced tea Kate handed her and slipped the extra sugar packets into her pocket so she could squeeze the lemon slice.

"The nurse let me call you after I called Mom."

"The nurse's office, huh?"

"I got a black eye."

"Ouch. Did you get a bloody nose too?"

"Huge." He sounded proud of it.

"Did the nurse give you an ice pack?" He'd gotten hurt somehow and called her after calling his mom for a reason. She was picking up the sounds of a nervous boy.

"It's freezing. Would you tell Tim it's not his fault? He kind of did it. We were playing volleyball in gym class, and the kids were laughing at him. He got mad. He didn't mean to hit me when he threw the ball." Adam was rushing his words, trying to protect his friend.

"Accidents happen all the time. I'll be glad to talk to Tim. I bet he feels awful about what happened. Would you like me to come by when school gets out?"

She looked over the seat at Jennifer as she made the offer, trying to decide if she was going to be getting a cab to keep this promise.

"Please. Mom is coming to get me. Could you kind of smooth things out with her too?"

"I would be glad to. Why don't I meet you by the bike rack?"

"Okay. Tim and I will be there."

Rachel hung up the phone.

"Trouble?" Jennifer asked.

Rachel put away the phone. "I need to swing by the school. Let me call a cab. I'll catch up with you guys back at the hotel."

"The school is on the way to the hotel. We'll wait for you," Jennifer said.

"Are you sure? You need to get some rest before dinner."

Jennifer nodded to Lisa. "I'm resting. Ask my doctor."

Lisa smiled at her. "You need to listen to your doctor more."

"You need to work on your bedside manner," Jennifer suggested with laughter.

"We'll stop at the school," Kate decided, the driver settling the matter. Kate's milk shake arrived. She put it in the cup holder and pulled to the street exit. "Are the streets still one way around the school?" she asked Rachel.

"Yes. Take Buckley Street to Converse. You'll avoid the traffic."

Rachel shifted her sacks, looking for the one with the gift for Marissa. She'd found the perfect beaded clutch purse for her to take to the prom. "Does anyone see the sack with the wrapping paper?"

"Back here. Which one is your pleasure?"

"The gold foil. And a white bow. And somewhere back there is a roll of tape."

"Found it."

Rachel had small scissors on her keychain. She tugged them out and cut off the tags from the gift. "What do you think?" She held the purse out for Kate to see.

"Marissa will love it."

Rachel slipped it into the tissue paper and back into the small box. "She deserves a great prom." Rachel wrapped the gift and added a bow. "Park at the ice cream shop. You won't get stuck in traffic since you can exit with the light."

They were a few minutes early. Rachel checked that she had her phone and her pager as Kate parked. "If you see Marissa while I'm over at the middle school, will you get her attention? I won't be long."

"We will."

"Do you want to sit out at a table, Jen, or stay in the car?"

As that question was debated, Rachel got out of the car and leaned against the side, watching the gathering parents. She could see the bike rack at the middle school from here; it was one of the reasons she had suggested that meeting place. She didn't want to head over too early for the shade wasn't great and kids had a way of being late coming out, given there were lockers to get to, gym things to collect, and friends to find.

Kate came around the car to join her. "Remember when you were in high school?"

"I'm doing my best to forget."

Lisa opened the car door and shifted pillows around so Jennifer could stretch out. The high school bell rang. Kids began streaming out. Rachel kept an eye out for Marissa as the high school parking lot became crowded. Then the middle school bell sounded. Rachel watched the growing crowd of kids meeting up with parents until she saw girls from Adam's class appear. "If I'm going to be more than twenty minutes, I'll call you," she told Kate.

"Tell Adam hi for me."

Rachel lifted a hand in acknowledgment and headed toward the middle school.

Gunshots erupted.

Seventeen

Cole listened in on a conference call with family services and the district attorney regarding an arson fire last week while he worked on the department budget. It felt odd to be back at his desk, but he was trying to clear the paperwork.

"He set his tree house on fire the first time; this time he started a fire in the trash bin behind his apartment building. You can call them accidents as much as you like, but if we don't pursue charges, we're going to be unable to stop him before someone gets hurt," the lawyer with the district attorney's office weighed in.

"He's eight. He needs counseling," the family services officer protested.

This was the third call concerning Rusty Vale in the last year. It wouldn't be the last. Cole revised budget numbers trying to squeeze in another set of wet gear. The flooding had demonstrated they didn't have as many guys trained as they needed.

Outside the fire station the long ladder truck warned with tones that it was backing up. It was Tuesday, and on Tuesdays that rig got a full checkout. A sticking valve had been reported, and four guys led by Jack were working the problem. It sounded like they had it resolved.

"The family refuses to discuss it and I can't sit by and do nothing."

"Captain, do you have an opinion?" The family services officer was looking for help.

Cole agreed the boy needed help, but he wasn't sure the counseling she had in mind would be enough. "You said he's been having trouble at school. He's going to run afoul of the zero tolerance policy and face expulsion. His parents may be more willing to agree to counseling if faced with the headache of finding a new school."

The prosecutor and counselor began discussing the school counselor's report. Cole leaned back and reached for the fax coming in from the lab on evidence collected Friday.

"We'll go back to the parents one more time," the prosecutor agreed.

Tones sounded.

"I've got to go, folks. Let's touch base next week."

Cole cut off the call. He reached for his fire coat. They were short handed today as men who had been on full-time flood relief finally got a few days off. Cole was backing up Frank, the other captain on this shift, on the fire runs. He walked into the equipment bay as the huge doors rose.

"We've got a fire alarm at the middle school," Jack called over.

Cole swung up on the newly polished ladder truck, praying this was another in a string of false alarms. If Rusty was behind this, the discussion Cole had just listened to was moot. Hundreds of kids, panicked, with smoke filling the halls of the buildings… A fire at a school was something they all dreaded. It was policy to always roll a full response for a school alarm. "We'll take the east side; you take the west."

Jack nodded and Engine 81 rolled out.

Eighteen

G et down!"
Pain flared through the center of Rachel's back as Kate shoved her down, knocking them behind a nearby car. Gravel tore into Rachel's palms and glass bottle fragments on the pavement ripped into the knees of her jeans. Kate landed beside her and reached over to push her head down. Lisa slammed the open doors of their car to hide Jennifer and dove to the ground near them. The screams were terrifying as teenagers in the parking lot tried to get to cover and horrified parents across the street pulled their children to safety.

"Jen, keep your head down," Kate ordered, all cop, as she tugged out her sidearm. "Where's it coming from?" she shouted to Lisa who had better visibility in the other direction.

A car window in the school parking lot shattered with an explosion of glass. Someone was shooting in the midst of the kids. Rachel wanted to cry.

"Two o'clock," Lisa yelled back.

"Call this in!" Kate ran toward the high school parking lot.

"I'm calling," Lisa shouted back.

Rachel scrambled to the front of the car. Her heart broke as she saw the faces of the terrified kids. Incredible fear was frozen on their faces as they didn't know which way to run to get out of the way. She recognized the shock. They thought they were invincible, and someone had just ripped away that sense of safety.

"Marissa!" Rachel saw her stumble as she tried to hurry down the stairs, lose her balance, and tumble down the final six concrete stairs to the ground off the side of the stairs. Rachel wanted so badly to go help her friend.

The gunshots stopped. For good, for the moment... Rachel couldn't breathe. Beside Marissa she could see kids in the parking lot on the ground not moving. *Oh, God, what do I do?*

Jennifer pushed open the car side door. "Jen, close the door," Rachel pleaded.

"Kids are hurt. Get me to the kids." There was determination in her face and she wasn't thinking about the danger to herself, just the need. "Lisa, get someone to help carry me. We can both help them."

"Not yet," Rachel urged, "not until Kate has stopped this." She knew the counsel of the experts on this critical moment. *Think about your own safety. Realize if you get hurt, you can't help and will in fact slow down help getting to victims by becoming one yourself.* She couldn't stand to follow the advice. More gunshots erupted, and this time it sounded like shots and returned shots. Kate would get hurt trying to stop this and they wouldn't know. Rachel looked back at Lisa. "Stay with Jen. I'm going." She headed after Kate.

She could feel herself exposed to the danger, could feel the slowness in her movements as she struggled to hurry. She could feel her heart pounding and her breath coming in short gasps. Kate spent her life doing this, running into danger. She understood why Kate did it, but not how she lived with these moments of fear.

Rachel passed a blue Chevy with its back passenger door open. A gray Ford had backed into a white Honda and stood abandoned. Under her tennis shoes she could feel the sharp edges of glass from the shattered car windows. Backpacks lay where they had been dropped, spilled books and papers fluttering in the wind. Rachel passed kids crouched down and hiding behind vehicles and memories flashed back to the Colorado holdup years before. The kids were afraid to move for fear they would attract gunfire. She silently pointed back the way she had come.

Rachel caught up with Kate crouched behind a van.

"I told you to stay put," Kate whispered angrily.

"I couldn't."

Her sister peered around the front of the van again, trying to sort out the scene and find the shooter. "There! Past the blue Lincoln. A school jacket, black jeans. The kid has a crew cut. That's the first gunman, but there are at least two. Stay here. I mean it."

Rachel leaned against the side of the van and struggled to catch her breath. She was halfway to Marissa. Her friend had landed in an awkward angle and it looked as if her leg was broken. She was exposed, and the shooter appeared to be moving in Marissa's direction. Rachel crept from behind the safety of the van to the sedan in the next row.

She bit her lip to keep from crying out.

A boy had been shot in the thigh and lay where he had fallen across a white parking space stripe. He was using his elbows to edge himself toward safety. Before she could move, two of the boy's friends rushed back toward him to grab and carry him behind the cars. "Pressure," she called urgently, "put pressure on the wound to stop the bleeding."

She hurried back the way she had come. "Lisa! Over here." Rachel waved to attract their attention. Jennifer was out of the car with Lisa and the manager of the ice cream shop helping her. Lisa waved back.

Rachel caught up with Kate as she crouched behind the car in the handicap parking place.

Kate looked at her and there was dread in her voice. "The two boys are heading *into* the high school."

Rachel recoiled at what that might mean. They had to stop this, now. "I'm coming with you. I've been in the school. I know the layout."

Nineteen

The school building was brick and rough against her back as Rachel leaned against the wall to the east of the front doors. Behind them in the parking lot the screams had been replaced with soft calls for help. Kate was on her phone, trying to raise through dispatch any security officer that might have been assigned to the school.

Kate pushed her phone into her pocket and looked over at her. "They can't raise anyone. The wise thing is to wait." The blare of fire engines and police sirens were coming from all directions through the subdivision as help rushed toward the scene. They were coming to help, but they weren't here yet.

Rachel already knew Kate's decision. "There are innocent kids in there," she replied softly.

"Two shooters entered."

Kate didn't want her going in, and yet to stay here would be nearly impossible. "It's all the more reason to have someone watching your back." They had to stop the shooters so they could safely help the injured, and it was worth the price that had to be paid. She could help after a tragedy, but for the first time she was in a position to prevent one. Rachel had spent a lifetime desiring to be able to stop some of the pain rather than just help people recover from it. "I'm coming with you, Kate."

Her sister looked back at the glass doors. Alarms going off inside the building were making the glass vibrate. "Describe the layout."

"The school cafeteria is the center of a large square of hallways. Around the outside of the buildings are classrooms, and lining most of the hallways are rows of lockers. Behind the cafeteria is the kitchen and then the music room."

"Stairs?" Kate asked.

"Immediately on your left and at the middle of the building on your right. Locker rooms and access to the gymnasium complex is on the far left."

"Okay." Kate thought about her plans. "I'm going to open the door and prop it open with a backpack. When I signal, you come through fast. I want you keeping an eye on the stairs. Any kids I point out, your job is to get them out these doors."

Rachel prayed she didn't freeze under fire. It wasn't the first time she had walked into a shooting, but this time it would be deliberate. Kate was showing her trust by not even objecting.

Kate reached for one of the numerous abandoned backpacks. She ducked and rushed forward, yanking open the door, dropping the backpack, and darting to the right. When Kate signaled, Rachel rushed after her, the glass door heavy as she squeezed through.

She flattened herself against the wall beside Kate. The sound of the fire alarm was deafening. The hallway was deserted. Rachel had not been expecting that. Only several dozen open locker doors swinging back and forth suggested this had not been a normal exit of students. Books had spilled out of a couple lockers, a wastebasket had been overturned, and there were a couple sodas that had been dropped, the liquid running slowly down the hallway to the lowest point.

Kate checked the staircase and peered around the first hallway. She pointed Rachel to the first doorway between lockers where there was a little protection. Rachel hurried that way. She passed beneath one of the alarm horns and her ears hurt. School had just been letting out. There had to have been hundreds of people still in this building when the shooting started. It was eerie the way they had vanished.

Kate tried the doorknobs one by one as they passed rooms. They were locked. Teachers had barricaded themselves and students inside the classrooms.

Kate pointed across to the cafeteria where a door was still swinging. Rachel nodded. She stayed behind Kate as they crossed the hallway to the doors.

"Mark, where are you? Come out here, you jerk." A door slammed. A gunshot hit something metal.

She gasped. Kate silenced her with a hand across her mouth.

Rachel leaned against her sister. "I know that voice," Rachel whispered, horrified. "That's Greg Sanford."

Twenty

Kate could feel a piece of glass that had worked its way inside her tennis shoe cutting through her sock as she shifted her weight. She grasped Rae's shoulder, feeling her sister's tension in the damp shirt. She leaned in so she could be heard. "You recognize the boy speaking?"

"Greg is Marissa's prom date. Kate, he's a good kid."

"Who's got a gun in his hand. Describe him."

"Tall, lanky. Blue eyes. Brown hair, wavy. He's not the crew cut kid you saw in the parking lot. Kate, he fits none of the profiles of a school shooter. He's been helping take care of his younger brother Tim and little sister Clare; he's been there for Marissa. You've got to figure out a way to negotiate a peaceful ending to this."

Kate wished there was some way she could promise that. "Do you know who Greg is yelling at?"

"No. Marissa never mentioned anyone named Mark."

Kate pointed to the recessed doorway to the chemistry lab. "Stay over there, away from these doorways. No matter what you hear, Rae, stay out here."

Rachel nodded and reluctantly moved away. Kate took a deep breath. Her hand was sweating. The shouting inside the cafeteria grew louder but was indistinguishable. Shots rang out again inside, the overlapping staccato of gunfire and return fire. She was walking into a beef between two kids being solved by bullets.

Movement at the end of the hall caught Kate's attention. Another cop was in the building. Kate held up her badge, knowing he couldn't read it but would at least understand the meaning. She pointed at the cop and the far doors, then pointed at herself and the near doors. He nodded. They would have to get into the cafeteria and sort it out under fire.

Kate eased open the doorway a crack and saw an overturned table and chairs. She pushed the door open and slipped inside as fast as she could. Kate looked fast around the large room and dashed toward the serving counter. The floor was tile and her tennis shoes squeaked. It was the end of the school day rather than the lunch hour. Most chairs had been stacked and put away on the side of the room so that the floors could be mopped. Two rows of tables had been in use. The floor was sticky from spilled drinks around a few of the overturned tables.

The shouting was coming from the kitchen area.

She made it ten feet inside the cafeteria and found her first victim. A girl had been struck in the head, the open book in her hand suggesting she died where she had been surprised when the gunmen burst in.

Shots slapped into the metal supply carts near the salad line. "Police! Drop it!" The cop coming in the other end of the cafeteria took incoming fire and returned it.

Kate rushed to the end of the counter to help him. "Police! Put it down!"

The tall lanky kid went crashing over the counter. Kate moved toward him and barely ducked in time as the crew cut boy crashed atop her. A shot went off so close her ears rang. And then the pain registered. "Rachel!"

Twenty-one

Jennifer struggled to remember her residency days in the ER. She wasn't used to this degree of trauma, but she knew how to keep the girl shot in the side from bleeding to death. She worked as a one-person trauma team trying to assess and treat the injury, knowing she was in a fight against time even as she listened to the shouts of firemen and paramedics and police surging into the area. She needed a medevac flight and a good surgeon.

Jesus, I could use Your healing touch right now. It was a desperate prayer as she packed off the injury with the lining torn from a school jacket. "Hold on, Kim."

"It hurts."

The girl was crying and moving her legs against the agony. Both were blessings. Her lungs were clear and she had good mobility. Jennifer could feel the exit wound. This was a clean gunshot that had gone straight through and had luckily missed her liver.

"Were you planning to ride the bus home? Was your mom coming to meet you?"

"Ride with Theresa," she gasped. "She lives on my block."

"Theresa Wallis, she's over there by the oak tree," the baseball player who had been helping her pointed out. There were heroes in this group of high school students, those who had rushed back to help despite the risks. Jennifer had seen adults doing the same thing, shielding students as they helped them get away.

Jennifer turned. "Light green blouse and jeans?"

"Yes."

"Go get her. If asked, tell the cops she's coming to help me."

The boy nodded and took off at a sprint.

Across the high school parking lot paramedics and firemen were rushing to help kids, the first arriving officers covering them. They were working toward the school as fast as they could, getting the kids who could be moved back to where they could be treated. Jen was relieved to see her brothers. Jack and Stephen were both working the front lines. Kate and Rachel had disappeared inside that building too long ago for comfort. A few teachers had broken out windows and were getting kids out of first floor classrooms, trying to avoid the school hallways.

The boy came running back with Theresa beside him.

Jennifer added another layer to the bandage covering the injury. She had the bleeding under control. That was rule one. "Kim, Theresa's here." She smiled at the friend and nodded to Kim's other side. "I'm Jennifer. Can you hold her hand and relay messages to Kim's mom? I've got my phone here you can use."

Theresa gladly complied, her relief at seeing her friend alive obvious. "Hi, Kim."

"Mom...the community pool. She teaches the tadpole class."

Her friend dialed the number information gave her.

A police officer reached them. "Can she be transported by ambulance? General Hospital has a trauma center; it's a six-minute drive with escort. Air is still minutes away."

"As long as she goes now."

He nodded and got on the radio. The logistics of containing a site that encompassed two schools and several hundred students that had yet to be secured was huge, as the number of responding police and ambulance grew each moment and already in the mix were parents trying to reach their children.

"Doc. We need you over here!" an officer yelled.

"I've got my hands full, Jennifer," Lisa called. "Can you—"

Jennifer turned and looked. "Yes." They were working like a MASH unit doing fast triage and trying to keep students alive until more help could get here, and right now there was a desperate need for more doctors. Jen could see the ambulance coming. She reached for the hands of the boy. "Keep pressure here, steady and firm. Don't lighten up until the paramedic takes over. Can you handle that?"

The boy nodded.

The owner of the ice cream shop was working alongside her. "Get me over there please."

Jennifer clenched her teeth against the pain of moving as she was lifted to the wheelchair. She wished Tom were here. They not only needed another doctor but she needed her husband. She hoped he didn't get himself killed running red lights rushing here from the hotel. She'd promised him to take it easy this afternoon. The pain was growing as she tried to get her body to bear up under the strain.

Jack and Stephen were both in the group helping the girl, which was the first clue of what Jennifer was getting into. She eased to the ground beside the girl lying facedown on the concrete beside the stairs. Jennifer battled tears as she saw who was injured.

"Marissa, this is my sister Jennifer." Jack eased a blood pressure cuff around the girl's arm, trying to rapidly get an assessment of how severe the shock was hitting her.

"Bad," Stephen mouthed, shifting the bandage on her leg.

Her leg had an open compound fracture below the knee. Stephen was working to stop the bleeding from the long gash while trying not to make the break worse. Jennifer could see the intensity in Stephen's face as he worked: He knew the reality—he was trying hard to insure Marissa did not face amputation in order to save her life. Jennifer checked the tourniquet and nodded to Stephen then checked the other leg. When Marissa had tumbled on the stairs, her prosthesis had twisted around and broken at the ankle. Jennifer leaned down so the girl could see her. "Hi, Marissa."

The girl's face was pasty white and she was sweating, both bad signs. Jennifer ran her hand lightly along Marissa's arm, reassuring that the worst was over. A splint on her hand protected fingers broken in the fall. Jack had been able to lift her head just enough to put a soft cloth beneath her face, and it was absorbing the blood from the scrapes that had marred her face during the fall.

"You're the doctor. Rachel's sister."

"Yes. You broke your leg pretty badly," Jen said, at least able to reassure the girl she hadn't been one of the unlucky ones shot. Caught in the rush to get out of the way of the shooters, badly hurt, and forced to lay and watch her friends in the parking lot fall to the shootings, Marissa was fighting to overcome the shock now absorbing her. Stephen held up a note. Jennifer nodded agreement. Stephen filled a syringe and provided the first shot of pain relief.

"Both of them, I didn't think it was possible." Marissa tried to smile. "No more dreaded leg exercises to improve my gait. No more trying to carry my backpack and not tip over as I walk. It's okay. It's just a few months of sitting down. I can do this."

Marissa's words were slurring and her breathing grew more labored. "Don't you hate that they make most wheelchairs gray instead of in a rainbow of colors?" Jennifer asked, reading the latest vital readings from Stephen's clipboard. The teenager had spirit. Jennifer could see her sister's influence in the calm responses and optimistic attitude. Marissa would have to endure months in plaster, but she'd be able to do it with humor. They had to get her stabilized or she wouldn't make it that far.

Jack and Stephen carefully placed an air splint around the leg break.

"We're going to turn you over, Marissa. You'll feel a little dizzy as we do. I just want you to relax into the pain. It's going to pass."

Stephen pointed to the guys helping him to make sure they did this smoothly. "On three." They turned her with care.

There was a scramble of hands as they realized the lower front of her shirt was bloody. Jack ripped material. She had a penetrating wound from something she had fallen on. They struggled to stop the bleeding.

While they worked, Jennifer carefully wiped the blood from Marissa's split lip, then ran her hand gently across the facial injuries making sure they weren't covering broken bones. "You got yourself a couple nice bruises. How does it feel?"

"Not bad." Marissa breathed out in relief as the pain subsided.

Stephen was checking vitals. Jennifer knew the numbers were stabilizing. She could see the relaxation of stress on Marissa's face and the return of some color. Her breathing began to ease.

"Does your mom carry a phone with her?"

"Most of the time," Marissa whispered.

"She's probably on her way here. Let's give her the good news and a chance to hear your voice before we give her the bad news."

"What's a phone number to try?" Stephen asked Marissa, being passed a phone by the one of the officers. He was able to get through to her mom, and the conversation began with a calm reassurance that Marissa was with him and able to talk with her. He held the phone for the girl.

"Mom, I love you." The words came accompanied by tears. Jennifer gently wiped them away so the salt wouldn't burn her scrapes.

Jack helped her tuck a blanket around Marissa. They had to get her to the hospital, but for the moment giving her vitals a chance to come up and stabilize mattered more than moving her. Jennifer would prefer to take her to the hospital by air so that jarring movement during the trip would be minimized. She wasn't sure where the air ambulances would land but guessed they would use the football field. The leg break would have to be dealt with by a great surgeon.

"How are you doing, Jen?" Jack asked.

"I can last until more doctors get here." She could feel an incredible exhaustion now taking over, her hands quivering at times, and a deep burning pain in her back. The agonizing pain building in her side nearly doubled her over. Jennifer looked toward the school, wishing Rachel and Kate were out here. It would do Marissa good to see Rachel before she left for the hospital. "Jack, they've been in there a long time."

"I put out a family emergency page. Marcus and Quinn will be here soon."

"Where's Cole?" She had seen him earlier with Stephen. Rachel would need someone to hold her when this was over, and Cole was the perfect choice.

Jack looked over at her and he shook his head. "You don't want to know."

Twenty-two

Rachel walked out of the high school cafeteria stunned. The blood on her hands was Kate's, and her hands trembled as she tried to wipe it off but couldn't feel it through the rush of adrenaline. Kate had screamed her name, and Rachel had risked entering the cafeteria. The image wasn't going to fade. *Jesus, I need...* She reached for the wall to steady herself.

"Easy." Gloved hands caught her and steadied her. Cole wrapped his arms around her. She was enveloped deep in a fireman's coat and broad chest. She collapsed into the breadth of the man, knowing it was a safe place to hide.

"Cole..." She struggled to form the words. "Kate needs a doctor. Her arm is ripped up and bleeding. And Greg—" her hands coiled into the stiff fabric—"is dead."

She shuddered at the images seared into her memory. Greg had been on the floor near Kate with two bullets in his chest and a gun in his hand. Her sister had been feeling for signs of a pulse. Rachel tried to help, only to have Kate gently take her hands and stop her, shaking her head.

Reaching for a towel, Kate wrapped it tightly around her arm to staunch the bleeding and rose to check on the other boy. Lying face-down, he'd been hit in the head and there had been no hope, but Kate still checked. From there Kate headed over to the other officer, who had been hit in the shoulder. He'd already been struggling to his feet. They began a sweeping of the school cafeteria to make sure no trapped students were still inside.

What had happened here?

Cole moved Rachel back against the wall to keep her upright, his hands rubbing her back.

"Greg and another boy are dead. They were shooting at each other," she whispered. She couldn't get the image of the girl who had been caught by surprise and killed with a book in her hand out of her mind. It was senseless. It was a school day, and there were kids dead in the cafeteria.

Kids.

She struggled to get beyond that horrifying thought. Rachel looked up at Cole's face, and a chill settled across her heart at his expression. "How bad is it out there?"

His hands tightened. The man she cared about had faced arson fires and car deaths, and the calm she depended on had been replaced with incredible distress.

"Tell me."

"Rae, it started at the middle school."

Twenty-three

A dam is dead," Rachel whispered, terrified. There was a scene like this at the middle school. Tears began to flow as the shock reached unbearable levels.

Cole's hands shook as he cupped her face. "No."

She braced herself for the words coming.

"It's his friend, Tim. He was shot once in the chest. We found him in the boys locker room."

"Adam's best friend? Greg's brother?" Rachel struggled to get her thoughts around the information. How was she going to tell Clare the news that both her brothers were dead? That precious little girl with a smile that beamed and who had so adored her older brother… And the boys' parents—this news was going to further tear apart their lives already damaged by the divorce.

Rachel leaned against Cole, feeling sick. She rubbed numb hands on her jeans, trying to get sensation back. "What about Adam? Was he hurt?"

Cole slid his hand around the back of her neck and tenderly cradled her against him. She could feel him trying to absorb the pain she was in, and she didn't know how to release it to him. "I didn't see him, but it's chaotic out there."

"I was supposed to meet Tim and Adam at the bike rack. Maybe if I had been over there—"

"Don't," Cole interrupted her. "We don't know what happened yet to cause this. Don't start the if-onlys yet."

She forced herself to face reality. "How many others are hurt?"

He hesitated before answering her. "There were six high school students injured in the parking lot. How about inside the building?"

She eased back and struggled to get a deep breath. "I know of one girl killed. The two shooters. I haven't heard about the building sweep." Someone finally killed the building alarm and the school became eerily silent. Rachel rested her hands against Cole's chest and felt it rise and fall with his breathing. He was here, alive, well. She was going to hold on tightly to that reassurance. "You got called."

"Someone pulled the fire alarm at the middle school and a short time later the high school."

She was grateful for whoever had thought to do so, for it had triggered the emergency units to come even before phone calls could reach 911. "Marissa was among those hurt."

"She broke her leg, Rae. It's bad, but she wasn't one of the shooting victims."

The cafeteria doors opened behind them and Kate stepped out. Her sister was furious. Rachel could see it in the tight control and contained expression with her jaw clenched. Kate's impassive distance in a crisis had given way to the reality of this one. It was kids. Her sister would be haunted by the deaths. Her arm was already bleeding through the next towel. Rachel wrapped her in a hug. "I am so sorry."

Kate hugged her back. "Are you okay?"

"Shaky."

Kate ran her hands across Rachel's arms, trying to reassure. "It's over, Rae. Keep telling yourself that."

"You need Jennifer to look at that arm."

"Two minutes," Kate said. "We're sealing the cafeteria and then they'll start clearing classrooms. They'll need a full debriefing at some point tonight," she said softly. "I'll come find you."

Rachel nodded.

Kate looked over at Cole. "Would you tell Lisa I need her inside as soon as she can break free?"

"I will."

"Take Rae out of here."

Rachel wasn't sure she could walk that far.

Cole's arm around her waist tightened. "Come with me, Rae."

She had met one of the shooters in Greg. She knew one of the casualties in Tim. And she knew one of the victims in Marissa. Outside there were hundreds of students who had just gone through the most traumatic moment of their lives, who needed to be held, and she wasn't sure she had it in her to cope with her own experience and also theirs. She wasn't ready to face the questions.

"Trust me, honey," Cole said gently.

She let him lead her outside, her muscles still quivering just to walk straight. The sunlight made her blink.

"I want you to sit in my vehicle until Stephen can check you out."

"I need to get to work." She had to get past the incredible shock of what happened and work was something that would force that distance.

"You're walking wounded at the moment. Others can do your job for a short while."

"I need to see Marissa and Adam. Then I'll sit down." She tightened her grip around his arm. "Please." She had to see for herself that they were safe.

He studied her face, and then he nodded. "This way."

She spotted Jack amid a small group near one of the ambulances. "Marissa?"

"They're transporting her to the air ambulance."

Rachel headed that direction. She took a deep breath and forced herself to smile as the group parted to let her through. If ever she was going to help someone, it had to be here, now. She saw Jennifer first. Her sister looked much better than Rachel had expected. Jennifer was in pain, that was clear in the white tenseness in her face, but her sister was focused on the job at hand.

"Hi, M. How are you doing?" Rachel knelt beside the stretcher.

Marissa tried to smile. "You bought me a purse for the prom."

"A pretty one." Rachel brushed back her hair. It was wet. Marissa was alert, but she was in a lot of pain.

"Do you think Greg will mind if I spend it sitting down?"

Rachel held back her tears. Marissa didn't know about Greg's death, and Rachel wasn't about to tell her in these circumstances. "He won't mind." Her friend had already endured so much, and asking her to endure this as well was heartbreaking.

"Jack helped me talk to Mom."

"I'm glad. Hearing your voice is the thing that matters the most in this situation."

"Can you come with me to the hospital?"

Rachel sent a pleading look to Jennifer and then looked back to her friend. "It may be a while before I can come. I'll send Jennifer with you until I can get there."

"It's okay. The orthopedic doctor will have to get creative. I don't know which leg will take longer to fix. My artificial foot broke off."

"You've been down this road successfully before. Remember to take it one hour at a time today."

"Our ride has arrived. Ready to go take your first helicopter ride?" Jack asked.

Marissa nodded. Rachel moved back out of the way as Marissa was lifted into the ambulance. Jack lifted Jennifer into the ambulance to sit on the bench. "Page me?" Rachel asked Jennifer.

"I will."

Jack closed the ambulance doors. Rachel watched it pull out.

A crowd of kids stood on the other side of the yellow police tape. Weeping kids, some watching in silence, some standing defensively with arms crossed and trying not to show the emotion, but none of the kids were able to walk away. Rachel was overwhelmed at the numbers, knowing all of them needed someone to help them deal with this. She could see the Red Cross jackets of those on the response team already mingling with the crowd of students and parents. This school district was like others in the country; there was a folder with a plan for how to respond to an unthinkable event like this. It was being implemented.

The sun was still shining, and outside the five-mile radius that comprised this school district the afternoon was proceeding as normal. It was hard to put normal and chaos together. What had just happened would have to be integrated into the fabric of this community and into the lives of those present. They were still alive, she was still alive, and there would be a week anniversary, a year and five-year anniversary.

She wanted to sit down and cry. She'd been part of this tragedy, not just a witness to it. Who would be putting her name in a composition book to check back with her and ask how she was doing? Who would listen to her painful memories of what it had been like to sit by the chemistry lab and watch doors through which her sister had gone? To listen to multiple gunshots ring out from behind those doors? To hear Kate scream her name?

Cole's hand tightened on her shoulder. "Let's go see Adam."

She wiped the back of her hand across her eyes.

He left his hand on her shoulder in a firm grip until she nodded, and then he slid his hand down to grip her hand. "Come on, honey."

She tried not to look at the destruction in the parking lot as she walked, the damaged cars and the shattered windows. She tried hard not to look at the bloodstains on the pavement. She saw people in those reflections and kids' faces as they ran.

Cole led her across the blocked-off street to the middle school.

Yellow police tape was up now around the building and across part of the parking lot. On the other side of the tape parents were clustered in groups, talking about what had happened, and holding tight to their children. Word had spread that a child was dead; she could tell by the way parents talked in hushed tones. They were feeling relief that it wasn't their child and guilt for thinking that.

Rachel saw her sister Lisa enter the middle school. "They've gone through the school? Was Tim the only victim?"

"I was part of the two walk-throughs. The tragedy here was contained to the boys' locker room and Tim," Cole said.

Rachel looked around for Ann, Adam and Nathan. How was she going to tell Adam about Tim? The two boys had a tight friendship with sleepovers and scavenger hunts and shared secrets. The news would be devastating.

"Cole—" She stopped him when she spotted Ann. Rachel had seen a lot of distraught parents in her days. She released Cole's hand and ran toward Ann.

"Where's Adam?" Ann was panicked. "Rae, I can't find Adam."

Twenty-four

"A nn." Rachel rested her hands on the sides of Ann's face, knowing the contact would serve not only to reassure but also to block out much of the chaos around them. Her own terror dropped away in the face of a friend she had to help at all costs. "They've been through the school and they haven't found him hurt. We'll find Adam. He's just lost in the crowd. You can help us by describing what he was wearing today at school." Nathan was crying, holding on tight as Ann held him equally tight. Rachel didn't offer to take him to help Ann, for the boy desperately needed the reassurance of his mom's embrace. This had terrified the little boy. He would have been here when the students ran screaming from the school.

"Adam had on his short sleeve blue-and-white baseball shirt, with...jeans. His black tennis shoes. He was carrying a dark green backpack and a blue lunch bag."

"Tell me the five best friends he has."

Ann's eyes filled with tears. "Tim."

Rachel was fighting the tears too. "I know. Who else?"

Ann struggled to think. "His soccer friends, Scott and Jay. Mike from his homeroom. Our neighbor, Mrs. Sands."

"Let's talk with his homeroom teacher, his friends, find out where Adam was when the bell rang. He knew to get out of the building when the fire alarm rang. He must have gotten outside and wasn't sure where to go. What did you teach him to do if he got lost?"

Ann's panic was fading. "To sit down. To wait for me to find him."

"That's what he did then," Rachel said.

She looked around and spotted Nora from the local Red Cross office. Rachel waved her over. "Do you remember Nora? She was helping out at the flood scene."

Ann gave a shaky nod.

"I want you to walk with Nora through the parking lot. Check every row, look around the cars. Ask every parent you know to be on the lookout for Adam. Cole and I will search the school building one more time. We'll find him."

Ann nodded, looking relieved to have a plan.

"Nora, do you have a radio? Add Adam's description to the lost list. They'll canvas four blocks around the school for us, Ann." They were looking for a scared little boy whose best friend had died. They had to find him quickly before he heard rumors and misinformation about what had happened. The truth was awful enough. "Either Cole or I will check in with you every fifteen minutes."

Ann took a deep breath and nodded. "Okay."

Rachel waited until Ann and Nora had begun their walk before she looked at Cole. She took a painful breath. "I need to see what happened. I need to see Tim."

"It's a crime scene, Rae."

"If I'm going to find Adam, I have to see the scene. The boys were coming to meet me at the bike rack after school. Both of them."

"We don't know Adam was with Tim. They may not have met up yet."

"It's best to assume the worst."

She was relieved he didn't try further to dissuade her. "Come on."

They entered the school.

The hallway bulletin boards were covered with pictures from art class. Children had dropped backpacks and fled when the fire alarm went off. The hallway leading to the gym and locker rooms had been limited to personnel from the state crime lab. Lisa came back to meet them. The boys' locker room was at one end of the hall, the girls at the other, with the PE teacher's office in the middle. Large boards on the hallway walls were posted with information and schedules for basketball, soccer, and baseball. Rachel spotted Wilson talking with the fire captain and was grateful he was one of the homicide officers working the case.

The window in the PE teacher's office was open, adding fresh air to what was otherwise a stale and sweaty hall. The office was cramped with a desk and a line of chairs, but it was well lit with sunlight and cheery in its colorful posters and neat desk. The line of chairs inside the office was disrupted, but it was hard to tell if the teacher had shifted them when the chaos started or if it was the result of the normal visits of children to her office during the day.

There was no indication of how many children might have been back in this area when the shooting happened.

Rachel followed Cole into the boys locker room.

She flinched.

Tim had yet to be moved.

Cole tightened his grip on her arm. The boy lay between one of the benches and a row of lockers. He was slumped on his back, his face still showed his surprise even in death. He'd been shot in the center of the chest. Death must have been instantaneous. The way he lay suggested he had been standing by one of the lockers and had fallen backward when he was hit. There was an open gym bag with a towel half out the top resting on the bench near him.

Remembering the boy as he had been with Adam and now seeing him still and lifeless was crushing. She scanned the locker room but saw no obvious evidence of a fight. Lockers were dented, but from this event or simply wear and tear from use could not be determined. The photographer was still documenting the scene. The technicians working with Lisa were using bright lights to search the room for any signs of another bullet.

"Cole, if Adam saw this happen—his reactions are going to be intense. Even if he's hurt, his instinct would be to hide. You'll pass by calling his name and he won't answer. We need to go through this area again searching for him—this locker room, the girls locker room, and the classrooms outside this hallway."

"Lisa?"

·"We'll get a third search underway," Lisa promised, "including the gym itself. A few minutes delay won't matter for Tim."

"Where would Adam go if he ran?" Cole asked. "If he was here or he simply heard the shooting, where would he likely go?"

"Outside. The parking lot. His mom's car. A friend's house. He'll seek familiar things and familiar places that give him a sense of distance and safety."

"Let's start outside. It's the most likely place he would be. There are people who may have seen him that we can talk with, and they may not be here in an hour."

He wanted her out of here and she wanted to leave. His suggestion made sense. Rachel nodded.

Cole walked with her out of the boys locker room, down the hall, and back into the school's main corridor. He stopped her. "Give yourself a chance to absorb this before you add another layer."

She stepped into the hug he offered and squeezed him hard, knowing how hopeless this felt. He was fighting tears himself. "A little boy is dead. Across the street his brother is dead. What do you tell a mom in this situation? A dad?" she asked.

"A heartfelt 'I am so sorry for your loss.'"

"And tonight, when the police go through Greg's room looking for a motive? When the press starts hounding? How do parents get through it then?" She hurt just thinking about it, for she had been through many such media spectacles after tragedies. The grief would be aggravated by the search for someone to blame, the simplistic analysis of news reporters, and the extended focus on the most sensational images of the scene.

She forced herself to focus on the task on hand and eased back from Cole. "We need to check the soccer field. It's one of Adam's favorite places to go."

"We'll start there and work our way around the building."

He led her outside.

Jesus, it didn't occur to me to pray. It didn't occur to me that Cole would be with one of the units responding. I didn't even think to put out an emergency page to the O'Malleys to alert them to come. In the midst of a crisis when I think myself organized and ready to be there for people, I wasn't even thinking about the obvious steps I could take. Her steps slowed and stopped.

Cole's hand warmed between her shoulders. "Worry the problem in a straight line, honey."

"I didn't think of you. I didn't pray. I didn't even think to page family."

"You were focused on keeping yourself and Kate alive."

"I watched her go into a room where two shooters were exchanging gunfire."

Cole rubbed the back of her neck and, when her tension didn't fade, settled his arms around her in a hug and kissed her forehead. "Let it go. I thought of you, I prayed, and God knew you were busy."

She wanted to absorb Cole's steady assurance and wear it like a cloak around herself. "I saw Marissa fall. And they tried to shoot Kate."

"I know." He turned her hand and brushed his fingers across her palm where the gravel had torn the skin. "It looks like you took a tumble too."

She looked at the injury and found it odd she hadn't even realized it had happened. "Kate tackles hard."

"I'm giving her a hug when I see her next."

"Give her a long one. This has devastated her." She took a deep breath and started walking again. The soccer field was beside the ball diamond and beyond it the groundskeeper's equipment shed. They walked toward the ball diamond.

Rachel stopped. "Over there."

Adam was beneath the bleachers by the ball field. She squeezed Cole's hand. "Go get Ann," she whispered. She crossed the field to the bleachers and looked for how he had gotten under there and crouched to crawl in after Adam. His face was streaked with tears, his clothes dirty.

Adam's eye still needed ice, and the nurse hadn't been able to totally wash out the drops of blood on his shirt from the nosebleed. The bruise on his arm looked recent, like someone had grabbed his arm to hurry him along during the rush to get kids from the school building. She wasn't worried about the things that would heal; she was worried about the pain she could see simply in how he sat, hunched over his knees.

"Tim was supposed to see the PE teacher after school," Adam said. "He got a detention for throwing the volleyball." She sat down beside him, having to crouch not to hit her head on the bench. "I was coming to sit with him, but the teacher wouldn't let me. Tim still thought I was mad at him because he hit me with the ball." The boy's heart was breaking. Rachel mopped his eyes with her shirtsleeve cuff and then solved the distance by swallowing him in a hug.

Adam cried, his bony arms wrapped around her.

"Where were you when the shooting happened?" she asked as the tears slowed.

"I was waiting for Tim." Adam wiped the back of his hand across his eyes. "Greg had heard about the detention. He stopped me in the hall to ask if my eye was okay. He wanted to see it and told me to get another ice bag when I got home." Adam paused for a long time. "I waited. The fire alarm went off. The art teacher said I had to leave." Adam turned his face into her shoulder and his small body shook. "I should have waited for him. I didn't, and Tim is dead."

Twenty-five

Marcus felt like he was looking over a war zone as he walked the path the shooters had taken, following the destruction with Quinn and Lisa.

Lisa knelt by one of the white evidence markers and picked up a shell casing. "This one is a .45."

"Two guns and a lot of ammunition in the midst of hundreds of kids—it's a wonder the number of injured and dead aren't higher." Overhead the sounds of helicopters signaled the arrival of more media.

Lisa rose to her feet. "We were there when it started—" she pointed—"standing by our car. I heard the first shot. A pause. Then several more shots. That's when I saw the first boy running toward the high school. Moments later, I saw another boy run into the school after him."

Marcus listened intently, seeing it, and dreading what they had lived through. He had to get over to the hospital to see Jennifer as soon as he could. Quinn looked angry and in his partner that visible emotion was rare. Quinn hadn't handled that emergency page they'd received any better than he had.

Marcus rubbed his sister's shoulders, finding comfort in the contact. "Lisa, I need to know what happened here. It started in the middle school and spilled this way. Who shot Tim? Give me the fundamentals as soon as you can." Rachel was going to need the information, and

Detective Wilson was already on scene heading the investigation. Marcus knew he'd be open to a couple days of outside help. It wouldn't be the first time Marcus had joined Wilson on a case that touched the O'Malleys.

"You'll have it. I'm putting a priority on tracing the guns."

Marcus saw Kate walk down the steps from the high school, her hands shoved in her pockets, her head bent. From behind the police tape came a chorus of reporters' voices trying to get her to come over and answer questions. Kate ignored the reporters, spotted their group, and came to join them. He was relieved she'd finally stopped long enough to have her arm dressed properly. She met his gaze, and it was the beaten-up Kate he saw, the one who appeared when she felt she had failed and was struggling to get her perspective back. He'd talk to her later when he could get her away from this, but nothing would be able to take that weight off her. It was the price she paid for being a cop.

"We've got a problem. Where's Rachel?" Kate asked.

Marcus turned and looked back toward the middle school. He spotted Rachel sitting on a bench beside Ann, deep in conversation. Adam was sitting on Stephen's lap. While he watched, Nathan walked over to Rae and leaned against her knees. She boosted him onto her lap, hugging him. It looked like she had been able to turn the emotion and find that focus on work. It was good to see. "She's over with Ann."

"Jack." Kate waved their brother over. "I need you to hear this." She led the way to Rachel.

Adam's eye had swollen with the tears and the black eye was coming in colorfully. Rachel accepted the new ice pack Cole brought them with a quiet thanks. She offered it to the boy, smiling at him, even as she wondered what Adam had really seen and heard this afternoon. He was already trying to protect his mom—Adam hadn't mentioned to her that he had seen Greg in the hallway. And when Adam had first seen Nathan, Adam hugged his brother long enough Nathan started to squirm.

Adam was already showing the early signs of detachment. At his age his emotions wouldn't be able to absorb the impact of his best friend's death, so as a natural defense his mind shoved the details and the emotions of the experience to the side and cut them off until he was better able to cope.

Rachel reached over and brushed the hair back from his forehead. One of her tasks was to help him cope with what had happened. She could feel the desire to be holding a notebook and pen again and was relieved to find her own reaction to the incident wearing off. Her thoughts had been drifting, her concentration poor. Crying with Adam had probably saved her own sanity. She'd helped him from under the bleachers feeling heavy at heart but at least ready to engage in the work she spent her life training to do. To do that, she needed to find a lot more answers to what had really happened here.

Stephen helped the boy adjust the ice pack. "I know it's cold. Just relax against it and it will get better."

"Did you ever get a black eye?" Adam asked, his voice finally coming back to normal pitch.

"Several," Stephen said, "most of them when Jack and I went after the basketball at the same moment."

"Tim didn't mean to give me this one."

"Accidents happen. I spend my days at work helping people after accidents. I'm sorry about this, buddy. Tim was a good kid. The guys at the station liked him. We're all going to miss him."

Adam leaned back against Stephen, finding comfort.

"Rachel."

She looked over and saw her family coming to meet them. Their expressions were enough to warn her. She hugged Nathan and shifted him to Ann. "I'll be back in a moment."

She looked at Cole and her hand motioned him to join her. They met her family at the sidewalk.

Kate looked around to make sure she would not be overheard and then around the group. "They've identified the second shooter. It's Mark Rice."

The news stunned the group. "Carol Iles's son?" Lisa asked.

"A lady is murdered during the flood and today her son is in school with a gun. Anyone here want to speculate on the odds that this is a coincidence?"

Twenty-six

Rachel tucked the phone against her shoulder as she scrawled another note in her composition book and ducked beneath the yellow police tape. "Nora, I've got nine kids who were in the school cafeteria when Mark and Greg ran in. Who do we have that can talk to them tonight?"

She read off the names. They were trying to make sure everyone who had been caught in the path of the two boys had someone debrief them before they had to try to sleep tonight.

Rachel felt like she had been working this scene for days, but a glance at her watch showed that it had been just over three hours. Most of the parents and children had already left for home. Spectators from the community were beginning to disperse, leaving the scene to the investigators under the watch of the media.

Rachel had made Lisa's car her temporary command center. She tugged out the rough sketch of the school buildings' layout and penciled in the information on where the boy shot in the thigh had fallen. She had just spoken with the boy's two friends. The fact that they had rushed back to help him was making it easier for them to adjust to what happened.

She was asking every student she spoke with three questions: "Where were you when the shooting started? What did you see? Who was around you?" From dozens of answers she was piecing together a mosaic. She underlined in red three names on her sketch. She hadn't spoken with them yet, and from the information she had, they would have been standing next to a girl who had been one of those shot. That kind of grief—*why her and not me?*—would be hard to manage without someone to share it with who understood what it was like.

The goal of the first eight hours was to make sure the kids did not feel like they were alone to cope with the experience and to identify anyone who was at immediate risk. Teens who had already spent the hours since getting home calling friends to talk about what had happened were not the ones who had her worried. It was the teens who had just lost their best friends and were having trouble doing anything but crying who needed immediate intervention. Finding those kids among the hundreds at the middle and high schools wasn't a simple task, for their instinct was to withdraw from people under the weight of that grief.

"Nora, I'm heading out now to start the hospital rounds. Would you ask the police chaplain to page me when he leaves Greg and Tim's mom?" She wanted to have positive news about Marissa to take with her when she met Mrs. Sanford and hopefully got a chance to see Clare again. The boys' father was flying today, the Boston to Chicago route, and someone was now at the airport to meet the return flight. The death of his sons was not something they wanted to tell him while he was in the air piloting a plane with two hundred passengers aboard. "I'll check in again in an hour."

She closed the phone. "Cole, I'm ready to go. At which hospitals are the kids?"

He was helping Jack pack up the last of the equipment Engine 81 had used in treating the injured. "Lutheran has three, Mercy has one, and General has two."

"I need to be back here at nine. There's a coordinators' meeting at the church down the street."

He glanced at his watch. "Not a problem." He stowed the medical kit. "Jack, I've got the incident paperwork with me to finish up. Anything you need before I go?"

"We're set, boss. They've released us. We'll head back to the station."

"Page me before you go off shift?"

"Will do."

"Rachel, let's take my car." Cole pointed it out on the street. "Frank brought it over."

She nodded and gathered up her growing collection of paperwork. The school counselor had brought her a recent yearbook and current class rosters.

"Need a hand?"

She passed Cole the folder of sketches she had collected. Most students found it easier to draw a sketch to show her where they had been and who had been near them, and she encouraged it. Anything with pen and paper and an analytical question to answer helped them start thinking like students again.

Cole held open the passenger door for her. And then she saw Gage. He was standing by the grassy knoll near the soccer field overlooking the school grounds. He wasn't working—he was simply standing there with his hands in his back pockets, watching the investigators. "Cole, go on ahead. I'll catch a lift later."

He had seen the man too. "There's work here. I'll wait." Rachel reached for her notebook and a pen and picked up two cold sodas from the cooler one of the students had brought over to her an hour ago, one of the many gestures from students who wanted to do anything they could to help out.

Gage saw her coming but he didn't speak, just watched as she joined him. She loved this man, and she had a good idea what was going on behind that solemn expression. She sat down on the grass beside where he stood and set aside the composition book. She opened one of the sodas.

He sat down without care for the dress slacks and grass stains and picked up the other soda. "I can't handle kids killing kids."

She let her silence be her agreement. They had already shared a sadness so overwhelming they needed no words to convey the depth of this new one. The weeks after Tabitha's death and that of his unborn son had already plowed this ground. She rested her head against his shoulder for a moment and sighed. "Today was the stuff of nightmares."

He rubbed her back.

"Where were you when you heard?" she finally asked.

"Doing the stuff in life that is irrelevant now. I was talking with the mayor's press secretary about a rumor the mayor is going to try to move the parking for the new stadium. You?"

"Enjoying a rare day shopping with Jennifer. We stopped by the school on the way back so I could see Adam and Tim."

She watched the fireman who was hosing down the areas where there were bloodstains. It was a fine balancing line. The men wanted to erase the physical evidence of the day and support students to give them time to heal. While at the same time they had to also slow down their own rush to forget and move on. She watched the man work and wondered what would erase her memories of the four deaths she had seen up close.

"I know you had to go in with Kate, but I wish you hadn't."

"I'm jumping when a door slams or a book drops."

"Give yourself a lot of room in the midst of this to recover. You took it on the chin."

"I hear an echo of my own advice coming back."

He smiled. "So I actually listened over the last two years." Gage nudged the sack beside him over to her. "I brought you some things."

There was a clean shirt, a wrapped toothbrush, a small tube of toothpaste, and a hairbrush. Her emergency duffel bag was still at her apartment. She knew she wouldn't be home for the next twenty-four hours, if not the next forty-eight. She'd been planning to hit the hospital gift shop if she could get there before it closed. Rachel hugged him.

"Call me early in the morning and let me know where you're heading? I'll bring you breakfast and the latest news update."

"Deal."

He nodded toward Cole. "Go on. I know the next twelve hours will be very hard. He'll take good care of you."

She studied her friend. "Will you be okay?"

"Will you?"

"Maybe in six months."

He smiled. "Give me a couple years."

She rubbed his arm and got to her feet. She left him there and crossed the field to join Cole.

He opened the car door for her again and then circled around to take the driver's seat.

"Who do you want to see first?"

"Marissa."

She flipped open the composition book and went back through what Janie had told her as Cole drove. She wanted to stay with Gage and grieve, but she couldn't. Her job was now beginning in its most intense way.

She understood what was coming. Unexpected, sudden violence had frozen a moment in time. Now time would speed up. In the days to come the rush of events would overwhelm: the investigation, the media, the funerals, the reopening of the schools. An emotional roller coaster had begun: denial, anger, despair, and acceptance. How she and the other counselors approached this mattered, for others would take cues from them. And on a day when she most needed to be strong, she had never felt so weak.

Jesus, I treasure those words you proclaimed in Exodus, "I am the LORD your Healer." Remember us today. It is Your healing touch we now desperately need. There was comfort in her new faith. No matter how great the need, she was finally learning to lean against someone who could meet it in full. And on days such as this, that awareness was what kept her going.

"Is your system settled enough you could handle a bite to eat?" Cole asked.

"I'll pass on food, but I'd love another drink." Her voice was already hoarse.

Cole stopped on the way to the hospital and pulled into a drive-thru. He bought her a large iced tea and a small fry. "Try to eat something anyway. It's going to be a long night."

Rachel took a long drink. "Forget sleep tonight. Once the media plays this for twenty-four hours, I'm going to have two schools full of students struggling to adjust to what happened. What they didn't see today, they'll unfortunately have seen by tomorrow."

She searched the radio stations to find one of the news stations so she could listen to how the local reporters were covering the shooting. "How are your guys handling it?"

"I was fortunate. Most of them only dealt with the injured. Once the lead guys saw Tim, they checked the locker room for injured and then sealed off the area."

"How are you handling it?"

Cole looked over at her, then back at the road. "How about you?"

Rachel understood exactly what he meant. "Better a discussion for tomorrow?"

"I think so."

She rubbed her forehead. "What are the odds you have aspirin available?"

"Try the glove box."

She dug around for the packets. "You know, batteries go bad when they get hot."

"Considering I tossed them in there two years ago, they're already goners."

She found the aspirin.

"Hand me two please. My headache is a bear too."

She shook out two for him and passed him her drink.

"Eat some of these." She offered the fries.

She pulled out another stack of blue cards and began marking the back with numbers. She had already handed out dozens. Her pager went off. She slipped it off and read the number, then immediately reached for her phone. "Marcus, how did the walk-through go?" She tucked the phone against her shoulder and reached for the composition book.

"There was a bullet in the chemistry lab room door. Someone was shooting at you, Rae, and you failed to mention it?"

She really didn't want to know. "It must have been before I got there." She'd tell herself that and hope it was true.

"Good. That was my update; the rest I'll give you when I see you at nine," Marcus said. "What do you have for me?"

She flipped back in her composition book to the summary pages. She scanned the information, trying to limit what she had learned to only what Marcus would need in order to resolve the shooting. "Tim was a kid who got picked on. That's the consensus of the kids who knew him. There was genuine surprise when I asked if Tim ever talked about a gun or showed a fascination with guns. If he had any interest that way, it's not showing among those who knew him. I'll talk more with Adam about it tomorrow."

She read her notes. "Did Tim have enemies? Yes and no. He was getting harassed by some freshman kids who were neighbors of his, but it was the *you're fat, have freckles, and you can't even catch a ball* type taunting. Tim would have been the one to retaliate to such taunting, but all I've got so far is the fact that he was looking forward to going to a private school next year."

Rachel hated her final conclusion. "Marcus, for now I'm leaning toward Tim being in the wrong place at the wrong time."

"The wrong place at the wrong time—how many obituaries do we see that should include that statement?" Marcus asked grimly.

"I know," Rachel replied, hearing and sharing the ache in his heart. A child had died and it looked to be an unfortunate chance.

"Regarding Mark Rice." She turned to the center section of the book. "He's the classic school shooter, Marcus. Cole already has him down as a budding arsonist who was a significant contributor to his parents' divorce. The murder of his mom—we'll set aside the question of whether he had anything to do with that—it was a definite trigger in his life. I've got two teachers and the vice principal describing his behavior in the last month as unpredictable with a hair-trigger temper. A notebook in his backpack had doodles of dead people; he's been talking to other kids about guns; and he's angry at authorities and cops in particular. Guns appear to be a long-term fascination of his. Mark's best friend is Chuck Holden. Three boys who knew Mark have volunteered that same name. The boys hung out together. Maybe he knows something or heard Mark say something."

"I'll get someone to track down Chuck," Marcus promised.

"Good. Let me know what you find."

"What do you have on Greg?"

Rachel read her notes and sighed. "Confusion. Kids are stunned at the idea of Greg shooting someone. He's the one kids describe as law and order, follow the rules, right versus wrong. They joke about the fact that he was careful to round his time card at work down five minutes in favor of his boss. He's a classic caretaker, Marcus. He looked after his brother and sister and got a job after his parents' divorce so he could help pay his way to college. He's an A student with an occasional B. For temperament most people say he's patient, especially with his little sister Clare. If Greg knew Mark, it was in passing in the halls. They had no classes in common. They don't appear to have friends in common."

"Your best guess?" Marcus probed.

"I don't like it."

"Tell me anyway."

Rachel chewed on the end of her pen. "Okay. I heard Greg shout at Mark inside the cafeteria. He was furious. Not just angry, but furious. Like Kate going after someone who caused her to lose a hostage type furious. Greg was out of control. Adam said he saw Greg at the middle school, that Greg had heard about Tim's detention and come over to get his brother. Marcus, I'm thinking it's something as simple as Greg was nearby when Tim was shot. For whatever reason Greg blamed Mark, and he took out after Mark to make him pay for it. The chase went from the middle school back to the high school and ended in the cafeteria with both Greg and Mark dead."

"How did Greg get a gun?"

"Greg wasn't the type to carry one. I'm sure of that. But I could see Mark bringing one to school. Why do kids most often bring guns to school? To show them off to friends, to trade or sell them. I think Mark was trading guns with someone at the middle school, and they were in the locker room. Tim would have been at the PE teacher's office, which puts him right there too, and as a result Tim was in the wrong place at the wrong time. He got killed."

"If Mark handled both guns, we should be able to prove it from prints. Lisa's got the guns as a top lab priority," Marcus said.

"How many shots did each boy fire? Did Greg shoot at anyone other than Mark?" It was awful to think she was trying to put all the blame on Mark and make him the villain when Greg had clearly been carrying a gun and was chasing Mark. But Rachel couldn't get past the fact she had met Greg and her heart was torn up at the fact he'd been involved.

"We all want those answers, Rae. It's going to take time to figure out. I'll see you at nine, and hopefully I'll have something by then. Would you keep an eye on Kate tonight? Make sure she gets something to eat?"

"I already have. She groused because I ordered mustard on her cheeseburger." Rachel smiled at the memory.

"She has to give you grief about something."

"She's bouncing back just fine. I'll see you at nine."

Rachel closed the phone. Kate was bouncing back. Rachel wished she was doing as well. She cautioned every victim not to get stuck on the question: What could I have done to change what happened? And she was getting stuck.

"So you think Greg was avenging his brother."

Cole broke into her thoughts and she tried to refocus. "It's the only logical answer. He was a caretaker. His job was to protect Tim and he failed."

"Kids don't pick up guns and just go after someone without a reason."

Rachel had seen kids react this way before, if not taken to the extreme of killing someone. "Maybe Greg thought Mark would get away with it, and he wasn't going to let that happen."

Cole reached over and squeezed her hand. "Let it go, Rae. The boys made their choices. You can't undo their decisions." He turned into the hospital parking garage past a row of satellite television trucks.

"How many reporters are now covering this shooting?" Rachel turned in her seat to see if she could catch station initials.

"Two schools involved, brothers among the dead, a slow news day otherwise—they'll make this story the headlines for the week."

"Which means copycats," Rachel observed, knowing it was inevitable. "I don't want to end up in the middle of the media tonight."

Cole parked on the fourth floor of the garage. "We'll go through the geriatrics ward. That wing still has its own elevators."

"I like the sound of that plan. Where will we find Jennifer and Tom?"

"She said the hospital had set aside a waiting room near the ICU for the families of the students brought here."

Rachel checked her watch and gathered the items she needed to take in with her. "Marissa went into surgery forty-eight minutes ago. There should be news by now."

"It was a bad fracture. Don't expect her to be in recovery yet."

Cole escorted her through the hospital. They were directed to the private waiting room. She was relieved to see Jennifer in her wheelchair over by the window, not trying to be in the middle helping the families. Rachel crossed to her sister and knelt beside her wheelchair. Jennifer was pale and in pain, her exhaustion apparent, but her smile when she saw Rachel was still there. Rachel leaned over and gently hugged her. "Marissa?"

"The surgeon is excellent, Rae. She should be in recovery shortly."

"I didn't see her mom."

"She just went to meet Marissa's grandmother downstairs."

Rachel rubbed Jennifer's arm. She had been holding back the emotions until a safe moment and looking at Jennifer the tears returned. "Thank you for being there at the school. For saving so many lives. You and Lisa—"

Jennifer smiled. "God knew," she said softly. "He knew I needed to be back in Chicago. I've been watching the coverage. It's been rough."

"Yes." Rachel had been dodging the media, well aware that the scene was being transmitted live to the city.

"How are the kids doing who saw it?"

"Divided between those who felt they were able to help and those who felt like they froze. Between those who were in the parking lot and saw someone get hurt and those who only heard the shooting and were trapped not knowing what was going on."

"You need to make sure to get some sleep tonight."

"I'll try." Rachel held her sister's gaze. "Would you let Tom take you back to the hotel? I'm going to need you as a sounding board this week."

"I've learned my limits, Rae. We'll leave just as soon as Marissa gets to recovery. Have you seen Kate?"

"She's mad about someone shooting her, about all of us being there when it started. Give her a day to get past that. Lisa is busy at the scene tonight, and she promised to keep an eye on Kate for me too. I did nag her into eating since the painkillers were making her queasy." Rachel looked around the room. "Tell me who's here. I need to start making the rounds."

A movement at the door caught her attention. Marissa's mom came in, accompanied by her grandmother. Following them was a man Rachel was overjoyed to see. "Marissa's dad came."

"I was talking with Marissa's mom when he called. He was in Milwaukee when he heard the news."

"Marissa will be so relieved to see him."

"Go talk with them; I'll be a phone call away when you want to talk later."

"Thanks, Jen." Rachel leaned over and hugged her. "I love you."

"I love you too. Go to work. And feel free to call tonight if I can help."

Twenty-seven

Marcus parked the car down the block from Mark's home Tuesday evening. "This is going to be interesting." Brian Rice stood in his front yard having a heated exchange with a police officer, all of it happening under the view of the reporters across the street. Two officers were standing back a few feet ready to step in if needed.

Lisa stepped out of the car. "His son is dead at school, and we're executing a search warrant on his home. We already know from Carol's murder investigation that this guy has a bad temper. The warrant covered the entire grounds?"

"Yes," Quinn confirmed.

"Let's make sure more than a couple officers search that utility shed and the backyard," Lisa noted, glancing into the backyard.

"Also the attic and the utility room," Quinn added.

They ignored the verbal shouting match going on as they walked up the drive. Marcus held up his badge and led the way inside the house. It was well lit up as officers conducting the search worked room to room. "Mark's bedroom?"

The nearest officer pointed. "Down the hallway, second door on the left."

The photographer was just finishing up his work.

Marcus expected an angry kid with rock music posters, video games, a huge collection of music, and an emphasis on sports. "This is a dichotomy." Mark Rice was into rock collecting. The bookshelf in his bedroom had two handbooks on rocks, and the rest of the shelves contained samples, neatly collected and labeled, some on display, others stored in clear plastic cubes. Quartz, graphite, pieces of fool's gold.

"Don't change your impressions too quickly." Quinn picked up one of the rocks and blew off the dust. "Some of these boxes have labels from before Mark was born."

Marcus watched over the technician's shoulder as the computer was turned on. "Strike out here. He's got it password protected. We'll have to take it in." He pushed around the books and loose papers on Mark's desk. "Restaurant delivery menus, school papers, most of it out of date."

Lisa pulled a box from beneath the bed. "His more current reading." She pushed aside the magazines the boy wasn't old enough to own. "Quinn." She picked up a thin rod and a rag and sniffed the cloth. "He was cleaning something that smells of gunpowder."

She handed it to a technician to bag as evidence.

Marcus opened the closet. "Do you think Mark shot his mom?" he asked Lisa, sorting through T-shirts and jeans, checking pockets.

"He proved today he would carry and use a gun," Lisa replied. "His alibi for the night of Carol's murder is that he was playing at a high school basketball game and his dad was with him. We're still trying to get a time line that tells us if that's airtight."

"Carol was shot with a .38. Neither gun recovered at the school was a .38."

"Which means if the gun turns up in this house, I would be very interested."

Marcus found nothing in the closet beyond clothes and shoes. "This place was cleaned up. How many kids have closets where you can see the floor?"

"I'm getting that same feeling." Lisa flipped through the boy's music tapes. "We didn't get here in time."

"Let's go see what the other search warrants turn up among Tim and Greg's things," Marcus said.

———⦻———

Cole walked out to the parking lot after the 9 P.M. update meeting. This Tuesday felt like a very long year. He was accustomed to disasters where he could do something, but he could do so little here. His work was over, and Rachel's was just beginning.

What he understood about her job had been transformed in the last few hours. She walked among the teenagers and they instinctively turned to her. They clustered around her in groups, seeking reassurance and a chance to share what they had experienced. She took the terror and the pain they felt and absorbed it. And when she wrapped her arm around the shoulders of a teenager, her empathy got through the pain and touched the sorrow. Her calm reassurance that the moment was over made it safe to grieve. She loved them and they knew it. She pointed the way to how to recover.

Lord, Rae's going to need Your strength. She's carrying a difficult burden, and it's not going to end anytime soon.

She was one of many counselors but a vital one. She had worked the aftermath of other school shootings, but the realization of the expertise she had developed was just becoming clear. He'd watched her at the coordinators' meeting. When the National Crisis Response Team began the briefing only six hours after the shooting, they sought Rachel's advice for such questions as how best to reopen the school and when, based on her assessment of which grades and students were most affected.

He knew how to fight a fire; Rachel knew how to heal a school— let students talk about it, grieve, and then help them get back to normal life. On big things and small she had practical advice. She recommended against the school using the normal bell to signal class changes during the first week, but to instead have a woman's voice on the intercom; for security to be in uniform walking the halls to create a solid presence; that a memorial wall be set up in the cafeteria for students to share their memories; that updates be posted on the bulletin boards twice a day for how the injured students were doing. Information, consolation, and for the anger, direction for how to release it.

Cole was grateful Rachel had her family intimately involved in this crisis. He'd left her talking with Marcus. Cole spotted Gage in the parking lot and headed over to see him. A press conference was scheduled after the meeting, and the parking lot had become a gathering place. "How are you doing, Gage?"

Gage considered him. "About as well as you."

"That bad, huh?" Cole gave a rough smile. He leaned against Gage's car and ran a hand through his hair. "I feel a bit like I got kicked by a mule."

"Marcus thinks a bullet missed Rachel by a matter of about three inches."

Cole nodded. "I heard. That kind of news ages a man."

"Tell me about it." Gage tossed him a soda. "The O'Malley ladies took it on the chin. I was there when Kate finally sat down to let someone look at her arm. And Lisa paused to pass word that Jennifer may have to be admitted back to the hospital tonight to try to get the pain under control. She's at the hotel now, but it's not going well."

"I hadn't heard about Jennifer."

"I spoke with her about an hour ago. She's hurting." Gage opened a soda for himself. "Any truth to the rumor you were the first one inside the boys locker room?"

"I was there," Cole replied. He didn't want to ever again see something that tragic.

"Want to trade information?"

Cole broke a long-standing practice of avoiding the press without a qualm. "Deal."

Gage studied him. "It's going to be that ugly of a case."

"Those boys got the guns from somewhere. This isn't over, Gage."

"You want to meet tomorrow and exchange news?"

"Page me. I'm going to try to get by the station house to move what I can from my calendar. Come by. If there are homemade cinnamon rolls, I'll set a couple back for you."

"I'll take you up on that." Gage reached into his briefcase and pulled out a folder. He handed it to Cole. "Show these to Rae. On-line versions of the newspapers are a pretty good indication of what will be running in the papers tomorrow morning. The coverage looks to be over the top. The kids being interviewed are calling this a shooting gallery."

"From what I've seen that's a pretty good description."

Gage nodded toward the church. "Rae's going to have a long night."

"She wants to head back to the hospitals from here."

"Her kids are hurt. She couldn't be anywhere else. If you get a fire call and need someone to relieve you, call me. I can spend a couple hours playing double solitaire with her in the hospital waiting room while she keeps students and their parents company."

"Thanks, Gage."

"It's one thing for Rachel to work a natural disaster; it's another to have her deal with kids killing kids."

"I hear you."

Twenty-eight

Stephen tapped on Jennifer's hotel suite door at 1 A.M. Wednesday. He'd been awake when her page came, unable to sleep, still trying to cope with the memories of having treated students who were shot. The suite door opened. He was met by Tom still wearing yesterday's shirt and jeans, carrying a cup of coffee. "Is she still awake, Tom?"

"Unlike me, Jen is wide awake. She's starting a late night movie. The pain pills have finally kicked in but not the rest of it." Tom stepped back to let him into the suite. "She has taken over the living room." He turned. "We've got company, Jen."

"Company as in many?" Jen called.

Tom looked over at him and Stephen just smiled. "What's she need, ice packs?"

"And the next meds in…twenty minutes."

"Go find a pillow and a bed. I can handle it for an hour." Stephen walked into the living room. "Hi, precious." He had expected to see her an emotional basket case, but there wasn't a tissue box in sight. She looked a bit like she had the night as a resident when she had delivered her first baby. She had saved lives today. "Or should I say, Doctor Precious?"

She smiled. "What's that you're carrying?"

He set down the squirming jacket. "Your puppy sleeps in the strangest places."

Delighted, Jennifer picked up the puppy and cuddled. "I found him curled up around my cactus once, using the sticky points to scratch his head." She nodded to the TV. "Sit and watch *Godzilla versus Mothra* with me."

"Let's not and say we did. How are you faring?"

She rubbed the puppy's head. She glanced up, then back at the puppy. "I'm dying, Stephen."

There was no good way to answer that matter-of-fact statement. He leaned over and kissed her forehead. "Tom showed me your last blood work panels. I'm not burying you yet." He didn't want to have a serious discussion tonight if he could avoid it. Too much had happened today.

He settled down on the floor beside her and picked up a pretzel. "How are you doing?"

He shrugged. "I was awake when you called." He smiled at her. "You were the one who paged. What's on your mind?"

"I want you happy. Why don't you get serious about seeing Ann? I like her."

He blinked and then laughed. "This is one of those middle-of-the-night pages." He leaned over and tucked another pillow behind her so she wouldn't wince as she turned her head. The entire O'Malley family felt the freedom to meddle, and they inevitably did it for the best of reasons. Jennifer had always been one of them who liked to meddle for a purpose. "I'm not interested in settling down, Jen, but your suggestion is noted. And Ann says she already has two guys in her life. Sorry. I like her and the boys, but getting serious? She's more than an acquaintance but not nearly what you hope for. Anything else on your mind?"

"I've got a list," she admitted with a laugh. "But it's just because I love you and you've got me curious. Why haven't you moved yet? You've been talking about it for so long."

"Find my place in the country where I'm more likely to treat broken arms and heart attacks than gunshot wounds?"

Jennifer nodded.

He thought about it. "Someone else would have to watch out for

Kate and the inevitable trouble she gets into. I've patched her up too many times this last year to want to move very far away. I think I'll hold off on any decision until she's settled."

"She'll be settled soon with Dave. You should think about it some more. Go find yourself a small town somewhere and find out if the peaceful life you dream about is out there, or if what you're really searching for is something spiritual."

Stephen sighed. "How many times have we talked about God?"

"Apparently not enough."

"I know who He is, Jen. I just want to live my own life." He understood the price religion demanded of a man, and he was honest enough to know he didn't want to pay it. But he knew well how badly she wanted him to say yes. "It's my choice. That doesn't mean I don't appreciate the thought." Her gaze held his and there was sadness there, and pity, neither of which settled well with him.

"I'm not giving up on you."

He made himself smile. "Which is one of the reasons I love you. You always were the stubborn one in the family. And quite persuasive. Is that it?"

She dug out a piece of paper she had tucked in the cushions of the couch. She read it, refolded it, and offered it to him. "When I die. Tom doesn't need to worry about the funeral. I planned it."

He took it but scowled. "Don't get morbid on me."

"Stephen."

He looked from the note back at her.

"I've watched many people die during my lifetime. This energy— it isn't natural," she said softly. "I'm dying. Soon."

He wrapped his hand around hers. "It's also likely adrenaline," he said gently. "You saved lives today. It's a high like no other."

She studied him in silence and then smiled. "Yes. I can see why you do it."

Jen nestled down into the cushions with the puppy. "Get me another ice pack and then let's play some Scrabble."

"Only if medical words aren't allowed. It's too easy for you to use the hard letters." He got up to get the ice pack.

"*Latex* is not a hard word."

"You and your *X*s. You want the lumpy ice pack or the thick one?"

"Whatever hits the center of my back the best."

He got the ice pack and retrieved cold sodas.

"How's Rae?"

"I saw her a couple hours ago making a hospital cafeteria table her temporary office," Stephen replied. "The girl who died in the cafeteria? She was the oldest in a family of immigrants. Rae's Spanish has improved in the last year. She's nearly fluent."

"How traumatically is it hitting the students?"

"She's got five girls red slipped. Given the number of students, I'm surprised there aren't more." He found more pretzels. "I saw card number sixty-eight get passed out to one of the injured students. Her pager was definitely getting a workout. Try this ice pack."

Stephen handed it to her and sat back down. He tugged over the table so she could play Scrabble without having to reach too far. He dumped the letters from the board back into the draw bag. "Low letter goes first?"

"Sure." Jennifer drew out an A. "I go first."

"I hope that doesn't represent your luck for the night." They selected letters.

"Stephen, I want a favor." She played the word *TITAN*.

"On top of your list? This *is* an interesting evening. What's the favor?"

"You were a fireman and it wasn't enough to make you content, so you became a paramedic. You're still restless. Go be a carpenter. Go prove to yourself the restlessness won't go away until you finally listen to the truth."

"Run away to find myself?"

"You're smart enough to know I'm right."

"I'm smart enough to know *TITAN* to *TITANIUM* is worth a small fortune in points." He laid down the three tiles and tallied his score.

She laughed and played the word *CHEATING*.

Stephen looked at her empty rack of letters and at 2 A.M. wouldn't put it past her to have palmed a letter. She just smiled at him. He played *HEXAGON*. A brother would let a sister win at only so many things, but Scrabble wasn't one of them. "Do you want me to call the others?" he asked. All the O'Malleys should be here tonight.

She squeezed his shoulder. "Your company is just fine."

Stephen didn't know how to take that.

"I don't plan to die alone. Other than that, it's not that scary, Stephen. I'm on earth one moment and walking around heaven the next. I'm sure it will be a captivating enough place that I won't have more than just a thought or two about the fact it means I just died. You're here so you can assure the others that my death was peaceful."

"Don't talk like this, Jen."

"You're afraid because you don't believe."

"I'm not the one you should ask for this."

"Who better to ask? Lisa? Rachel? Marcus?"

He looked from his letters over to her.

"You've got the strength to deal with death. You've seen that moment of death so many times, when an accident victim stops living. I want you to have one good memory to replace all those horrible ones. I want you to know what it's like to die peacefully when Jesus is waiting to meet you."

Man, she really thinks she is dying. "I thought I had days with you to say good-bye, and now you're telling me there may not be a tomorrow."

"Today, this week, this month," she answered gently. "It's soon, Stephen." She squeezed his chilly hand. "Hand me the remains of Tom's hamburger, will you? Butterball is hungry."

Stephen was relieved to have her change the subject. "Thirsty maybe. That mutt shared my dinner on the drive over here." If she so much as sneezed wrong tonight, he was going to page the family. She hadn't told Tom; otherwise the man would be sitting in the chair beside him talking with her. Jen was a doctor, Tom was a doctor, and there was a hospital across the street. In a pinch, Stephen would call 911, but he was the one they would send to respond. "It's your turn."

"Now we're playing proper names." She laid down *OMALLEY*.

She had boxed him in on the board so he could only play a two letter *ME*. "I wish Marcus had suggested a different name."

Jen switched around her letters, looking for ideas. "Was he the one who first mentioned O'Malley? Rachel and I found one of the earlier lists, but we didn't find the one with that name."

"Remember the St. Patrick's Day party where Jack made the 7UP vivid green?"

"How could I forget?" Jen asked. "Jack ate clam chowder later that night and got sick."

"It was a midnight meeting in the hallway where we drew short straws to see who had to check on him. Marcus made that statement, 'O'Malleys take care of their own' and it stuck."

"I thought he said, 'Men take care of their own' and you were supposed to take the short straw. Everyone knew it was the toothpick with the red on the end."

"You're kidding."

Jennifer laughed. "All these years and you didn't know? You drew the short straw."

"Purely by accident. Jack is not fun when he's sick."

"I know what you mean," Jen agreed. "I think O'Malley came up at the meeting that next weekend. Maybe you suggested it."

"I've no idea. It's your play."

"I'm thinking." Butterball knocked over her rack of letters.

"Puppies can't help. I plan to win this one."

She played *XEROX*. "Triple points." She reached for more letters. "I'm very glad you were there yesterday. It was a relief to look up and see you and Jack heading into the fray."

He leaned over and hugged her. "The next crisis, I'll try to be there even earlier."

Twenty-nine

R achel had trouble reading her own writing. She unwrapped another cough drop, hoarse from hours talking on the phone with kids. She was updating Nora on what she had learned about the network of friends so the other counselors could sort out the follow-up plans. Rachel had on her short list for this Wednesday morning to visit Marissa and Adam and then get some much needed sleep.

"Lisa's back," Nora noted as they finished work.

Rachel turned. She hadn't realized her sister was planning to come back to the command center this morning. She glanced back at Nora as her friend got up from the table. "Do you need help with the morning briefing?"

"I'm ready."

"I'll be over to help with the hotline in a minute."

"It's covered for now," Nora said. "Protect what remains of your voice."

"And eat. You look awful," Lisa encouraged. Rachel took the ham croissant Lisa offered and watched her sister take a seat on the edge of the table.

"It's been a long night." She had spent it moving from one hospital to the other with Cole, for two students were still on the critical list.

"Let me make it a more interesting day."

"Wait a minute." Rachel waved over Cole. "I want him to hear the update."

"Your new-couple side is showing."

"I don't know how I ever worked a disaster without him. Last night—I'm talking with Greg and Tim's mom and Clare is flirting with Cole. It wasn't how I expected that session to go, but Cole making Clare laugh was a delight to see."

"Sandy is a nice lady. I met her when they were executing the search warrant."

"She's convinced if she had never divorced, her boys would still be alive. I'm worried about her, but at least she has Clare as a reason to get up every day. Their father Peter is a bigger concern. He's feeling enormous guilt and facing an indefinite leave at work. No one is going to put him behind the cockpit of a plane with two hundred passengers while he's facing this."

"It's going to get rougher before it gets better," Lisa said.

"I know. The funerals are being scheduled for this weekend. The girl killed in the cafeteria will be buried on Saturday. Greg and Tim will be buried together in a Sunday morning service, and Mark will be laid to rest later in the afternoon." The boys' funerals were being kept private to limit the media pressure on the family.

The counselors were gearing up to be ready for those tough days. The command center was in full operation. Her friends on the National Crisis Team were here. The relationships among the group had been forged through hurricanes, plane crashes, and wildfires. Her friends stopped by to squeeze her shoulder and share wordless sympathy that she'd seen this one up close, and then they settled in to learn the kids, the parents, to handle the media, and assist with the restoration of the crime scene back to a school.

The two schools would be cleaned up, painted, and reopened for classes on Friday. Rachel had recommended it. Parents and students alike needed to get back into the schools before the memories became bigger than they had to be. The hotline was already lit up with calls from kids who had struggled to cope overnight.

Cole joined them. He offered Lisa a cup of coffee. "Thanks for coming this way."

"I need to walk through the scene again."

Rachel studied her sister. "You've got news."

"Very bad news."

What could be worse than what they already had?

"We recovered two guns from the boys in the cafeteria, both .45s. Tim was killed with a .38." Lisa let that sink in. "We never found that gun. Someone else was there. And ballistics say the .38 is the same gun used to murder Carol Iles."

Rachel walked with Cole up the driveway to Ann's home. The recovery from the flood was still going on in the more subtle changes. New bushes had been planted along the walkway and new gutters to replace those torn away by the waters had arrived and were being installed. Nathan's tricycle was out on the driveway and the flag was flying by the doorway. A yellow-ribbon wreath was on the door. Rachel and Cole had taken a chance and just come over. They had a gun missing.

Jesus, I can't afford to make a mistake. There were kids making rash decisions to bring guns to school, to use them, and somewhere out there was a missing gun and another kid who had to be an emotional mess right now. She had to get control of this situation. She should have seen the shooting coming; she knew Marissa, and through her Greg, and had met Tim. She had known something about Mark and his history and his parents' divorce but still she hadn't realized there was trouble coming within the group. She was desperately afraid she wouldn't be able to figure out what other students had been involved in this event before another shooting occurred.

Cole squeezed her hand. "Adam would have said something to his mom if he knew details."

"Maybe." But she hadn't needed to convince Cole to bring her straight here, and that told her Cole was worried about the possibilities too.

Cole rang the doorbell. Rather than a scurry of feet inside, which was the norm; Ann came to the door. "Rae, Cole. Hi. Please, come in."

Rachel hugged her friend. "How are you this morning?" She knew it wasn't just Adam's reaction weighing on her, but the fact that Ann had been working at the dispatch center when the emergency calls had come in about a shooting at the school. Ann didn't look like she had slept much last night.

"I was just going to ask you the same question," Ann said.

"You get through an event like this one day at a time."

"I know the feeling. I found myself baking this morning at five o'clock."

Nathan tugged Rachel's pant leg and held up his arms. She hoisted him up and hugged him. "Hi, sweetie."

Nathan offered her a bite of his cookie.

"Thank you."

He grinned at her and shoved the rest of it in his mouth with his fist.

"You are priceless, you know that."

Ann laughed and ruffled her son's hair. "He's been helping me."

Rachel was grateful Ann had been able to keep her equilibrium. She was going to need it when they talked about the status of what happened. "How's Adam?"

"He's in his room drawing. I think it helped that Stephen came over last night. Adam slept pretty well. Feel free to pop in and say hi. Can I get you two some breakfast?"

"You've been baking bread."

Ann smiled at Cole. "Rolls actually. Come on back to the kitchen. They are best eaten hot."

Rachel set down Nathan. "Go with your mom. I want to say hi to Adam. And save me one of those cookies," she told Nathan, hugging him and getting in a tickle, sending the boy into a fit of laughter.

Rachel walked back to Adam's room. Whatever he knew, he hadn't said anything to his mom or Stephen.

The bedroom had been transformed into the hideout of a little boy.

Adam's comic collection was proudly displayed on the shelves, there were posters of soccer players on the walls, and his schoolbooks were piled beside the desk. Shoes peeked out from beneath the bed and gum wrappers had missed the wastebasket. A shirt had slid off its hanger in the closet and Scrabble game letters had become roadways for Matchbox cars. She tapped softly on the open door. "Hi."

He looked up from his drawing. His face looked solemn, old.

"May I come in?"

He nodded.

"What are you drawing?"

"Just a picture."

She looked over his shoulder. "You draw very well." She rubbed his back. "You like baseball?" He had a baseball set on a cup coaster and was trying to capture what the seams looked like.

"Cole brought me over the baseball and a glove."

"He's nice that way." She sat down on the made bed and kicked off her shoes so she could pull up her feet.

"How's your friend Marissa?"

"Doing better. I saw her after she came out of surgery last night. They were able to set her broken leg."

"I wanted to call Tim's mom, but Mom said I should wait."

"What would you like to talk to her about?"

"Tim's funeral. Will I be able to go?"

"Yes," she reassured softly. "I saw Sandy last night. She would be glad to talk with and see you, Adam. The police just needed her time last night. She wanted to know if you would come over and help her choose items for Tim's memorial chest. You know what he loved the most."

"Do you think I could contribute one of my comic books?"

"I'm sure she'd appreciate it." Rachel rested her chin on her drawn-up knees. "Could we talk about yesterday, Adam?"

He looked back at his drawing.

"It's important." She understood the pain in those memories. From the black eye in gym class to the painful terror of the shooting, he was overwhelmed. He was retreating. It had begun yesterday when he limited what he told his mom about the events so he wouldn't have to talk about them. It showed itself today by his solitary occupation and the care in his drawings. Rather than be with his mom and brother in the kitchen baking cookies, he had chosen to be alone. She had learned enough about Adam since the flood to know a few basics of his personality. It wasn't a bad way to cope. Solitude was a positive for him, as was a tight circle of friends. He had lost his best friend in Tim, and she wasn't surprised he wanted time on his own to come to terms with it. Adam's sadness was deep.

He reluctantly nodded.

"Where were you when the fire alarm went off?"

"On my way to meet Tim. I met Greg in the hall, and he stopped me to ask about my eye."

"Did you go in and see what had happened to Tim? Were you there?"

"I just heard about it."

The boy wouldn't meet her eyes. But he sounded tired, resigned, rather than anxious as if he had lied. "You wish you had been there."

Adam looked up and nodded. "If I had been, I could have helped Tim."

She was grateful he hadn't been there. The thought of a little boy trying to stop his friend from bleeding to death from a gunshot wound... That reality was hard enough on a doctor accustomed to working on trauma victims. "You were not responsible for Tim's death," she said softly.

"He was my friend and he died alone." Adam started to cry.

She reached for the tissue box and offered it to him.

"I know it hurts. I promise he wasn't really alone; God was with him." She waited for him to gain his composure. "I need to ask you something that's hard. Okay?"

He wiped his eyes.

"A gun is missing that was used at the school. Did you take it? Did you bring it home?"

His head jerked up. "No! I wouldn't do that. Nathan plays with anything he finds."

She watched Adam—the flush of anger that showed with his words and the way he dropped his eyes and bit his lip for having yelled at her.

"If you hear anything about it, will you tell me?" She waited but he didn't look at her.

He finally nodded.

She could tell he was upset by the questions. "I need to know and I had to ask."

"It's okay."

His voice said it was anything but. "Not if you feel like I don't trust you. I know how hard you try to do the right thing. I'm just scared because I can't find the gun. I don't want anyone else to get hurt."

Adam looked up as she spoke. "It's okay." He sounded like he meant it this time. He wiped his eyes again. He was nearly breaking the pencil he had picked up. The stress this boy was under was intense. Rachel moved him up to the top of her watch list.

"I'm so sad that this happened to you and your friend. Is there anything you need or want me to tell your mom for you?"

He thought about it then shook his head.

"Is there anything you're not telling me I should know?"

He bit his lip. "Could I ask you something?"

"Sure."

"Why did you go into the high school with Kate?"

"Because she's my sister and I wanted to do anything I could to protect her."

"Were you scared?"

"Very." She paused to see if he wanted to ask anything else. "You know you can page me if you need me, right?"

He pulled her card from his pocket. "Mom laminated it for me."

"I'm glad." Rachel got up and hugged him. "It's going to be okay, Adam."

"I want my friend back."

"I know." She tightened her hug. "Cole came with me. Would you like to come say hi?" She wasn't sure if he would want to, but he nodded.

They joined Ann and Cole in the kitchen. Cole came over and knelt down to greet him. Rachel was relieved to see Adam rebound and start to smile under Cole's attention. It was a tough call to make, but Rachel decided to talk to Ann later that afternoon when it could be a private conversation. Rachel sampled enough cookies Nathan had helped bake that she edged toward queasiness with the sugar and lack of sleep. After half an hour, Rachel hugged the boys farewell.

Cole walked with her outside.

"Does Adam know anything?"

She was still struggling to figure out the answer to that. "He says no, but I'm not sure. I think he knows more about what happened than he's willing to say. If he thought he was protecting Tim by taking the gun, he might have hidden it. I do know it's not in the house. He wouldn't want Nathan to get hurt."

"Who else may have it?"

"Mark's friend Chuck is still a possibility. Wilson was going to talk to him. Do you have time to take me by the hospital to see Marissa?"

"I'll drop you off and go check in with my office, then come back for you."

"Thanks."

He lifted her hand to his lips and kissed it. "We'll find the gun and the student who has it, Rae."

"Before someone else takes a rash action?"

The .38 had already been used in a murder and a school shooting. They needed a lead. And she felt like she was missing it. *Jesus, I'm going to fail without Your help. We need to find who has this gun.*

Thirty

Rachel eased the door open to Marissa's hospital room. She'd been given a private room on the orthopedics floor. Marissa's mom said she had had a peaceful night and was resting. The fever she had begun to run after surgery had come down. Marissa's mom and dad had spent the night here but had stepped down to the private waiting room to have a cup of coffee.

"Hi, M," Rachel whispered.

"Rae." She opened her eyes, still drifting in and out and smiled.

"How are you?"

"They gave me something to help me to sleep last night. It worked."

Rachel sat down in the chair next to the bedside and slipped her hand under Marissa's. "You look better than the last time I saw you." Her pallor had eased. Around the room were numerous gifts of flowers and dozens of get-well cards. Rachel could hear the sound of the automated pressure cuff around Marissa's ankle inflate and deflate every few minutes to keep a blood clot from forming.

"Tomorrow I'll look even better. Janie was by. She brought me makeup and a pair of wonderful earrings."

"I'll bring fingernail polish. What color?"

"Peach."

Rachel reached for a glass of water and held the straw for Marissa.

"Thanks," Marissa said. "Janie said the press was asking about me. All I did was fall down some stairs. But because I only have one leg, the press thinks I'm a better story than one of the kids who got shot."

"Trust me, they are interested in everybody," Rachel said. "You can decide when and if you want to talk to them."

"Maybe after my leg is in a cast and it's covered with signatures. Did you see my dad? He's here. He helped me with breakfast."

"I talked with him for a few minutes. He's coping, M."

"He promised to be the first one to autograph my cast."

"I'm glad." Rachel squeezed her friend's hand. "I have some hard news for you."

Marissa nodded. "I thought you might. Mom and Dad were doing a good job of not answering my questions directly."

Rachel hurt for the news she had to share. "Greg is dead. And Tim."

The monitor behind Marissa captured the shock as her heart rate jumped. There was a moment of disbelief, and then tears filled her eyes. "Both of them."

"I'm so sorry, M," Rae said, her own eyes filling with tears.

"Were they shot?"

"Yes."

"What happened?" Marissa wailed.

Rachel rubbed her arm. "We're not sure yet," she said softly. "Tim died in the boys' locker room at his school. People saw Greg chasing Mark Rice. There were gunshots exchanged. They both died at the high school."

"No." Marissa's voice trembled.

Rachel leaned across the bed and hugged her. "I know, honey. I know." She would feel the same way if something had happened to Jennifer. Rachel got Marissa tissues and sat quietly, letting her friend absorb the news.

"I told Greg he should go to the principal."

Rachel stilled at the mention of his name. "Was something going on?"

"Mark picked on Tim. Greg and Mark got into a fight once about it. It just got worse. I know Greg talked to Mark's mom about it."

"Carol Iles?"

Marissa nodded. "It was after Tim came home with skinned knees. He'd been skateboarding at the park and Mark and one of his friends hassled him."

"When was this?"

"A couple months ago. I thought it was getting better. Tim hadn't said anything lately, and Greg hadn't mentioned it." Marissa's hand tightened on hers. "Greg promised his mom he would look after Tim. Did Greg die because of that?"

Rachel brushed back Marissa's hair. "I don't know. But we'll find out." She could offer so little comfort but her presence. Marissa's mom and dad would be the ones to help her through this loss, but there was one part of the shock she could help alleviate. "When did you last see Greg?" Rachel tried to pull out the happy memories, knowing there was comfort in them.

"Greg was teasing me over lunch that he was going to get me to dance with him at the prom, even if he had to hire the band to stay around after everyone else went home."

Rachel shared a smile with Marissa and leaned against the bed railing. She rested her chin on her hand. "I'll tell you about my first date with Cole if you share your first one with Greg."

"Greg took me to a movie."

Rachel reached forward and gently wiped away a tear slipping down Marissa's cheek. "Romance or adventure?"

Marissa smiled. "Romantic comedy. He was pulling out all the stops."

The fire station was humming with activity Wednesday. It had become the staging area for the extra police who were assigned to patrol the community and deal with the intense media and community interest in the schools. The scene yesterday had taken its toll, for more than one member of the department had children attending those schools.

Cole set down his coffee and moved the stack of phone messages on his chair so he could sit down. He wasn't staying long, but he needed to get a feel for what else had happened in the last twenty-four hours. "Did you get any sleep?" Jack asked. His friend leaned against the office door.

"A catnap or two. I'll cut out later this afternoon. I dropped Rae off at the hospital to visit with Marissa, and I'll pick her up in an hour to give her a lift home."

"What can I handle for you?"

Cole appreciated the offer. He handed Jack the top folder. "That diner fire last Saturday? I heard the lab reports came in. They're somewhere on Terry's desk. Would you see what's there?"

"Glad to."

His assistant poked her head in the doorway and leaned around Jack. "Cole, line 5. The district attorney."

"I'm not here."

She smiled back at him. "I already tried that one."

Cole reached for the phone. "Jeffrey, what can I do for you?"

Jack followed Terry out of the room.

Life didn't stop because a school shooting happened. Cole moved as much paper as he could as he talked about an arson case coming up on appeal. No wonder Rachel was so often exhausted. He'd been working the school shooting for twenty-some hours, and the idea of going another five days through the funerals before the first break came felt impossible. He had to make sure Rachel got at least six hours of solid sleep this afternoon.

He wished the rest of her team would get here soon so someone better at debriefing could help her talk through what she had seen. What Rachel had been through was more than just traumatic, and he worried about the aftereffects. She had pulled herself together to focus on the job at hand. But when her pager went off and the next crisis came? He dreaded the day she got word of another disaster. She wasn't nearly as far from danger in her job as he would like.

He hung up with the district attorney and then started returning phone calls.

He was hanging up the phone after his ninth call when he heard his assistant say in surprise, "Rachel. Hi." It gave him time to turn toward the door just as Rae appeared.

"I told...Marissa said..." She was crying in such deep sobs her breath was missing. His first thought as her grief sucked him in was that she'd been driving while she cried. He had to break her of that habit. Whoever had brought her a car when she was this tired hadn't been thinking. Since his guest chair was stacked with books, he caught her hand and led her to sit on the credenza so he could mop her tears. "What did Marissa say?"

"Everything okay in here—" Jack froze in the doorway.

Cole met Jack's gaze over Rachel's bent head. "Go away." Cole kicked the door closed.

He wiped Rae's tears. She was losing it. He tilted up her chin and held her gaze, awash in the depths of what she was feeling.

"It could have been prevented."

"I know."

"Earlier. Greg talked to Mark's mom. It's linked somehow, Cole. Carol's death and the blowup at the school. There is history there going back months."

He'd been expecting a wave of emotion from her, but this... "Oh, honey." He pulled her onto his lap and held her tight as she sobbed, resting his chin against her hair. One person should only have to be asked to carry so much, and Rachel... "Shh, it's going to be okay."

Her hands curled into his shirt. "Why, Cole? Why do kids have to be the victims?"

He rubbed her back. "I don't know, precious." How he wished he did.

Cole eased her to her feet. He picked up the keys he'd tossed beside his dying cactus. "Come on; I'll take you home."

"I need to talk with Lisa and Marcus. I'm sorry I'm crying all over you."

"We will. And I don't mind." He wrapped an arm around her shoulders and opened the door. She had hit the wall, and the best hope he could offer was some desperately needed sleep. "Would you like to guess what Jack was doing this morning?"

Rachel leaned against the door of her apartment after saying good-bye to Cole. *Lord, thank You for sending me a man who understands the comfort found in a hug.* She would have asked Cole to stay a while, but she desperately needed some sleep. She was turning to Cole in ways she'd never asked of someone other than family before, trusting him to take this explosive grief and carry her. Even with family she had tried not to lean too hard. With Cole she was dumping it all and hoping he could bear it. She loved him and trusted him even with her breaking heart.

She loved him...

The words were welling up from a place in her heart where dreams were born. For the first time she trusted someone with everything, and she was finding in Cole that the trust was well placed. It felt right.

Lord, thank You.

The peace in her thoughts lasted until she looked down and saw the faint remnant of blood on her shoes. She stepped out of them where she stood and left them there.

Rachel went straight to bed, so tired it felt like a weight was pressing on every inch of her body. She buried herself between the pillows and closed her eyes. Instead of the relief of sleep, she felt a fierce tension build. She couldn't shut off the images or the sounds. She could hear the school alarm blare and Kate scream her name. The harder Rachel tried to forget, the more the memories sped up—of Kate shoving her, of the agonizing images of an injured boy trying to pull himself to safety, and of the girl lying dead where she had fallen.

Rachel stumbled out of the bed and went into the living room to curl up on the couch. She'd left the apartment Tuesday morning expecting a laughter-filled day with Jennifer and her sisters, and thirty hours later she couldn't remember how to smile. She needed to sleep, but she was scared of what it would be like to dream.

God, would You please take away this panic? Death came and it was unexpected and it was random and this time I witnessed it firsthand. She wiped at tears. *I'm not even sure what it is I'm afraid of. I just can't stop the memories.*

It helped knowing at this moment she wasn't alone. In the last hours the only peace she'd been able to offer many of the students and their parents was that God was strong enough to handle this. She was doing her best to lean hard against that strength.

She reached for the phone and placed a page. *Please, Kate, be somewhere you can answer.*

The phone rang back in less than a minute.

"Rae, what's wrong?"

She closed her eyes and exhaled. "I just needed to hear your voice."

Kate's voice gentled. "That bad, huh?"

"I'm trembling."

"I've had the shakes today too. Where are you?" Kate asked.

"Home. Cole brought me about an hour ago."

"Want me to get him back for you? He can hold your hand until it passes."

"I don't want him to worry about me any more than he already is."

"Guys are in our lives to worry about us."

Rachel hugged one of the couch pillows against her, her favorite huge lavender one that had a soft center. "Maybe if it doesn't pass. Are you doing okay?" She hadn't stopped long enough to do the follow-up with her family that was normally her role. Everyone had been there and was affected in various ways, but she didn't know other than generally how they were doing today.

"Dave brought me roses and dinner late last night, and he gift wrapped a bulletproof vest for me."

Kate had the ability to get shot and a day later chuckle about getting a bulletproof vest as a gift. For Kate the school shooting was only one of many incidents she would deal with this month. Rachel was grateful Dave was there to help Kate in a way that best supported but didn't limit her. "Dave's good for you."

"Three weeks and the stitches will be gone. I'll recover, Rae."

Rachel felt herself relaxing as Kate's calmness became hers. "What did I interrupt?"

"I'm at my desk looking at ballistics reports. Those .45s that were recovered at the school have a long history. At least this time they'll be melted down."

"Thankfully. Have you talked to Jennifer today?"

"I spoke to Tom at about noon. Jennifer is really worn out. He's hoping she'll sleep the majority of the next few days."

"Is she going to bounce back from this?"

"She saved lives. She's jazzed, Rae. More than I've seen since she had to quit seeing patients last year when the chemotherapy began. She'll find a way to recover from the exhaustion."

Rachel leaned her head back against the couch cushions and looked toward the ceiling. "I hope so."

"Go to sleep, Rae. Think about Cole. There should be enough good memories to take the place of the tough ones."

She had some wonderful memories and was holding on tight to them. "Please tell me the shakes go away."

"They do. I promise you that."

"I hope you get a boring day stuck at your desk."

"I appreciate the wish. I'll talk to you later, Rae."

Rachel said good-bye to her sister. She had hoped to avoid this backlash of emotions until after the funerals were past. She was going through her own decompression at the same time the kids were. When they described having been in the parking lot when the shooting was going on, she heard and saw those same memories. She had to stop this reaction. She had so much she needed to do in the hours ahead.

She took a deep breath and hugged the pillow against her chest. *God, life is so hard.* She had to see Jennifer. Rachel knew how rough this crisis had been on her sister's health, and yet Rachel had never been so relieved to have someone with her. Jennifer and Lisa had saved lives.

Rachel went to take a long hot shower, for the chill had reached into her bones. She took time to dry her hair and brush it out, then went back to her bedroom. After some thought, she reached for the phone beside the bed and made a second call.

"Cole?" She'd taken a chance that he would be home. She needed the reassurance of hearing his voice.

"Hi, honey." He sounded like he had been dozing.

"You know that verse Kate likes to quote: *The Lord is my helper, I will not be afraid; what can man do to me?*'"

"You're making me think on twenty minutes of sleep." He was quiet for a moment. "I think it's in the last chapter of Hebrews."

"*What can man do to me?* One thing he can do is shoot at me. It's scary."

"Bad dreams, huh?"

"I haven't gotten that far. I wasn't ready for yesterday, and I'm a basket case just trying to sleep because I keep thinking about it. My hands are trembling."

"You have to let yourself feel the emotion, accept it's a justified reaction, and then let it go."

"I wish you could make this go away," she whispered.

"Rae, you'll never be able to stop the evil people do, any more than Lisa can stop the murders. But what you do does matter. Kids are coping today because you have been there for them."

She wiped her eyes. "I can't do this anymore. It hurts too bad."

He didn't answer her for a long time. She wasn't sure what she wanted from him. But it mattered, what he said. She was looking hard for a way out of this pain. There had been too many tragedies coming too close together and they were burying her under their weight.

"Rae, another wise thing my dad taught me was don't make decisions when you are tired or upset."

Tears flowed. She was both. She blew her nose. "It's good advice."

"You want me to come over and bring a video? We can eat popcorn and you can pretend to be interested in my choice of movie."

She laughed, appreciating the soft offer more than he knew. "I need to sleep. And so do you."

She shifted pillows around.

"You're exhausted, honey. What do you tell your kids when they're struggling to sleep like this?"

It was hard to remember. "Sometimes the memories start to repeat less once they are written down."

"Want to try that? Or better yet, when they start to race on you, call me back and tell me about them. I'll share it with you, Rae."

She was comforted just by the offer. "I'm going to try to sleep now."

"I'll be a phone call away. Always. Call me when you wake up later? Let me get you dinner?"

"Your optimism is showing."

"Yeah. Sleep well, beautiful."

"Good night, Cole," Rachel whispered. She hung up the phone and put her head down on the pillow.

God, I'm so grateful You put Cole in my life.

She sighed and closed her eyes, her thoughts on the man she had let inside her heart. She finally slept.

Cole pulled his arm back, faked a throw, and then tossed the tennis ball toward the garage. Hank raced after it.

"He has to go crashing through that bush rather than around it," Rachel remarked.

"What he lacks in smarts, he makes up for with enthusiasm," Cole replied, smiling. Rachel had slept through the afternoon and early evening, and he was relieved to see the calmness, even laughter, in her expression. Her phone call hadn't come until after 8 P.M. It hadn't been that hard to talk her into coming over for a bite to eat.

The dog loped back. Cole leaned down and tugged the tennis ball free from Hank's jaws. "Were you intending to feed Hank your sandwich?"

Rachel looked down at the paper plate she'd set on the ground. "Sorry." The ham sandwich had disappeared.

Cole had seen her eat the cookies but not the sandwich. "I'll fix you another if you like."

Her pager went off. She glanced at it but didn't reach for the phone. "This one can wait."

Hank tried to climb onto her lap.

"You're supposed to throw the tennis ball," Cole pointed out.

"It's icky."

She tossed it toward the garage, and this time Hank got stuck when he tried to plow through the bush. "You're going to have to replant that somewhere else to give him a clear path. It's like leaving a piece of furniture in the middle of a hallway—it's not fair."

"Move the bush and the dog is going to crash full speed into the side of the garage. It's like his eyesight is myopic. He's got a lousy sense of distance."

Hank came back with the tennis ball. "Poor boy." Rachel picked twigs and leaves out of his coat.

"What's on your plate for tomorrow?" Cole asked, working on how he could best help her in the next couple days.

"Work the pager and the phone primarily. Join a walk-through at the school. After that, a day spent visiting kids. They are going to try to have the school open in the afternoon for students to collect belongings, so they can have a regular school day on Friday."

"Will you be working at the schools the first day?"

"Probably not in a formal way. There are other counselors who are better at mass debriefing and reassurance. My list for the day will include talking with the students we know are going to need extra help. I'm hoping the missing .38 is recovered by then. I'm terrified of holding school classes again without us having found who has that gun. I've got dread in the pit of my stomach over there being another school shooting just as kids come back."

"The police will do everything they can to find it, but it's not the only gun out there."

Her pager went off. She glanced at the number. "I need to answer this one."

"I'll fix you another sandwich."

"Can you make it to go? I want to stop by and see Marissa on my way home."

"Sure. You'll get through this, Rae."

"I wonder sometimes." She returned the page.

Thirty-one

The middle school smelled of fresh paint Thursday afternoon. The hallways were being repainted white with a blue stripe to match the school colors. Rachel walked around the painters, drop cloths, and ladders. She could think of a lot of places she would rather be at the moment. She had a sketch of the school grounds with a hundred stories to go with it—students terrified by what had happened when the fire alarm sounded and then realizing there was someone shooting in the parking lot.

She hadn't been focused on the investigation, but it was clear seeing Wilson, Lisa, Marcus, and Quinn that it had been proceeding full force. This walk-through was an attempt to take a final look at the time line of the shooting before the children returned.

"The answers to what happened start here." Lisa led the way into the boys locker room. "An unknown number of boys were present. Tim was killed with a .38. Coincident to that someone pulled the alarm."

"Cole, which fire alarm was pulled?" Marcus asked.

"Interesting question. Hold on." Cole searched his reports. "Number 18, which is…the alarm by the PE teacher's office."

"So someone yanked this alarm after the shooting."

"Or before the shooting," Rachel offered, shoving her hands in her pockets.

"Or maybe someone pulled the alarm, and a kid with a gun jerked at the sound and pulled the trigger," Quinn suggested.

"An ugly possibility." Lisa walked the hall from the PE teacher's office to the boys locker room. "Tim is in the locker room with someone who eventually shot him. We know some shoving was going on because Tim has bruises that had just begun to form no more than a few minutes before his death. Someone else came into the locker room, realized what was going on, and pulled the fire alarm trying to break up the fight. Then the gun goes off."

"Someone pulled the alarm, someone took the gun. But who was it?" Marcus asked.

"Adam?"

They looked to Rachel. "He's heartbroken over Tim's death," she replied. "He's not a hider by nature. If he saw something more than just Greg in the hallway, if he saw the boys who hurt Tim, I think he would have told me."

"What about Greg taking the .38?"

"If he did, we would have found it somewhere at the scene."

"Maybe someone else was here with Mark."

"How about Mark's best friend, Chuck Holden?" Rachel suggested. "If Mark brought a gun with him to school, Chuck would know about it."

"We talked with him," Marcus replied. "He denied any knowledge of it or of a problem between Mark and Tim."

"Do you believe him?"

"Not entirely. Are we confident we would have found the .38 if it's still here?"

"We've turned this place upside down," Lisa replied.

"Then we need to go back and figure out what kids were doing in that half hour before the shooting. Someone had to have seen the boys come over here from the high school." Marcus looked at his watch. "It's about time for the afternoon briefing. The press will know soon that a gun is missing."

"If we don't have a lead on it by morning, we may have to put the word out ourselves. We can't reopen the schools and not alert the public. Rachel, are there enough counselors to cover both schools tomorrow?" Wilson asked.

"We'll be as ready as we can." Rachel looked with longing back at the hall door. This place was making her claustrophobic. Cole reached for her hand.

She held on tight.

Rachel used the trunk of her car as a worktable Thursday afternoon and held down the corners of her map with a flashlight, two decks of cards, and her soda can. She bit into the cheeseburger she'd been handed. "Gage, you forgot the onions again."

"But I remembered the mustard this time." He tossed a couple yellow packets to her. They had gotten into the habit of catching a meal together whenever they were in the same vicinity. "Where are you heading next?"

"I have no idea. I've got nine more house calls to make and rush hour traffic is starting." Her street map was wearing out. School resumed tomorrow morning, and Rachel was making an effort to talk to the girls she had identified as the natural leaders among the teenagers.

The teenagers had latched on to the idea of doing something special in memory of the girl who had died in the cafeteria. They wanted to hold the charity rubber duck float that had been canceled due to the flooding, and they had already contacted the chamber of commerce to see if it would be possible. It was a great idea. There were enough rubber ducks that every student at the middle school and the high school could participate.

She swiped some of Gage's french fries. "In your article this weekend would you mention the duck memorial?"

"Sure. Do you have a date arranged?"

"Saturday, May 5. The girls are putting it together so I should have details later tonight."

He pulled out his notebook to jot down the date and information.

"Have you even read a newspaper this week?"

"I'm avoiding the press whenever I can." She glanced over at him and smiled. "No offense."

"None taken, LeeAnn."

She wrinkled her nose at him for shortening it to just her middle name. "I need you at the school tomorrow morning when they reopen the doors. Can you come?"

"What do you need?"

"A reporter to work with the five teenagers who put out the school newspaper to help them create an issue that can be kept as a memorial of the event." She knew the student body needed closure and a way to express themselves as a group. The school paper was the most important collective voice they had. It needed the touch of someone who understood how to pull together the event and the memories and to also point the way forward. Gage was the right man to help those kids.

"Me, going back to high school?"

She smiled at him. "Please?"

He finished the fries. "You would have to say that magic word. I'll be there. Did you remember to get gas in your car?"

"You are never going to let me forget last month are you?"

He smiled back.

"I'm set." She folded up her map. "Thanks for dinner. I've got to get going."

"Drive carefully, Rae."

She gave him a hug.

The hotel suite Jennifer called home was quiet. Cole relaxed in a chair and watched her sleep on the couch. She rested on her side, hands tucked under her cheek. Cole hurt just watching her. She'd saved lives, but at what cost to her own health? Did those students know the gift she had given them, the full price that had been paid?

Tom rejoined him and handed him one of the glasses he carried.

"She's running a fever. You should admit her to the hospital, Tom."

"It's 100.6 and responding to medication. She's stubborn. And there are too many germs for her to catch if I did admit her." Tom shifted the ice pack against her back and checked the time. "I can give her more pain meds in twenty minutes. That will help."

Jennifer slept through pain that had tears sliding down her cheeks. It was a hard thing to face. If only the O'Malley's hadn't been caught right in the middle of the shooting… The stress of that moment had taken so much from her.

"She got a chance to be a doctor again in a critical role, Cole. She considers this price minor to that joy."

"Do you?"

Tom looked at the ice in his glass but didn't answer.

Cole finished his drink. "Rachel is coming by as soon as she can."

"There's no imminent crisis to this flare-up," Tom said. "If there was I'd call Rae. Jennifer understands well the time pressure her sister's under. She's frankly more worried about Rae than she is about her own situation."

Cole shared that concern. "Rae copes by keeping busy."

Jennifer stirred. Tom rose and helped her. He changed the ice and she took the medication he offered gratefully.

"Cole," her voice was soft, almost inaudible, "I'm glad you came." Her smile was still the breathtaking one he remembered.

"I'm glad you called."

She lifted her head and Tom shifted the pillow to support her head. "Better, thanks." She relaxed into the new position, her breaths slow and even as she absorbed the pain. "The bedroom gets so boring," she offered. "It's easier to rest here."

"You're sleeping; that's good."

She smiled. "Dozing. You worry about me as much as Tom does." Her eyes closed and she fought to reopen them. "I'm drifting on the meds. Sorry."

"Don't be." Cole waited as she rallied. "How can I help you, Jen?" She'd called him for a reason. He would help and get out of here. She needed that sleep she was fighting.

"I didn't need anything. I just wanted your company."

He blinked and then chuckled. "Did you?"

"I thought we might talk about Rae."

Cole relaxed in his chair, smiling back at her. "One of my favorite subjects."

"I just need a distraction from the pain," Jennifer whispered. "Tom's running out of stories."

"I'd be glad to help," Cole replied, following her rationale and touched that she'd called him instead of one of the other O'Malleys. "Why don't you start at the beginning about Rae? When did you two meet?"

"I really like you." Jen tucked her hands under her chin. "At Trevor House. She headed the welcoming committee."

Thursday evening, Rachel leaned back against the lawn chair that now had her name taped to the back webbing and worked on updating her composition notebook by penlight while she waited for Cole to return from work. He had been out on a fire run when she called the station. She hoped it wasn't a severe fire. The guys had already had a tough few days, and a deadly fire would layer hurt on hurt.

Faced with the choice of returning home or stopping by to see Cole, there hadn't been much need for thought. She was attached to his company, wanted to be with him.

The breeze ruffled the pages and Hank got up to plop two big feet on her knees. "Your breath is bad," Rachel offered as she reached out and scratched under his chin. She picked up the tennis ball and tossed it, and he took off after it.

"You look comfortable."

She leaned her head back as Cole joined her. She hadn't heard his car, but since the driveway had a stack of lumber on it at the moment, he'd parked on the street. "I wanted to watch the full moon."

"It's a beautiful night." He bent down and softly kissed her. She slipped her hand around the back of his neck and leaned against him, absorbing the fact the man was a rock in the middle of a chaotic day.

"You need a shower."

He shook his head and ash fell on her notebook. "Yep, I guess I do. We had a hot fire in a restaurant kitchen."

"Arson?"

"An accident. It took about ten minutes of searching to confirm it had started on the stovetop where a gas feeder line had a pinhole break. Come on in. I'll get cleaned up."

"Why don't you clean up and come back out. It's nice to just sit and enjoy the calm night."

His thumb soothed her shoulder blade. "Ten minutes," he promised and headed into the house.

She returned to the work in her notebook updating observations and contacts made throughout the day. She would have to go to volume two tomorrow, for this notebook was almost full.

Her pager went off. It was from the National Crisis Response Team. She returned the call. The first vandalism of the crisis had been a threat against the high school principal spray-painted on the back of the gym. It was inevitable that some of the anger against what had happened would manifest itself in vandalism and threats. The big problem would be the inevitable bomb threats. The counselors already had the school staff prepared.

Cole slid his arm across her shoulders as she spoke with Nora, and Rachel lifted her hand to grip his. It had been a twenty-hour day, but she wouldn't have missed coming here for anything.

She closed the phone, and he offered her a lemon drop. "You've almost lost your voice."

"Close to it."

She relaxed. She didn't feel a need to put into words the simple fact that she hadn't wanted to be alone. Cole already understood.

He broke the comfortable silence. "Jennifer called me today."

Rachel stiffened. She knew she should have figured out how to make it to the hotel today. "What's wrong?"

"Relax." He eased her back into the chair. "Her recovery is still pretty iffy on the pain levels. Tom wanted you to know they might admit her to the hospital for a couple days, but if they did, it would just be a precaution. A couple weeks recovering and Jen should be okay. She just wanted company between catnaps."

She warily looked at him. "What did you talk about?"

He tucked a wisp of hair behind her ear. "Besides her dog, Stephen, and what Boston is like in the winter?" He smiled. "She loves you."

"Well…" She'd been expecting to hear some comment about her past, and his answer threw her. "That's good. Fine. Okay."

He laughed and hugged her.

On Friday morning, Rachel walked into the hotel where Jennifer and Tom were staying, relieved they hadn't had to admit Jennifer overnight. Tom met her at the suite door. "It's good to see you, Rae."

"I should have been here yesterday."

"Don't. I know what your day was like. I would have called if it was urgent." He tipped up her chin. "I'd prescribe about ten hours of sleep and some good news."

She smiled at his comforting words. "School started today with over 70 percent attendance. I've had several hundred hugs this morning. That was pretty great. Can I borrow your wife for a minute?"

"She's in the bedroom. Can I get you some hot tea for that sore throat?"

"I'd love some."

Rachel walked through the suite to the bedroom and leaned around the doorway to see if Jennifer was awake.

"Hi," Jen whispered. "I heard you come in."

"Can I get a hug?"

"You can get one for as long as you like."

Rachel sat down on the bedside and leaned over for a very, very long hug. She finally sat back. "You look horrible," Rachel said softly. The jaundice had grown worse in the last twenty-four hours. There was no benefit to ignoring the reality they had to deal with.

"I don't feel so hot today," Jen admitted. "Doctoring takes a lot of energy." Jen closed her eyes and rallied. She smiled and reached up to brush a lock of Rachel's hair aside. "You've got gray hair coming back."

"It's going to come in white this time." Rachel kicked off her shoes and stretched out beside Jennifer on the bed. She reached for one of the huge extra pillows. Jennifer had a stack of pillows behind her to support her and three ice packs against the worst of the pain in her back. "Are you numb?"

"It comes and goes in my legs," Jen admitted. "It doesn't take much swelling for it to press against a nerve."

"Is there anything else we can do?" Rachel asked.

"Tom can go to even stronger pain meds if I need them." Jennifer smiled. "I'll get past this one. It just makes me feel kind of mushy, like my hands aren't quite sure they want to move."

Rachel wished she could hide out here with Jennifer for the rest of the day. "The funerals start tomorrow."

Jennifer rubbed her shoulder. "You'll get through them, Rae."

She wished she had that kind of confidence. "The one tomorrow is for the girl killed in the cafeteria. Practically the entire school body is going to be there, as well as the community. It will be televised."

"Was she a Christian?" Jennifer asked.

"Yes."

"How are her parents doing?"

Rachel sighed and wrapped her arm tighter around the pillow. "Better than I expected. The grief is... Remember what it was like when we were fourteen and Shelly got adopted? How awful it felt that she was gone and yet how overjoyed we were that she had gotten her wish for a home?"

"I remember."

"Those are the dual emotions her parents are feeling. They miss her terribly. She's okay in heaven, but they are having to realign their entire lives without her."

Jen nodded. "When you have kids, you expect them to outlive you."

"Yeah. Are you doing okay with what you saw?" Rachel asked.

"No."

She reached for Jennifer's hand. "I thought that might be the case."

"I wish I had been able to do more. Kim is still heavy on my mind."

"The surgery went well, and she's listed in good condition. She's got a very close family. I visited with them last night."

"She was terrified. You really think she'll be okay?"

"I've got many kids on my list having a harder time coping than Kim."

They rested in quiet. Rachel leaned her chin against her hands. "Do you want to go ahead with the wedding date of May 19? We can move it if you'd like."

"This family needs something positive to look forward to. I know I do."

"Do we need to move it forward?" Rachel whispered.

Jennifer held her gaze and squeezed her hand. "The nineteenth should be okay. I want to celebrate their weddings, but Lisa and Kate need time to solve this case. It should give me a chance to get my strength back." Jen reached over to wipe one of Rachel's tears away. "I'm ready, Rae. If God says now is the time, I'm okay with that. I haven't given up on a miracle, but my trust has returned that God is indeed good. He knows what's best. I saved kids, Rae." Her smile grew. "They've got names and faces and it felt really great."

"Is Tom prepared?"

"My husband is my hero. Tom has more courage about this than I do. He asked me to marry him knowing it would take a miracle to avoid a funeral. He's ready because he has to be. That's the best kind of love."

"He's wading into the deep waters with you."

"He is." Jennifer studied her, then smiled. "Cole is a lot like Tom."

"Trouble flows around him, never breaking his calm. It's reassuring."

"You're falling in love."

Rachel smiled back as she nodded. "And in the midst of this pressure, I'm finding out just how much of a blessing it is."

⸺◦◦◦◦⸺

Rachel studied the picture Stephen was hanging for Ann Friday afternoon. "A little higher on the right. There. Good." She was waiting for Adam to get home from school to see how his first day had gone. She had stayed at school this morning helping students, but she didn't want to get in Adam's space this afternoon unless he paged her.

Assuming he would be okay was part of what made it possible for him to be okay. Treat him as overwhelmed and he would stay overwhelmed. Adam needed his routine back, his sense of life moving on.

"Jennifer planned her own funeral," Stephen said, returning to the tough discussion of the afternoon.

"Ann wants the next picture hung over there." Rachel pointed to the spot on the wall. "What did you think Jennifer was doing with her spare time?"

"Something better than being morbid."

"I've got my funeral planned."

"But you think that way. Jen thinks about what wrapping paper will look color coordinated with the gift she bought."

"Stephen, she's got terminal cancer. The doctors told her to go home. Without a miracle she doesn't have much time left."

"Preparing for death is wishing that it would come."

"Denial isn't going to make it go away."

He looked away and didn't comment. Rachel squeezed his shoulder.

"What time did Nathan go down for a nap?" Stephen asked.

"A little over an hour ago." She was keeping an ear open for sounds over the intercom that he was waking up. She'd offered to watch him while Ann went to get Adam from school.

Car doors slammed.

"It looks like there might have been some trouble," Stephen said, getting the first look as Ann and Adam got out of the car. "Adam added another shiner to go with the one he already had."

Rachel set down the picture and caught up with Stephen as he headed outside to the driveway.

"What happened, buddy?" Stephen knelt in front of Adam.

"He called Tim a coward, so I hit him."

The defiance in Adam's tone said he didn't care if it was wrong. He was glad he'd done it.

"And he hit you back."

"He's the coward."

Stephen took a good look at the eye. "Nice shiner. Remember where you put the ice pack?"

Adam nodded.

"Go get it. You earned it. Then you'd better head to your room so Nathan doesn't see you and start to cry."

Adam's defiance faded a bit.

"Nathan's a little sensitive to you getting hurt right now," Stephen said softly. "You might want to think about that next time. Protecting him is probably more important than getting people who don't know better to think well of Tim."

"I'm sorry."

Stephen hugged him. "Just get cleaned up before Nathan sees it."

Adam headed to the kitchen to get the ice.

"Thanks, Stephen," Ann said. "He didn't want to talk with me."

"I should have warned him about the comments. They were inevitable. Mind if we stay for dinner?"

"You're welcome to. It's—"

"Hot dogs and Jell-O," Stephen finished for her. "You let Adam decide since it was a hard day."

She gave a small smile. "But on the grill outside tonight." Ann led the way back inside. "Thanks for hanging the pictures. It's impossible to do by yourself."

"Rae helped." Stephen put away his tools. "I'll go find charcoal and start the grill."

Rachel helped Ann in the kitchen get out items for dinner. "Adam will get through this, Ann."

"He isn't sleeping well. He's restless. I find him up in the middle of the night getting himself a drink or sitting in the living room in the dark. I've seen him check on Nathan at night. It's odd. Rae, it sounds crazy, but it's like he just became twenty. He's solemn, calm, protective. He needs to know where people are."

"He's got a tender heart, Ann. He wants to make it better; he wants people around him to be okay. His world as it existed has taken a huge blow too. The sadness is a good sign, for it shows he's admitting it hurt; the trouble sleeping—part of that is the depression he's feeling. He went back to school without his best friend. The anger today was probably a good thing, considering. He just needs to get through it."

"I don't know what I should be doing."

Rachel wrapped an arm around her friend's waist and squeezed. "Just give him lots of love." The sounds over the monitor signaled that Nathan was awake. He was talking to himself. "What is he saying?"

Ann smiled. "Sounds like *hot*. Nathan wakes up talking to the world. Unlike Adam who doesn't say much, Nathan doesn't have that problem." Ann went to get him.

They took dinner outside to the patio table. Rachel was glad Stephen was here, for he gave Ann and the boys one more piece of assurance that everything would work out. Adam brought out his baseball and glove so he could play catch with Stephen after they ate.

"What do you like on your hot dog, Adam?" Rachel asked, opening the bun.

"Everything."

"A big everything like Stephen, or a small everything like Cole?"

"A kid's everything. No peppers."

"Got it."

She handed him a paper plate.

He carried it over to sit with Stephen. Her brother made room for him and said something that made Adam laugh. Rachel relaxed. Adam would be okay. She glanced at her pager. It was time for her to start her evening rounds visiting kids. She made her hot dog to go. Nathan just about strangled her as the two of them exchanged a giggling good night.

Thirty-two

Nearly the entire school population had turned out for the funeral of the girl killed in the cafeteria. Cole couldn't find Rachel. It took a while to search the crowds. Cole walked the sidewalk in front of the memorial wall. The students needed a way to express their grief, and it had appeared in the spontaneous memorial of flowers and cards and stuffed animals at the high school track, where she had been a member of the track and field team. Rachel never made it into the large auditorium where the funeral service was held. She had spent the time walking the halls of the church and the parking lot, talking with those who came but had been unable to get through the service.

Unable to locate Rachel among those lingering at the memorial wall, he returned back to the church. Rachel had driven herself over early this morning, and it was possible a situation had arisen where she had left to help one of the students. She'd parked on a side street to leave the parking lot for guests. One more walk-through of the building and he would head over to check for her car. Several of those hospitalized had been able to come by ambulance for the hour-long service, and he paused as the last ambulance pulled from the parking lot for the return trip to the hospital.

Marcus joined Cole as he made his way into the auditorium. "Rachel left about twenty minutes ago. She got a page."

"One of the students?"

"Kate," Marcus replied. "Rachel just said it was urgent."

"Any idea where she went?"

"No. But given that Kate called her, it's probably someone struggling to get through the televised funeral."

Cole glanced at his watch. "Marissa called. She was watching the funeral on TV. I was planning to stop by the hospital and see her. She's having a rough afternoon."

"I suggest you go on. When I hear what's going on, I'll give you a call."

Cole didn't particularly want to leave; the odds were good that Rachel would be back to walk the memorial wall again. She'd been gearing up all week to handle this day, and he'd gotten a sense in the first half hour of how intense the day would be for her. The funeral was hard on those who attended, but it was even harder on those unable to handle entering the auditorium. "Call me just as soon as you hear."

Marcus squeezed Cole's shoulder. "She's been through many days like this."

It wasn't the reassurance Marcus meant it to be. Cole was still learning how to support a lady whose job required her to shoulder the weight of grief from events like this on an ongoing basis.

"Peter, think what this will do to Clare. She loves you." Kate leaned against the door between the garage and the house. It was getting hot in the garage. The deck of cards she was using to keep herself alert was starting to stick together. She could hear the TV through the door. Her partner had line of sight through the patio doors into the kitchen, and so far Greg and Tim's father had shown no willingness to back away from the threat of using the gun he held on himself.

Rachel was brought into the garage by one of the undercover cops. They were trying hard to make this look routine without squad cars in the drive and street. Two men stood in the front yard talking, idly walking the sidewalk keeping media from the house. One was walking around the backyard. If asked, they were simply there to make sure something didn't happen after the funeral as emotions among the students ran high.

Kate pointed to the stool against the wall. Rachel took a seat. "What's going on?"

"Greg and Tim's father has a gun, and he's having a very bad day."

"Is it the missing .38?"

Kate raised one eyebrow at the question. "Oh, that would be just wonderful. Three deaths from one gun." Kate unwrapped a piece of gum and offered one to Rachel. She accepted it and Kate saw her sister's tension begin to fade.

"Who called it in?"

"His ex-wife Sandy. She was over this morning to talk to Peter about the funeral arrangements for tomorrow. She called me when she left because she was worried about him. By the time I got here, Peter had already acquired the gun."

"The man is grieving."

"Tell me about it. He watched the funeral of that girl on TV, and he's crying his eyes out."

"I thought you searched his house."

"Trust me, we did." Kate already had the same discussion with the officer on the scene. "Wherever that gun was, it was very well hidden."

It was quiet inside the house, too quiet. Kate turned toward the doorway. "Peter, Rachel is here. You said you wanted to talk with her about Clare."

Silence met her call. Kate cut the deck of cards, the rhythm of the movement helping with the passage of time. She eventually hoped to get an answer to one of her statements. She kept the comments coming at regular intervals. She wanted to reassure him that he was not alone. He'd lost two sons, and the house was a silent reminder as he mourned.

"Can we talk face-to-face?" The question came from Peter, tired and slow.

"If you set down the gun and open the door, we can sit right here and talk for as long as you like," Kate replied calmly. The odds were slim that he'd do so, but she'd take any step she could get. She moved on the stairs from leaning against the door to instead lean against the upright deep freezer.

Her partner was on the radio seconds later. "He's moving. He left the gun on the counter."

"Stand easy, people." He wasn't a violent man, and she wasn't planning to treat him as such. There was a sharpshooter who had line of sight to the doorway.

The doorknob turned.

A glance up from the deck of cards she was cutting confirmed the man had had very little sleep in the last week and looked as though he had aged a few years. "Peter, I'm Kate O'Malley. You remember my sister Rachel." She gave him a moment to look over and see Rae. "There are cold sodas if you happen to like orange."

"Those are Clare's favorites."

"I know," Kate replied. "She brought them over."

The man sat down heavily on the tile inside the doorway. He'd cried himself out. It was hard to see on a proud man, who from everything she had been able to learn had tried to be a good father. Kate handed him a soda. "I'm sorry about your sons."

"Greg did not kill Tim."

"The ballistics prove that," Kate reassured again as she had done many times. "You need to let someone help you."

"I'm tired." He looked at Rachel. "I can't go to the funeral tomorrow. And I can't tell Clare that."

"She understands when you have to fly and are often gone," Rachel replied. "Call her and let her know when you will be over to see her and then keep your word. That's what she needs. To know that you and Sandy are still there for her."

"Sandy doesn't blame me, but she should."

"I met your sons, Peter. Would you remember the fact that your boys loved you? The fact that Greg helped Marissa get through this last year? That Tim was Adam's best friend? They were good kids."

"There's nothing left. My boys are gone, my job."

Kate handed him a note. "Sandy asked if you would stay with her and Clare for the coming week. I think you should take her up on it."

"I can't do that."

"Peter, you said you've got nothing left. What do you have to lose? I don't know what caused the divorce, but Sandy was your wife for eighteen years, and it takes about three minutes in her company to realize she still cares about you a great deal. Spend a week with her and your daughter. Clare would find your presence when she came home from the funeral a great help."

He rubbed his swollen eyes. "What about all this?"

"I don't know about the other guys, but I'm on my day off." Kate cut the deck of cards and turned up a four of hearts. "You take Rachel's card and promise to call her if the grief gets bad. You allow me to take that gun, show me where you had it hidden, and give me your word that there are no others in this house. We don't need to make something of today beyond what it is."

He nodded. "I need a shave."

Kate offered a smile. "Eat something first. I don't know about you, but orange soda isn't the same as what I remember from childhood."

Peter chuckled. "I thought it was just my sense of taste dying."

"You like pizza?" Kate asked. "The guys say the pizza place on the corner is good. They bought a large hamburger and sausage."

Rachel got to her feet. "Is that what I've been smelling? If he's not hungry, I am. I'll get it."

Kate slid her cards into her pocket. "Peter, where did you have the gun hidden?"

"There's a safe in the floor in my office. When Sandy last moved furniture she had covered it with the couch."

Kate walked into the kitchen first and over to the counter. The gun was a .22 caliber. She unloaded it and secured the weapon. "Show me where that safe is."

Rachel handed Kate a bottle of ice water and opened the passenger door for her sister. "You did a great job."

Kate took a seat and reached for the seat belt. She buckled in. Rachel could tell Kate's arm was bothering her as she cradled it against her chest. "I owed his boys." Kate lowered her head and wiped at the dust that had stuck to the back of her neck with a wet tissue. It left a streak of grime.

"We've got a ton of pages to return, starting with Marcus," Rachel mentioned as she started the car.

"You want to do the talking for both of us?" Kate asked.

"I'm the one losing my voice."

"They can find us later." Kate picked up her phone and turned it off. "I stopped by and saw Jennifer this morning."

Rachel looked over at her sister to share a look. "What did you think?"

"I wish I'd taken that vacation two years ago and gone snorkeling with her in the Gulf."

"I've got a few of those moments I wish I had taken too," Rachel replied.

"When did we stop praying for a miracle?" Kate asked quietly.

"I felt it start to change when it became clear that God had a plan in mind for Jennifer much more complex than just healing her cancer."

"I've found myself praying more for us than Jennifer, for those staying behind."

"This is going to be a much harder transition than I think any of us are ready for," Rachel said. "Are you ready for this, Kate?"

"I'm glad I believe in heaven."

"I worry about Stephen." Rachel knew he was already finding it hard to adjust to the fact the rest of them believed and he did not. He was left out of something that gave them hope, and he had no one to relate to who felt the kind of grief he did—believing that life ended at death.

"So do I. We'll keep praying for him."

Rachel drew to a stop beside the building where Kate was meeting Dave.

"Are you heading home next?" Kate asked.

Rachel held up the hotel card Marcus had given her months before. "I'm going to do follow-up with those students visiting the memorial wall, answer the pages that have come in, and then I'm going to disappear for a few hours. I need some sleep before Tim and Greg's funeral in the morning. Reporters found my home."

Rachel checked into the hotel. As much as she wanted to be in her own home tonight, Gage's warning that reporters were waiting for her there had made her decision. She wanted privacy more than she did her own pillow.

She had spent much of her life in hotels and there was a routine for making them comfortable. She hung up her garment bag in the closet as she continued her fifth phone conversation of the evening. "Marissa, did Janie bring by the needlepoint?"

"It was exactly what I was looking for," her friend said. "I want to add something to the memorial wall. Someone needs to remember Greg."

Rachel knew how hard it was going to be on Marissa not to be at the funerals in the morning. "I have your memorial gift for Sandy. It will make a difference, Marissa, for both Sandy and Clare."

"I hope so. Cole came by this afternoon."

"Did he?" Rachel had seen him only briefly this morning before the funeral and wasn't sure what his plans for the day were.

"He talked with my parents for several hours. I like him, Rae."

"So do I." Rachel sat on the side of the bed. "Is there anything I can do to help you with tomorrow?"

"Mom and Dad are both going to be here. I'm glad in many ways that their funeral is being kept private. I don't know that I could handle watching another one on TV."

Rachel understood exactly what she meant. "It's draining." She checked numbers queued on her pager. "I'll call you in the morning, M. Don't hesitate to page me if there is anything I can do for you or one of your friends."

"I will. I'm grateful you are a phone call away."

"You've been making a big difference just calling and talking with your friends, reassuring them. Keep it up, honey. You're a huge help to me."

"And you're sweet. Cole said I could tell you that."

Rachel smiled. "Really? I'm keeping him. Good night, Marissa."

"Night, Rae."

She hung up the phone, paused to open the carton of orange juice she had bought, and then dialed the next number on her list. The calls now were the second and third follow-up calls after the shooting, most of them simply a reassuring contact to see how the students had handled the funeral this afternoon. Only one student was still on Rachel's high-concern list, and one of the other counselors, who had worked with her the day of the shooting, was following up in person daily.

Rachel opened her diary and her Bible, looking for the notes she had made the evening before. In finding reassurance for Adam about heaven, Rachel had found reassurance for herself as well. Heaven was as real as earth. She also made a note to spend some time with Nathan. He was young, but he knew something was wrong and that his brother was sad. Nathan needed the reassurance too.

Her pager vibrated and she checked the number. Other calls could wait a few more minutes; she dialed back. "Hello, Cole."

"Where are you, darling?"

The endearment made her feel so special. She pushed pillows into a backrest and leaned against the headboard. "Hiding."

"I figured that out two hours ago," he replied, amused.

"It's kind of nice seeing your numbers come across my pager." She could no longer imagine her life without Cole in it; his presence had so profoundly changed things. There was comfort just in hearing his voice.

"You're not going to tell me."

"I'm hardly hiding if someone knows where I am," she teased. "I've got two dozen calls to return over the next few hours." She wanted to be able to give him her full attention when she next saw him. She wanted another one of those long hugs.

"Are you holding up?"

"I took your suggestion on the orange juice. I'll make it. What about you?" Rachel asked.

"I had a good visit with Marissa and her parents. I can tell why you enjoy her company so much."

"I've made some great friends over the years. I appreciate you going over to spend time with them."

"Kate told me where you were this afternoon," Cole said.

"She handled the problem with her usual skill." Rachel looked at her watch. "Can I attend the funeral with you tomorrow?"

"Sure. Come over for breakfast if you like and we can go from here."

"I appreciate it."

"Anything else I can help you with?" Cole asked.

"I want a hug tomorrow."

"A long one," Cole promised.

Another page came in. "I'll see you in twelve hours." Rachel said good-bye and took a deep breath. She began working the network of friends, arranging the pages so that one after the other she could talk to a cluster of students who knew each other. It allowed her to gather information even as she gave it out. From her discussions with students at the memorial wall, she had known that this would be a busy night. She hadn't been ready for this.

Thirty-three

The private funeral service for Greg and Tim was scheduled to begin at 10 A.M. Sunday. Rachel was grateful she was with Cole as they entered the cemetery grounds. She came to help ease a family through the grief of saying good-bye. She had to do it when her own heart was incredibly heavy. The funeral service was held in the small chapel on the cemetery grounds so it could be kept out of the range of the media. Cole parked, and they walked over to join Stephen, who had brought Ann and Adam.

The chapel held about a hundred guests and it had begun to fill. As they entered and Adam saw the flowers and the closed caskets, he stopped. Ann knelt and whispered to him and he gripped her hand. They moved to seats reserved for them at the front right of the chapel. Rachel helped them get settled, asked Cole to save her a seat, and moved back outside to meet the arriving family.

Four cars came in together. Sandy and Clare were accompanied by Sandy's sister and husband. Rachel met the group and hugged the boys' mom. "I'm so sorry, Sandy."

"Thank you for sending friends to be with Peter this morning."

"Whatever I can do," Rachel promised from the depth of her heart. She took from her pocket a red-white-and-blue ribbon formed into a heart. "Marissa wanted very much to be here. She sent this for you."

Sandy teared up when she saw it and pinned it to her lapel. "Greg

261

was so happy to have her in his life. Please tell her that."

"I will." Rachel knelt down. "Hi, Clare." She offered the white stuffed rabbit she had brought.

"It's sad without my brothers."

"I know, honey," Rae whispered. "Adam is here. You said you wanted to sit with him?"

The girl solemnly nodded.

Rachel offered her hand. And the small hand gripped hers.

Rachel escorted Sandy and Clare and their family into the chapel and to the front row. Clare was clearly relieved to see Adam and sit with him. Rachel had attended many funerals over the years. It was hard for a child to absorb the emotions of such a day and the feeling of anxiousness about what was coming. Adam was feeling the same. He leaned over to talk to Clare and smile at the rabbit she held. Clare smiled back. Sandy settled her arm around her daughter to try to reassure her.

Rachel slid into her seat beside Cole and was embraced with the comfortable weight of his arm around her shoulders. He was a safe harbor in the midst of this emotional storm. Two caskets, two brothers. The sea of flowers around them and the pictures that remembered the boys as they had been just made the loss heavier. Greg had died with a gun in his hand, angry. No one could go back and give him another chance to make a different decision. Yesterday's funeral had been tragic, but this one was weighted with a deeper grief.

The chaplain rose to start the service.

Sandy did not try to speak during the program. Her sister, brother-in-law, and pastor spoke for her. It was a beautiful service in its music and its words, remembering the love of both a mother and a father for their sons. That Sandy had been able to gather herself to plan it while trying to help her ex-husband through his own crushing grief was all the more a tribute to her sons. For Clare's sake, Sandy was dealing with it. And Rachel knew that no matter how many people were here to offer support, for Sandy the loneliness of the moment was stark. She leaned forward to rest a hand against Sandy's shoulder.

When the service concluded, friends of the family joined together to carry the coffins from the chapel to begin the short trip to the graveside. A solemn procession gathered to follow.

Chairs had been set up under the canopy where the boys would be laid to rest. Rachel watched Clare cross to take Adam's hand. He leaned over and whispered something, touching the rabbit she clutched, and for a moment Clare smiled. The two children were leaning on each other and bonding together through this morning.

The graveside service was mercifully brief.

When the pastor said the final prayer, silence descended as Sandy lifted Clare in her arms and they walked forward to the side of the caskets to say a final good-bye. As they stepped back, Clare wrapped her arm around her mom's neck and laid her head down against Sandy's shoulder.

In small groups, guests came forward to say private condolences. Rachel walked around the chairs to join Ann and Adam.

"Can I go up to the grave?" Adam whispered to his mom.

"Go ahead, honey." Rachel stood with Ann and watched as Adam walked to Tim's coffin to say his own farewell to his friend. It was painful to watch—Rachel wiped her eyes with her fingers, and Ann offered her a tissue.

"You have a son to be very proud of."

"I am."

Adam walked back, and Rachel could see in his entire body the sadness that gripped him. He was no longer trying to bravely hold back the tears; he wiped his eyes. "Mom, can I come back and see Tim tomorrow? He's going to be so lonely here."

The question broke Rachel's heart and everyone else's who heard it. Ann hugged her son. "I'll bring you."

Adam wrapped his arms around her. "I left Tim my good comic book in his memorial box. I still owed him for the baseball card he gave me after the flood."

"That was nice of you."

Stephen knelt beside them and rubbed Adam's back. "Come on,

buddy. Let's go home." He picked up the boy.

Rachel struggled to stop her tears. Cole hugged her. "I know, honey. I know."

Cole stopped Rachel from returning to the chapel after the cars carrying Sandy and her family pulled out of the parking lot. "Stop for a moment. Catch your breath."

She leaned against him. "I'm okay."

Cole wrapped his arms around her and just held her.

"Jennifer has planned her funeral."

He rubbed her back. "She told me." It had been a heartbreaking phone call as he called to hear how Jennifer was doing and she passed on the news in her quiet, calm way.

"I like the music Sandy chose. It wasn't trying to pick you up or lead you somewhere. It was just peaceful and let you remember the music."

Cole blinked away tears. "Anything you need to tell Jennifer you haven't already told her?"

"Good-bye has been said many times and in many ways. But the day that comes when Jennifer isn't a phone call away... It's going to hurt so bad."

"I know, Rae."

He loved this woman. And if he could take away the pain of the moment, he would do so in an instant. How did you tell someone you loved good-bye? It just wasn't something you were ever prepared to do. Over twenty years of history would be broken if Rachel lost Jennifer.

"I've got to shift focus and get ready for Mark's funeral. I'm working the hotline for the afternoon."

He loved her enough to release her to go do that job. "God will give you the strength you'll need," he whispered. Rachel had been given the gift of knowing what and how to reach out to touch a heart. She had given Adam and Marissa the gift that she'd be just a page away as long as they needed help. Rae had handed her cards to numerous students.

She had to go. "Come over tonight. Let me fix dinner, and we'll sit outside and watch the stars."

"I love you, Cole."

He'd been hoping to hear those words for so long. They were the most precious gift she could give him, and today, when her heart was full with so many emotions, he knew she trusted him with her heart. Cole hugged her tight. "I love you too." He wasn't sure when his emotions had fully turned to that reality, but there was no distance anymore between his dreams for his future and his feelings for her. She was the one person he had been praying to find. He loved her smile, and the way she gave without reservation, the way she loved him enough to trust him with everything going on. He brushed back her hair and kissed her. He wasn't going to let her down.

Cole fixed Rachel dinner around seven Sunday night, keeping it to basic spaghetti, salad, and hot bread. He ate quietly and watched her nibble at a salad she was too tired to eat.

She eventually just set down her fork. "I appreciate this, your quietness. Gage pushes."

Cole thought about that. "Gage likes to listen to himself talk."

She paused in lifting her glass and laughed. "You're right. He does."

"He's also worried about you."

"Join the crowd." She rested her chin on her hand and circled her glass, pushing the moisture around. "I'm tired, Cole, deep inside bone tired."

He leaned over and rubbed her back. "You've been doing a great job. And try to remember that God designed us to sleep for a third of our existence, and you are woefully behind." A few hours at a time over the last week were not enough to keep her going.

"I'm getting a crash course in how to lean hard against His strength," Rachel said. She shifted away her plates and lowered her head onto her arms. "I'm just going to rest here a while before I go back to the hotel for the night. Wake me when the brownies are done?"

He glanced at the timer he had set. "You've got fourteen more minutes."

"I'll take it."

He rose to get the teapot as it began to whistle. Rachel had stressed her voice to the limit today. Hank barked once and Cole went to let his dog in. He turned on the backdoor light. The weight Rachel had to carry wasn't over, for the coming week would be uniquely stressful. With the funerals over and school back in session, it would be a struggle for the students to accept normalcy in life. They still felt overwhelming grief and had to return to the schools where the violence had occurred.

Cole shut off the timer and pulled out the brownies to cool.

"Rachel."

She didn't stir.

Cole brushed her hair back and realized she had already fallen asleep. He thought about moving her but in the end decided to simply let her rest where she was. He kissed her forehead. "Sleep well."

He quietly put dinner away.

The lights shining across the window warned him. He moved to the back door to meet the unexpected company.

"Can I come in, Cole?"

"Sure, Lisa."

She knelt to greet his dog. "Where's Rachel?"

He nodded to the kitchen. "She came over for dinner, laid her head down on her arms, and fell asleep."

"She's exhausted."

"Past it. You've got news."

Lisa pushed her hands into her back pocket. "More of the inevitable, we're back to looking at the evidence that Brian Rice murdered his ex-wife and that probably started this rolling crisis of events."

"I hate to wake her up."

"I'm awake," Rachel said, reluctantly stirring. "It's going to be hard to prove since Brian's alibi for the night was his son, and Mark is dead. He's not around to admit he lied."

Lisa tugged out a chair beside Rae. "We've had harder challenges.

If you can handle it, Marcus would like to meet tomorrow afternoon to go over what we've found."

"I'll be there."

Lisa looked at him.

"We both will," Cole agreed.

Cole had sent brownies with her to the hotel. Rachel let herself into the room she had made her home, balancing the package, grateful for the freedom that came with being anonymous. Now that the funerals were over and the schools were reopened, the reporters had probably moved on from her apartment, but she was too tired to go check. Marcus's gift of the hotel voucher had become a source of refuge for her.

She pushed off her shoes and left them at the end of the bed. She laid her pager and phone on the dresser. She only had a few calls to return and they could wait a few minutes.

Her hardest work of this crisis was coming up in the next week. She had to walk the fine line to teach how it was possible to continue to grieve while at the same time you went on with life. One action did not contradict the other. But for students stuck on either side of that line, it was hard to understand those on the other.

In a sea of people wanting to move on, there were many who weren't ready yet. Rachel had cried herself out during the day, sharing tears with students struggling with the fact that their lives were torn apart and yet a new week was coming and it was time for them to get back to the routine of being a student. The sympathy of last week would give way to encouragement, which would appear like pushing to those who needed to move more slowly.

Rachel turned on the television for the first time in a week and listened to the late news as she got ready to turn in.

She picked up her diary from the bedside. She tried to keep a diary during a crisis if only because it was a safe place to process her own emotions. She turned to a blank page.

Day 6.

The last funeral was today.

Jesus, I am so glad I saw the verse in the Bible when You saw Lazarus's tomb. It said, *"Jesus wept."*

I cried today.

My heart breaks for the four children who were lost.

Every night I have come to You for strength for the next day.

I come tonight to ask for sleep, renewal, and strength.

Send Your healing, dear Lord. You understand what is happening here much more profoundly than I.

R.

She closed the diary. News about the funerals came on the television and Rachel reached for the remote to turn it off. She couldn't handle any more sadness today. Instead of hitting the off button, she accidentally changed the channel. The laughter on the show stopped her and she watched for a moment, smiling. She moved pillows around and settled down to watch the old comedy. Her emotions lifted as she listened to the soundtrack of laughter.

Rachel wasn't setting aside the sadness as she normally did. It remained heavy on her heart, a burden that was difficult to lift. In the nearby hotels there were other counselors from the National Crisis Team similarly ending their evenings. Only they were carrying the weight of this crisis not knowing beforehand the community and students they had come to help. They came because of the need. There were days it was easier not to know the community you were trying to help.

Rachel reluctantly reached over to the side table and picked up the composition book that recorded this crisis. Over time, every crisis brought a change to her life, and this one was bringing a change to her focus and a reexamination of where she was heading. For the first time a tragedy was teaching her that maybe she was at her limit of what she could absorb for a while.

Life was short. Sometimes cut shorter. She traced the names in the book. So many kids had been impacted by this event.

She knew what drove her desire to help. She saw a child hurting and couldn't stop herself from putting her arm around that child. In the midst of her own personal tragedy as a child, she'd been chosen by the O'Malleys. For years she had been giving back by choosing children from within a tragedy she would give her card to with a promise to help no matter what the cost, what the duration, what the need.

She had found that same kind of lifeline with God. No matter what the need or when she called for help, He was there with everything she required. There was never any lack either in His love or His provision.

She had returned to the cemetery before going over to see Cole. She sat by the gravesides of Greg and Tim, and she began to face the hardest question: Did she have it in her to sit beside the graveside that was coming, one for Jennifer, for the first O'Malley to die? This family would need her then in a very big way, and she wasn't sure if she could meet that need.

Jesus, it's a lonely time tonight.

The phone rang as Rachel dozed watching TV. She reached for it and offered a sleepy "hello," knowing only a few people had this number.

"Rae, I'll be by to pick you up in ten minutes," Cole said, his voice tense, a total change from when she had last seen him.

She swung her legs over the edge of the bed. "What's going on?"

"They found the missing Amy Dartman."

All the implications of that news settled in. She'd known since last week that Amy was missing and that Marcus and Quinn were part of the investigation. She'd known then that the answer would be terrible news when it came. A missing person had been found, and they had contacted Cole. She didn't ask questions. There would be time for those soon. "I'll be waiting by the lobby door when you get here." She glanced out the window and changed to jeans and a sweatshirt, adding a windbreaker. She pushed keys and cash into her jeans pocket and tucked her phone and pager in her jacket pocket. She headed downstairs.

Cole pulled to a stop before her building eight minutes later, driving a fire department SUV. He leaned over and opened the passenger door as the vehicle was left running. She was hit with the strong smell of pine air freshener. The attempt to kill the smoke smell had been a bit overdone. Cole waited until she was buckled in and then picked up the radio and called in to dispatch.

"Where are we going?"

"Carillon Estates. The river finally abated enough to get into the cut-off homes that had taken the brunt of the flood damage."

The expensive homes. She'd been meaning to get down there to see the situation but never had. Another team had been working that subdivision. "Who called you?"

"Lisa. She asked that I pick you up."

Rachel huddled in her jacket. They had found Amy Dartman. Rachel had hoped it would be alive, that Amy had somehow been gone by choice, but with Lisa involved, that clearly wasn't the case. "Do you know why Lisa asked for me?"

"No."

It was a quiet drive that took twenty minutes. The area was crowded with vehicles: police, the coroner's office, rescue personnel, and the media. Cole flipped on his blue light and a cop waved him through toward the center of the scene.

The river had not given up its turf without a fight. The stretch of homes on this block was badly damaged. Near the river four homes had been destroyed, the walls knocked out and roofs caved in. The water was receding, but it remained several feet deep in homes at the end of the block. The devastation had left a river of mud and piled debris.

Rachel got out and stood by the vehicle, scanning the area. She saw Marcus and Quinn talking with a cop and eventually spotted Lisa and Jack. The fire department rescue boat had been brought in. "Stay here for the moment," Cole requested.

She nodded and leaned against the vehicle, watching as Cole crossed over to the assembled group. It was a long conversation, but eventually Cole broke free to rejoin her.

"The collapsed house on the far left—a car crashed through the windows and ended up in the living room. The driver is unidentifiable as the vehicle has been underwater three weeks, but the ID on her is for Amy Dartman. They need the car hauled out of there."

"How?"

Cole opened the back door of his vehicle and took out his heavy gear. "We're going to haul a chain in there by boat, attach it to the car, and pull the wreck out. At this point the river has beaten the car to pieces. Dragging it out isn't going to change the evidence much."

She held his coat and helmet as he pulled on boots. "Do you ever get asked to do simple jobs?"

"I was asked to rescue a cat once," Cole offered. "Lisa's going to have another tough case to solve."

"No wonder they couldn't find Amy. The car was inside a collapsed house."

"Not something they considered," Cole agreed. He slipped on the coat.

"Be careful out there."

His gloved hand touched her cheek. "Always. Lisa needs to talk with you about Amy's parents before she calls them. It may be a few minutes though before she's free to come over."

"I'll wait here."

Cole joined Jack at the boat. Rachel watched them push off for their grim task.

They worked their way to the destroyed home and Cole slipped from the boat. He waded in to attach the chains. Cole came back and signaled the tow truck. The winch started. They hauled the car out of the destroyed house.

The river had beaten the car into a hunk of metal.

When it was pulled clear of the water, Lisa and her team moved in. Quinn and Marcus joined the group. Rachel watched as a photographer came in, the car door was forced open, and a body bag was brought in. When the body was removed, a preliminary search of the vehicle began.

How could Lisa do this job? It was one thing when someone had just died and looked very much as if they were asleep, but when they had been underwater for so many days...

Quinn was the first one to break free and come to join her.

"Is it Amy?"

"Yes. Her seat belt was half off like she was trying to get out of the car," Quinn said. "I can see how it happened. Carol's murder happened late on a Friday night; it's raining; Amy witnessed the murder; and she's driving on roads at high speed trying to get away from the killer chasing her. We know Rosecrans Road was flooded that night, as were several others. She drove into water and thought she could get across, not realizing how deep it was or how powerful, and got swept into the river."

Quinn pointed to the wreckage. "See how the back fender and trunk is crushed in? Something hit that car hard, or the car hit something hard. That impact jammed the doorframe so even if she could get leverage against the force of the water, she couldn't get the door open. It looks like she was trying to get out the window but she drowned before she succeeded."

"Does this help solve what happened that night?"

"It only explains the mystery of what happened to Amy. The real work will happen at the lab to see if there are any clues that can still be found in all this water-soaked evidence."

The drive back to the hotel was quiet. "Would you like a dry towel? I've got a couple in my emergency bag," Rachel asked Cole as he pulled to a stop in front of her building.

"I'll clean up at the fire station. I'm getting accustomed to being wet and uncomfortable."

He had to be miserable. "It has been an unusual couple weeks for water. Oh—" she dug in her pocket—"for you." She held out his new watch. "I kept it nice and dry." She'd had it in her hand most of the night and the metal still felt warm.

Cole slipped it back on. "I appreciate it."

"I hope you get a chance to go home before dawn." She didn't want to say good night, but it was very late. He needed time to decompress from this.

"I'll help Jack get the boat cleaned up and then call it a day."

She slipped from the vehicle so he could get going. "Good night."

"If it's not too late when I get home, I'll give you a call and let you say good night to Hank."

She closed the door and leaned against the window so she could smile over at him. "Do that."

They looked at each other, neither one ready to close the evening with action. "Want to talk about the weather awhile so we don't have to call it a night?" he asked, hopeful.

She stepped back with a laugh. "Go to work, Cole."

"Yes, ma'am."

Thirty-four

Lisa, take the whiteboard." Marcus pitched her a marker as more people came into the conference room to join them Monday afternoon. "I want to go back as far as we have leads on the missing gun, and that starts with the murder of Carol Iles."

Cole looked around the assembling group. From the breadth of people Marcus had pulled together Cole could see how rapidly the school shooting was rolling together with the other investigations into one very broad case.

"Just a sec, Marcus." Lisa leaned over to confer with Detective Wilson and then moved to the board. "I'm going to give a brief summary of the time line and then come back to discuss the details within each. Hold the questions for a moment." She pushed a pad of paper down the table. "Dave, scribe this for me. Some of this information has been coming in over the last hour."

Lisa wrote the date March 16. "Carol Iles was shot with a .38 that Friday night. That same night Amy Dartman disappeared. The lab evaluation on her vehicle came in last night—Amy's car was probably run off the road. You can see where her vehicle was hit from behind. Her death is also considered a homicide."

Lisa drew a line connecting the two names. "We have placed Amy at Carol's house that night. We believe she was there when Carol was murdered and tried to run from the scene. We assume the same man who shot Carol also ran Amy off the road. We know Carol was shot in her living room, by someone who stood a few feet inside the front door. The floodwaters have limited what we've been able to recover about that shooter."

Lisa drew a line on the board.

"From there we have nothing on the .38 until it is used again on April 24 to kill Tim at the middle school. Where was it in between those times? Where did it go after the twenty-fourth? Those remain central questions to resolve."

She connected with an arrow the school shooting back to the murder. "We're coming back to the original theory that Carol's murder was a domestic case—Brian Rice killed his ex-wife. His son is just too strong a link to ignore. Brian's alibi for the night of her murder is his son Mark. We have them confirmed at a basketball game at the high school, but the coach said Mark was ejected from the game and sent back to the locker room early in the first quarter. While parents report Brian did take Mark home after the game, Brian left the gym when his son was ejected, and we've not been able to confirm where he was for a period of time during the game. We know he wasn't with his son in the locker room when the coach got back there after the game. Wilson is not ready to say Brian's alibi has been broken, but he's close."

Cole watched Rachel's head nod down against her chest as she fell asleep. He gently pushed Rachel's chair. She jerked awake and shook her head, then tipped her chair back on two legs to rock and keep moving. She'd been returning pages throughout the night and her sleep had been sporadic.

"Can you break his alibi through tracing the guns?" Marcus asked.

Lisa looked to Wilson. "The most likely theory is that Brian killed his ex-wife Carol with the .38, and he kept the gun. Mark lifted the guns from his dad and he brought the .38 to school along with the two .45s."

"What do the prints show on the two .45s that were recovered?" Marcus asked.

"Mark handled the guns and loaded the clips of both. Greg's prints were found only on the grip of the .45 caliber gun he had picked up."

"But what set off the school shooting? There had to be a triggering event, and Tim, Mark, and Greg aren't around to tell us what it was." Quinn nodded to the board. "What's between March 16 and April 10? A river and a flood. No one who murdered Carol is going to hold on to the weapon used in the crime. It got pitched in the river. Only the floodwaters left items behind when it receded."

Rachel's chair fell back to four legs with a small crash. "At Adam's sleepover with Tim, he said they were taking Greg's metal detector to search the riverbanks. Adam was excited about the chance to go exploring again. They had already found three silver dollars."

Marcus turned toward her. "If Tim found that .38, Adam would know about it."

She rubbed her eyes. "He wouldn't want to darken the memory of his friend by saying Tim had taken the handgun to school. In an awful way this makes sense. Tim was getting bullied by Mark. What does a boy getting bullied do? He boasts, 'Back off, I've got a gun.' That might be the trigger that led to the school shooting. We've got two boys goading each other to prove it."

"What time does school get out? Talk to Adam and find out if that .38 was in Tim's possession."

Rachel looked at her watch. "Ann will be picking him up in forty minutes."

"Quinn, Cole, as soon as we finish the general update go with Rachel to meet them at the school. We need to know."

Rachel nodded. Cole reached under the table and squeezed her hand.

Quinn set down the report he'd been scanning. "Was it a truck that hit Amy's car?"

"The car trunk was crushed downward when it crumpled and you can see the height of the bumper on the other vehicle," Lisa confirmed. "They're working on a warrant for Brian's truck now."

"I want to turn to the time line of what happened at the school. Are there any general questions before we do so?" Marcus asked the room at large. Quinn closed his folder and nodded toward the door. Cole and Rachel joined him to head to see Adam.

"I can't read my notes." Rachel struggled to make out the information in her composition book as Cole drove them to the school. "My handwriting wasn't even legible through a few of the days last week."

"Relax, Rae."

"I misread Adam. I asked him my standard follow-up question, and rather than answer me, Adam asked about Kate and why I had gone into the school with her. I should have seen it."

"We've known ever since Lisa figured out the gun was missing that someone had taken it. In an odd way, I hope it was Adam who took it. He's not someone who would use it. If he took it, at least Adam will have the smarts to hide it well."

Rachel looked over at the man she loved and took a deep breath. "Thank you. I appreciate your optimism."

"As bad as the school shooting was, it could have been much worse." Cole reached for her hand. "This is coming to an end, Rae. You'll get a chance to breathe again."

Rachel's pager went off. She looked at the number and tensed. It was an emergency code, and there had been only a handful of them over the years. "Not for a while. There's trouble."

Thirty-five

Rachel flipped to a blank page in the composition book as she returned the call. "I'm here, Kate."

"Are you driving?"

A chill traveled up her spine. "Cole is."

"I was at the high school when the middle school reported a problem with a number of backpacks left behind after school was let out. With everyone a bit spooked, I've been helping clear them. I found Adam's and gave his mom a call to let her know it had been left behind. Rae, Adam is missing. He called his mom and asked to go home early, that he wasn't feeling well. Ann said when they got home Adam asked her if she would fix some macaroni and cheese and then he went to lie down. When she went to check on him ten minutes later, she found his bedroom window wide open and he was gone. Stephen's on his way to Ann's now, and I'm pulling together a search group."

Rachel reached out and touched Cole's arm. "Hit the car horn and warn Quinn. I need you to divert to Ann's home."

"What's wrong?"

"Adam's missing."

She didn't have time to explain beyond that as she dropped the call with Kate and turned her attention to the composition book she had been assembling. She traced back the web of notes she had for Adam's friends and began placing calls, looking for anyone who might know his plans.

But as she spoke with each friend, it became obvious that Adam had told no one. He would have shared his secret with his best friend Tim, but his best friend was dead. And in trying to protect Tim, Adam was trying to take an adult-sized problem on his own shoulders.

She closed the phone, feeling lost, not knowing what else to do.

"Rachel, what do you need?"

"Wisdom. Where does a little boy go when he's overwhelmed?"

"We'll find him."

"We need to check Tim's grave site."

Cole reached over and squeezed her hand. "We'll start at his neighborhood first."

They turned onto Governor Street. "Cole." Rachel pointed toward the bridge. "I thought the bridge was still closed."

"It is." He slowed to look down the street. "Is that Adam?"

"I think so." The boy was trying to climb under the railing.

Rachel spotted Stephen and Ann running toward the bridge from the opposite direction.

Adam lost his balance and disappeared from the bridge. "No!"

Cole threw the car in park and was out and running along the riverbank before she got her door open. Moments later he went into the river after the boy.

Rachel ran down the riverbank and joined Ann, trying to keep up with Stephen as he raced ahead to help Cole. Rachel saw Cole grab the boy in the swift-moving current.

Cole angled himself and Adam toward the shore. Dirt crumbled beneath Rachel as she slid down the bank to the river's edge. Her feet slipped into the water as she stopped her descent. She reached for Adam as Cole dragged him close to the bank. She pulled Adam from the water, turned, and passed him up to his mom. He coughed up water.

"Go on, help Ann," Stephen urged as he pulled Cole ashore. Rachel left them and scrambled back up the riverbank.

Adam was crying in his mom's arms. Rachel ran her hand across his wet hair and dried his face with her shirtsleeve. "Adam, please, what's going on? What were you trying to do? Where were you going?"

"I didn't want Tim blamed for bringing the gun to school." His voice quivered. "I was going to put it back where Tim had first found it." Adam looked at his mom, pleading for her to understand.

"You took the gun after the shooting?" Rachel asked softly.

"I told Tim I'd meet him in the gym after he got out of his detention. I was bouncing a ball, practicing. Mark came in the back gym doors and went through to the locker room. I heard Tim and I went to see what was going on. I heard the shot and saw Mark run out, being chased by Greg. Mark dropped the gun in the hall as he ran by."

"Where is it now?"

Adam pointed back toward the bridge. "Under the bridge span. I was trying to reach it."

Stephen had joined them. "Come and show me, buddy." Stephen reached down and picked up the boy. In that simple gesture, Adam got the first assurance that the grown-ups had arrived to take over.

Ann offered Rachel a hand up.

"I'm sorry, Ann. I should have been able to help sooner."

Ann patted her shoulder. "Adam left a note on his desk. It said: '*Don't worry, Mom. I have Rachel's card.*' He knew he could count on you even if he was hiding what had happened."

Rachel wiped away tears. "You have a wonderful son, Ann. Two of them."

Ann wrapped her arm around Rachel and hugged tight. "And I've got a great friend."

"You better go join Stephen and Adam. Get Adam a hot shower and then feed him macaroni and cheese. I'll wait down here until Lisa arrives to take the weapon to the lab, and then I'll come talk to him."

Ann nodded. "Take care of Cole."

Rachel smiled. "I'll try."

Cole brushed mud from his jeans. Climbing up that riverbank had left him a mess.

"You're dripping."

"Quit laughing, Rae. I'll lean over and hug you, then you'll be dripping too," Cole threatened, even as he smiled. The river water stank. He slipped off his watch with a sigh. Water dripped from it. This one hadn't even survived a month.

Rachel offered the napkins she had found in the car. With her shirtsleeve she reached up and rubbed his cheek. "That looks like slimy mud."

"You're really finding this amusing."

"Relief. Pure relief. You did great. I want to give you a hug, but I don't want to get that wet."

"Adam's going to be fine, Rae. He's a smart kid. If you want to stay with Ann and Adam for a while, I'll head back to the fire station and get a shower."

"It might be best. Why don't we meet for dinner later?"

"I'd like that."

Tones sounded on the radio he'd left on the front seat of his car. "Get that for me please," he requested as he mopped mud and water away.

She retrieved the radio and Cole listened to the traffic. "I'm sorry, Rae. I may be gone for a while."

"What is it?"

He opened the driver's door and pulled out his keys. "A house fire. I'll call you." He gave a rueful laugh. "At least the heat will dry me out."

Thirty-six

The address of the fire was one Cole knew well, and there were some things he didn't want to tell Rachel. Carol Iles's house was burning.

The intersection of Rosecrans Road and Clover Street was closed to traffic. Cole could see in the blackness of the rising smoke and the height of the flames that the house would likely be a total loss. He parked out of the way and walked down to the scene, annoyed by the wet clothes. The house was brick, but the major parts of the structure in the roof and rooms were wood, and as they burned through they collapsed onto the bricks, bringing down part of the outside walls.

There were enough firemen trying to drown the fire it was creating another miniflood as the water that didn't turn into steam drenched the fire and ran back into the yard. Cole picked his way across the mud, seeing remnants of the police tape that had marked the home as a crime scene. "What do you know?" Cole asked the commander on the scene, shouting to be heard over the noise.

"We got here and the front of the house was fully involved with the roof of the garage smoking," he yelled back. "By the time we got hoses laid, the fire had jumped to the back. It's been burning dark smoke the entire time. Two small explosions ripped through the kitchen area. Gas pockets possibly. They both blew out as much as up."

Cole studied the blaze. "One problem—gas to the house was

turned off." The black smoke told him more than even how fast the fire spread that he was likely looking at arson. The carbon particles not burning but rather turning into black smoke told him gasoline probably wasn't used as the accelerant. "Tell your guys as they come off the fight that I'll need descriptions of what they saw. This was a crime scene, and now it's likely also an arson case."

Cole set out to circle the scene. He already knew the suspect he had in mind. Carol's ex-husband Brian Rice. Proving it wouldn't be so simple. A house known to be empty, set a distance away from neighbors, a house floor plan Brian knew: It would require coming prepared, but he could have been on scene mere minutes to set up the arson if he knew what he wanted to do. And the ignition source could be on any kind of timer, making it possible to be long gone before the house went up.

Cole walked back to his vehicle to get his gear. He had to check the chemical composition of the smoke to give him a clue of what he wanted to look for.

"Wilson, I thought you might be this way."

The detective stepped out of his car. "Arson?"

"Looks like it to me, and smells like it."

"We went to serve the material search warrant for Brian's truck and found that apparently he hadn't been home in the last three days. The newspapers and mail were piled up."

"He's at the top of my suspect list for this," Cole said.

"It's one way to destroy evidence, whatever might have been left at the house—burn it down. He's running," Wilson said.

"If he's guilty, he murdered Carol, ran Amy off the road, his son died in a school shooting, and now he's burned down Carol's home. I wouldn't stay around either. He shot his wife and threw the gun into the river. Tim found the gun and thought he could use it to get Mark to back off. Only Mark was already angry and ready to react to such a threat. He brought a gun to school too. Whether Mark ever thought he would fire the gun or not, no one will ever know, but it was a recipe for tragedy from the time Brian shot his wife. Mark was as much of a casualty as Tim."

They walked down the street to the house together. As the garage crashed in, a vehicle appeared in the wreckage. "What do you want to bet that's the truck I'm trying to serve a warrant on?"

"Tires are melted, paint is burnt off, it's crushed under the weight of rubble. Your evidence just got destroyed."

"This guy is annoying me. How long before you can sort through this?" Wilson asked.

"Tomorrow morning at the earliest. We'll cordon off the scene and let it cool for the night."

Cole walked across his backyard, carrying iced tea for himself and Rachel. She had moved her lawn chair to the side of the yard where she could watch the evergreens in the neighbor's yard. She had seen two rabbits there shortly before sundown, and for once Hank had listened to her soft admonition not to give chase. Cole had a pretty good idea his dog hadn't been able to see them.

The moon was huge as it rose in the sky tonight. He paused to enjoy the sight.

It had taken him some weeks to realize why she preferred to sit outside rather than inside during an evening. She worked so many disasters she was braced for unexpected events even when she relaxed. She preferred not to have something over her head that could fall on her. Firemen had similar learned behavior in the routines they maintained.

Cole offered her the drink. "Here you go."

"Thanks."

She was tired but relaxed to the point that she was melting into the lawn chair. Cole moved his chair over beside Rachel's and leaned down to greet Hank. The dog was flourishing under the attention.

"He's growing into his name."

Cole smiled. "He's working on it. How's Adam?"

"I spent an hour walking with him along the river, talking about Tim. He's got a few hard months coming, but he'll get through this. Can you tell me about the fire?"

He'd considered what to say during the drive home, not wanting to add this to her day, but it would be public knowledge with the morning papers. "There was an arson fire at Carol Iles's home. And Wilson recovered the truck Brian drives. Both were destroyed."

"Brian is trying to run."

"I somehow don't think he'll get far."

"While he runs, a thousand people try to cope with the chain of events he began." Rae leaned her head back and sighed. "The right answer to this is to try to let it go?"

"There's not much you can do tonight about any of it," Cole agreed.

She nodded. "The memorial rubber duck float is coming together for Saturday the fifth. Will you be able to come?"

"I've already rearranged my schedule," Cole said.

A comfortable silence stretched between them.

The dog took off barking only to get stuck in a bush. Rachel snapped her fingers at him, laughing. "Hank, leave my bunny rabbits alone."

Cole caught the dog's collar as he raced back. "Yes, I know this is your turf. But you have to learn to share."

"I'd like to take him with us next time we visit Adam and Nathan."

"He'd like that," Cole agreed. One hand holding his dog still, Cole leaned over and kissed Rachel.

Her hand tightened around his wrist to keep him close. She kissed him back. "Thanks. I've been thinking about that for days. I've missed you."

"Same here."

Her pager went off.

He laughed at her expression. "Answer it."

She reluctantly released his wrist. She picked up the pager and her phone and tugged Cole over to listen in to the call. "You'll want to hear this."

"Hi, Jen."

"Tom is on board."

Rachel picked up her notebook and flipped to the short list of wedding plans. "That just leaves the puzzle of getting Kate there. She's already getting a bit suspicious."

"Lisa wants to handle it."

"Tell her not to make assumptions. Surprising a cop can elicit an interesting reaction."

Jennifer laughed. "I'll warn her. Let me talk to Cole a minute."

Rachel raised an eyebrow.

"Give me the phone," Cole said, chuckling. He walked toward the house so the conversation would remain private.

When he rejoined Rachel a few minutes later, he handed her the closed phone.

"I'm like Kate," she mentioned. "I don't like surprises."

Cole smiled. "You'll like this one."

Marcus followed Kate into her apartment. He bent to scoop up her tabby cat and ruffled his ears as Marvel waffled between hissing back and purring. Kate was still talking on the phone with Wilson about the nationwide search for Brian Rice. Marcus bet he'd be picked up within twenty-four hours. The system was designed to find murderers trying to flee.

Since Kate's conversation sounded like it would take a while, Marcus stepped into the kitchen and raided the cupboards. The smell of tuna fish turned the ambivalent cat into his new best friend. Marcus admired the rascal. This family had a habit of adopting pets that were...interesting. He fixed himself a peanut butter and jelly sandwich and made a mental note to get Kate a new calendar. She was still on last year.

"Bring me something to eat, will you?" Kate called from the living room.

Marcus fixed her a sandwich and himself a second one. He carried the plate and two glasses of milk into the living room and set them on the end table.

She had collapsed facedown on her couch. He tickled the bottom of her foot. "Who else is coming over tonight?"

Kate leveraged herself up to reach for the late dinner. "Stephen was going to come by after his shift. Jack and Lisa are working. I didn't want to bother Rachel. She desperately needs a night off."

Marcus sprawled in the corner chair. "What decisions need to be made?"

Kate reached for her Bible and retrieved the envelope inside the cover. She handed over a small slip of paper. "Jennifer found it in the old scrapbooks." Marcus read the list and was smiling as he got to the bottom.

Lisa had been scribing during the family meeting where they chose a last name. Her handwriting had been legible in those days. They had settled on the name O'Malley, and in the margins she had scrawled a note about their twenty-fifth family anniversary.

"We should move up the anniversary celebration."

Marcus looked at Kate. He folded the note and handed it back.

"She's not going to get another remission, Marcus."

"I would not bet against Jennifer. She's been beating what her own doctors thought was possible time and time again."

"I want us to have one final celebration as a family before we face losing her. This would be perfect. I'm worried about how everyone is going to react to her death, and a gathering like this would be a good thing."

"Stephen is the wild card," Marcus agreed.

Kate picked up her cat and Marvel sprawled on the couch, taking a full cushion. "Stephen has nowhere to put the pain he feels. It's bottling up in him."

"He's going to retreat emotionally," Marcus predicted.

"I think so."

"He doesn't want to accept Jesus, and with the rest of us having made that commitment, he's feeling pretty alone through this. He doesn't have the same confidence we do that Jesus will carry this. Kate, we don't need to have a celebration for Jennifer's sake. She is already comfortable with the day-to-day time she has left with us. We do need something to look forward to as a family for after her death. You and I have to make sure this family sees a future together and that twenty-fifth anniversary will be well timed. Far enough in the future to make it a place to be our turning point."

"I don't want to look that far out."

"I know." He had guarded this family for years, and his toughest challenge was coming. "The same thing that holds us so close together is the one thing that will threaten to tear us apart. Will we still risk loving each other this much after we take the pain of losing Jennifer? Or will we start to hold back a little just because it hurts so badly to take the loss?"

Kate didn't answer him for a long time. "I don't know what we will do."

Marcus finished his drink. "In that honesty is a scary reality."

"Remember those first days at Trevor House?"

Marcus nodded. "A common enemy. Loneliness."

"We'll rise to this occasion."

"The O'Malley spirit?"

She smiled. "We're a stubborn group."

"I'll grant you the stubborn." He reached into his pocket and pulled out an item. He tossed it to her.

By reflex, she caught the bullet.

"You came a hair's breadth away from being the first O'Malley we buried."

"Where did you find this?"

"We dug it out of your pager."

Kate paled. He was perversely pleased to see it. "Dave wasn't too happy with you."

"He knows?"

"Why do you think he bought you the bulletproof vest?"

She buried her head under a pillow.

Marcus smiled. They were a family of survivors. He was depending on that.

Ann had made her final decorating decision to do the living room in bold blue and white, with red accents in the fabrics. Rachel had come over Tuesday to see Adam to reassure herself he was getting over his dunking in the river, but it wasn't long before she had picked up a paintbrush to help out. Rachel thought the color combination was excellent, and she found painting therapeutic. She edged the door frame in blue. Not for the first time she considered taking it up as a hobby. Cole had baseball; she needed a hobby too.

Nathan peeked around the doorway. Rachel held up her paintbrush to keep from dripping on his hair. He put his hand over his mouth in an exaggerated motion for silence. Rachel smiled. The boy was adorable. She pointed toward Ann who was painting the window frame. The boy tiptoed across the room. Small hands reached around to cover Ann's eyes.

"Who is it?"

Nathan giggled.

"Adam, you've shrunk. Oh, no."

Ann reached behind her to Nathan and tickled him. He broke into peals of laughter as he was pulled around onto her lap. "You've had chocolate milk."

"Come play."

Ann hugged him. "In five minutes, sweetie. Turn on the egg timer."

"Go see the river?"

Ann looked over at Rachel.

"Yes, it's important they both be comfortable down there and know how to be there safely."

"Okay, we'll walk down to see the river. Tell Adam."

Nathan ran to find his brother.

"Adam will be fine with it. I intentionally walked with Adam down by the river yesterday."

Ann smiled. "It's Nathan who will be the challenge. He thinks his big brother got a special treat by being able to swim in the river."

"Then we definitely want to take the boys to the river and remind Nathan how muddy it is," Rachel agreed.

Ann closed her paint can. "Thanks for coming over today. It helped, just to remind Adam even after the crisis at the bridge that the day after really is normal and he's getting treated the same as before."

Rachel knew exactly what she meant; it was one of the reasons she had come. "You're very welcome, Ann."

Thirty-seven

The Saturday of the rubber duck charity memorial was sunny and bright, with a steady breeze from the west. Rachel was proud of the students. From an idea to an event, they had drawn together to plan something that was an honor to the students who had been hurt and killed. They had drawn together in unity. The streets by Governor Bridge had been closed off and lawn chairs and blankets lined the riverbanks. The proceeds of this event were being dedicated to fund the arts and sports programs at the schools. It was fitting that Brian Rice had been arrested that morning in Ohio. There was finally truly closure to the events of the last month.

Rachel uncapped her black waterproof marker. She had decorated her yellow rubber duck with a bright red ribbon.

Nathan landed against her knees. "Look at mine."

He had added a big black stripe down the back of his yellow duck. "What's his name?" she asked, smiling at him.

"Skunk. The river is icky."

"Muddy," Rachel agreed. She added her name to the bottom of her duck. "Okay, Adam, you can add mine to the truck." The boy took it and headed toward the collection site. The huge truck set at the center of the bridge was filling up with thousands of ducks. It would soon lift and dump its load into the water and the race would be on. Adam had already dedicated one for Tim.

Cole was still working on his duck. She leaned against him. "What did you put on your rubber duck?"

Cole turned it over. "Cole & Rachel" was inscribed inside a heart. "Oh."

He laughed and leaned over to kiss her. There was a point of stability in her daily life now and it centered on Cole. Up until this point the stability in her life had been her family, but now Cole was also there as a solid wall to lean on. She loved him so much.

"Yuck."

Rachel leaned down and tickled Nathan for that comment.

Cole offered his duck to Adam to take to the truck. "Here's another one." A cheer went up across the street as the school band began the school song. "They did a great job organizing this. How many ducks were bought?"

"Over nine thousand, I think."

He picked up another duck to decorate.

"How many did you buy?"

Cole smiled. "A few." He dedicated a duck to each of the students who had been injured and then started on one for each guy at the fire station. Adam took handfuls of ducks to the truck, slowing his steps on his last trip so Nathan could keep up carrying the final duck Cole had decorated.

The program began at noon. Rachel kept an eye on the crowd of students. They had come out in school colors to show a unified spirit, and for the first time she saw more smiles than tears in the clusters of students. They were turning the corner two weeks after the shooting, coming together to help each other move on.

Adam took Nathan's hand and led the way down to join Stephen and Ann. They had set out a blanket on the riverbank where there would be a good view.

Cole took Rachel's hand and pointed to the fire truck behind them. "Let's get higher." The department had brought the boxes of ducks over, and a crew was staying at the event on the off chance there was need for a medical presence. Cole gave her a boost up onto the fire truck.

Sitting up on the hose bed they had a great view. Jack joined them.

On the bridge a long solemn whistle blew. The truck raised its bed and the rubber ducks slid out into the river. A huge cheer erupted. A river of rubber ducks with black sunglasses began their journey.

"There's mine." Jack pointed. His had been spray-painted fluorescent blue.

"Trust you to get colorful." Rachel watched the ducks drift in the water, bounce off each other, swirl together in eddies, and then continue their journey downstream.

Rachel picked up her program. She was going to be adding it to her memory box.

"Did you read Gage's tribute this morning?" Cole asked, unfolding his newspaper to show her.

Rachel nodded. "He did a magnificent job." She had expected nothing less from her friend.

She looked around the crowd of students one last time. They were turning the corner today in a corporate way, giving each other permission to go on with their lives. It was the right memorial and at the right time.

Rachel looked down at her pager. For the first time in weeks it was quiet.

Rachel was asleep on a gym bleacher at the community center. Cole paused beside her to read her sweatshirt. Something about honey and cream. Rachel's arms were folded across her chest and she was holding a towel even in her sleep.

Stephen shot a basket from near the half-court line. It hit the rim, and he went after the rebound to grab it and put up another shot. "Come on, Cole. Let's play some one-on-one."

"Is she going to fall off that bench?"

"Doubtful. It's her spot. She's gotten lots of practice ignoring a basketball game. She comes to hold the towels."

Cole set down his gym bag. "I can see that."

He slipped off his watch and added it to the towel Rachel was guarding. He let a finger brush her cheek as he smiled, and then he crossed to join Stephen on the court. "What are we playing to?"

"Whoever is ahead in half an hour."

Cole nodded and caught the basketball. He shot a few practice hoops. "No one else is coming?"

"The guys will dribble in over the next hour if they're free."

Cole tossed Stephen the ball and settled in to play the game. It felt good to be back on the court.

As she awoke, Rachel was aware that a rather intense basketball game was going on. She could hear Jack and Stephen doing their floor chatter as they tried to figure out how to get the ball around their opponents and to the basket. It was a familiar sound, for basketball was an O'Malley family tradition. She opened an eye at the sound of bodies making contact and got a good look at her brother Marcus as he crashed into the wall a short distance away from her perch. The basketball bounced from the rim toward the far wall and got scooped up by Cole. Shirts were plastered by sweat and the guys were breathing hard.

She'd been tired enough to sleep through it.

Rachel sat up, realizing she had become the guardian of two towels, a watch, and someone's sunglasses. Lisa on a bleacher above her handed down a water bottle. "Thanks."

Stephen noticed. "Hey, sleeping beauty is waking up."

Quinn ran past. Rachel slipped on the glasses and found there was no corrective prescription. "Who's winning?"

Jack laughed. "Depends on which scorekeeper you listen to."

Cole used the fact Jack was distracted to score from the baseline.

"I see I'm bringing you good luck," she called as Cole ran back the other way on defense.

"Just sit there and keep smiling, honey."

The *honey* paused Marcus in his tracks and Cole stole the ball.

Lisa laughed. "You are good luck."

"Why aren't you playing?" Rachel asked her sister.

"Too much sweat on the court. You were exhausted."

"It's catching up with me," Rachel admitted. "This is a nice place to hide." She settled her elbows back on the bleacher behind her and watched the guys run the court. "I wish Jennifer were here to see this."

Lisa held up the camcorder on the bench beside her. "I caught about twenty minutes of it for her."

Rachel held out the water bottle the next time Cole ran by, and he took it with a grateful smile. He had a moment to grab a drink and toss it back to her before Jack invaded his corner of the court.

Cole had been accepted into her family. It was comforting not to just know it but to see it.

Lisa moved down to sit beside her. "Are we ready?"

"The wedding dresses arrived," Rachel replied. "My list is complete. We're ready."

Thirty-eight

Rachel circled the hotel suite, mingling. It felt good to laugh with family. The double wedding they had been planning for weeks was an hour away, and the party had already started. It had begun as something the O'Malleys could look forward to with joy and had become a powerful healing moment for them all. In their own way they were allowing each other permission to enjoy the day even as they corporately worked to accept the fact Jennifer's days were numbered.

Jennifer had been in charge of the guest list and she had cast a wide net. "Marissa, can I get you anything?" Rachel stopped beside her friend.

"I'm fine. Clare is helping me out with the decorations." Marissa smiled at the girl drawing a heart on her cast below the knee.

"See?" Clare asked, pausing to show off the artwork.

"Absolutely gorgeous."

The little girl beamed at her.

Marissa nodded around the suite. "Do you think Kate will be surprised?"

Rachel looked around the transformed hotel suite. "She's going to be overwhelmed." Roses were everywhere. The wedding plans had been cut back in light of how Jennifer was feeling—they had set aside original plans from a dinner together to a large reception. But even so it was going to be a wonderful evening. There would be a beautiful double wedding ceremony with two great wedding cakes. The kids had been awed at the wedding cakes.

Gage was perched on the arm of the couch, sharing a moment with Nathan that had both the man and boy smiling at each other. Nathan could wrap anyone around his finger, and Gage already had an incredibly soft spot in his heart for little boys. Ann was talking with Marcus's fiancée Shari. Rachel saw Adam tugging at his tie and Stephen knelt to help him straighten it.

Jennifer had rallied for this day and was now sitting comfortably in a plush chair set strategically to allow her to be fully involved in the coming evening events without having to move. She was talking with Dave's sister Sara and her husband Adam Black, Jack and Tom both nearby.

Cole joined her. He held out a handful of the mints he had asked her to add to the list. "I think you have managed to pull it off."

She smiled at him. She'd been dragging him all over the city in the last couple days getting the last details figured out. He'd been an incredibly good sport about it. She had so enjoyed the time with him, a chance to decompress from the stress of the last month with a man who had become so important to her. "Come here," she whispered. He kissed her and he tasted like mint. There was a time and a place for everything, and tonight she was enjoying Cole's company.

She accepted some of the mints and wished she had paused to eat dinner during the racing around to get the final details finished. "Now if the brides would just arrive." Lisa was responsible to bring Kate without letting her know what was coming. It was a tough assignment, but so far keeping this a surprise appeared to have been successful. And if Kate for some reason truly got cold feet and couldn't handle the surprise, it would simply be Lisa and Quinn getting married tonight. No one wanted to back Kate into a corner she really wasn't ready for.

"Relax. She's going to love it," Cole assured her.

"I hope so."

The grooms were pacing by the windows. Dave and Quinn were handsome men in their matching tuxes and tails. Rachel smiled as she watched them. Quinn still had on his cowboy boots.

The suite phone rang once and stopped. It was Lisa's signal that they were arriving at the hotel. Kids scurried to their planned greeting positions.

The door to the suite opened. "Surprise!" A number of flashbulbs went off to capture the moment, and only because Lisa had her arm around Kate's shoulders did the initial reaction of a surprised cop not result in something more than Kate instinctively taking a step backward out of the doorway.

Lisa laughed and hugged her. "Welcome to my wedding."

Kate looked around the suite and her smile bloomed. "Really?"

"I'm getting married tonight. And if you would like to join me, Dave has it all planned."

Kate turned a startled gaze toward Dave, who had crossed to join them.

"Kate O'Malley, will you marry me tonight?" Dave asked softly.

Her jaw didn't drop but it quivered. She threw her arms around his neck. He picked her up, holding her tight. "I love you," he whispered.

"Yes, I would love to marry you tonight." She leaned back. "Lisa didn't give away a clue. You really planned a double wedding?"

Dave kissed her. "With a lot of help." He reluctantly lowered her to her feet. He slipped off her pager. "You won't need this for a week."

"Really?"

He slipped it into his pocket. "Really."

Lisa took Kate's hand. "Come on, Kate. You've got to see the dresses. Go cool your heels guys; we'll be half an hour." With a lot of laughter Kate was pulled toward the bedroom. Rachel joined them. The dresses were center stage, laid out on the bed. White intricate lace and silk, flowing skirts, and long sleeves—they were exquisite.

Kate lifted hers up, overwhelmed. "You found it."

Rachel handed her sister a tissue. It had taken a series of long phone calls, but they had found the designer of the wedding dress she had marked in the bride's book. "Dave hasn't seen it yet. He just gave us a blank check."

"How long have you been planning this?"

"Weeks," Rachel replied, sharing a smile. "And it has been so much fun. Jennifer loved it."

Lisa turned Kate toward the mirror. "Hair first. Marissa is going to do our makeup."

They got ready, laughing as they tried to move around the bedroom in their wedding dresses. Rachel helped Marissa move around in her wheelchair and helped her as she did a beautiful job on their makeup.

"Aren't we supposed to have a rehearsal or something?" Kate asked as she studied her image in the mirror.

"Sure." Lisa stepped into white slippers. "Join Dave and say yes."

Kate laughed and picked up her bouquet.

Rachel stepped out of the bedroom to alert the guests that they were ready.

Marcus was waiting at the door to escort them. He was giving away the brides. Rachel gave the sign to Adam and he pushed the button on the tape deck. The wedding march filled the room.

It was hard to tell who was more proud, Dave or Quinn, as they came to meet their brides. The group gathered around the two couples. Rachel joined Jennifer, sitting beside her and just holding her hand, sharing the joy. The ceremony began.

Rachel had never seen Kate so emotional. Kate struggled not to cry through most of the ceremony even as her smile grew wide. Twice Kate turned and buried her face against Dave's shoulder. He rested his head against hers, whispering something that drew a silent laugh. For Kate this was a day that would transform her life forever.

Lisa's gaze rarely left Quinn's as they shared a private conversation of their own without needing to say a word.

Wedding vows were spoken. The O'Malley family expanded. They had been seven, and with Tom they had become eight. Now they were formally ten. Rachel blinked away her tears.

The couples kissed and on cue Adam started the music and Nathan cheered, a happy little boy that made them all laugh.

They moved to cut the wedding cakes amid a lot of laughter and photographs.

Rachel watched Jennifer. She had set her heart on reaching this day. Jennifer was having to conserve her energy, but she was enjoying the evening enormously.

Cole slipped his arm around Rachel's shoulders. "Good job, honey."

"I'm closing my wedding planning book for a while," she said. She was incredibly relieved to have this event successfully over.

The O'Malleys and their guests lingered and laughed and eventually by silent agreement began to disperse. Lisa and Quinn came over to say good night to Jennifer, exchanging a long hug. They were heading to Montana tonight. Dave and Kate came to say farewell and then left for a destination unknown. The other guests followed soon after, with Marcus and Shari taking Marissa and Clare home and Stephen walking down with Ann and her boys.

Jennifer wisely allowed Tom to help her turn in.

With Cole's help Rachel restored the suite to normal. She called the hotel coordinator, who had offered to refrigerate the wedding cakes and transport the wedding dresses. Rachel made arrangements for help to come up in twenty minutes. Only the multitude of roses remained to mark the weddings.

"They were gorgeous brides," Rachel remarked, kicking off her shoes.

Cole draped his tie across the arm of her chair and settled on the couch as she returned the family photo albums to their boxes. "Very. And it was an evening that filled Jennifer with joy."

"Part of this is your credit. You suggested the idea."

"I enjoy weddings," he replied, smiling. He reached in his jacket pocket and offered her a small box. "For you."

She set aside the photo album and took the small box, surprised. She opened it. There was a gorgeous bracelet inside. She lifted it from the box. On the inside was an inscription: 'A time to love' and today's date. She leaned over and wrapped her arm around his neck. "Thank you," she whispered, overwhelmed.

"Come here." Cole tugged her from the chair to the couch beside him. He took the bracelet and fastened it around her wrist. "This day needed a memory marker."

"It's a beautiful one."

His hands cupped her face. "I love you, in my mind where my thoughts reside, in my heart where my emotions live, and in my soul where my dreams are born. I love you."

Her smile quivered. She held his gaze, absorbing his expression. He meant it. And part of her began to hope as she never had before in her life. The tears began to fall as her smile grew even wider. "Oh, Cole... I love you too."

He wiped her tears for her, his hands gentle.

She laughed and helped him. "I'm sorry. All I've done is cry on you lately."

"You're smiling this time," he said tenderly, smiling back. "It's a nice improvement."

Cole settled his hands on her shoulders and rubbed his thumbs along her shoulder blades. "I'm old-fashioned, Rae. I want a family with you, and nights watching the stars, and quiet moments like this one at the end of long days."

"I've longed for such a future."

"We're going to make it together, and it's going to be special."

"I like that word *special*. A lot." She kissed him. "My brothers are going to meddle. Or have they already?"

He chuckled but he didn't deny it. "I like your brothers. I always have."

"You're going to fit in quite well. I think of them as the chivalrous sort, my brothers. They didn't have an example; they just had an idea of what a brother was supposed to be. And they have never believed in doing something partway."

"Honey, I understand family. I may not have a big one of my own, but I've got the big picture down." He brushed her hair behind her ear. "I like your friends. I like your family. It's a pretty good beginning."

"Where is Gage in that list?"

"Unique." Cole smiled. "Rae, I understand Gage. He's already been hit hard by life. As a result, he's solid. You can't intimidate him. You can't budge him. That's a man who isn't going to move from what he decides is right. I like him."

"I was afraid you wouldn't understand."

"You have a friend there that is a lifelong friend. But he can still irritate a saint when he's working on a story."

"True."

Cole interlaced his fingers with hers. "Are you ready for the next weeks? The next few days?" he asked softly.

"I have to be." She tried to capture in words what had filled her heart in the last days. "We're a strong family Cole, but if Jennifer dies... You can't replace the links that will be lost. The scar in this family will be deep and lasting. I don't know how we rebuild around such a tear."

"You'll adapt."

"Eventually. But I worry about how hard that will be and how long it will take."

"Rachel, have you ever given up on someone you gave a card to?"

She looked at him, puzzled. "No."

"The very first cards you gave out were to your family. They've got your pager number in red. You'll get your family through this."

"It feels like an incredible task."

"You'll get through it."

Thirty-nine

The roses had begun to droop. Rachel made a circle of the hotel suite removing those roses that would not last another day. She'd bring new ones tomorrow. She did her work with care, taking her time on each decision. In the month since the wedding, Jennifer had become bedridden. And with that change, there had been a shift in priorities. Rachel's pager was somewhere at home, her phone turned off, the rest of her life blocked off from today. She stayed at the hotel now, having taken a room next door to the suite.

She had been joined at the hotel by all the O'Malley's. Jennifer refused to let it be a sad gathering. The honeymooners were back, and Jennifer loved listening to the stories they had to tell.

Tom joined Rachel. He rested his hand on her shoulder and she covered it with her own. She loved this man who loved her sister. He had not slept much in the last week. "The guys said they'd meet you in the coffee shop," she passed on. Tom had begun the practice of giving Jennifer a gift each night to mark the day. The gifts were lined up on Jennifer's bedside table, small markers of victory, things to make her smile and laugh and give her joy. He wanted to buy his wife a good piece of jewelry for today, and the guys in the family had offered to keep him company for the excursion. Rachel had a pretty good idea that Tom would not be the only one opening his wallet.

"I won't be long."

"I brought a book. Don't feel like you need to hurry."

She finished the flowers and straightened pillows, then sorted magazines. Rachel stepped into Jennifer's room, moving quietly in case her sister was asleep.

"I'm awake."

"I just wanted to see if you needed anything else tonight."

Jennifer patted the bed. "Your company," she whispered.

Rachel stretched out on the bed beside her sister, tugging over one of the big throw pillows to wrap her arms around. "What are you reading?" Jennifer had her Bible open, resting against her chest.

"Ephesians. It's a wonderful book."

Jennifer was drifting in and out of sleep, the medication to stop the pain now powerful enough it wasn't uncommon to have her drift off midsentence. Rachel straightened the edge of the blanket spread over Jennifer, pink and soft, one of her sister's favorite colors.

"I was thinking…"

Rachel waited as Jennifer drifted between asleep and awake.

"…that heaven will probably be colorful."

Rachel rested her chin against her hand. "God likes colors: deep green grass, bright blue sky, vibrant red roses. I bet He made heaven beautiful like that."

"I'm ready to go, Rae," Jennifer said softly.

Rachel interlaced her fingers with Jennifer's. Her sister's hand was chilly. Rachel warmed it with hers. "Tom appreciates every day he has with you."

Jennifer smiled. "It's mutual." She touched the bracelet Rachel now wore. "Cole is a good man."

Rachel knew how blessed she was. "A veteran in a profession of heroes. I love him so much. And the best part is that he loves me too. Do you know how long I've waited to be able to say those words?"

"It makes your heart go mushy," Jennifer agreed. "You'll make a wonderful mom someday."

Rachel struggled to keep her voice steady. "I wish you were going to be here."

Jen's hand tightened on hers with what little strength she had left. "Tom promised to take very good care of you when you do someday have children; he'll be your doc a phone call away in my place. I think Cole will be a wonderful father." Jen's hand slackened around hers. "Tomorrow, would you ask Stephen to bring over my puppy…" Jen drifted to sleep.

Rachel stayed holding her hand until the clock on the dresser moved to the top of the hour. She kissed the back of Jennifer's hand and settled it below the covers, making her sister as comfortable as she could. Rachel moved the Bible and letter Jennifer had been writing to the bedside table. The tears were close but she didn't let them fall.

Jesus, give her another night of peaceful sleep, and in the morning a beautiful dawn.

This family would share her life until her last breath. And there was peace in that for both Jennifer and for them. Peace, and if not acceptance yet, at least peace.

Tom,

My dear husband, I love you with every fiber of my being. I've told you that a few times and basked in the light of your smile as I do so, but I haven't written it nearly as much as I should have. I know the lasting value of words. Your letters to me are of priceless value, sentimental and rich in shared memories. The honor of being your wife is hard to convey. There is a picture of life as it was before I met you and a picture of life as it is with you now. The cancer cannot mar what is obvious to all. I'm blessed. In your love I have found joy beyond words.

Every night you hold my hand to share a prayer with me, and every morning I watch you pray alone. When this pattern began in our marriage, why, I do not remember. But I know an evening is coming when you must pray alone because I will not be there.

I felt it important to leave with you one last prayer for when that moment comes.

It's hard to be alone. I tasted it when my parents died, and as deeply as I grieved for them, I grieved for myself even more. I was alone and I knew it. My knees shook at the idea of facing the world alone. I stiffened my spine and tried, not because I thought I could do it, but because I had no choice.

God knew. He knew that loneliness.

"Surely he has borne our grief and carried our sorrows."

I walked into Trevor House on the most terrifying morning of my life, and I ended that day still in the same place but with the O'Malley's for comfort. I didn't know God until you introduced me to Him, but I understood years later when I met Him just how much He loved me. He acted on my behalf when I didn't even know He was there. He placed me with the O'Malleys. For years they have been the source of my strength. In years to come, they will be yours.

I wish I knew what God had planned for the evening of your hardest day. I know it is coming. I am afraid I will be the cause of that deep, dark night.

My prayer on that night you must pray alone is very simple: I pray for the return of your joy.

All my love, my beloved,

Jennifer

Jennifer woke early Friday with an odd feeling in her chest. The pain that coiled around her back and numbed her legs had not changed, but something else had. *Jesus, You woke me early. Why?* It was odd to awake with an urgency and yet not have a sense that it was to pray for someone. It was for herself.

"Tom," Jennifer called softly.

He was asleep, the heavy sleep of exhaustion. Jennifer reached over and brushed her hand lightly along his jaw, loving him. He'd been holding her family together even as this day came close. She settled her hand on his pillow. "Tom."

He awoke and kissed her palm.

She loved him so very, very much. He'd filled up her life with so much joy that it brimmed over. She wore the ring he had bought her last night, a simple gold band that was beautiful. "I'd like to go outside."

He turned his head and looked at her. She loved him too much not to let him see the truth. Tears filled his eyes. She gently wiped them away.

He leaned over and kissed her. "I love you."

She slid her arms around his neck and returned his kiss. She held him, resting in the depth of that love.

"I'll get dressed," he said softly.

He took his time with the simple steps of buttoning his shirt, sitting to slip on socks and shoes. Tom wrapped her in a blanket and lifted her from the bed.

Dawn cracked the sky.

Tom took her down to the bench near the rose gardens in the park beside the hotel and sat with her in his lap. Jennifer rested her head against his shoulder. "You kept your promise. I cherished every day of our marriage."

He laid his head against hers. "Life is too short. You never got to see Paris."

"I did through your memories."

They sat in quiet, sharing without needing words. She loved this man and knew how his heart beat and what this day would be like for him. "Would you do something for me?"

"Sure." She could feel him wrestling with the emotions.

"There's a package with my diary. Give it to Stephen a year from now?"

"My promise."

She worried about her brother. She wanted so badly to see him in heaven one day. She had done what she could. The rest would have to be left to God and the other O'Malleys.

The sun appeared over the hillside. "I'm tired, Tom."

"It's okay to go home," he choked.

"Hold my hand?"

His arms tightened around her and his fingers interlaced with hers. She closed her eyes against the brightness. "I love you."

"I love you too," he whispered.

Jennifer died feeling the warmth of the rising sun.

Forty

"I am the resurrection and the life; he who believes in me, though he die, yet shall he live.'" The sun broke through the afternoon clouds as the graveside service concluded. Tom turned the pages in Jennifer's Bible, reading the Scriptures she had chosen, the pink fabric-covered book looking odd in his hand.

"'If any one serves me, he must follow me; and where I am, there shall my servant be also; if any one serves me, the Father will honor him. In my Father's house are many rooms; if it were not so, would I have told you that I go to prepare a place for you? And when I go and prepare a place for you, I will come again and will take you to myself, that where I am you may be also. For this perishable nature must put on the imperishable, and this mortal nature must put on immortality.'"

Rachel reached for Cole's hand as the final words were spoken. She wiped her eyes as "Amazing Grace" began to play. Jennifer had chosen the words as much for her husband as for them. Just listening to Tom's solemn voice as he laid his wife to rest was enough to bring the grief she had long borne back to the surface. Cole's free hand slid behind her neck and turned her face into his shoulder. How she would have survived today without him…she couldn't imagine it. She took a deep breath and turned back to listen to the service.

Jennifer was being buried next to her parents. Marcus and Stephen lifted the bouquet of roses from atop the casket and moved it to the family headstone. Jennifer had requested carnations, roses, and a simple, very private service. She had chosen the verses, the songs, keeping it short. It was a beautiful service.

Tom stepped to the casket to make his private good-byes.

Her family didn't want to stay to see the coffin lowered into the hole in the ground. But no one wanted to say the service was over either.

Stephen was the first to walk forward, touch the casket, and then walk away, back toward the chapel where the service had been held. Rachel watched him go. Stephen had already lost his younger birth sister, and now he was burying the youngest O'Malley. Even Nathan last night strangling him in a sticky hug good night had not been able to get more than a brief smile from him. Her brother was suffering the deepest of them all, for the words of hope they heard in the Scriptures he wasn't able to share.

Marcus and Shari joined Tom as he moved to place flowers in front of the inscription already added to the headstone. *Wife, friend, and beloved sister.* For Tom's sake Rachel was grateful that this long weekend journey of farewell was now concluded. Tom had accepted as much sadness and grief as he could absorb.

Lisa lifted one of the white carnations from the basket to have as a keepsake. She broke the silence among their group. "I don't know about the rest of you, but cemeteries give me the creeps."

Rachel blinked and then smiled, for Lisa was right. They had all lost and buried family and when it was personal, a cemetery was a depressing place. Too many memories were pulled back to the present.

"I thought I was the only one feeling it," Kate said. She glanced at her husband. "Shall we gather at our place for dinner?"

Dave nodded. "It would be best. Tom needs a place to relax."

"Why don't you all go, catch up with Stephen. Cole and I will be there in a minute."

"You'll give Ann a call?" Kate asked.

Rachel nodded. Stephen was the one who suggested it was best if they didn't come to the funeral today, for Adam didn't need to experience a second one in such a brief period of time.

Lisa and Quinn, Kate and Dave, walked back toward the chapel's parking lot.

Rachel released Cole's hand and walked to the side of the casket, struggling to find the final words to let Jen go. Everything she could have said had already been said while Jennifer was alive. She rested her hand against the coffin, enormously comforted that God had already given her the opportunity to say the words. *Jen, I miss you already. The O'Malleys will get through this. And we'll take good care of Tom for you, I promise you that. You led us to a hope that will endure even in this grief.* She wiped away a tear. *I love you.*

Cole rested his hands on her shoulders as she began to cry. She leaned back against him and lifted her face to the sky. He'd absorbed enough of her tears in the last month; she wasn't going to break down again, not here.

"Good-byes are hard."

Rachel rested her hand over his. He'd buried firefighters, friends killed on the job, in accidents, and even a friend who had turned to the dark side of arson. He didn't need to say words to empathize; he just had to be with her. "I've said them all. Let's catch up with the others," Rachel said, looking after where Stephen had gone.

The empty chair was haunting him. Stephen shifted his chair so the chair where Jennifer should be sitting was no longer in his line of sight. If she were here right now, she'd be kicking him under the table, trying to get him to smile. She'd taken being his little sister as a serious role. Nathan sitting on his lap bounced and pointed. "M&M?" he asked, hopefully.

Stephen tugged over the dish. He'd made the wooden candy dish for Kate as a wedding gift and the candleholders. "Which color this time?"

"Blue."

"I should have guessed that." Stephen had to dig to find one. Nathan loved the blues.

Stephen could see why Rachel loved working with kids. They were good for making sure even miserable days at least stayed on an even keel.

The family was lingering over coffee: Marcus and Shari, Kate and Dave, Lisa and Quinn, Jack and Cassie, Rachel and Cole. He could hear Tom and Ann laughing in the kitchen. They were fixing homemade milk shakes that Tom swore turned little boys into angels. They had asked Adam to help with the cherries and vanilla and flavorings. Stephen was grateful they had come. Adam was sensitive to the sadness of another funeral, but Tom and Ann were doing a good job distracting him.

Stephen wasn't sure how Tom had handled this last weekend with the equilibrium he had. *Jennifer, you married a good man.* Tom planned to return to Houston next week and the pediatrics practice he and Jennifer had shared. He'd married Jennifer knowing this day might come, and Tom had still let himself love her completely until the very end. He'd never drawn back to separate himself from the pain of this day. How Tom had found the focus to be able to read the Scripture passages and say the final amen… Stephen knew he couldn't have done it. Tom's last act of love for his wife had been to help her take care of them.

Stephen watched his family, and he struggled to make a decision. Stay, or go.

He'd been wrestling with the decision all night. The arrangements were made; they just awaited his action. And as he hugged Nathan it became simple. He couldn't handle seeing someone else die, not another man-made tragedy like the shooting, not an accident, not even another death from illness. He'd promised Jennifer, and he was going to keep his word. There was no better time than now.

Stephen hugged Nathan again and moved his chair back. "Go to Rachel, buddy. She's got the cookies."

His sister turned in her chair and accepted Nathan onto her lap. The boy mashed her in a hug and peals of laughter ensued as she tickled him. Stephen caught Cole's gaze and shared a smile with him. Rachel had found a good man too. All his sisters had.

Stephen rose and stepped into the kitchen to say good-bye to Ann. "Does this taste okay?" Adam asked, offering a long spoon and a chance to sample the just completed milk shake.

Stephen tried it. "Great."

"Not too much vanilla?"

He took a second spoonful to taste and shook his head. "Perfect."

Tom helped the boy pour the milk shakes. Adam had a long line of glasses waiting and a cup with a lid for his brother Nathan.

Ann put away the ice cream and stepped over to join him. "You're heading out?" she asked softly. They'd driven over separately.

"Yes."

Ann hugged him, not asking how he was doing, not pushing. Stephen relaxed into the hug, appreciating her comfort. She'd been there for him this month. That friendship had helped more than he could explain. "When you get home, check the back patio," he said softly. He'd made a set of bar stools for her kitchen counter.

"You finished them?"

He smiled. "The paint finally dried. The pattern choice was Jennifer's." The rose and ivy pattern had taken days to paint. He stepped back, absorbing the memory of her face, then simply nodded his good-bye.

In the dining room, Stephen paused at the head of the table by his eldest brother. "Marcus, I'm heading out."

"You want to join us for a basketball game later? Jack wants to run off dinner."

"I'll take a pass. I promised the guys at work I'd swing by and sign off some paperwork."

Marcus's gaze held his and Stephen wondered what the odds were Marcus knew he was lying. Probably pretty good. Marcus slowly nodded. "You need me, call."

"Will do." The last thing he wanted to do was give this man something else to worry about. His brother had carried the weight of arrangements for the last few days and made it possible for all of them to get through today.

With rapt attention Nathan was listening to one of Rachel's made-up stories. Stephen pointed to Jack and got a thumbs-up back. He wasn't saying good-bye. Everyone he said good-bye to died. His parents, his little sister, now Jennifer. As close as this group was, as powerful as it was to be an O'Malley, he still walked out of here knowing he was alone.

He walked out the front door, not letting himself slow or glance back. The clouds had rolled back in and a spitting rain was in the air. There would inevitably be car accidents tonight as the weather changed and people didn't slow down enough to make adequate allowances for the changing road conditions. He couldn't handle the idea of going back to work, not now, not anytime he could see in the next weeks. He tugged on the baseball cap, which was his concession to the weather.

"Stephen."

He turned as Kate called his name. She came running down the stairs to catch up with him. "You're leaving early."

"Some." He shifted his car keys in his hand. He didn't want her prying into his plans for the night, so he smiled at her and reached out to catch her hand and hold up the ring he was still getting used to seeing on her hand. "You never mentioned: What do you think of being married?"

"Marriage suits me just fine," she replied, smiling. She looked at the keys in his hand. "Are you sure you won't join us later at the gym? We'll be there quite a while."

"I'm sure."

"Where are you going?"

"For a drive," he said, telling her the truth.

He was nearly toppled by her hug. "Hey."

"Don't go."

She hadn't cried at the funeral and now Kate was threatening to bawl on him. He tried to pat her back and ease her away at the same time. "It's not forever, I promise," he said, desperate to stop the emotions and get this back to the teasing, which was about the only thing he could take tonight.

"You'll need a navigator."

He had to laugh. He'd never been able to keep a secret from her. He took off his hat and dropped it on her head, tugging the bill straight. "You're a lousy navigator."

"When will you be back?" she asked. "You haven't quit a job in my lifetime. Your boss called this morning," she explained. "He was worried."

"It's just a leave of absence." There wasn't a good explanation for his actions, and given the turmoil of the last month, he didn't feel a need to figure out a good one. "I made a promise to Jennifer; it's time I keep it. I want to drive awhile, see some of the country, think. I'll be gone until I get the answers I'm looking for."

"You'll call more than just occasionally?"

"You know I will," he reassured. "I'll have to call just to make sure you're not getting yourself in trouble, something that happens with regularity."

"Ann's going to miss you, the boys too."

"Rachel and Cole will be there for them." He glanced up at the deteriorating weather. Kate was trying to stall him and talk him out of this. He'd been on the other end of her negotiating skills too many times to miss the subtle signals. "I've got to go."

"Don't drive too far tonight."

"You've been a rock for this family since it first formed. Keep them together and strong."

"We'll be waiting for you to come back." She framed his face with her hands. "And if you're gone too long, we'll come find you."

He loved her for having become his family.

She hugged him. "Find your answers, Stephen."

He hugged her back. "Later, Kate," he whispered.

He walked to his car. His bags were in the trunk. On the seat beside him were a map and a very old note from Jennifer. "Stephen, this spot has to be seen to be appreciated. Remember the church in the southwest with the spiral staircase, built without a single nail? I met a man who built a modern day one like it. You'll need your sketch book." The note was over ten years old, and he could still hear Jennifer's joy even in her written words.

Jennifer had given him a place to begin his wandering. The O'Malleys would be fine. They had found others to share their lives with. He was the last with a restlessness inside that would not settle. He'd spent his life, first as a fireman and then as a paramedic, pouring his efforts into rescuing people. *I'm the one who needs rescuing now.* He wanted a job as far away from life-and-death decisions as he could get. He'd never figured out what it was he was after. It was time to find out.

He drove north.

Dear Reader,

Thank you for reading this story. Rachel O'Malley has been my partner throughout the O'Malley series, helping me understand her family that she loves and knows so well. Cole is the man I instinctively knew had the depth and patience for Rachel and the burdens she carries for others. They were a wonderful couple to get to know through the two books *The Protector* and *The Healer*. It was a pleasure to write their love story.

Disasters happen all around us each year, and the first responders that arrive to help—firemen, police, paramedics, and Red Cross volunteers—make the critical difference in how people recover. I'm pleased to know there are many like Rachel setting aside creature comforts and sleep to be there for others in need.

This was also by far the hardest O'Malley book to write. Jennifer is the special O'Malley, the youngest, and her death hit not only this family, but also the author, hard. I believe God heals. I've seen many examples during my lifetime. For those fighting cancer today I offer the hope of James chapter 5—prayer has great power. I know the story with Jennifer getting well would have been very powerful. But I chose instead to let her die, for death is the one thing everyone fears: dying alone, afraid, before we are ready, leaving things undone. I wanted to let Jennifer show us how to handle those last days, to be an example of living life so you do not have regrets at the end. I know firsthand that Jesus is able to carry us through floodwaters and tragedies, unbearable pain and overpowering grief. He's trustworthy with the deepest hurts of our lives. It's a bittersweet parting as she enters heaven for a joyful eternity and the other O'Malleys now must adapt to the loss.

I hope you'll join me for Stephen's story in *The Rescuer.* He already lost a birth sister to death, now Jennifer is gone, and he's feeling bereft inside. The O'Malleys have stuck together for years, but Stephen is running now…from the pain, from the grief, from himself. The other O'Malleys are going to have to find him, for he isn't sure he ever wants to come back. He's looking for anonymity and space. Only he's about to run into Meghan.

As always, I love to hear from my readers. Feel free to write me at:

Dee Henderson

c/o Tyndale House Publishers

351 Executive Drive

Carol Stream, IL 60188

e-mail: dee@deehenderson.com

or on-line: http://www.deehenderson.com

First chapters of all my books are on-line. I invite you to stop by and check them out. Thanks again for letting me share Rachel and Cole's story.

God Bless,

Dee Henderson

The publisher and author would love to hear your comments about this book. *Please contact us at:* www.deefiction.com

The Protector

Jack O'Malley is a fireman who is fearless when it comes to facing an inferno. But when an arsonist begins targeting his district, his shift, his friends, Jack faces the ultimate challenge: protecting the lady who saw the arsonist before she pays an even higher price. . . .

The Healer

Rachel O'Malley works disasters for a living, her specialty helping children through trauma. When a school shooting rips through her community, she finds herself dealing with more than just grief among the children she is trying to help. One of them saw the shooting. And the gun is still missing. . . .

The Rescuer

Stephen O'Malley is a paramedic who has been rescuing people all his life. His friend Meghan is in trouble: Stolen jewels are turning up in interesting places and she's in the middle of it. Stephen's about to run into a night he will never forget: a kidnapping, a tornado, and a race to rescue the woman he loves. . . .

And visit www.DeeHenderson.com to find first chapters and more!

More great fiction from

SUSAN MAY WARREN

THE NOBLE LEGACY SERIES

After their father dies, three siblings reunite on the family ranch to try to preserve the Noble legacy. If only family secrets—and unsuspected enemies—didn't threaten to destroy everything they've worked so hard to build.

THE DEEP HAVEN SERIES

Romance, suspense, and adventure on Minnesota's North Shore . . .

THE TEAM HOPE SERIES

Meet Team Hope—members of an elite search-and-rescue team who
run to the edge of danger to bring others back. Unfortunately,
they can't seem to stay out of trouble. . . .

have you visited tyndalefiction.com *lately?*

Only there can you find:

- → books hot off the press
- → first chapter excerpts
- → inside scoops on your favorite authors
- → author interviews
- → contests
- → fun facts
- → and much more!

Sign up for your **free** newsletter!

Visit us today at: **tyndalefiction.com**

Tyndale fiction does more than entertain.
- → *It touches the heart.*
- → *It stirs the soul.*
- → *It changes lives.*

That's why Tyndale is so committed to being first in fiction!

TYNDALE FICTION